Passions & Reflections

A Collection of 20th-Century Women's Fiction

PASSIONS & REFLECTIONS

A Collection of 20th-Century Women's Fiction

EDITED BY JUDY COOKE

With an introduction by
DEBORAH MOGGACH

VOLUME I

BCA
LONDON · NEW YORK · SYDNEY · TORONTO

This edition published 1991
by BCA
by arrangement with
Lime Tree

CN 1002

Typeset by Falcon Typographic Art Ltd.,
Edinburgh & London
Printed in Great Britain
by Clays Ltd., St Ives Group

Cover Illustration:
Volume I Henri Matisse:
Interieur à Nice, Jeune Femme Lisante, c. 1919
© Succession H. Matisse/DACS 1991
Philadelphia Museum of Art:
Given by Mr and Mrs R. Sturgis Ingersoll

Volume II Henri Matisse:
Femme Assise, le Dos Tourné Vers la Fenêtre Ouverte,
1921-3, oil on canvas, 73 x 92.1 cm
© Succession H. Matisse/DACS 1991
The Montreal Museum of Fine Arts; purchase, Tempest
Fund; 1949. 1915
Photo Marilyn Aitken, MMFA

Contents

Acknowledgements

The original publication details of the texts in this anthology are given below. Copyright material is reproduced by kind permission of the publishers and authors. Every effort has been made to trace copyright owners correctly and credit them accordingly. Apologies are made for any errors or omissions.

Margaret Atwood, *Cat's Eye*. First published 1989 by Bloomsbury Publishing Ltd; copyright © 1989 Margaret Atwood.

Elizabeth Bowen, *The Death of the Heart*. First published 1938 in Great Britain by Jonathan Cape Ltd. Copyright © Elizabeth Bowen 1966.

Anita Brookner, *Latecomers*. First published in Great Britain by Jonathan Cape Ltd; copyright © Anita Brookner 1988.

Angela Carter, *The Magic Toyshop*. First published 1967 in Great Britain by William Heinemann Ltd; copyright © Angela Carter 1967.

Colette, *The Cat*. First published 1933 as *La Chatte*. This translation from the *Fleuron* edition first published in England in 1953 by Martin Secker and Warburg Ltd. Reprinted by permission of Martin Secker and Warburg Ltd.

Anita Desai, *Clear Light of Day*. First published 1980 in Great Britain by William Heinemann Ltd; copyright © Anita Desai 1980. Reprinted by permission of William Heinemann Ltd.

Margaret Drabble, *The Millstone*. First published 1965 in Great Britain by Weidenfeld & Nicolson; copyright © Margaret Drabble 1965.

Daphne Du Maurier, *The Birds*. First published 1952 by Victor Gollancz Ltd. in *The Apple Tree and some stories*; © 1952 The Estate of Daphne Du Maurier. Acknowledgement is also made to Curtis Brown on behalf of the Estate of Daphne Du Maurier.

Marguerite Duras, *The Lover*. Translated from the French by Barbara Bray, Collins 1985. Originally published in France as *L'Amant* by Les Editions de Minuit. Copyright © 1984 Les Editions de Minuit. Translation copyright © 1985 by Random House Inc. and William Collins.

Buchi Emecheta, *Second Class Citizen*. First published 1976 by Allison & Busby; copyright © 1974 Buchi Emecheta.

Zoë Fairbairns, *Daddy's Girls*. First published 1991 in Great Britain by Methuen London; copyright © Zoë Fairbairns 1991.

Nadine Gordimer, *Blinder*. From the collection *Something Out There*, first published 1984 in Great Britain by Jonathan Cape Ltd; copyright © Nadine Gordimer 1984.

Georgina Hammick, *People for Lunch*. From the collection *People for Lunch*, first published 1987 in Great Britain by Methuen London; copyright © Georgina Hammick 1987.

Patricia Highsmith, *Something You Have to Live With*. First published in *Ellery Queen's Mystery Magazine*, July 1976. From the collection *Slowly, Slowly in the Wind*, published in Great Britain 1979 by William Heinemann Ltd. Copyright © 1979 Patricia Highsmith. Reprinted by permission of William Heinemann Ltd.

Ruth Prawer Jhabvala, *How I Became a Holy Mother*. From the collection *How I Became a Holy Mother*, John Murray, 1976. Copyright © 1976 Ruth Prawer Jhabvala.

Rosamond Lehmann, *Invitation to the Waltz*. First published 1947; copyright © The Albatross Ltd 1947. Acknowledgement is made to The Society of Authors as the literary representative of the Estate of Rosamond Lehmann.

Doris Lessing, *The New Man*. From the collection *A Man and Two Women*, first published 1958 in Great Britain by Michael Joseph; copyright © Doris Lessing 1958.

Olivia Manning, *The Spoilt City*. First published 1962 in Great Britain by William Heinemann Ltd; copyright © Olivia Manning 1962. Reprinted by permission of William Heinemann Ltd.

Introduction

I was sitting in a pub one day, eavesdropping on two couples. The women were discussing the marital traumas of some mutual friends; it emerged that the husband had run away with somebody else, and the wife was finding solace with the local builder. The two men looked increasingly bored and uncomfortable. Finally one leaned across to the other and asked loudly: 'So how does it feel, Alec, to be driving the Car of the Year?'

Ten guesses *he* wasn't a novelist. If there is a difference between men and women, it's that women are more like writers. When Brian Moore was asked why he writes so many novels from a woman's point of view he replied that he found them more interesting. 'In a curious way they are more honest when they talk to you. Women live in a personal world, a very, very personal world . . . When a woman tells me a story about something that happens to her, you often get a sudden flash of frankness which is really novelistic. It is as if a woman knows when she tells a story that it must be personal, it must be interesting. Men often see the story as something about them, rather than the true story.'

Even amongst potential writers I have noticed this. Occasionally I have taught at a residential creative writing course. By the end of the first evening the women have invariably revealed vast areas of their private lives, how they feel about their sisters, their parents, their lovers. Whatever its quality, their writing reflects this. On the other hand, days can pass and the most intimate thing the men have revealed is the make of their CD player. Many men, by the nature of their upbringing and the demands of their lives, are cut off from the hot centre of things, from child-rearing, and from the inexhaustible, and exhausting, tangles of family relationships, which are the life-blood of the novelist.

This feeds back into the work. Only Anthony Burgess still believes that women novelists write about adultery in Hampstead. One look at the contents of this anthology confirms that women no longer confine themselves – if they ever did – to the domestic arena. Nadine Gordimer is a powerful political writer. Jeanette Winterson's bold and playful imagination can dance across centuries, inhabiting characters ranging from a young boy during Charles II's reign to a Napoleonic cook.

It is more that women writers reflect experience at a deeper level than the domestic, somewhere in what Richard Ford calls 'the normal applauseless life of us all'. They are absorbed by personal relationships, by feeling rather than things, by ambiguities and doubts rather than certainties (perhaps that's why there are so few women in politics).

But isn't this true of all good novelists? Now that the feminist battle has been won, in writing if in nothing else, and nobody has to call herself Currer Bell in order to be taken seriously by a publisher, it may be as arbitrary to distinguish writers by gender as by their postal address or the size of their feet.

When I really think about it, there is only one indisputable difference between men and women writers. It is not to do with the nature of their work, but the circumstances in which it is written. To put it simply: women writers don't have wives.

Male writers are *Writers*. Their office hours are sacrosanct and they usually have a devoted partner who fends off phone calls, washes their socks and brings them mugs of Nescafé. Women writers are a mass of people, only one of whom is allowed to be a writer. They don't have a wife to look after them – if only they had! Their life is a battle against constant interruptions – the plumber, the neighbour who has lost her key, the child who has been sent home from school. They are pulled in all directions by emotional and physical needs.

For instance, I had just started writing this when the phone rang and a friend asked me to look after two Russian students for a couple of days. An hour later the phone rang again and somebody asked if I could look after their daughter's hamster, Shakespeare, while they went away on holiday. Halfway through the morning the phone rang again – the Russian girls had lost their way to my house and there followed a long conversation, in broken English, about Tube lines. Half an hour later the doorbell rang and Shakespeare arrived, in his cage. Another half hour later the Russian girls arrived, one of them so ill she had to be put to bed. The other turned out to be vegetarian so I had to rush out to the shops to buy something else for lunch, tripping over all their plastic bags on the way through the living-room. The next hour was spent cooking for them and politely asking questions about Georgian farming methods. They were delightful; so was Shakespeare. But somehow I couldn't imagine somebody phoning up Martin Amis in the middle of a working morning and asking him to look after two Soviet students and a hamster.

The only way to cope is to become a mistress of opportunism and compromise. I scribble things on the back of my cheque books when I'm waiting in the supermarket queue; I write cryptic scraps of conversations, on my wrist, when I'm waiting at the school gates. You draw nourishment from the life around you, at home and in the streets; you scavenge and live on your wits. Recently, in the changing room at the local swimming baths, I saw a child pointing to a plastic trough and asking its mother: 'What's that for?' She replied: 'It's for changing babies.' The child's eyes darkened; thoughtfully it gazed at the trough. And somewhere a short story stirred.

In the end, the only thing that matters is the truth of the work. Men can write about women; women can write about men. I often think that fiction writing is like driving in the dark – a process it sometimes unnervingly resembles. It is one of the few activities where nobody need know your sex; you are simply a pair of headlights probing the blackness. Enjoying this anthology, marvellously varied as it is, readers will find confirmed something they probably realized long ago: that the world isn't divided into two sexes, but into three – men, women and writers.

Deborah Moggach

Margaret Atwood

extract from

Cat's Eye

Elaine Risley is alone in Toronto, her home town, attending a retrospective of her work at an avant-garde gallery. She finds herself 'in the middle of my life', enjoying a successful career as a painter with two grown-up daughters from her first marriage and a second husband, Ben, whom she loves. 'He is not any kind of artist, for which I am grateful.' Sensing that the memories evoked by the trip will challenge her in a number of ways, she is nevertheless unprepared for the vivid ambivalence of her feelings towards Cordelia and Grace, childhood companions, and that part of her past shared with them.

I walk along Queen Street, past used comic book stores, windows full of crystal eggs and seashells, a lot of sulky black clothing. I wish I were back in Vancouver, in front of the fireplace with Ben, looking out over the harbour, while the giant slugs munch away at the greenery in the back garden. Fireplaces, back gardens: I wasn't thinking about them when I used to come down here to visit Jon, over the wholesale luggage store. Around the corner was the Maple Leaf Tavern, where I drank draft beer in the dark, two stoplights away from the art school where I drew naked women and ate my heart out. The streetcars rattled the front windows. There are still streetcars.

'I don't want to go,' I said to Ben.

'You don't have to,' he said. 'Call it off. Come down to Mexico.'

'They've gone to all the trouble,' I said. 'Listen, you know how hard it is to get a retrospective anywhere, if you're female?'

'Why is it important?' he said. 'You sell anyway.'

'I have to go,' I said. 'It wouldn't be right.' I was brought up to say please and thank you.

'Okay,' he said. 'You know what you're doing.' He gave me a hug.

I wish it were true.

Here is Sub-Versions, between a restaurant-supply store and a tattoo parlour. Both of these will go, in time: once places like Sub-Versions move in, the handwriting's on the wall.

I open the gallery door, walk in with that sinking feeling I always have in galleries. It's the carpets that do it to me, the hush, the sanctimoniousness of it all: galleries are too much like churches, there's too much reverence, you feel there should be some genuflecting going on. Also I don't like it that this is where paintings end up, on these neutral-toned walls with the track lighting, sterilized, rendered safe and acceptable. It's as if somebody's been around spraying the paintings with air freshener, to kill the smell. The smell of blood on the wall.

This gallery is not totally sterilized, there are touches of cutting edge: a heating pipe shows, one wall is black. I don't give a glance to what's still on the walls, I hate those neo-expressionist dirty greens and putrid oranges, post this, post that. Everything is post these days, as if we're all just a footnote to something earlier that was real enough to have a name of its own.

Several of my own paintings have been uncrated and are leaning against the wall. They've been tracked down, requested, gathered in from whoever owns them. Whoever owns them is not me; worse luck, I'd get a better price now. The owners' names will be on little white cards beside the paintings, along with mine, as if mere ownership is on a par with creation. Which they think it is.

If I cut off my ear, would the market value go up? Better still, stick my head in the oven, blow out my brains. What rich art collectors like to buy, among other things, is a little vicarious craziness.

Face-out is a piece I painted twenty years ago: Mrs Smeath, beautifully rendered in egg tempera, with her grey hairpin crown and her potato face and her spectacles, wearing nothing but her flowered one-breast bib apron. She's reclining on her maroon velvet sofa, rising to Heaven, which is full of rubber plants, while a moon shaped like a doily floats in the sky. *Rubber Plant: The*

Ascension, it's called. The angels around her are 1940s Christmas stickers, laundered little girls in white, with rag-set curly hair. The word *Heaven* is stencilled at the top of the painting with a child's school stencil set. I thought that was a nifty thing to do, at the time.

I caught some shit for that piece, as I recall. But not because of the stencil.

I don't look at this painting for very long, or at any of them. If I do I'll start finding things wrong with them. I'll want to take an Exacto knife to them, torch them, clear the walls. Begin again.

A woman strides towards me from the back, in a modified blonde porcupine haircut, a purple jumpsuit and green leather boots. I know immediately that I should not have worn this powder-blue jogging outfit. Powder-blue is lightweight. I should've worn nun black, Dracula black, like all proper female painters. I should have some clotted-neck vampire lipstick, instead of wimping out with Rose Perfection. But that really would make me look like Haggis McBaggis. At this age the complexion can't stand those grape-jelly reds, I'd look all white and wrinkly.

But I will tough out the jogging suit, I'll pretend I meant it. It could be iconoclasm, how do they know? A powder-blue jogging suit lacks pretensions. The good thing about being out of fashion is that you're never in fashion either, so you can never be last year's model. That's my excuse for my painting, too; or it was for years.

'Hi,' says the woman. 'You must be Elaine! You don't look much like your picture.' What does that mean, I think: better or worse? 'We've talked a lot on the phone. My name is Charna.' Toronto didn't used to have names like Charna. My hand gets crunched, this woman's got about ten heavy silver rings strung on to her fingers like knuckledusters. 'We were just wondering about the order.' There are two more women; each of them looks five times more artistic than I do. They have abstract-art ear-rings, hair arrangements. I am feeling dowdy.

They've got take-out gourmet sprout-and-avocado sandwiches and coffee with steamed milk, and we eat those and drink that while we discuss the arrangement of the pictures. I say I favour a chronological approach, but Charna has other ideas, she wants things to go together tonally and resonate and make statements that amplify one another. I get more nervous, this kind of talk makes me twitch. I'm putting some energy into silence, resisting the impulse to say I have a headache and want to go home. I should be grateful, these women are on my side, they planned this whole thing for me, they're doing me an honour, they like what I do. But still I feel outnumbered, as if they are a species of which I am not a member.

Jon comes back tomorrow, from Los Angeles and his chainsaw murder. I can hardly wait. We'll circumvent his wife, go out for lunch, both of us feeling sneaky. But it's merely a civilized thing to do, having lunch with an ex-husband in a comradely way: a good coda to all that smashed crockery and mayhem. We've known each other since the year dot; at my age, our age, that's becoming important. And from here he looks like relief.

Someone else comes in, another woman. 'Andrea!' says Charna, stalking over to her. 'You're late!' She gives Andrea a kiss on the cheek and walks her over to me, holding her arm. 'Andrea wants to do a piece on you,' she says. 'For the opening.'

'I wasn't told about this,' I say. I've been ambushed.

'It came up at the last minute,' says Charna. 'Lucky for us! I'll put you two in the back room, okay? I'll bring you some coffee. Getting the word out, they call it,' she adds, to me, with a wry smile. I allow myself to be herded down the corridor; I can still be bossed around by women like Charna.

'I thought you would be different,' says Andrea as we settle.

'Different how?' I ask.

'Bigger,' she says.

I smile at her. 'I am bigger.'

Andrea checks out my powder-blue jogging suit. She herself is wearing black, approved, glossy black, not early sixties holdover as mine would be. She has red hair out of a spray can and no apologies, cut into a cap like an acorn. She's upsettingly young; to me she doesn't look more than a teenager, though I know she must be in her twenties. Probably she thinks I'm a weird middle-aged frump, sort of like her high school teacher. Probably she's out to get me. Probably she'll succeed.

We sit across from each other at Charna's desk and Andrea sets down her camera and fiddles with her tape-recorder. Andrea writes for a newspaper. 'This is for the Living section,' she says. I know what that means, it used to be the Women's Pages. It's funny that they now call it Living, as if only women are alive and the other things, such as the Sports, are for the dead.

'Living, eh?' I say. 'I'm the mother of two. I bake cookies.' All true. Andrea gives me a dirty look and flicks on her machine.

'How do you handle fame?' she says.

'This isn't fame,' I say. 'Fame is Elizabeth Taylor's cleavage. This stuff is just a media pimple.'

She grins at that. 'Well, could you maybe say something about your generation of artists – your generation of woman artists – and their aspirations and goals?'

'Painters, you mean,' I say. 'What generation is that?'

'The seventies, I suppose,' she says. 'That's when the women's – that's when you started getting attention.'

'The seventies isn't my generation,' I say.

She smiles. 'Well,' she says, 'what is?'

'The forties.'

'The forties?' This is archaeology as far as she's concerned. 'But you couldn't have been . . .'

'That was when I grew up,' I say.

'Oh right,' she says. 'You mean it was *formative*. Can you talk about the ways, how it reflects in your work?'

'The colours,' I say. 'A lot of my colours are forties colours.' I'm softening up. At least she doesn't say *like* and *you know* all the time. 'The war. There are people who remember the war and people who don't. There's a cut-off point, there's a difference.'

'You mean the Vietnam War?' she says.

'No,' I say coldly. 'The Second World War.' She looks a bit scared, as if I've just resurrected from the dead, and incompletely at that. She didn't know I was *that* old. 'So,' she says. 'What is the difference?'

'We have long attention spans,' I say. 'We eat everything on our plates. We save string. We make do.'

She looks puzzled. That's all I want to say about the forties. I'm beginning to sweat. I feel as if I'm at the dentist, mouth gracelessly open while some stranger with a light and mirror gazes down my throat at something I can't see.

Brightly and neatly she veers away from the war and back towards women, which was where she wanted to be in the first place. Is it harder for a woman, was I discriminated against, undervalued? What about having children? I give unhelpful replies: all painters feel undervalued. You can do it while they're at school. My husband's been terrific, he gives me a lot of support, some of which has been financial. I don't say which husband.

'So you don't feel it's sort of demeaning to be propped up by a man?' she says.

'Women prop up men all the time,' I say. 'What's wrong with a little reverse propping?'

What I have to say is not altogether what she wants to hear. She'd prefer stories of outrage, although she'd be unlikely to tell them about herself, she's too young. Still, people my age are supposed to have stories of outrage; at least insult, at least put-down. Male art teachers pinching your bum, calling you *baby*, asking you why there are no great female painters, that sort of thing. She would like me to be furious, and quaint.

'Did you have any female mentors?' she asks.

'Female what?'

'Like, teachers, or other woman painters you admired.'

'Shouldn't that be mentresses?' I say nastily. 'There weren't any. My teacher was a man.'

'Who was that?' she says.

'Josef Hrbik. He was very kind to me,' I add quickly. He'd fit the bill for her, but she won't hear that from me. 'He taught me to draw naked women.'

That startles her. 'Well, what about, you know, feminism?' she says. 'A lot of people call you a feminist painter.'

'What indeed,' I say. 'I hate party lines, I hate ghettoes. Anyway, I'm too old to have invented it and you're too young to understand it, so what's the point of discussing it at all?'

'So it's not a meaningful classification for you?' she says.

'I like it that women like my work. Why shouldn't I?'

'Do men like your work?' she asks slyly. She's been going through the back files, she's seen some of those witch-and-succubus pieces.

'Which men?' I say. 'Not everyone likes my work. It's not because I'm a woman. If they don't like a man's work it's not because he's a man. They just don't like it.' I am on dubious ground, and this enrages me. My voice is calm; the coffee seethes within me.

She frowns, diddles with the tape-recorder. 'Why do you paint all those women then?'

'What should I paint, men?' I say. 'I'm a painter. Painters paint women. Rubens painted women, Renoir painted women, Picasso painted women. Everyone paints women. Is there something wrong with painting women?'

'But not like that,' she says.

'Like what?' I say. 'Anyway, why should my women be the same as everyone else's women?' I catch myself picking at my fingers, and stop. In a minute my teeth will be chattering like those of cornered mice. Her voice is getting farther and farther away, I can hardly hear her. But I see her, very clearly: the ribbing on the neck of her sweater, the fine hairs of her cheek, the shine of a button. What I hear is what she isn't saying. *Your clothes are stupid. Your art is crap. Sit up straight and don't answer back.*

'Why do you paint?' she says, and I can hear her again as clear as anything. I hear her exasperation, with me and my refusals.

'Why does anyone do anything?' I say.

* * *

The light fades earlier; on the way home from school we walk through the smoke from burning leaves. It rains, and we have to play inside. We sit on the floor of Grace's room, being quiet because of Mrs Smeath's bad heart, and cut out rolling-pins and frying pans and paste them around our paper ladies.

But Cordelia makes short work of this game. She knows, instantly it seems, why Grace's house has so many Eaton's Catalogues in it. It's because the Smeaths get their clothes that way, the whole family – order them out of the Eaton's Catalogue. There in the Girls' Clothing section are the plaid dresses, the skirts with straps, the winter coats worn by Grace and her sisters, three colours of them, in lumpy, serviceable wool, with hoods: Kelly Green, Royal Blue, Maroon. Cordelia manages to convey that she herself would never wear a coat ordered from the

Eaton's Catalogue. She doesn't say this out loud though. Like the rest of us, she wants to stay on the good side of Grace.

She bypasses the cookware, flips through the pages. She turns to the brassieres, to the elaborately laced and gusseted corsets – foundation garments, they're called – and draws moustaches on the models, whose flesh looks as if it's been painted over with a thin coat of beige plaster. She pencils hair in, under their arms, and on their chests between the breasts. She reads out the descriptions, snorting with stifled laughter: '"Delightfully trimmed in dainty lace, with extra support for the mature figure." That means big bazooms. Look at this – *cup* sizes! Like teacups!'

Breasts fascinate Cordelia, and fill her with scorn. Both of her older sisters have them by now. Perdie and Mirrie sit in their room with its twin beds and sprigged-muslin flounces, filing their nails, laughing softly; or they heat brown wax in little pots in the kitchen and take it upstairs to spread on their legs. They look into their mirrors, making sad faces – 'I look like Haggis McBaggis! It's the curse!' Their wastebaskets smell of decaying flowers.

They tell Cordelia there are some things she's too young to understand, and then they tell these things to her anyway. Cordelia, her voice lowered, her eyes big, passes on the truth: the curse is when blood comes out between your legs. We don't believe her. She produces evidence: a sanitary pad, filched from Perdie's wastebasket. On it is a brown crust, like dried gravy. 'That's not blood,' Grace says with disgust, and she's right, it's nothing like when you cut your finger. Cordelia is indignant. But she can prove nothing.

I haven't thought much about grown-up women's bodies before. But now these bodies are revealed in their true, upsetting light: alien and bizarre, hairy, squashy, monstrous. We hang around outside the room where Perdie and Mirrie are peeling the wax off their legs while they utter yelps of pain, trying to see through the keyhole, giggling: they embarrass us, although we don't know why. They know they're being laughed at and come to the door to shoo us away. 'Cordelia, why don't you and your little friends bug off!' They smile a little ominously, as if they know already what is in store for us. 'Just wait and see,' they say.

This frightens us. Whatever has happened to them, bulging them, softening them, causing them to walk rather than run, as if there's some invisible leash around their necks, holding them in check – whatever it is, it may happen to us too. We look surreptitiously at the breasts of women on the street, of our teachers; though not of our mothers, that would be too close for comfort. We examine our legs and underarms for sprouting hairs, our chests for swellings. But nothing is happening: so far we are safe.

Cordelia turns to the back pages of the catalogue, where the pictures are in grey and black and there are crutches and trusses and prosthetic devices. 'Breast pumps,' she says. 'See this? It's for pumping your titties up bigger, like a bicycle pump.' And we don't know what to believe.

We can't ask our mothers. It's hard to imagine them without clothes, to think of them as having bodies at all, under their dresses. There's a great deal they don't say. Between us and them is a gulf, an abyss, that goes down and down. It's filled with wordlessness. They wrap up the garbage in several layers of newspaper and tie it with string, and even so it drips on to the freshly waxed floor. Their clothes-lines are strung with underpants, nighties, socks, a display of soiled intimacy, which they have washed and rinsed, plunging their hands into the grey curdled water. They know about toilet brushes, about toilet seats, about germs. The world is dirty, no matter how much they clean, and we know they will not welcome our grubby little questions. So instead a long whisper runs among us, from child to child, gathering horror.

Cordelia says that men have carrots, between their legs. They aren't really carrots but something worse. They're covered with hair. Seeds come out the end and get into women's stomachs and grow into babies, whether you want it or not. Some men have their carrots pierced and rings set into them as if they are ears.

Cordelia's unclear about how the seeds get out or what they're like. She says they're invisible, but I think this can't be so. If there are seeds at all they must be more like bird seeds, or carrot seeds, long and fine. Also she can't say how the carrot gets in, to plant the seeds. Belly buttons are the obvious choice, but there would have to be a cut, a tear. The whole story is questionable, and the idea that we ourselves could have been produced by such an act is an outrage. I think of beds, where all of this is supposed to take place: the twin beds at Carol's house, always so tidy, the elegant canopy bed at Cordelia's, the dark mahogany-coloured bed in Grace's house, heavily respectable with its crocheted spread and layers of woollen blankets. Such beds are a denial in themselves, a repudiation. I think of Carol's wry-mouthed mother, of Mrs Smeath with her hairpinned crown of greying braids. They would purse their lips, draw themselves up in a dignified manner. They would not permit it.

Grace says, 'God makes babies,' in that final way of hers which means there is nothing more to be discussed. She smiles her buttoned-up disdainful smile, and we are reassured. Better God than us.

But there are doubts. I know, for instance, a lot of things. I know that 'carrot' is not the right word. I've seen dragonflies and beetles, flying around, stuck together, one on the back of the other; I know it's called 'mating'. I know about ovipositors, for laying eggs, on leaves, on caterpillars, on the surface of the water; they're right out on the page, clearly labelled, on the diagrams of insects my father corrects at home. I know about queen ants, and about the female praying mantises eating the males. None of this is much help. I think of Mr and Mrs Smeath, stark naked, with Mr Smeath stuck to the back of Mrs Smeath. Such an image, even without the addition of flight, will not do.

I could ask my brother. But, although we've examined scabs and toe-jam under the microscope, although we aren't worried by pickled ox eyes and gutted fish and whatever can be found under dead logs, putting this question to him would be indelicate, perhaps hurtful. I think of JUPITER scrolled on the sand in his angular script, by his extra, dextrous finger. In Cordelia's version it will end up covered with hair. Maybe he doesn't know.

Cordelia says boys put their tongues in your mouth when they kiss you. Not any boys we know, older ones. She says this the same way my brother says 'slug juice' or 'snot' when Carol's around, and Carol does the same thing, the same wrinkle of the nose, the same wriggle. Grace says that Cordelia is being disgusting.

I think about the spit you sometimes see, downtown, on the sidewalk; or cow's tongues in butcher's shops. Why would they want to do such a thing, put their tongues in other people's mouths? Just to be repulsive, of course. Just to see what you would do.

* * *

I go up the cellar stairs, which have black rubber stair-treads nailed on to them. Mrs Smeath is standing at the kitchen sink in her bib apron. She's finished her nap and now she's upright, getting supper. She's peeling potatoes; she often peels things. The peel falls from her large knuckly hands in a long pale spiral. The paring knife she uses is worn so thin its blade is barely more than a crescent-moon sliver. The kitchen is steamy, and smells of marrow-fat and stewing bones.

Mrs Smeath turns and looks at me, a skinless potato in her left hand, the knife in her right. She smiles. 'Grace says your family don't go to church,' she says. 'Maybe you'd like to come with us. To our church.'

'Yes,' says Grace, who has come up the stairs behind me. And the idea is pleasing. I'll have Grace all to myself on Sunday mornings, without Carol or Cordelia. Grace is still the desirable one, the one we all want.

When I tell my parents about this plan they become anxious. 'Are you sure you really want to go?' my mother says. When she was young, she says, she had to go to church whether she liked it or not. Her father was very strict. She couldn't whistle on Sundays. 'Are you really sure?'

My father says he doesn't believe in brainwashing children. When you're grown up, then you can make up your own mind about religion, which has been responsible for a lot of wars and massacres in his opinion, as well as bigotry and intolerance. 'Every educated person should know the Bible,' he says. 'But she's only eight.'

'Almost nine,' I say.

'Well,' says my father. 'Don't believe everything you hear.'

On Sunday I put on the clothes my mother and I have picked out, a dress of dark-blue and green wool plaid, white ribbed stockings that attach with garters on to my stiff white cotton waist. I have more dresses than I once had, but I don't go shopping with my mother to help pick them out, the way Carol does. My mother hates shopping, nor does she sew. My girls' clothes are second-hand, donated by a distant friend of my mother's who has a larger daughter. None of these dresses fits me very well; the hems droop, or the sleeves bunch up under my arms. I think this is the norm, for dresses. The white stockings are new though, and even itchier than the brown ones I wear to school.

I take my blue cat's eye marble out of my red plastic purse and leave it in my bureau drawer, and put the nickel my mother's given me for the collection plate into my purse instead. I walk along the rutted streets towards Grace's house, in my shoes; it isn't time for boots yet. Grace opens her front door when I ring. She must have been waiting for me. She has a dress on too and white stockings, and navy-blue bows at the ends of her braids. She looks me over. 'She doesn't have a hat,' she says.

Mrs Smeath, standing in the hallway, considers me as if I'm an orphan left on her doorstep. She sends Grace upstairs to search for another hat, and Grace comes back down with an old one of dark-blue velvet with an elastic under the chin. It's too small for me but Mrs Smeath says it will do for now. 'We don't go into our church with our heads uncovered,' she says. She emphasizes *our*, as if there are other, inferior, bareheaded churches.

Mrs Smeath has a sister, who is going with us to church. Her name is Aunt Mildred. She's older and has been a missionary in China. She has the same knuckly red hands, the same metal-rimmed glasses, the same hair crown as Mrs Smeath, only hers is all grey, and the hairs on her face are grey too and more numerous. Both of them have hats that look like packages of felt carelessly done up, with several ends sticking into the air. I've seen such hats in the Eaton's Catalogues of several years back, worn by models with sleeked-back hair and high cheek-bones and dark-red, glossy mouths. On Mrs Smeath and her sister they don't have the same effect.

When all of the Smeaths have their coats and hats on we climb into their car: Mrs Smeath and Aunt Mildred in the front, me and Grace and her two little sisters in the back. Although I still worship Grace, this worship is not at all physical, and being squashed into the back seat of her car, so close to her, embarrasses me. Right in front of my face Mr Smeath is driving. He is short and bald and hardly ever seen. It's the same with Carol's father, with Cordelia's: in the daily life of houses, fathers are largely invisible.

We drive through the nearly empty Sunday streets, following the streetcar tracks west. The air inside the car fills with the used breath of the Smeaths, a stale smell like dried saliva. The church is large and made of brick; on the top of it, instead of a cross, there's a thing that looks like an onion and goes around. I ask about this onion, which may mean something religious for all I know, but Grace says it's a ventilator.

Mr Smeath parks the car and we get out of it and go inside. We sit in a row, on a long bench made of dark shiny wood, which Grace says is a pew. This is the first time I've ever been inside a church. There's a high ceiling, with lights shaped like morning glories hanging down on chains, and a plain gold cross up at the front with a vase of white flowers. Behind that there are three stained-glass windows. The biggest, middle one has Jesus in white, with his hands held out sideways and a white bird hovering over his head. Underneath it says in thick black Bible-type letters with dots in between the words: THE·KINGDOM·OF·GOD·IS·WITHIN·YOU. On the left side is Jesus sitting down, sideways in pinky-red, with two children leaning on his knees. It says: SUFFER·THE·LITTLE·CHILDREN. Both of the Jesuses have haloes. On the other side is a woman in blue, with no halo and a white kerchief partly covering her face. She's carrying a basket and reaching down one hand. There's a man sitting down at her feet, with what looks like a bandage wound around his head. It says: THE·GREATEST·OF·THESE·IS·CHARITY. Around all these windows are borders, with vines twining around and bunches of grapes, and different flowers. The windows have light coming in behind them, which illuminates them. I can hardly take my eyes off them.

Then there's organ music and everyone stands up, and I become confused. I watch what Grace does, and stand up when she stands up, sit when she sits. During the songs she holds the hymn book open and points, but I don't know any of the tunes. After a while it's time for us to go to Sunday School, and so we file out with the other children in a line and go down into the church basement.

At the entrance to the Sunday School place there's a blackboard, where someone has printed, in coloured chalk: KILROY WAS HERE. Beside this is a drawing of a man's eyes and nose, looking over a fence.

Sunday School is in classes, like ordinary school. The teachers are younger though; ours is an older teenager with a light-blue hat and a veil. Our class is all girls. The teacher reads us a Bible story about Joseph and his coat of many colours. Then she listens as the girls recite things they're supposed to have memorized. I sit on my chair, dangling my legs. I haven't memorized anything. The teacher smiles at me and says she hopes I will come back every week.

After this all the different classes go into a large room with rows of grey wooden benches in it, like the benches we eat our lunches on at school. We sit on the benches, the lights are turned off, and coloured slides are projected on to the bare wall at the far end of the room. The slides aren't photographs but paintings. They look old-fashioned. The first one shows a knight riding through the forest, gazing upwards to where a shaft of light streams down through the trees. The skin of this knight is very white, his eyes are large like a girl's, and his hand is pressed to where his heart must be, under his armour, which looks like car fenders. Under his large, luminous face I can see the light-switches and the top boards of the wainscoting, and the corner of the small piano, where it juts out.

The next picture has the same knight only smaller, and

underneath him some words, which we sing to the heavy thumping of chords from the unseen piano:

> I would be true, for there are those who trust me,
> I would be pure, for there are those who care,
> I would be strong, for there is much to suffer,
> I would be brave, for there is much to dare.

Beside me, in the dark, I hear Grace's voice going up and up, thin and reedy, like a bird's. She knows all the words; she knew all the words to her memory passage from the Bible too. When we bend our heads to pray I feel suffused with goodness, I feel included, taken in. God loves me, whoever he is.

After Sunday School we go back into the regular church for the last part, and I put my nickel on the collection plate. Then there is something called the Doxology. Then we walk out of the church and stuff back into the Smeath's car, and Grace says carefully, 'Daddy, may we go and see the trains?' and the little girls, with a show of enthusiasm, say, 'Yes, yes.'

Mr Smeath says, 'Have you been good?' and the little girls say, 'Yes, yes,' again.

Mrs Smeath makes an indeterminate sound. 'Oh, all right,' says Mr Smeath to the little girls. He drives the car south through the empty streets, along the streetcar tracks, past a single streetcar like a gliding island, until finally we see the flat grey lake in the distance, and below us, over the edge of a sort of low cliff, a flat grey plain covered with train tracks. On this metal-covered plain several trains are shunting slowly back and forth. Because it is Sunday, and because this is evidently a routine after-church Sunday event for the Smeaths, I have the idea that the train tracks and the lethargic, ponderous trains have something to do with God. It is also clear to me that the person who really wants to see the trains is not Grace, or any of the little girls, but Mr Smeath himself.

We sit there in the parked car watching the trains until Mrs Smeath says that the dinner will be ruined. After that we drive back to Grace's house.

I am invited for Sunday dinner. It's the first time I've ever stayed for dinner at Grace's. Before dinner Grace takes me upstairs so we can wash our hands, and I learn a new thing about her house: you are only allowed four squares of toilet paper. The soap in the bathroom is black and rough. Grace says it's tar soap.

The dinner is baked ham and baked beans and baked potatoes and mashed squash. Mr Smeath carves the ham, Mrs Smeath adds the vegetables, the plates get passed around. Grace's little sisters look at me through their eyeglasses when I start to eat.

'We say grace in this house,' says Aunt Mildred, smiling firmly, and I don't know what she's talking about. I look at Grace: why do they want to say her name? But they all bend their heads and put their hands together and Grace says, 'For what we are about to receive may the Lord make us truly thankful, Amen,' and Mr Smeath says, 'Good food, good drink, good God, let's eat,' and winks at me. Mrs Smeath says, 'Lloyd,' and Mr Smeath gives a small, conspiratorial laugh.

After dinner Grace and I sit in the living-room, on the velvet chesterfield, the same one Mrs Smeath takes her naps on. I've never sat on it before and feel I'm sitting on something reserved, like a throne or a coffin. We read our Sunday School paper, which has the story of Joseph in it and a modern story about a boy who steals from the collection plate but repents and collects waste-paper and old bottles for the church, to make reparations. The pictures are black and white pen and ink drawings, but on the front is a coloured picture of Jesus, in pastel robes, surrounded by children, all of different colours, brown, yellow, white, clean and pretty, some holding his hand, others gazing up at him with large worshipful eyes. This Jesus does not have a halo.

Mr Smeath dozes in the maroon easy chair, his round belly swelling up. From the kitchen comes the clatter of silverware. Mrs Smeath and Aunt Mildred are doing the dishes.

I reach home in the late afternoon, with my red plastic purse and my Sunday School paper. 'Did you like it?' says my mother, still with the same air of anxiety.

'Did you learn anything?' says my father.

'I have to memorize a psalm,' I say importantly. The word *psalm* sounds like a secret password. I am a little resentful. There are things my parents have been keeping from me, things I need to know. The hats, for instance: how could my mother have forgotten about the hats? God is not an entirely new idea for me: they have him at school in the morning prayers, and even in 'God Save the King'. But it seems there is more to it, more things to be memorized, more songs to be sung, more nickels to be donated, before he can be truly appeased. I am worried about Heaven though. What age will I be when I get there? What if I'm old when I die? In Heaven I want to be the age I am.

I have a Bible, on loan from Grace, her second-best. I go to my room and begin to memorize: 'The heavens declare the glory of God; and the firmament sheweth his handywork. Day unto day uttereth speech, and night unto night sheweth knowledge.'

I still don't have any bedroom curtains. I look out the window, look up: there are the heavens, there are the stars, where they usually are. They no longer look cold and white and remote, like alcohol and enamel trays. Now they look watchful.

* * *

The girls stand in the schoolyard or up on top of the hill, in small clumps, whispering and whispering and doing spoolwork. It's now the fashion to have a spool with four nails pounded into one end, and a ball of wool. You loop the wool over each nail in turn, twice around, and use a fifth nail to hook the bottom loops over the top ones. Out of the other end of the spool dangles a round thick wool tail, which you're supposed to wind up like a flat snail-shell and sew into a mat to put the teapot on. I have such a spool, and so do Grace and Carol, and even Cordelia, although her wool is a snarl.

These clumps of whispering girls with their spools and coloured wool tails have to do with boys, with the separateness of boys. Each cluster of girls excludes some other girls, but all boys. The boys exclude us too, but their exclusion is active, they make a point of it. We don't need to.

Sometimes I still go into my brother's room and lie around on the floor reading comic books, but I never do this when any other girl is there. Alone I am tolerated, as part of a group of girls I would not be. This goes without saying.

Once I took boys for granted, I was used to them. But now I pay more attention, because boys are not the same. For example, they don't take baths as often as they're expected to. They smell of grubby flesh, of scalp, but also of leather, from the knee-patches on their breeks, and wool, from the breeks themselves, which come down only to below the knee, and lace up there like football pants. On the bottom parts of their legs they wear thick wool socks, which are usually damp and falling down. On their heads, outdoors, they wear leather helmets that strap under the chin. Their clothing is khaki, or navy-blue or grey, or forest green, colours that don't show the dirt as much. All of this has a military feel to it. Boys pride themselves on their drab clothing, their drooping socks, their smeared and inky skin: dirt, for them, is almost as good as wounds. They work at acting like boys. They call each other by their last names, draw attention to any extra departures from cleanliness. 'Hey, Robertson! Wipe off the snot!' 'Who farted?' They punch one another on the arm, saying, 'Got you!' 'Got you back!' There always seem to be more of them in the room than there actually are.

My brother punches arms and makes remarks about smells like the rest of them, but he has a secret. He would never tell it to these other boys, because of the way they would laugh.

The secret is that he has a girlfriend. This girlfriend is so secret she doesn't even know about it herself. I'm the only one he's told, and I have been double-sworn not to tell anyone else. Even when we're alone I'm not allowed to refer to her by her name, only by her initials, which are B.W. My brother will sometimes murmur these initials when there are other people around, my parents for instance. When he says them he stares at me, waiting for me to nod or give some sign that I have heard and understood. He writes me notes in code, which he leaves where I'll find them, under my pillow, tucked into my top bureau drawer. When I translate these notes they turn out to be so unlike him, so lacking in invention, so moronic in fact, that I can hardly believe it: 'Talked to B.W.' 'Saw HER today.' He writes these notes in coloured pencil, different colours, with exclamation marks. One night there's a freak early snowfall, and in the morning when I wake up and look out my bedroom window there are the supercharged initials, etched in pee on the white ground, already melting.

I can see that this girlfriend is causing him some anguish, as well as excitement, but I can't understand why. I know who she is. Her real name is Bertha Watson. She hangs around with the older girls, up on the hill under the stunted fir trees. She has straight brown hair with bangs and she's of ordinary size. There's no magic about her that I can see, or any abnormality. I'd like to know how she's done it, this trick with my brother that's turned him into a stupider, more nervous identical twin of himself.

Knowing this secret, being the only one chosen to know, makes me feel important in a way. But it's a negative importance, it's the importance of a blank sheet of paper. I can know because I don't count. I feel singled out, but also bereft. Also protective of him, because for the first time in my life I feel responsible for him. He is at risk, and I have power over him. It occurs to me that I could tell on him, lay him open to derision; I have that choice. He is at my mercy and I don't want it. I want him back the way he was, unchanged, invincible.

The girlfriend doesn't last long. After a while nothing more is heard of her. My brother makes fun of me again, or ignores me; he's back in charge. He gets a chemistry set and does experiments down in the basement. As an obsession I prefer the chemistry set to the girlfriend. There are things stewing, horrible stinks, little sulphurous explosions, amazing illusions. There's invisible writing that comes out when you hold the paper over a candle. You can make a hard-boiled egg rubbery so it will go into a milk bottle, although getting it out again is more difficult. *Turn Water to Blood*, the instructions say, *and Astound Your Friends*.

He still trades comic books, but effortlessly, absent-mindedly. Because he cares less about them he makes better trades. The comic books pile up under his bed, stacks and stacks of them, but he seldom reads them any more when the other boys aren't around.

My brother exhausts the chemistry set. Now he has a star map, pinned to the wall of his room, and at night he turns out the lights and sits beside the darkened, open window, in the cold, with his maroon sweater pulled on over his pyjamas, gazing skyward. He has a pair of my father's binoculars, which he's allowed to use as long as he keeps the strap around his neck so he won't drop them. What he really wants next is a telescope.

When he allows me to join him, and when he feels like talking, he teaches me new names, charts the reference points: Orion, the Bear, the Dragon, the Swan. These are constellations. Every one of them is made up of a huge number of stars, hundreds of times bigger and hotter than our own sun. These stars are light-years away, he says. We aren't really seeing them at all, we're just seeing the light they sent out years, hundreds of years, thousands of years ago. The stars are like echoes. I sit there in my flannelette pyjamas, shivering, the back of my neck hurting from the upward tilt, squinting into the cold and the infinitely receding darkness, into the black cauldron where the fiery stars boil and boil. His stars are different from the ones in the Bible: they're wordless, they flame in an obliterating silence. I feel as if my body is dissolving and I am being drawn up and up, like thinning mist, into a vast emptying space.

'Arcturus,' my brother says. It's a foreign word, one I don't know, but I know the tone of his voice: recognition, completion, something added to a set. I think of his jars of marbles in the spring, the way he dropped the marbles into the jar, one by one, counting. My brother is collecting again; he's collecting stars.

Elizabeth Bowen

extract from

The Death of the Heart

It is London in the late 1930s and the sixteen-year-old orphan Portia is striving to hold her own in a coterie of rather grand early middle-aged people. She is especially in awe of her sister-in-law, Anna.

The Marx Brothers, that evening at the Empire, had no success with Portia. The screen threw its tricky light on her unrelaxed profile: she sat almost appalled. Anna took her eyes from the screen to complain once or twice to Thomas, 'She doesn't think this is funny.' Thomas, who had been giving unwilling snorts, relapsed into gloom, and said, 'Well, they are a lowering lot.' Anna leaned across him, 'You liked Sandy Macpherson, didn't you, Portia? – Thomas, do kick her and ask if she liked Sandy Macpherson?' The organist still loudly and firmly playing had gone down with his organ, through floodlit mimosa, into a bottomless pit, from which 'Parlez Moi d'Amour' kept on faintly coming up till someone down there shut a lid on him. Portia had no right to say that people were less brave now. . . . Now the Marx Brothers were over, the three Quaynes dived for their belongings and filed silently out – they missed the News in order to miss the Rush.

Anna and Portia, glum for opposing reasons, waited in the foyer while Thomas went for a taxi. For those minutes, in the mirror-refracted glare, they looked like workers with tomorrow ahead. Then someone looked hard at Anna, looked back, looked again, registered indecision, raised his hat and returned, extending a large anxious delighted hand. 'Miss *Fellowes*!'

'Major Brutt! How extraordinary this is!'

'To think of my running into *you*. It's extraordinary!'

'Especially as I am not even Miss Fellowes, now – I mean, I am Mrs Quayne.'

'Do excuse me –'

'How could you possibly know? . . . I'm so glad we've met again.'

'It must be nine years plus. What a great evening we had – you and Pidgeon and I –' He stopped quickly: a look of doubt came into his eyes.

Portia stood by, meanwhile. 'You must meet my sister-in-law,' said Anna at once: 'Major Brutt – Miss Quayne.' She went on, not with quite so much assurance, 'I hope you enjoyed the Marx Brothers?'

'Well, to tell you the truth – I knew this place in the old days; I'd never heard of these chaps, but I thought I would drop in. I can't say I –'

'Oh, you find them lowering, too?'

'I dare say they're up-to-date, but they're not what I call funny.'

'Yes,' Anna said, 'they are up-to-date for a bit.' Major Brutt's eyes travelled from Anna's smiling and talking mouth, via the camellia fastened under her chin, to the upturned brim of Portia's hat – where it stayed. 'I hope', he said to Portia, '*you* have enjoyed yourself.'

Anna said, 'No, I don't think she did, much – Oh, look, my husband has got a taxi. Do come back with us: we must all have a drink. . . . Oh, Thomas, this is Major Brutt.'. . . As they walked out two-and two to the taxi, Anna said to Thomas out of the side of her mouth, 'Friend of Pidgeon's – we once had an evening with him.'

'*Did* we? I don't – When?'

'Not you and I, silly. I and Pidgeon. Years ago. But he really must have a drink.'

'Naturally,' said Thomas. Putting on no expression, he steered her by one elbow through the crowd at the door – for whenever you come out, you never avoid the Rush. In the taxi, infected by Major Brutt, Thomas sat bolt upright, looking hard at everything through the window in a military way. Whereas Major Brutt, beside him, kept glancing most timidly at the ladies' faces flowering on fur collars in the dark of the cab. He remarked once or twice, 'I must say, this is an amazing coincidence.' Portia sat twisted sideways, so that her knees should not annoy Thomas. Oh, the charm of this accident, this meeting in a sumptuous place – this was one of those polished encounters she and Irene spied on when they had peeped into a Palace Hotel. As the taxi crawled into Windsor Terrace, she exclaimed, all lit up, 'Oh, thank you for taking me!'

Thomas only said, 'Pity you didn't like it.'

'Oh, but I did like being there.'

Major Brutt said firmly, 'Those four chaps were a blot – This where we stop? Good.'

'Yes, we stop here,' Anna said, resignedly getting out.

The afternoon mist had frozen away to nothing; their house, footlit by terrace lamps, ran its pilasters up into glassy black night air. Portia shivered all down and put up her hands to her collar; Major Brutt's smart clatter struck a ring from the pavement; he slapped his coat, saying, 'Freezing like billy-o.'

'We can slide tomorrow,' said Thomas. 'That will be jolly.' He scooped out a handful of silver, stared at it, paid the taxi and felt round for his key. As though he heard himself challenged, or heard an echo, he looked sharply over his shoulder down the terrace – empty, stagy, E-shaped, with frigid pillars cut out on black shadow: a façade with no back. 'We're wonderfully quiet up here,' he told Major Brutt.

'Really more like the country.'

'For God's sake, let us in!' Anna exclaimed – Major Brutt looked at her with solicitude.

It was admirably hot and bright in the study – all the same, indoors the thing became too far-fetched. Major Brutt looked about unassumingly, as though he would like to say, 'What a nice place you've got here,' but was not sure if he knew them well enough. Anna switched lamps off with a strung-up air, while Thomas, having said, 'Scotch, Irish or brandy?' filled up the glasses on the tray. Anna could not speak – she thought of her closed years: seeing Robert Pidgeon, now, as a big fly in the amber of this decent man's memory. Her own memory was all blurs and seams. She started dreading the voice in which she could only say, 'Do you hear anything of him? How much do you see him, these days?' Or else, 'Where is he now, do you know?' Magnetism to that long-ago evening – on which Robert and she must have been perfect lovers – had made her bring back this man, this born third, to her home. Now Thomas, by removing himself to a different plane, made her feel she had done a thoroughly awkward thing. The pause was too long: it smote her to see Major Brutt look, uncertain, into his whisky, clearly feeling ought he not, then, to drink this? Ought he not to be here?

Otherwise he could wish for nothing better. The Quaynes had both seen how happy he was to come. He was the man from back somewhere, out of touch with London, dying to go on somewhere after a show. He would be glad to go on almost anywhere. But London, these nights, has a provincial meanness bright lights only expose. After dark, she is like a governess gone to the bad, in a Woolworth tiara, tarted up all wrong. But a glamour she may have had lives on in exiles' imaginations. Major Brutt was the sort of man who, like a ghost with no beat, hesitates round the West End about midnight – not wanting to buy a girl, not wanting to drink alone, not wanting to go back to Kensington, hoping something may happen. It grows less likely to happen – sooner or later he must be getting back. If he misses the last tube, he will have to run to a taxi; the taxi lightens his pocket and torments him, smelling of someone else's woman's scent. Like an empty room with no blinds his imagination gapes on the scene, and reflects what was never there. If this is to be all, he may as well catch the last tube. He may touch the hotel porter for a drink in the lounge

– lights half-out, empty, with all the old women gone to bed. There is vice now, but you cannot be simply naughty.

'Well, here's luck,' Major Brutt said, pulling himself together, raising his glass boldly. He looked round at their three interesting faces. Portia replied with her glass of mild-and-soda: he bowed to her, she bowed to him and they drank. 'You live here, too?' he said.

'I'm staying here for a year.'

'That's a nice long visit. Can your people spare you?'

'Yes,' Portia said. 'They – I –'

Anna looked at Thomas as much as to say, check this, but Thomas was looking for the cigars. She saw Portia, kneeling down by the fire, look up at Major Brutt with a perfectly open face – her hands were tucked up the elbows of her short-sleeved dress. The picture upset Anna, who thought how much innocence she herself had corrupted in other people – yes, even in Robert: in him perhaps most of all. Meetings that ended with their most annihilating and bitter quarrels had begun with Robert unguarded, eager – like that. Watching Portia, she thought, is she a snake, or a rabbit? At all events, she thought, hardening, she has her own fun.

'Thanks very much, no: no, I never smoke them,' Major Brutt said, when Thomas at last found the cigars. Having lit his own, Thomas looked at the box suspiciously. 'These *are* going,' he said. 'I told you they were.'

'Then why don't you lock them up? It's Mrs Wayes, I expect; she has got a man friend and she's ever so good to him.'

'Has she been taking your cigarettes?'

'No, not lately; Matchett once caught her at it. Besides, she is far too busy reading my letters.'

'Why on earth not sack her?'

'Matchett says she is thorough. And thorough chars don't grow on every bush.'

Portia excitedly said, 'How funny bushes would look!'

'Ha-ha,' said Major Brutt. 'Did you ever hear the one about the shoe-tree?'

Anna swung her feet up on the sofa, a little back from the others, and looked removed and tired – she kept touching her hair back. Thomas squinted through his glass of drink at the light: now and then his face went lockjawed with a suppressed yawn. Major Brutt, having drunk two-thirds of his whisky, in his quiet way started dominating the scene. Portia's first animation was in the room somewhere, bobbing up near the ceiling like an escaped balloon. Thomas suddenly said, 'You knew Robert Pidgeon, I hear?'

'I should say so! An exceptional chap.'

'I never knew him, alas.'

'Oh, is he dead?' said Portia.

'*Dead?*' Major Brutt said. 'Oh, Lord, no – at least, I should think that is most unlikely. He had nine lives. I was with him most of the war.'

'No, I'm sure he wouldn't be dead,' Anna agreed. 'But do you know where he is?'

'I last had actual news of him in Colombo, last April – missed him there by about a week, which was bad. We are neither of us much of a hand at letters, but we keep in touch, on the whole, in the most astonishing way. Of course, Pidgeon is full of brain: the man could do anything. At the same time, he is one of those clever fellows who can get on with almost anyone. He is not a chap, of course, that I should ever have met if it hadn't been for the war. We both took it on the Somme, and I got to know him best after that, when we were on leave together.'

'Was he badly wounded?' said Portia.

'In the shoulder,' said Anna, seeing the pitted scar.

'Now Pidgeon was what you could call versatile. He could play the piano better than a professional – with more go, if you know what I mean. In France, he once smoked a plate and did a portrait of me on it – exactly like me, too; it really was. And then, of course, he wrote a whole lot of stuff. But there was absolutely no sort of side about him. I've never seen a man with so little side.'

'Yes,' Anna said, 'and what I always remember is that he could balance an orange on the rim of a plate.'

'Did he do that often?' said Portia.

'Very often indeed.'

Major Brutt, who had been given another drink, looked straight at Anna. 'You haven't seen him lately?'

'No, not very lately. No.'

Major Brutt quickly said, 'He was always a rare bird. You seldom hear of him twice in the same place. And I've been rolling round myself a good bit, since I left the Army, trying one thing and another.'

'That must have been interesting.'

'Yes, it is and it's not. It's a bit uncertain. I commuted my pension, then didn't do too well out in Malay. I'm back here for a bit, now, having a look round. I don't know, of course, that a great deal will come of it.'

'Oh, I don't see why not.'

Major Brutt, a good deal encouraged, said, 'Well, I've got two or three irons in the fire. Which means I shall have to stick around for a bit.'

Anna failed to reply, so it was Thomas who said, 'Yes, I'm sure you're right to do that.'

'I'll be seeing Pidgeon some time, I dare say. One never knows where he may or may not turn up. And I often run into people – well, look at tonight.'

'Well, do give him my love.'

'He'll be glad to hear how you are.'

'Tell him I'm very well.'

'Yes, tell him that,' Thomas said. 'That is, when you do see him again.'

'If you always live in hotels,' said Portia to Major Brutt, 'you get used to people always coming and going. They look as though they'd always be there, and then the next moment you've no idea where they've gone, and they've gone for ever. It's funny, all the same.'

Anna looked at her watch. 'Portia,' she said, 'I don't want to spoil the party, but it's half-past twelve.'

Portia, when Anna looked straight at her, immediately looked away. This was, as a matter of fact, the first moment since they came in that there had been any question of looking straight at each other. But during the conversation about Pidgeon, Anna had felt those dark eyes with a determined innocence steal back again and again to her face. Anna, on the sofa in a Récamier attitude, had acted, among all she had had to act, a hardy imperviousness to this. Had the agitation she felt throughout her body sent out an aura with a quivering edge, Portia's eyes might be said to explore this line of quiver, round and along Anna's reclining form. Anna felt bound up with her fear, with her secret, by that enwrapping look of Portia's: she felt mummified. So she raised her voice when she said what time it was.

Portia had learnt one dare never look for long. She had those eyes that seem to be welcome nowhere, that learn shyness from the alarm they precipitate. Such eyes are always turning away or being humbly lowered – they dare come to rest nowhere but on a point in space; their homeless intentness makes them appear fanatical. They may move, they may affront, but they cannot communicate. You most often meet or, rather, avoid meeting such eyes in a child's face – what becomes of the child later you do not know.

At the same time, Portia had been enjoying what could be called a high time with Major Brutt. It is heady – when you are so young that there is no talk yet of the convention of love – to be singled out: you feel you enjoy human status. Major Brutt had met her eyes kindly, without a qualm. He remained standing: his two great feet were planted like rocks by her as she knelt on the rug, and from up there he kept bellowing down. When Anna looked at her watch, Portia's heart sank – she referred to the clock, but found this was too true. 'Half-past *twelve*,' she said. 'Golly!'

When she had said good night and gone, dropping a glove, Major Brutt said, 'That little kid must be great fun for you.'

* * *

Most mornings, Lilian waited for Portia in the old cemetery off Paddington Street: they liked to take this short cut on the way to lessons. The cemetery, overlooked by windows, has been out of touch with death for some time: it is at once a retreat and a thoroughfare not yet too well known. One or two weeping willows and tombs like stone pavilions give it a prettily solemn character, but the gravestones are all ranged round the walls like chairs before a dance, and halfway across the lawn a circular shelter looks like a bandstand. Paths run from gate to gate, and shrubs inside the paling seclude the place from the street – it is not sad, just cosily melancholic. Lilian enjoyed the melancholy; Portia felt that what was here was her secret every time she turned in at the gate. So they often went this way on their way to lessons.

They had to go to Cavendish Square. Miss Paullie, at her imposing address, organized classes for girls – delicate girls, girls who did not do well at school, girls putting in time before they went abroad, girls who were not to go abroad at all. She had room for about a dozen pupils like this. In the mornings, professors visited her house; in the afternoon there were expeditions to galleries, exhibitions, museums, concerts or classical *matinées*. A girl, by special arrangement, could even take lunch at Miss Paullie's house – this was the least of many special arrangements: her secretary lived on the telephone. All her arrangements, which were enterprising, worked out very well – accordingly Miss Paullie's fees were high. Though Thomas had rather jibbed at the expense, Anna convinced him of Miss Paullie's excellent value – she solved the problem of Portia during the day; what Portia learned might give her something to talk about, and there was always a chance she might make friends. So far, she had made only this one friend, Lilian, who lived not far away, in Nottingham Place.

Anna did not think Lilian very desirable, but this could not be helped. Lilian wore her hair forward over her shoulders in two long loose braids, like the Lily Maid. She wore a removed and mysterious expression; her rather big pretty developed figure already caught the eye of men in the street. She had had to be taken away from her boarding school because of falling in love with the cello mistress, which had made her quite unable to eat. Portia thought the world of the things Lilian could do – she was said, for instance, to dance and skate very well, and had at one time fenced. Otherwise, Lilian claimed to have few pleasures: she was at home as seldom as possible, and when at home was always washing her hair. She walked about with this rather fated expression you see in photographs of girls who have subsequently been murdered, but nothing had so far happened to her. . . . This morning, when she saw Portia coming, she signalled dreamily with a scarlet glove.

Portia came up with a rush. 'Oh dear, I'm afraid I have made us late. Come on, Lilian, we shall have to fly.'

'I don't want to run: I am not very well today.'

'Then we'd better take a 153.'

'If there is one,' said Lilian. (These buses are very rare.) 'Have I got blue rings under my eyes?'

'No. What did you do yesterday evening?'

'Oh, I had an awful evening. Did you?'

'No,' said Portia, rather apologetic. 'Because we went to the Empire. And imagine, quite by chance we met a man who knew someone Anna used once to know.

Major Brutt, his name was – not the person she knew, the man.'

'Was your sister-in-law upset?'

'She was surprised, because he did not even know she was married.'

'I am often upset when I meet a person again.'

'Have you seen a person make an orange balance on the rim of a plate?'

'Oh, anyone could: you just need a steady hand.'

'All the people Anna always knows are clever.'

'Oh, you've brought your handbag with you today?'

'Matchett said I was such a silly not to.'

'You carry it in rather a queer way, if you don't mind my saying. I suppose you will get more used to it.'

'If I got too used, I might forget I had it, then I might forget and leave it somewhere. Show me, though, Lilian, how you carry yours.'

They had come out into Marylebone High Street, where they stood for a minute, patiently stamping, on chance of there being a 153 bus. The morning was colder than yesterday morning; there was a black frost that drove in. But they did not comment upon the weather, which seemed to them part of their private fate – brought on them by the act of waking up, like grown-up people's varying tempers, or the state, from day to day, of their own insides. A 153 did come lurching round the corner, but showed every sign of ignoring them, till Lilian, like a young offending goddess, stepped into its path, holding up a scarlet glove. When they were inside the bus, and had settled themselves, Lilian said reproachfully to Portia, 'You do look pleased today.'

She said, in some confusion, 'I do like things to happen.'

Miss Paullie's father was a successful doctor; her classes were held in a first-floor annexe, built for a billiard-room, at the back of his large house. In order that they might not incommode the patients, the pupils came and went by a basement door. Passers-by were surprised to see the trim little creatures, some of whom hopped out of limousines, disappear down the basement like so many cats. Once down there, they rang Miss Paullie's special bell, and were admitted to a fibre-carpeted passage. At the top of a flight of crooked staircase they hung their hats and coats in the annexe cloakroom, and queued up for the mirror, which was very small. Buff-and-blue tiles, marble, gilt-embossed wallpaper and a Turkey carpet were the note of the annexe. The cloakroom, which had a stained-glass window, smelt of fog and Vinolia, the billiard (or school) room of carpet, radiators and fog – this room had no windows: a big domed skylight told the state of the weather, went leaden with fog, crepitated when it was raining, or dropped a great square glare on to the table when the sun shone. At the end of the afternoon, in winter, a blue-black glazed blind was run across from a roller to cover the skylight, when the electric lights had been turned on. Ventilation was not the room's strong point – which may have been why Portia drooped like a plant the moment she got in. She was not a success here, for she failed to concentrate, or even to seem to concentrate like the other girls. She could not keep her thoughts at face-and-table level; they would go soaring up through the glass dome. One professor would stop, glare and drum the edge of the table; another would say, 'Miss Quayne, please, *please*. Are we here to look at the sky?' For sometimes her inattention reached the point of bad manners, or, which was worse, began to distract the others.

She was unused to learning, she had not learnt that one must learn: she seemed to have no place in which to house the most interesting fact. Anxious not to attract attention, not to annoy the professors, she *had* learned, however, after some weeks here, how to rivet, even to hypnotize the most angry professor by an unmoving regard – of his lips while he spoke, of the air over his head. . . .

This morning's lecture on economics she received with an air of steady amazement. She brought her bag into lessons, and sat with it on her knee. At the end of the hour, the professor said good morning; the girls divided – some were to be taken round somebody's private gallery. The rest prepared to study; some got their fine pens out to draw maps; they hitched their heels up on the rungs of their chairs, looking glad they had not had to go out. Some distance away from the big table, Miss Paullie sat going through essays, in a gothic chair, at a table of her own. Because the day was dark, a swan-necked reading lamp bent light on to what Miss Paullie read. She kept turning pages, the girls fidgeted cautiously, now and then a gurgle came from a hot pipe – the tissue of small sounds that they called silence filled the room to the dome. Lilian stopped now and then to examine her mapping nib, or to brood over her delicate state. Portia pressed her diaphragm to the edge of the table, and kept feeling at her bag against her stomach. Everybody's attention to what they were doing hardened – optimistically, Portia now felt safe.

She leant back, looked round, bent forward and, as softly as possible, clicked open her bag. She took out a blue letter: this she spread on her knee below the table and started to read for the second time.

Dear Portia: What you did the other night was so sweet, I feel I must write and tell you how it cheered me up. I hope you won't mind – you won't, you will understand: I feel we are friends already. I was sad, going away, for various reasons, but one was that I thought you must have gone to bed by then, and that I should not see you again. So I cannot tell you what a surprise it was finding you there in the hall, holding my hat. I saw then that you must have been seeing how depressed I was, and that you wanted, you darling, to cheer me up. I cannot tell you what your suddenly being there like that in the hall, and giving me my hat as I went away, meant. I know I didn't behave well, up there in the drawing-room, and I'm afraid I behaved even worse after you went away, but that was not altogether my fault. You know how I love Anna, as I'm sure you do too, but when she starts to say to me 'Really, Eddie', I feel like a wild animal, and behave accordingly. I am much too influenced by people's manner towards me – especially Anna's, I suppose. Directly people attack me, I think they are right, and hate myself, and then I hate them – the more I like them this is so. So I went downstairs for my hat that night (Monday night, wasn't it?) feeling perfectly black. When you appeared in the hall and so sweetly gave me my hat, everything calmed down. Not only your being there, but the thought (is this presumptuous of me?) that perhaps you had actually been waiting, made me feel quite in heaven. I could not say so then, I thought you might not like it, but I cannot help writing to say so now.

Also, I once heard you say, in the natural way you say things, that you did not very often get letters, so I thought perhaps you might like to get this. You and I are two rather alone people – with you that is just chance, with me, I expect, it is partly my bad nature. I am so difficult, you are so good and sweet. I feel particularly alone tonight (I am in my flat, which I do not like very much) because I tried just now to telephone to Anna about something and she was rather short, so I did not try any more. I expect she gets bored with me, or finds me too difficult. Oh Portia, I do wish you and I could be friends. Perhaps we could sometimes go for walks in the park? I sit here and think how nice it would be if –

'*Portia!*' said Miss Paullie.

Portia leaped as though she had been struck.

'My dear child, don't sit hunched like that. Don't work under the table. Put your work *on* the table. What have you got there? Don't keep things on your knee.'

As Portia still did nothing, Miss Paullie pushed her own small table from in front of her chair, got up and came swiftly round to where Portia sat. All the girls stared.

Miss Paullie said, 'Surely that is not a letter? This is not the place or the time to read your letters, is it? I think you must notice that the other girls don't do that. And, wherever one is, one never does read a letter under the table: have you never been told? What else is that you have on your knee? Your bag? Why did you not leave your bag in the cloakroom? Nobody will take it here, you know. Now, put your letter away in your bag again, and leave them both in the cloakroom. To carry your bag about with your indoors is a hotel habit, you know.'

Miss Paullie may not have known what she was saying, but one or two of the girls, including Lilian, smiled. Portia got up, looking unsteady, went to the cloakroom and lodged her bag on a ledge under her coat – a ledge along which, as she saw now, all the other girls' bags had been put. But Eddie's letter, after a desperate moment, she slipped up inside her woollen directoire knickers. It stayed just inside the elastic band, under one knee.

Back in the billiard-room, the girls' brush-glossed heads were bent steadily over their books again. These silent sessions in Miss Paullie's presence were, in point of fact (and well most of them knew it), lessons in the deportment of staying still, of feeling yourself watched without turning a hair. Only Portia could have imagined for a moment that Miss Paullie's eye was off what any girl did. A little raised in her gothic chair, like a bishop, Miss Paullie's own rigid stillness quelled every young body, its nervous itches, its cooped-up pleasure in being itself, its awareness of the young body next door. Even Lilian, prone to finger her own plaits or to look at the voluptuous white insides of her arms, sat, during those hours with Miss Paullie, as though Lilian did not exist. Portia, still burning under her pale skin, pulled her book on the theory of architecture towards her, and stared at a plate of a Palladian façade.

But a sense of Portia's not being quite what was what had seeped, meanwhile, into the billiard-room. She almost felt something sniffing at the hem of her dress. For the most fatal thing about what Miss Paullie had said had been her manner of saying it – as though she did not say half of what she felt, as though she were mortified on Portia's behalf, in front of these better girls. No one had ever read a letter under this table; no one had even heard of such a thing being done. Miss Paullie was very particular what class of girl she took. *Sins* cut boldly up through every class in society, but mere misdemeanours show a certain level in life. So now, not only diligence, or caution, kept the girls' smooth heads bent, and made them not glance again at Irene's child. Irene herself – knowing that nine out of ten things you do direct from the heart are the wrong thing, and that she was not capable of doing anything better – would not have dared to cross the threshold of this room. For a moment, Portia felt herself stand with her mother in the doorway, looking at all this in here with a wild askance shrinking eye. The gilt-scrolled paper, the dome, the bishop's chair, the girls' smooth heads must have been fixed here always, where they safely belonged – while she and Irene, shady, had been skidding about in an out-of-season nowhere of railway stations and rocks, filing off wet third-class decks of lake steamers, choking over the bones of *loups de mer*, giggling into eiderdowns that smelled of the person-before-last. Untaught, they had walked arm-in-arm along city pavements, and at nights had pulled their beds close together or slept in the same bed – overcoming, as far as might be, the separation of birth. Seldom had they faced up to society – when they did, Irene did the wrong thing, then cried. How sweet, how sweetly exalted by her wrong act was Irene, when, stopping crying, she blew her nose and asked for a cup of tea. . . . Portia, relaxing a very little, moved on her chair: at once she felt Eddie's letter crackle under her knee. What would Eddie think of all this?

Miss Paullie, who had thought well of Anna, was sorry about Portia, and sorry for Anna. She was sorry Portia should have made no friend here but the more than doubtful Lilian, but she quite saw why this was, and it really could not be helped. She regretted that Mrs Quayne had not seen her way to go on sending someone to fetch Portia, as she had done for the first weeks. She had a strong feeling that Portia and Lilian loitered in the streets on the way home. Miss Paullie knew one must not be old-fashioned, but it gave better tone if the girls were fetched.

Any girls who stayed to lunch at Miss Paullie's lunched in a morning-room in the annexe basement: down here the light was almost always on. The proper dining-room of the house was a waiting-room, with sideboards like catafalques: where Dr Paullie himself lunched no one asked or knew.

The lunch given the girls was sufficient, simple and far from excellent – Lilian, sent to lunch here because of the servant shortage, always messed about at it with her fork. Miss Paullie, at the head of the table, encouraged the girls to talk to her about art. This Wednesday, this Wednesday of the letter, Portia seated herself as far away from Miss Paullie as she possibly could, whereupon Lilian seized the place next to Portia's with unusual zest.

'It really was awful for you,' Lilian said. 'I didn't know where to look. Why didn't you tell me you'd had a letter? I did think you were looking very mysterious. Why didn't you read it when you had your breakfast? Or is it the kind of letter one reads again and again? Excuse my asking, but who is it from?'

'It's from a friend of Anna's. Because I got him his hat.'

'Had he lost his hat?'

'No. I heard him coming downstairs, and his hat was there, so I gave it to him.'

'That doesn't seem a thing to write a letter about. Is he not a nice man, or is he very polite? What on earth were you doing in the hall?'

'I was in Thomas's study.'

'Well, that comes to the same thing. It comes to the same thing with the door open. You had been listening for him, I suppose?'

'I just was down there. You see, Anna was in the drawing-room.'

'You are extraordinary. What does he do?'

'He is in Thomas's office.'

'Could you really feel all that for a man? I'm never sure that I could.'

'He's quite different from St Quentin. Even Major Brutt is not at all like him.'

'Well, I do think you ought to be more careful, really. After all, you and I are only sixteen. Do you want red-currant jelly with this awful mutton? I do. Do get it away from that pig.'

Portia slipped the dish of red-currant jelly away from Lucia Ames – who would soon be a débutante. 'I hope you are feeling better, Lilian?' she said.

'Well, I am, but I get a nervous craving for things.'

When the afternoon classes were over – at four o'clock today – Lilian invited Portia back to tea. 'I don't know,' said Portia. 'You see, Anna is out.'

'Well, my mother is out which is far better.'

'Matchett did say that I could have tea with her.'

'My goodness,' Lilian said, 'but couldn't you do that any day? And we don't often have my whole house to ourselves. We can take the gramophone up to the bathroom while I wash my hair; I've got three Stravinsky records. And you can show me your letter.'

Portia gulped, and looked wildly into a point in space. 'No, I can't do that, because I have torn it up.'

'No, you can't have done that,' said Lilian firmly, 'because I should have seen you. Unless you did it when you were in the lavatory, and you didn't stay in there long enough. You do hurt my feelings: *I* don't want to intrude. But whatever Miss Paullie says, don't you leave your bag about.'

'It isn't in my bag,' said Portia unwarily.

So Portia went home to tea with Lilian and, in spite of a qualm, enjoyed herself very much. They ate crumpets on the rug in front of the drawing-room fire. Their cheeks scorched, but a draught crept under the door. Lilian, heaping coals of fire, brought down, untied from a ribbon, three letters the cello mistress had written to her during the holidays. She also told Portia how, one day at school when she had a headache, Miss Heber had rubbed with magnetic fingers Lilian's temples and the nape of her neck. 'When I have a headache I always think of her still.'

'If you've got a headache today, then ought you to wash your hair?'

'I ought not to, but I want it nice for tomorrow.'

'Tomorrow? What are you doing then?'

'Confidentially, Portia, I don't know what may happen.'

Lilian had all those mysterious tomorrows; yesterdays made her sigh, but were never accounted for. She belonged to a junior branch of emotional society, in which there is always a crisis due. Preoccupation with life was not, clearly, peculiar to Lilian: Portia could see it going on everywhere. She had watched life, since she came to London, with a sort of despair – motivated and busy always, always progressing: even people pausing on bridges seemed to pause with a purpose; no birds seemed to pursue a quite aimless flight. The spring of the works seemed unfound only by her: she could not doubt people knew what they were doing – everywhere she met alert cognisant eyes. She could not believe there was not a plan of the whole set-up in every head but her own. Accordingly, so anxious was her research that every look, every movement, every object had a quite political seriousness for her: nothing was not weighed down by significance. In her home life (her new home life) with its puzzles, she saw dissimulation always on guard; she asked herself humbly for what reason people said what they did not mean, and did not say what they meant? She felt almost certain to find the clue when she felt the frenzy behind the clever remark.

Outdoors, the pattern was less involuted, very much simplified. She enjoyed being in the streets – unguarded smiles from strangers, the permitted frown of someone walking alone, lovers' looks, as though they had solved something, and the unsolitary air with which the old or the wretched seemed to carry sorrow made her feel people that at least knew each other, if they did not yet know her, if she did not yet know them. The closeness she felt to Eddie, since this morning (that closeness one most often feels in a dream), was a closeness to life she had only felt, so far, when she got a smile from a stranger across a bus. It seemed to her that while people were very happy, individual persons were surely damned. So, she shrank from that specious mystery the individual throws about himself, from Anna's smiles, from Lilian's tomorrows, from the shut-in room, the turned-in heart.

Portia turned over records and rewound the gramophone on the shut seat, and Stravinsky filled the bathroom while Lilian shampooed her hair. Lilian turbaned herself in a bath towel, and Portia carried the gramophone back to the fire again. Before Lilian's cascade of hair, turned inside out and scented in the heat, was quite dry, it had struck seven; Portia said she would have to be going home.

'Oh, they won't bother. You rang up Matchett, didn't you?'

'You said I could, but somehow I never did.'

As Portia let herself into Windsor Terrace, she heard Anna's voice in the study, explaining something to Thomas. There came a pause while they listened to her step, then the voices went on. She stole over that white stone floor, with the chill always off, and made for the basement staircase. 'Matchett?' she called down, in a tense low voice. The door at the foot of the stairs was open: Matchett came out of the little room by the pantry and stood looking up at Portia, shading her eyes. She said, 'Oh, it's you!'

'I hope you didn't wonder.'

'I had your tea for you.'

'Lilian made me go back with her.'

'Well, that was nice for you,' said Matchett didactically. 'You haven't had your tea there for some time.'

'But part of the time I was miserable. I might have been having tea with you.'

'"Miserable!"' Matchett echoed, with her hardest inflection. 'That Lilian is someone your own age. However, you did ought to have telephoned. She's that one with the head of hair?'

'Yes. She was washing it.'

'I like to see a head of hair, these days.'

'But what I wanted was, to make toast with you.'

'Well, you can't do everything, can you?'

'Are they out for dinner? Could you talk to me while I have my supper, Matchett?'

'I shall have to see.'

Portia turned and went up. A little later, she heard Anna's bath running, and smelled bath essence coming upstairs. After Portia had shut her door, she heard the reluctant step of Thomas turn, cross the landing, into his dressing-room: he had got to put on a white tie.

Anita Brookner

extract from

Latecomers

Fibich and Hartmann have been business partners for more than twenty years but their friendship goes much further and deeper than their professional lives. They met as boys at an English boarding school and this shared childhood experience of being outsiders, refugees from Germany, has been as close a bond as their considerable success in later years. Happily married and enjoying a comfortable way of life, neither man has felt the necessity of exploring his past. Until Fibich makes a sudden decision.

At sixty-one Fibich grew old, perceptibly. No longer interested in his work, he put all his efforts into doing it, with fewer results. Because of his inherent meticulousness no one noticed this, but it seemed to him that the major exercise of the day was getting to the office, and then, after an aching interval, which he measured minute by minute, getting home again. He felt endangered by his absence from home, and, once home, was not much reassured. He begged Christine not to bother to devise meals for him; he would concentrate on trying to eat a little fish, which he would dismember with a tremulous knife and fork. He would discard his city clothes with a sigh of relief and put on his dressing-gown. Christine, trying to make a ceremony of this habit, which she saw as alarming, bought him a velvet smoking-jacket. He wore it once or twice to please her, and then relapsed into the dressing-gown. Once she saw him shuffling along from the bathroom, the cord tied loosely round his waist, and was thankful that Toto no longer lived at home to see his father in this condition. She wondered whether it was the prospect of Toto's imminent departure to Morocco, to make a film, and his absence for a projected six months, that had brought about this change. She even discussed this with Hartmann, since Fibich would say nothing. Hartmann, for once, was devoid of resource. 'The trip may have tired him,' said Hartmann. 'Let him rest. He'll be all right. We'll plan a holiday, take a house somewhere this summer. He will come round.'

So they let him rest. He slept voraciously, and sometimes dreamed. His dreams were not clear to him. In one he was being very kindly introduced by a companion to an aristocratic tailor who was to measure him for a suit. The fitting was to take place in Brighton, near the station. While he waited for the tailor to attend to him, which he never did, the scene abruptly changed to Copenhagen on a winter's morning. This was somehow significant. In the dream Fibich took photographs of Copenhagen which he later studied with the same companion who had introduced him to the tailor. But in one of the photographs the companion figured quite prominently, standing in front of a cottage in the grounds of a large mansion or hotel. There had been a displacement of some kind, a fobbing off, a lack of explanation. Fibich awoke from this dream with a sense of alarm, relieved to find himself in his own bed. The relief gave him a little energy with which to start the day, which he did with a factitious enthusiasm that he was forced to substitute for the real thing. At the office, where he still appeared to be effective, he sat for long periods at his desk, staring at his hands. 'He's a little tired,' explained Hartmann, who was thereby forced into regular attendance. Goodman, ever sympathetic, took most of the work off his shoulders.

It was Yvette's turn to appear with covered dishes. Turning bad into good, as was her habit, she regarded Fibich's malaise as a challenge to her psychological powers and excellent household management. Luxurious foods appeared, were discarded by Fibich as too elaborate, and were hastily eaten by Christine in order that feelings should not be hurt. 'Don't trouble yourself,' said Christine to Yvette, as a concoction of sole with mushrooms in a cream sauce was handed in. 'He has no appetite.' 'Then he needs building up,' said Yvette firmly. Her reassurance, though of a hollow nature, was balm to Christine's anxious spirit.

To Hartmann Yvette said, 'I don't think he eats enough.

Does he have a proper lunch?' 'He never has,' Hartmann informed her. 'Then you'd better see that he does. Take him to that place of yours. He'll eat if you're with him. After all, he is no longer young.' Hartmann was disgruntled, disturbed. He was the elder by five years, sixty-six to Fibich's sixty-one. Nobody remarked that he was no longer young. Of course he did not feel old. That, essentially, was the difference between Fibich and himself.

For the first time Hartmann was obliged to think about age, and about the future. He was not particularly inclined to make changes. Since his mother-in-law's revelations he no longer felt that France was a country to which he might wish to retire. This, he knew, was irrational. Nevertheless, he would wait a bit and see if the feeling passed. And if not, well, there were other places: Spain, Switzerland. And yet he had to confess that he had little taste for uprooting himself. Now that he was forced to acknowledge that he too got tired, that he was no longer eager to leave home in the mornings, that he always felt a sense of deliverance as the weekend approached, he thought it might be time to sell up, settle affairs, make arrangements, and then, perhaps, wait a little to see what everyone wanted to do. He would miss his little indulgences, his routines, but he was not without resource. By nature he was a man of pleasure, and he could see that there might be a voluptuous charm in simply filling the empty days as only he knew how: a morning of delicate shopping, a stroll, a decent lunch somewhere. Could it be that he was at last on the verge of that real, that ineluctable old age, in which he had never truly believed? If so, he thought, it had come suddenly and quickly. He pondered a moment in disbelief, looked around at Yvette's apricot walls, looked at Yvette herself, dressed in the bright colours she still loved, the hair an ever more ambitious gold, saw her, unconscious of his gaze, vigorously and importantly moving about her drawing-room, saw, in a flash, that he must stay alive for her sake, for she would never fare well as a widow. He felt an unaccustomed pang in the heart as he looked at her, never still, in her royal blue blouse and her black skirt, humming a little under her breath, beautifully concerned for his comfort and the perfection of his home. He sighed. Perhaps they would quietly remain here, and somehow carry on as they were. Perhaps Fibich would come out of his depression, if that was what it was, and resume his duties, bring his attention once more to bear on the present. Suddenly all that Hartmann required was to see smiles on the faces around him. It was, after all, what he had always required. In his own eyes he had changed very little, had always, even as a young man, had an adult sense of responsibility. He had always had the insight that if he organized the main structures of his life – work, home, marriage – in a satisfactory manner, then he was fully entitled to enjoy his liberty outside them. He had had an easy attitude to fidelity when first married, but now he realized that he had been faithful to his wife for so long that he would find anything else intolerable. He became aware that Yvette had made him happy. He looked at her, sitting at her little desk, making out her shopping list, her mouth firm with attention. She would never understand either *La Princesse de Clèves* or *Madame Bovary*, and he was glad of it. He went over to her and kissed her hair, put an arm around her thickening shoulders.

'You know,' he said gently. 'I think you have put on a little weight.'

'I may have filled out a bit,' she admitted. 'But no one could say that I haven't kept my figure.'

'No,' he agreed. 'No one could say that.'

He patted her arm, was suddenly reluctant to leave her. She was, however, as always, sublimely unconscious of his moods.

'Are you off?' she asked. 'Don't be late this evening. I might want to see Marianne.'

'What will you do today?' he asked her in his turn.

She looked at him in surprise. 'Oh, I have plenty to do, don't you worry about me. Are you all right, Hartmann? You're usually on your way by this time.'

'Yes,' he said. 'I'm all right. I'll see you later. Have a good day.'

But he hesitated by the door, looked back at her unrealistically golden head, bent once more over her list, and wondered suddenly what it would be like not to see her there. He shivered. But this was ridiculous! They were still young! This was the malaise that was afflicting Fibich: he must have caught it from him. He straightened his shoulders and left the room, took his hat and the cane he sometimes affected, decided to walk to the office to demonstrate how young and active he was. It was a clear day, mild but sunless: rain was forecast. The white sky reflected his mood, in which he detected a certain anxiety, and absence of joy. He put this down to the strain of Marianne's second pregnancy, which had worried him, but he was aware that this was not the only cause. If Fibich went . . . Again, he told himself, this was ridiculous. Because the man had had the absurd idea of going to Berlin and had understandably been shaken up by the experience, there was no need to regard him as endangered. He had always been nervous, and now he was just a little more nervous than he had been: it was as simple as that. And even if it were not simple, they had reached the stage in life in which matters had to be made simple if they themselves were to last out the course. How could Fibich have put them all at risk with his insane journey? And what had he proved? Striding up the tree-arching avenue in the park, Hartmann felt his heart expand with anger, and also with joy, as he recovered his normal equilibrium. Fibich must pull himself together. He must be told that he owed it to Christine, to his son, and to himself, Hartmann, to behave like a grown-up for once in his life. For that was the trouble with Fibich, he thought. Although recognizable as elderly, he had never grown up. Well now, he, Hartmann, would have to talk with Fibich, as man to man, not as the boys they had once been, would tell him about the sudden recognition of old age that he had had that morning, would remind him that they must make plans, settle affairs, and, most of all, preserve themselves so as to enjoy whatever future remained to them. Hartmann, gazing up proprietorially at the arching branches, the trees now in full leaf, felt his troubled thoughts leave him, and also his ill humour. This had always been his strength, he thought, his endless tolerance of idiosyncrasy in others. Nevertheless, he was determined to speak to Fibich quite firmly. He strode on, proud of his ability to cover the distance from Ashley Gardens to Spanish Place, at a steady pace, on this dull but cloudless May morning. And not even out of breath, he remarked to himself.

The morning passed without incident. Roger brought no news of Marianne's condition. She had been in the hospital for three weeks and now the baby was almost due. Hartmann felt a thrill of fear: if bad news were to come it would come from that quarter. It was only natural that his nerves were on edge, he thought. Perhaps if Fibich were to become a grandfather he might behave more sensibly, might realize that energies have to be reinvested in that new generation, not squandered on his own past. But he thought that Fibich might be denied the opportunity to see his grandchildren. He somehow knew that Toto would remain unmarried for a very long time, would indeed regard his youth, and in turn his youthfulness, as his stock in trade, and therefore remain professionally famous as a young man until at the very least in his late thirties. Hartmann realized with a shock that Toto was already twenty-nine, nearly thirty. Where had the time gone? Again with a shiver of disquiet he determined to bring Fibich to book, as if he alone were responsible for all this ageing, as if time had less purchase on Fibich than on the rest of them, as if it devolved upon Fibich to bring them all safely through to the untroubled prospect that was, by now, surely theirs by right.

At half-past twelve he knocked on Fibich's door. Fibich, his hands folded and resting on top of an almost empty desk, looked up mildly. Hartmann resented his inactivity, as if this were proof of some private decision to abandon serious matters, until he saw that it was not inactivity at all: in the background, by the safe, was John Goodman, their all too devoted company secretary, whose eagerness was out of all proportion to what Hartmann and Fibich saw, still, as the frivolous nature of the enterprise. A small fortune built on flair, nothing but flair: how could they take credit for it? They had always had an amiable attitude towards work, the two of them, both knowing that in another life they would have done something more sensible, more serious, recognizing what they actually did do as appropriate to their uncertain position in every sort of hierarchy. Hartmann had the ideas and Fibich did the worrying: it suited them both perfectly. It was something of an effort for them to accommodate the personal career ambitions of both Myers and Goodman, young men on whom, Hartmann thought, youth was wasted, but fervid in their belief that what they did in this toy empire was important. Dark-suited, their rolled umbrellas a mark of *gravitas*, Myers and Goodman treated each other in a perfectly affable manner but with a lack of intimacy that entertained Hartmann profoundly. 'Such senators!' he had once remarked to Fibich. 'Such men of the cloth!' For he thought that work should be tackled exuberantly, light-heartedly, or not at all. Fibich was more tolerant, at least of Myers. Goodman worried him more. It was Goodman's assiduity he found hard to bear, his almost feminine desire to be necessary and wanted. And those extraordinary pleading eyes, the eyes of a harem favourite, quickly cast down, at the merest hint of reproof, into a double arc of dense, almost tangled lashes.

Fibich had devised many ways to outwit Goodman's sensibility, and had been forced to improvise many others, but that sensibility had never been exhausted. Trying to spare Goodman's feelings frequently brought on one of Fibich's migraine headaches. Hartmann treated him more teasingly and suffered from him accordingly less. Fibich could hardly bear to think about Goodman's life with his mother, in their little house in Putney, the news of the day faithfully served up to her over the evening meal. He saw them as himself and Aunt Marie Jessop, all those years ago. Nevertheless he continued to enquire after Mrs Goodman's health, although the radiant answers made him uneasy. Hartmann quite simply saw him as unawakened, waited for him to break out. In the meantime, since there were no signs of Goodman's ever breaking out, he would sportingly assume the existence of several girlfriends. 'Still out and about, John?' he would say. 'Still fancy free? Still tormenting the women?' Goodman would modestly lower his fabulous eyelashes, uncertain as to how to respond. At an admonitory shake of the head from Fibich, Hartmann would relent. 'Leave early today, John,' he would say. 'Give your mother a surprise. Everything seems to be taken care of. You do an excellent job.' Fibich often wished he had so light a touch. Goodman always appreciated Hartmann's sallies, but it was to Fibich that he looked for praise.

'Lunch,' said Hartmann firmly, determined to get down to the matter in hand. 'I am taking you out to lunch. All right, John, get some lunch yourself. And tell Tania to go too. We'll be back about two-thirty.'

Fibich looked at him in surprise. 'I am not hungry,' he said. 'Yes, John, finish up here later. I don't really want to eat.'

'I am taking you to lunch,' said Hartmann, handing him his hat. 'That is what is the matter with you, Fibich. You're neglecting yourself. And it's time we had a talk.'

In the street he looked about him with displeasure at

the prolonged sunlessness, the absence of good weather. Brave girls were dressed in flimsy garments, their bare legs white, their shoes inadequate. Harsh light came down unmediated from the colourless sky: rain still threatened but refused to materialize. Turning into the hotel dining-room, Hartmann was mildly put out to see nearly all the tables occupied. He stood majestically by the door, waiting to be ferried over to safe keeping. Reaching a table that was not his usual table, he flourished his white napkin, waved away the menu, and said, 'Sole. Grilled. Is that all right with you, Fibich? Fish is what you like, isn't it?'

'Thank you, thank you,' said Fibich. 'Sole, by all means.'

They sat in silence for a while, Fibich staring at his hands. Eventually Hartmann, who knew him so well, sighed.

'What happened there?' he asked. 'What did you find?'

Fibich looked up at him, still mildly.

'I found a foreign city that I did not remember,' he said. 'Rather a pleasant one. It meant nothing to me whatever.'

'And yet, since you came back you've been different. Changed. Something must have happened. What was it?'

Fibich smiled painfully. 'The only memory came last of all,' he said. 'Do you remember a commotion at Heathrow? A woman fainting?'

Hartmann nodded.

'The last sight of my mother,' said Fibich finally. 'She fainted when she said goodbye to me. I seemed to see her again. And since thinking about that moment, I find that I cannot endure . . .'

He dropped his head, made a helpless gesture with his hand, and knocked over a glass of water.

'Fibich!' said Hartmann warningly, summoning a waiter.

'I should have gone back,' whispered Fibich. 'I should not have left. I should have got off the train.'

'Is everything all right, gentlemen?' asked the head waiter, removing the wet tablecloth.

'Quite all right,' said Hartmann, rather too loudly. 'But I'm afraid we are in rather a hurry.'

'Your lunch is served, sir.' And the table was put to rights, hastily, while another waiter dealt with the fish, taking it off the bone and decorating it with lemon wedges and tartare sauce. 'A little wine, perhaps? If Mr Fibich is not feeling well?'

'No, no,' said Hartmann, again too loudly. 'That will be all.'

'Thank you,' said Fibich, in a voice slightly higher than normal, feigning enthusiasm. But his face was pale, and as the smell of fish rose from the plate in front of him his eyes filled with tears.

Hartmann stared at him in alarm. A collapse here, in Durrant's Hotel, where he lunched every day? A breakdown, the end of Fibich? He watched as Fibich tried to eat, raising and lowering his fork, disguising the untasted fragments beneath the sauce, the tears sliding down his face. He glanced round to see if anyone were watching. Conversation had ceased at the adjoining table.

'Come, Fibich,' he said. 'Thomas. You are safe. You are here. Try to eat. You have such a good appetite. Make an effort.' He was distractedly torn between anger and pity. But as the tears continued to fall he summoned the waiter again. 'On my account,' he said. 'We have to go.'

'Of course, sir. I understand.' They were outside in what seemed like record time, their passage shielded by waiters, their hats handed to them silently. Hartmann was aware of a momentary cessation of activity, a collective holding of breath, before they reached the blessed anonymity of the street.

Somehow he got Fibich back to the office, his coat hanging off his shoulders, his hat on the back of his head. Hartmann could not bear to put him to rights, simply drew his arm through his own, walked him like a child, aware of what they must look like, an upright bourgeois with his dissolute brother. Two girls, passing, giggled, taking Fibich to be drunk. As they reached their building, Fibich stumbled on the step. Then they were inside, safe from alien eyes. Hartmann guided Fibich to his room, to his chair, removed his hat, stood there while Fibich wept.

Goodman, returning, and thinking to find the room empty, went in to finish his work at the safe. He stopped at the sight of Fibich, whose tears were now spent, sitting with his head lowered to his clenched hands, still in his coat. Hartmann lifted his hand in warning, putting his finger to his lips. But Goodman, who was all too naturally of a filial nature, disappeared, came back with a glass of water, knelt by Fibich's desk, and took his hand.

'Mr Fibich,' he said gently. 'Would you like me to make you some coffee?'

Fibich raised his head, looked around him, and then looked down into Goodman's extravagant eyes, while Hartmann eased his coat from his shoulders.

'John,' he said presently, in an almost normal voice. 'I think I must have turned a little faint.'

'Drink this, sir,' said Goodman, proffering the glass.

Fibich drank slowly, shuddering as the icy water reached his stomach. 'That's better,' he said, his face still ghastly. 'Did you have lunch, John?'

'Oh, yes, sir,' Goodman's voice was devoid of embarrassment. Life at home, even at the age he was, must have conditioned him to work of this nature. Hartmann's opinion of him rose.

'And do you look after yourself properly, John?'

'Oh, yes, sir,' said Goodman again. 'My mother sees to that. We eat very healthfully. Mother sees to it that I eat a lot of salads.'

'That's good,' said Fibich. 'Take care of your mother,

John.' Hartmann turned away and looked out of the window. 'Is she in good health? Do you keep her company?'

Goodman did not appear to find these questions unusual. 'We've always been close,' he replied. 'My father left home when I was little, so there's just been the two of us. We do everything together.'

'And what will you do this weekend?' asked Fibich.

'I dare say we shall go over and visit my married sister,' said Goodman. 'I'm an uncle, you see. My sister has a small girl. We like to see her as often as we can.'

'That's good, John, very good.' Fibich's colour was returning, as if the contemplation of Goodman's home life were gradually filling him with reassurance.

'Perhaps a cup of coffee, Mr Fibich?'

'Why, yes, John, if you would be so kind.' At a nod from Hartmann Goodman left the room.

'Hartmann,' said Fibich. 'Something has happened.'

Hartmann stood behind him, his hands on Fibich's shoulders.

'Nothing has happened,' he said. 'You're still here. And so am I. Perhaps you did what you had to do, faced facts, did your grieving. Perhaps it is over for you now. I was lucky,' he went on, wiping the moisture from his eyes. 'I dismissed it all. And I was able to do this, somehow. I don't know how. I can't explain it, any of it. Perhaps you had to go through this to be free of it. A little crisis,' he said, blowing his nose. 'One might even say it was overdue. And all managed without the benefit of psychiatrists. Think of that!'

Fibich looked around him wonderingly. 'I feel better,' he said. But he did not look well, Hartmann thought. Nevertheless, his colour was nearly back to normal, and he drank the coffee that Goodman brought. Both watched him as he replaced the cup carefully in its saucer.

'Perhaps you should go home, sir, when you've had a rest.'

'Yes,' said Fibich. 'I should like to go home.'

'We will both go,' said Hartmann. 'And you too, John. Finish what you have to do and go home.'

'Buy your mother some flowers,' said Fibich. 'Give her a nice surprise.'

'I usually do, at the weekends,' said Goodman. 'We always enjoy our weekends.'

They both watched him as he collected the cups. Doomed, thought Hartmann. Saved, thought Fibich.

They took a taxi, leaving Fibich's car behind. They sat in the back, two elderly gentlemen, Hartmann resting his hands on his cane. They said nothing, simply marking the passage from danger back to normal life. The streets were empty: it seemed as if most people had left early for the weekend, despite the unpromising weather. Fibich appeared to have recovered from his attack, or whatever it was, thought Hartmann. He cautiously allowed himself to hope for the best. He resolved, at some point during the weekend, to speak to him about retirement. They would both retire, he thought, remembering his melancholy of the morning. It was time. And it was unthinkable, in any event, that he might carry on without Fibich. Their day was done, he now saw, although it terrified him to think that this might be so. Nothing too precipitate, of course: perhaps a year to wind things up, convert themselves into shareholders, make provision for the children. It could be done, he saw, and all in due season. There was no need to get out immediately, no need to frighten anybody. Everyone would understand. And their wives would be glad of their company. He thought back to Yvette, as he had seen her that morning. All in due season, he thought. All in due season.

Fibich thought of his home, of Christine, of his son. How painfully he had missed them, he thought: how wrongly he had spent his time, trying to re-establish a life before the only life he knew. He longed to reach his home, which was the only haven he would ever reach, and yet how temporary, how unstable even that now seemed to him. In any event he had always had an ambivalent attitude towards his home, for while the idea was sacred to him, the reality of it always proved fugitive. This was nothing to do with its physical location, or the fashion in which it was arranged: he even liked Christine's hazy muted colours, although he regarded the rooms as belonging entirely to her, with himself as a visitor, agreeably housed, but, it seemed to him, on a temporary basis. When in the office he would sometimes think lovingly of his home, yet as soon as he was back there he was afflicted with a restlessness which had him seizing his hat again and calling to Christine that he was going to get a bottle of wine, or post a letter, or simply take a walk in an attempt to dislodge the beginnings of a headache. He would wonder if he might feel better somewhere else, would search the Sunday newspapers, go with Hartmann to visit blocks of flats in St John's Wood, in South Kensington, in Highgate or Chiswick. Hartmann enjoyed these visits as simple excursions – he was in any event curious about other people's living arrangements – but to Fibich they were a matter of greater importance. Would he feel better if he received the evening sun, if he had a balcony, a patio, a roof terrace, if there were a caretaker on the premises, if the shops were near to hand, if there were three bathrooms instead of two, if he faced the other way? He did not know. He only knew that he felt a dismay amounting to anguish at the thought that he was already experiencing the maximum amount of comfort to be derived from the concept 'home'. He worried that it loomed so large, yet filled him with despair. Whatever brief moments of satisfaction he had felt in his life were always lessened by the idea of going home. He could be sitting comfortably in his own chair, in his own drawing-room, doing something entirely pleasant – reading, listening to music – when the idea of home would strike through him with a pang, as if home were somewhere else. Thus the homesickness that had afflicted him in Berlin had nothing to do with any home that he had ever known, but rather as if his place were eternally elsewhere, and as if, displaced as he was, he was only safe when he was fast asleep.

Gliding down Park Lane in the taxi, with Hartmann silent beside him, he began again to wonder whether they should not all sell up and go to the sun. For surely he would feel safer in the sun, source of all life, all joy, drawing him out of that deathly sleep every morning, summoning him, challenging him, revivifying him? The white skies and the green leaves of London had never given him the comfort that burning heat and brilliant light would certainly supply. For ten months of the year he felt cold, and his longing for warmth, like his longing for home, seemed unconquerable. He was not like Hartmann, who had the gift of being able to enjoy everything, every change in the climate, every amusement in the working day, every prospect of a new life. Fibich wished only to be safe, and, once safe, to be free, and, once free, to be brave. He had always known this, but never so clearly, never so nakedly as he did in this taxi, which even now was at the bottom of Grosvenor Gardens, and was taking him home to his wife, who must not be told that he was gravely damaged, merely a little tired, a little over-stressed and in need of a holiday. Hartmann would see to it. Hartmann would know what to do, what to say. For his part he felt quite calm, as if that shameful weeping had sedated him, leaving him devoid of resource, devoid too of his habitual nervousness, but cold, very cold.

They found Christine arranging pink and white tulips in a square glass vase. 'I'm so glad you're early,' she said. 'Toto is coming to dinner. You're eating with us, Hartmann. Does Yvette know you are home?'

'No,' he said, 'I haven't been upstairs yet.'

'You are more than welcome to stay,' she said. 'Will you have tea? Or did you have some at the office? You look cold, Fibich. Take your coat off. You'll soon get warm.'

She was too busy to pay them much attention. Fibich

watched her, patting her tulips, straightening a couple of books on a side table, twitching curtains into place.

'Toto coming to dinner?' he asked. This was almost unprecedented.

'Apparently he is off on Monday. The dates are being put forward. And we shan't see him for six months.'

She put her hand to her heart, as if registering the full impact of this news.

Fibich smiled, went over to her. 'Then we must see that he has a nice evening,' he said.

It appeared that nothing would be mentioned of the affair of Fibich's day, for which Fibich was grateful. He had not yet decided what to make of it. He now viewed his conduct with distaste, the distaste of a rational man. He felt quiet and empty, had no desire to return to that moment of – what had it been? revelation? – which he had experienced in the hotel dining-room. Whatever it had been, he had a sense of finality, as if the episode were done with. The partial easing of his feelings (for he knew there might be more to come) had been violently registered as a physical upheaval over which he had no control, and, as with any other illness, he was too glad to have got it over to investigate it further. Health, he supposed, was an absence of physical despair, and for the moment he felt none. Like a restored invalid he welcomed the warmth of the room, the flowers in the vase, the tea in his cup. Like an invalid he drank greedily, ate, with a careful and painful exactitude, the slice of iced apricot flan that Christine made so well. Hartmann lingered, turning to the window, his cup in his hand.

'You are very quiet, Hartmann,' said Christine. 'What are you thinking?'

'I was thinking of a housekeeper we had,' he said. 'In Munich. Her name was Frau Dimke. I have just remembered it. And my nurse was Frau Zarzicki.'

But Fibich waved a hand at him, as if to say, 'That life is over. Leave it alone. It has no place here. Remember not to remember, or you will be like me.' And Hartmann nodded, as if he understood what Fibich did not need to put into words, so present was it in both their minds.

Hartmann smiled. Such smiles they both had, thought Christine. That was what had bound her to them in the first place, their wonderful smiles, eager in Hartmann's case, tentative, like an English sun, in Fibich's. And from the joyless world of her youth she had retained a nostalgia for joy, although she herself was untrained for such emotion, and was awkward with it. Toto had it, that smile, although in his case it came too rarely, and when it did come could be perverted to do duty for feeling. Latterly, she thought, smiling herself, he had begun to look more like Fibich, tall, inwardly pondering, so that the smile, when it came, had a thoughtful reflective quality to it. In her eyes Fibich had changed little: it was Toto in whom all the major changes could be observed. Fibich, just today, when his hair was a little untidy and beginning to grow long again, might have been the man she married, tall and spare, absent-minded, with the same loping walk that she had often and secretly observed from behind the curtains of her father's flat in West End Lane. If anything it was Hartmann who had changed, grown pear-shaped, silver-haired. But his face, beneath the expensively barbered and flattened hair, was still the same, the face of an impudent boy impatient to grow into a fully fledged roué. It was all a matter of expression, she thought. He still cocked his head to one side, pursed his lips as if to kiss someone, anyone, widened his eyes at the thought of treats to come. And Fibich, too, had kept his original expression. He had a characteristic way of smiling and shaking his head at the same time that she had always found endearing. She saw that in time Toto might come to have that little mannerism, although in Toto the family likeness had taken a long time to come to the surface. She hoped that there was nothing of herself in Toto, although many people had remarked on his brilliant eyes, so unusual with dark hair, and, in rare moments of exaltation Christine did suppose that he might possibly have inherited them from her.

'What are you smiling at, Hartmann?' she asked.

'I am smiling at you smiling,' he said. 'One can see your boy is coming home.' He sighed. 'If only Marianne were here. Then we could all be together. No news, I suppose?'

'Nothing in the last hour. You had better ring the hospital and give them this number. Then you can relax this evening.'

'Yes,' he said. 'I must go and change. What time do you want us, Christine?'

'Toto is coming at seven-thirty,' she told him.

He smiled again. 'Then we will come at eight.'

When Toto came in, on the stroke of seven-thirty, with a carrier bag, she almost cried out at the resemblance to his father. He had let himself in with his key, and was deep in thought, going through his lines, she supposed, for she had no notion of how films were made. He straightened up, with a visible effort, and smiled at her. That smile again! From the bag he produced a bottle of wine and a pot plant, which she put in the place of honour on a small table, sweeping aside her tulips in order to do so.

'My dear boy,' she said. 'My dear boy.'

He flapped his hand at her. 'It's only a plant, Ma,' he said. 'The wine is for Dad. Drink it when I'm not here. You're very quiet, Dad. Daddy? Are you all right?'

'Never better,' said Fibich.

This was new, he thought, this noticing. But because he now wished to preserve his son from those quaking feelings of loss and regret which were his almost constant companions, he said little, put away his anxiety and his solicitude, the enquiries about Toto's health, sleep, exercise that he longed to make and habitually did make. Now it was appropriate, on the eve of Toto's departure, to treat him like a man, and in order to do so he must behave like a man himself. For he knew, somehow, that Toto, who was about to leave them (and who knew if he, Fibich, would ever see him again?) must feel some of that melancholy experienced by all those who leave their known worlds behind, and leave behind, too, those who love them, exchanging them for the more brutal attitudes of casual acquaintances, acquaintances who might see him as a novice who must undergo some rites of initiation if he were to be one of them. For whom could Toto trust, since he loved no one? He would be for ever dependent, whether he knew it or not, on those who loved him. And Fibich, in the clarity of this unusual day, could see that Toto was beginning to be aware of this, and to begin his own life, in which the mourning process would not be entirely absent.

The arrival of Yvette, in a blast of 'Joy' and a black and gold striped dress that made her look like a wasp, lightened the atmosphere. 'Hartmann is still telephoning,' she said disgustedly. 'He telephones every hour. He is driving them all mad. I told him I would *know* when the baby was born. "I am a mother," I said. "I will *know*." He takes no notice, of course. As if I were not concerned myself.'

'And of course Roger would let you know,' said Christine.

'Oh, Roger,' said Yvette, with surprise in her voice. 'I'd forgotten about Roger, to tell you the truth.'

Toto laughed. 'I adore you, Yvette.'

'Well, of course, darling,' she smiled. 'You always did. And how's our clever boy, then?'

They ate roast lamb, with tiny carrots and turnips, and a pudding that consisted of squares of shortbread floating on a sea of fruit. Toto ate swiftly, his eyes on his plate. 'There is plenty more,' observed Fibich mildly, almost amused to see his appetite duplicated so exactly. The day had brought revelations, he thought. *Life* brings revelations. He remembered some inkling of this having come to him in Berlin. He had felt then on the verge of a great discovery. But perhaps that was the discovery, quite simply that life brings revelations, supplies all the material we need. And if it does not supply it in the right order, then we must simply wait for more to come to light. He felt a coldness at the thought that more might be revealed to him, was no longer so anxious to bring it about, might even be content, he thought, to wait, and even to hope that nothing more would be vouchsafed to him this side of the grave. He glanced at his wife, whose eyes were all for Toto. Yet Fibich knew that in those last days, if he were granted the grace to be aware of them, Toto would be his, entirely his. For at the end he knew, even if Toto were not there (and he could not help wishing, selfishly, that he might be) he would, with his knowledge, die a happy man.

'There is cheese, if anyone wants it,' said Christine. Nobody did. She put a dish of chocolate-covered marzipan on the table, and went out to make coffee.

'Why do you never put on weight?' wondered Yvette. 'You both have such a sweet tooth. Hartmann was saying this morning that he thought I had filled out a little.'

'I was mistaken,' said Hartmann gravely. 'You look to me as you looked when I first saw you. Voluptuous, sensual, a woman of mystery. You maddened us with desire, back there in the Farringdon Road. I had to tie Fibich down to his desk. He was like a werewolf. A lycanthrope,' he added, taking the last of the marzipan. 'We imagined men fighting duels over you. Not much of a typist, though, as I remember.'

'Oh, Hartmann,' protested Yvette. 'You are always making fun of me.'

'I?' He put his hand to his breast. 'Would I do that?'

'I think I ran that office very competently,' she said.

'My darling, I can safely say without fear of contradiction that we have never had another secretary like you.'

The evening passed as if there were to be no birth, no departure. Fibich reflected that it might well be the last of such evenings. He felt a sense of completion, not devoid of sadness. They would never move, he could see that now. They would stay as they were, for whatever changes would take place would take place in their children, not in themselves. He supposed that he and Hartmann would continue to go to the office, do a little less, perhaps, then a great deal less, until they could do no more. Then they would take their rest. He did not know which of them would be left to take care of the others. For himself now it would simply be a matter of trying his best. He looked around him, at the faces at the table. Toto had wandered off to watch television. Christine was flushed, as she always was in moments of pleasure. Yvette – and he could see that she was now quite plump – sat with her hand through Hartmann's arm. And Hartmann looked quite old. But just the same, still the same bold young man that he had been on leaving the army, ready for anything. Fibich turned and looked at his son, who sat, long legs stretched out in front of him, in front of the television.

'Remind him to take something warm for the evenings,' he said to Christine.

'But it will be hot!' said Yvette. 'Marvellously hot. We should go to the sun ourselves this year. What do you say, Christine?'

'It would be better to wait until the winter,' she answered. 'I don't want to be away until Toto comes back.'

'And have you forgotten Marianne?' said Hartmann. 'Oh, God. Should I telephone again?'

'Not yet,' Yvette told him. 'You know what would be nice? If we took a house somewhere, and the children came too. Would you like that, Toto? Would you come?'

'Leave him alone,' said Fibich, smiling. 'He will come if he wants to. And if not, not.'

Toto leaned forward and switched off the television.

'Rubbish,' he commented. 'And he wasn't good. What was that, Daddy? A house? Oh, yes, I'll come. I'll come. If you really want me, that is.'

Angela Carter

extract from

The Magic Toyshop

Melanie, orphaned together with her younger brother and sister, has already fallen in love with her Irish aunt Margaret (who cannot speak) and Margaret's brothers Finn and Francie. But the head of her new family, Uncle Philip, puppet master and creator of the magic toyship, is a tyrant. Melanie is more frightened than flattered to be cast in the leading role for his Christmas show.

One night, her aunt drew a length of white chiffon out of a paper bag. The painted dog's eyes shone with white lights, reflecting it. She gestured Melanie over to her and draped the material around her shoulders. All at once, Melanie was back home and swathing herself in diaphanous veiling before a mirror. But the cuckoo clock poked out its head and called nine o'clock and there she was, in Uncle Philip's house.

'Your costume,' wrote Aunt Margaret on a pad, to save herself getting up. 'For the show.'

'What am I?' asked Melanie.

'Leda. He is making a swan. He is having trouble with it. He says Finn is trying to spoil it.'

This seemed very likely to Melanie.

'How big is the swan?'

Her aunt sketched a vague shape in the air.

'I don't think,' said Melanie, 'that I want to be Leda.'

'That is how he sees you. White chiffon and flowers in your hair. A very young girl.'

'What kind of flowers?'

Aunt Margaret drew out a handful of artificial daisies, yellow and white like fried eggs. Melanie would be a nymph crowned with daisies once again; he saw her as once she had seen herself. In spite of everything, she was flattered.

'Needs must,' she said. 'I suppose.' Her aunt's scissors flashed in the light like exclamation marks as she snipped into the flimsy stuff.

When the dress was roughly tacked together, Melanie had to put it on and go down and show it to Uncle Philip. She had to take all her clothes off and wear just the chiffon tunic with the white satin ribbons criss-crossed between her breasts (which, she observed with interest, seemed to have grown and the nipples to have got rather darker.) Aunt Margaret brushed her hair with the silver-backed brush which, like Winnie the Pooh, had survived the crash; she brushed and brushed until Melanie's black hair swirled like the Thames in flood, and then she floated all the daisies on it. She took a cigar box from a cupboard, opened it and displayed a number of sticks of greasepaint. Melanie's eyelids were painted blue and her lips coral. She felt greasy, basted with lard.

'Have you any nice jewellery?'

'Only confirmation pearls.' They, too, had survived. Aunt Margaret stroked them and adored them and fastened them round Melanie's neck. A few pins left in the chiffon tunic scratched Melanie's flesh. She wriggled.

'The pearls are the finishing touch. You look so pretty!'

'Well, I wish I could see myself. It is a long time since I dressed up.' Recollecting, she bit her lip.

'Go down, now.'

'By myself?'

Aunt Margaret nodded. Melanie slung her coat round her shoulders for the thin silky stuff hardly kept out the draughts and the house was freezing cold. Tea was long over and, downstairs, the evening's work was well under way. The curtains were open and Finn stood on the stage surrounded by cans of paint, open eyes of pure of colour, working on a blackcloth showing a sea with a blood-orange sunset, something like the background to the picture of the dog in the kitchen. Under the crude strip lighting, Uncle Philip squatted on the floor with a mound of feathers on a spread sheet before him. He was sorting the feathers into smaller piles. His moustache was lightly furred with down.

'Here I am,' said Melanie.

He stayed on his heels, resting his bulky hands on his dirty white overall knees. Tonight, his eyes were the no-colour of old newspapers.

'Why, his head is quite square!' thought Melanie. She had never noticed before. This evening, some disarrangement of the pale hair emphasized the corners. His head was a jack-in-a-box. A pin stuck in her armpit painfully.

'Take off that wrap,' he said.

She obeyed, shivering, for the basement was heated only by a miserly, inefficient little oil stove. Finn painted on. She heard the slap-slap of his brush as he filled in a large area of sky.

'You're well built, for fifteen.' His voice was flat and dead.

'Nearly sixteen.'

'It's all that free milk and orange juice that does it. Do you have your periods?'

'Yes,' she said, too shocked to do more than whisper.

He grunted, displeased.

'I wanted my Leda to be a little girl. Your tits are too big.'

Finn flung down his paintbrush.

'Don't talk to her like that!'

'Keep your mouth shut and mind your own business, Finn Jowle. I'll talk to her anyway I please. Who is it pays for her board?'

'I can talk how I like, as well as you!'

Uncle Philip stroked his moustache thoughtfully, not looking at Finn at all.

'Oh, no,' he said calmly. 'Oh, no, you can't. Get on painting. You haven't got all day.'

The discord jangled between them. Melanie's head ached.

'Finn,' she said. 'Please. I don't mind.'

'You see?' said Uncle Philip with a queer inflection of triumph. Finn shrugged and picked up his brush.

'And wipe out that paint mark you just made!'

Scowling, Finn scrubbed at the brush-mark on the floor with the elbow of his paint-stiffened overall.

'You'll do, then,' Uncle Philip said to her. 'I suppose you'll have to do. And you've got quite nice hair. And pretty legs.' But he was resenting her because she was not a puppet.

'Turn round.'

She turned round.

'Smile.'

She smiled.

'Not like that, you silly bitch. Show your teeth.'

She smiled, showing her teeth.

'You've got a bit of a look of your ma. Not much but a bit. None of your father, thank God. I never could abide your father. He thought 'isself too good for the Flowers by a long chalk, he did. A writer, he called 'isself. Soft bastard, he never got his hands dirty.'

'But he was awfully clever!' protested Melanie, stung with defiance at last.

'Not so clever he thought to put a bit by to take care of you lot when he'd gone,' Uncle Philip pointed out reasonably. 'And so I've got his precious kids all for my very own, haven't I? To make into little Flowers.'

He began to sort the feathers again. Jesus wants me for a sunbeam, Uncle Philip wants me for a little flower. The feathers moved about in the current of air that blew in under the door. Uncle Philip sighed heavily, the sigh of a man being thankful for exceedingly small mercies.

'You'll do,' he said. 'I suppose. Now piss off.'

Finn looked up angrily and Melanie ran upstairs before the sharp words and blows began. Why was Finn standing up for her, quixotically acting her champion like this? Because it was such an easy way of rousing her uncle? But did Finn care how much it upset her to see them so fierce with each other? He probably did not even notice. She took the flowers from her hair and carefully stepped out of the tunic. She did not think she would like herself in it if she could see herself and she did not think she would like to see her face bright and thick with greasepaint.

'I wish the show was all over,' she said.

Her aunt nodded and her eyes strangely spilled over with quick tears. She thrust her fists into her eyes and her shoulders shook. She cried often, these days. The bull terrier at once left off lapping water from its baking dish and went and put its head on her knee. Melanie was again surprised at the quick, alert sympathy of the dog, how he combined the roles of guard dog and four-legged comforter. She wished she could act just as quietly, just as simply. She put her hand on the older woman's shoulder and Aunt Margaret blindly grasped it with her own bird-claw. They stayed together like this for a long time. Each time Aunt Margaret cried, she and her niece became closer.

Finn said: 'You must rehearse with me.' He did not raise his eyes to Melanie but stared at the backs of his hands. The chisel cut had left a broad, purple, crescent-shaped scar.

'What, on the stage?'

'Do you think he'd allow us on to his lovely stage? Never. We'll have to do it in my room.'

'Why with you and not the swan?'

'You're not to see the swan until the performance so that you will react to it spontaneously. But you've got to practise with me to get the movements right so I'm to stand in for the swan.'

His voice was softer than a goose's neck, almost inaudible, and he kept his eyes turned away.

'Are we to rehearse in costume?' she asked half apprehensively, thinking of the white chiffon and her own white flesh showing through like milk in white glass.

'What, you think I should feather myself?'

He looked like the petrol-soaked wreck of a swan come to grief in a polluted river. His trousers and shirt (an old-fashioned shirt of striped flannel which should have had a collar but did not) were motleyed with all sorts of paint and a welter of dirt and sweat. His bare feet were warty with dirt. There was a dark brown tidemark round his throat and heavy thumbprints of dirt under his ears. The fungus was on his chin again. He smelt sickening and stale, a sour-sweet stench as if he was going bad.

'You should take more care of yourself,' she said. 'Oh, Finn, wash yourself. And cut your hair, perhaps.' For orange tendrils of uncombed hair curled round the shoulders of his grimy shirt.

'Why should I?'

She could not answer that.

It was the becalmed middle of a Sunday afternoon. In the kitchen, Aunt Margaret sat in her grey dress and vicious collar, sewing at the Greek tunic with the finest of stitches. Tea was already laid in the dining-room, the calm white cloth laid with green-banded Sunday china, milk and sugar standing on tiptoe to be used in jug and bowl. Victoria napped in her cage beside the blossoming geranium. Jonathon made ships downstairs while Uncle Philip constructed his swan and planned how it should be strung. Francie had taken his fiddle and gone off about his own business in his Easter Rising trilby and mackintosh. The house rested.

'Come on, then,' said Finn.

They climbed the stairs together past all the closed doors of Bluebeard's castle. Finn's hoarse, snoring breathing echoed noisily. They went into his room and he kicked the door to behind him. His face was a picture of sulky boredom.

'Let's get this stupid game over with, then.'

She looked around her, disconcerted. The room was as bare as if all the brothers' possessions were packed up in trunks and cases and put away in preparation for imminent departure. On the wall which she had never seen because it was the one with the peephole in it was a shelf with the only small and personal thing in the room standing on it, a single, faded photograph in a black, badly fitting frame. The photograph was of a woman with a broad face who looked the camera squarely in the eye without a smile. She wore a Galway shawl and there was a baby in the fold of it.

'Our mother,' said Finn, 'with Maggie in arms.'

Behind her head was a desolation of rocks.

'Back home,' said Finn and said no more.

Next to the photograph was the Anglepoise lamp coiled up ready to spring. But for the strip of mirror and the portrait of her aunt, the walls were empty. There was no sign of the St Sebastian triptych. He must have hidden it. By the shelf was a built-in cupboard but everything else she saw was familiar. She sat down on the roses-and-castles chair with a ludicrous sense of formality, as if paying a polite call in a tailored suit and a small, veiled hat.

'This is how it goes,' said Finn. He seemed to grudge every word he spoke. 'Leda walks by the shore, gathering shells.'

From his pocket, he took a convoluted shell, all milky mother-of-pearl. He set it down on the bit of rug.

'Night is coming on. She hears a beating of wings and sees the approach of the swan. She runs away but it bears down and casts her to the ground. Curtain.'

'Is that all?'

'It is only a vehicle for his handsome swan, after all.'

She rose and stooped for the shell. She moved badly because he was watching her.

'Make it more fluid,' he said wearily. 'Move from the hips.'

She stooped again, waggling her backside, which was the only way she could think of moving from her hips.

'For Chrissake, Melanie. Did they teach you hockey when you went to school?'

'Well, yes. They did.'

He sneered.

'Move – ah, like this.' He scooped up the shell. But he no longer moved like a wave of the sea. He creaked, indeed, like a puppet. He had forgotten his grace was all gone. He stopped short, fingering the shell.

'Anyway,' he said. 'Try again.'

She tried.

'Better, maybe. Now, do it again. I'm the swan.'

She walked by the shore, gathering shells. Finn stood on his toes. His hair was all over his face; she could hardly see him. He made swishing noises indicating the beating of wings.

'When you hear that, you worry. You run a few steps.'

She ran a few steps.

'Right.'

He ran after her. It was charades. She giggled.

'No, don't be silly! You're supposed to be a poor frightened girl.'

'I can't take it seriously.'

'But, Melanie, he'll turn you out if you can't work for him. And what would you do then?'

'He wouldn't,' she said wondering. 'He couldn't.'

'Yes, he could and would.' He was reasonable and serious. 'We could do nothing for you. You would starve.'

'I hate him,' she said. She had not meant to say this. Their eyes met and looked away again.

'Start from the beginning. Pretend. Act.'

This time, things went better. She screwed her eyes up and pretended she saw evening coming on. And pretended she could hear gulls mewing and the squeak of sand under the balls of her feet and the rhythm of wings. So it was easy to look frightened and to run a little way.

'You run and stumble and I bear you to the ground.' He concealed a yawn. 'Put the shell down and we'll go through it all.'

She obeyed him. The gulls mewed and the sand shifted and the swan hurtled down and it was easy. She sprang away from Finn and it was no longer a pretence –

she stumbled over the knotted fringe of the rug. Overbalancing, she clutched at Finn to save herself but pulled him over with her. Clinging to each other, Melanie laughing, they toppled in slow motion to the floor.

But Finn did not laugh. And Melanie's laughter trickled to nothing when she saw his pale, bony face half-hidden by hair and could see nothing there, no hint of a smile or inflection of tenderness which might mean she would be spared. He lay as close as a sheet to a blanket; and he smelt of decay, but that no longer mattered. Shuddering, she realized that this no longer mattered. She waited tensely for it to happen.

She was seized with a nervous, unlocalized excitement. They lay together on the bare, splintered boards. There was no time any more. And no Melanie, either. She was utterly subdued. She was changing, growing. All that was substantial to her was the boy whom she touched all down the length of her but did not touch. The moment was eternity, trembling like a dewdrop on a rose, endlessly about to fall. Grudgingly, slowly, reluctantly, he put his hand on her right breast. Time began with a jolt, their time. She let her breath out in a hissing rush. He closed his Atlantic eyes. He looked like a death-mask of himself. It was killing him to leave his isolation, but leave it he must.

'This is the start,' she said to herself, clearly. She heard her own voice, certain and distinct, inside her head. No more false starts, as in the pleasure gardens, but the real beginning of a deep mystery between them. What would he do to her, would he be kind? She looked down with a fear that was also a pleasure at his stained, scarred hand. His workman's hand, which was strong and cunning. The light seemed to die about her, leaving her to see by her senses only.

'No,' said Finn aloud. 'No!'

He leapt to his feet and sprinted across the room. He jumped into the cupboard and shut the door. From the cupboard came a muffled cry. 'No!' again.

The tension between them was destroyed with such wanton savagery that Melanie fell limply back and struggled with tears. She still felt his five fingertips, five red cinders, burning on her breast. But he was gone. She felt cold and ill.

'No!' more faintly.

'What have I done wrong?' she asked the door of the cupboard. No answer. 'Finn?'

Still no answer. She felt a fool, lying on the floor with her skirt rumpled over her knees. She could see under the beds, a pair of shoes standing harmlessly under each one in no dust. The room was very clean although Finn was not. Francie's shoes were brilliant with polish but Finn's were caked with mud – though where could he have been, had he been walking in the pleasure garden by himself, talking to the broken queen and patting the stone lioness on the head? His shoes were lopsided with walking.

'Maybe,' she thought, 'he wouldn't because I never polished his shoes.' Anything was possible, when he went to earth in a cupboard to get away from her.

From the keyhole of the cupboard issued a blue trail of smoke. She was horrified until she guessed he had lit a cigarette. Probably, in the close confinement, he would suffocate in his own smoke. Or set himself on fire like a Buddhist monk, but accidentally.

'Isn't he *silly*,' she thought. She felt very old, but not mature.

'Don't smoke in the cupboard,' she said.

A fresh puff of smoke answered her. Grumbling beneath her breath, she dragged herself upright and went and opened the door. The cupboard was just deep enough to hold him sitting cross-legged, his head concealed in the pin-striped folds of Francie's second-best suit, which hung on a hanger. There were also some ghostly white shirts there. On a shelf at the top of the cupboard were piled paintings of all shapes and sizes. Finn's hand, with a cigarette in it, poked out of the folds of clothing and tapped ash on to the floor. He said nothing. She examined the crossed soles of his feet.

'Finn,' she said, 'there's a splinter in your left foot.'

'Go away,' he said.

'If you don't take the splinter out, it will fester. They will probably have to amputate your leg, in the end.'

'Please. Go away.'

'Why are you hiding in the cupboard, Finn?' she asked like a mother to an inexplicable child at the end of a hard day.

'Because there's room for me,' he said. The Lewis Carroll logic of this was too much for her; she ran up a white flag, acknowledging defeat.

'Oh, Finn, why did you run away from me?' And the words issued out on the wings of a wail.

'You are too young,' he said, 'to say things like that. You must have read it in a woman's magazine.' His voice was muffled in serge, dressed up for the Arctic in cap and muffler.

She pushed aside the clothing and revealed him, all small and disconsolate and shrivelled looking, knees drawn up under chin in a foetal position. He scowled with squinting ferocity, like a balked Siamese cat.

'You see,' he said, 'he wanted me to fuck you.'

She had only read the word before, in cold and aseptic print, never heard it spoken except in heat by rough farm-workers who did not realize she was walking by. She was deeply agitated. She had never connected the word with herself; her phantom bridegroom would never have fucked her. They would have made love. But Finn, she acknowledged with a sinking of her spirit, would have. She could tell by the way he ground out his cigarette on the floor.

'It was his fault,' he said. 'Suddenly I saw it all, when we were lying there. He's pulled our strings as if we were his puppets and there I was, all ready to touch you up just as he wanted. He told me to rehearse Leda and the swan with you. Somewhere private. Like in your room, he said. Go up and rehearse a rape with Melanie in your bedroom. Christ. He wanted me to do you and he set the scene. Ah, he's evil!'

Melanie kicked at a knot in the floorboards with the toe of her shoe. She noticed that the toe was scuffed and the shoes would need mending. Did the household have credit at a cobbler's shop? She tried to concentrate on this so as not to have to think about what Finn was saying.

'Well,' said Finn, parting the clothes in order to light a fresh cigarette, 'I'm not having any, see? I'm not going to do what he wants even if I do fancy you. So there.'

Melanie abandoned trying to think about cobbling.

'Oh, but Finn, why ever does he want you to—'

'To pull you down, Melanie. He couldn't stand your father and he can't stand you and the other kids being your father's children, though he doesn't mind you being your mother's. You represent the enemy to him, who use toilet paper and fish knives.'

'We never had fish knives,' said Melanie.

He disregarded this. He became distraught and incoherent.

'And you're so fresh and innocent, all of you, and so you're something to change and destroy. Well, Victoria is Maggie's baby, now, and he has Jonathon working all day and all night under his eye and there is only you left not accounted for. So he thinks I should do you because he despises me, too, and he thinks I'm God's scum. He does, really. A dirty beatnik and he'd turn me out if it wasn't for Maggie and if it wasn't for the painting, and I'd go, anyway, if it wasn't for Maggie. And so I should do you because you shave under your armpits and maybe you would have a baby and that would spite your father.'

'My father is dead.'

'He knows. All the same, it's all the same to him.'

'I don't shave under my armpits.'

'It's a manner of speaking.' His face twisted in a grimace of pain or pure disgust and he threw away his cigarette and buried his head in his arms. She shifted her weight from foot to foot, uncertain and bewildered. She hardly took in what he said. Without understanding, she said: 'And you don't want me, then?'

'That's got nothing to do with it,' he snapped. 'Besides, you're too young. I found that out in the pleasure garden. Later on, perhaps. But you're too young.'

'I know,' she said. 'It is my curse.'

'Isn't it terrible?' Finn said. 'This is a madhouse. He is making me mad.'

He hid himself with the clothes again, jerking them about on their hangers. Disturbed, the pile of paintings on the shelf slithered to the floor. Melanie picked them up wearily. She was exhausted with surprises. First the St Sebastian triptych, all finished, down to the last arrowhead and gobbet of blood. She made a face at it and thrust it away. Then she saw herself, and was touched.

She was taking off her chocolate sweater and was all twisted up, a rather thin but nicely made young girl with a delicate, withdrawn face, against a wall of dark red roses. Her wallpaper. She looked very scrubbed. She looked like a virgin who cleaned her teeth after every meal and delighted to take great bites from rosy apples. Her black hair exploded about her head in great Art Nouveau ripples. It looked as though Finn was trying his hand at curves. The picture was as flat and uncommunicative as all his pictures and seemed to be an asexual kind of pin-up. Round the bare upper part of her right arm was a black band. He did not see her precisely as she saw herself but it could have been very much worse.

'But why has he put in the mourning band?' she thought.

Nevertheless, she was pleased.

'Did you make sketches of me through the spy-hole when I was undressing?' she asked.

'Don't look at my pictures.'

'I'm only putting them away.'

Then she saw the horrible picture. It was a hell of leaping flames through which darted black figures. Uncle Philip was laid out on a charcoal grill like a barbecued pork chop. He was naked, gross and abhorrent. His flesh was beginning to crack and blister as his fat bubbled inside it. His white hair was budding in tiny flames. Beside him stood a devil in red tights with horns and a forked tail. He held a pair of red-hot tongs in his hands with which he was tweaking Uncle Philip's testicles. Uncle Philip's face was branded with a fiery hoofprint. His mouth was a black, screaming hole from which issued a banner with the words: 'Forgive me!' The devil had Finn's former, grinning face.

'So that is where his grin went,' thought Melanie. 'He wiped it off his face and slapped it on to the cardboard.' Finn would never grin again.

From Finn's painted lips, which were made of fire, came the one word: 'Never!' Over the top of the picture, in a white shield, was a title, also in Gothic script: 'In Hell, all wrongs are righted.' The inspiration of the whole was Hieronymus Bosch. Melanie dropped the picture with a sob.

'I told you not to look.'

'You are right. It is a mad house.' She began to cry. Finn crawled out of the cupboard on all fours and clasped her knees, burying his head between her thighs. She dug her fingers in his hair convulsively and said the words which floated on top of her mind, thoughtlessly; if she had thought about them, she would never have said them.

'I think I want to be in love with you but I don't know how.'

'There you go again, talking like a woman's magazine,' said Finn. 'What you feel is because of proximity, because I am here. Anyway, you are too young, we have been into that. And it would be a waste of your time, for I'm going to make him murder me, aren't I?'

Then the gong sounded for tea, which somehow had to be endured, the shrimps shelled, the bread buttered, the milk and tea poured into the cups, Victoria's cake to be cut into fingers so that she could eat it all up. In the witch-ball, they all sat, monstrously swollen, eating at a warped white table that stretched for ever. Melanie kept her eyes on the witch-ball so as not to have to look at Uncle Philip.

The next day was Christmas Eve but it was no different to any other day except that the shop was very, very busy. It was crowded all through the day and Melanie and Aunt Margaret tottered on burning feet by the time they turned the sign on the door round to read 'closed'. The shelves were almost bare, the stock almost gone. Even the hobby horse and the toy puppets had gone from the windows, leaving only the plastic holly behind. Notes spilled out of the money drawer. They were down to the last roll of flowered wrapping paper. The shop had the look of a battlefield the morning after. On its perch, the parakeet drooped as if it, too, had been worked off its feet.

'Well,' wrote Aunt Margaret, 'at least we shall have a day of rest tomorrow.'

Although nothing more. Melanie wrestled with self-pity and memory as she sat in the kitchen with her book while her aunt sewed the last seams of the Greek tunic. No holly in the kitchen, no mistletoe over the lampshade. No Christmas tree with small coloured lights. Uncle Philip received Christmas cards and calendars from traders and wholesalers with whom he dealt but he destroyed them as soon as they arrived so there were no cards on the mantelpiece. Nothing. And the house was peculiarly cold. Perhaps it was freezing itself out of spite.

Melanie wondered if they would go to church, to Midnight Mass, because she, in a muddled way, thought they must be religious if they believed so firmly in Hell.

But bedtime was at the usual time and, though Francie returned very late, he was slightly drunk so he could not have been to church. She heard his uncertain footsteps on the stairs and he was humming a hornpipe under his breath.

Finn must have been lying awake in the darkness, as she was, the wall separating them like Tristan's sword, for she could hear the soft murmur of him and Francie talking together for a little while, but she could not make out one word. Then a little light came through the uncovered spy-hole, a flickering, surreptitous light. And her nostrils caught the smell of charring wood. They were burning something. Guiltily, she got out of bed to look. Out of bed, it was colder than she would have thought possible, the temperature of Russia when nights are coldest there. The floorboards struck ice up through the unprotected soles of her feet. She felt gooseflesh rising up all over her.

The brothers' room was dim and shadowed; she made out their two shapes with difficulty. They were hunched together in the middle of the room. The strip of mirror suddenly flashed at a struck match. Francie's raincoat glimmered; he still wore his coat and hat. He knelt on the floor, steadying himself with one hand. In the other, he held upright a small, carved doll with a shock of yellowish white hair made from unravelled string. It had a small, dandyish white shirt with a bootlace tie. Aunt Margaret must have made the shirt, it was so small and fine. It must have been difficult to make it so small.

Finn was carefully applying matches to various parts of the doll. As soon as the clothing began to smoulder and glow, igniting the wood beneath, he pinched out the charred, burnt part and began again on another place. Both were quite silent and busy, absorbed. She saw the dog was also present, sitting watching them without blinking. When the matches shone out, its eyes were fluorescent raspberries. Its white fur looked unnatural, bleached on purpose, for a disguise. Finn put a match to the doll's trousered groin and he and Francie laughed very quietly. The Jowles were keeping Christmas in their own way.

Melanie went back to bed and pulled the covers over her head. But there was no warmth in the blankets and the stone hot-water-bottle had cooled in her absence. It was so cold she thought the mucus would freeze inside her nose and her brain congeal to a ridged knob of ice. She kept her head under the blankets so that she would not see the magic light.

Colette

The Cat

ONE

Towards ten o'clock, the family poker-players began to show signs of weariness. Camille was fighting against sleepiness as one does at nineteen. By starts she would become fresh and clear-eyed again; then she would yawn behind her clasped hands and reappear pale, her chin white and her cheeks a little black under their ochre-tinted powder, with two tiny tears in the corners of her eyes.

'Camille, you ought to be in bed!'

'At ten o'clock, Mummy, at ten o'clock! Who on earth goes to bed at ten o'clock?'

Her eyes appealed to her fiancé, who lay back, overcome, in the depths of an armchair.

'Leave them alone,' said another maternal voice. 'They've still seven days to wait for each other. They're a bit dazed at the moment. It's very natural.'

'Exactly. One hour more or less . . . Camille, you ought to go home to bed. So ought we.'

'Seven days!' cried Camille. 'But it's Monday today! And I hadn't given it a thought! Alain! Wake up! Alain!'

She threw her cigarette into the garden and lit a fresh one. Then she sorted out the scattered cards, shuffled them and laid them out as fortune-tellers do.

'To know whether we'll get the car, that marvellous baby roadster, before the ceremony! Look, Alain! I'm not cheating! It's coming out with a journey and an important piece of news!'

'What's that?'

'The roadster, of course!'

Without raising the nape of his neck from the chair, Alain turned his head towards the open french window, through which came the sweet smell of fresh spinach and new-mown hay. The grass had been shorn during the day, and the honeysuckle, which draped a tall dead tree, added the nectar of its first flowers to the scent of the cut grass. A crystalline tinkle announced the entrance of the ten o'clock tray of soft drinks and iced water, carried by old Emile's tremulous hands, and Camille got up to fill the glasses.

She served her fiancé last, offering him the misted tumbler with a smile of secret understanding. She watched him drink and felt a sudden pang of desire at the sight of his mouth pressing against the rim of the glass. But he felt so weary that he refused to share that pang and merely touched the white fingers with the red nails as they removed his empty tumbler.

'Are you coming to lunch tomorrow?' she asked him under her breath.

'Ask the cards.'

Camille drew back quickly, and began to act the clown a little over her fortune-telling.

'Never, never joke about twenty-four-hours! Doesn't matter so much about crossed knives, or pennies with holes in them, or the talkies, or God the Father . . .'

'Camille!'

'Sorry, Mummy. But one mustn't joke about twenty-four-hours! He's a good little chap, the knave of spades. A nice black express messenger, always in a hurry.'

'In a hurry to do what?'

'Why, to talk, of course! Just think, he brings the news of the next twenty-four hours, even of the next two days. If you put two more cards on his right and left, he foretells the coming week.'

She was talking fast, scratching at two little smudges of lipstick at the corners of her mouth with a pointed nail.

Alain listened to her, not bored, but not indulgent either. He had known her for several years and classified her as a typical modern girl. He knew the way she drove a car, a little too fast and a little too well; her eye alert and her scarlet mouth always ready to swear violently at a taxi-driver. He knew that she lied unblushingly, as children and adolescents do; that she was capable of deceiving her parents so as to get out after dinner and meet him at a night-club. There they danced together, but they drank only orange-juice because Alain disliked alcohol.

Before their official engagement, she had yielded her discreetly wiped lips to him both by daylight and in the dark. She had also yielded her impersonal breasts, always imprisoned in a lace brassière, and her very lovely legs in the flawless stockings she bought in secret; stockings 'like Mistinguett's, you know. Mind my stockings, Alain!' Her stockings and her legs were the best things about her.

'She's pretty,' Alain thought dispassionately, 'because not one of her features is ugly, because she's an out-and-out brunette. Those lustrous eyes perfectly match that sleek, glossy, frequently washed hair that's the colour of a new piano.' He was also perfectly aware that she could be as violent and capricious as a mountain stream.

She was still talking about the roadster.

'No, Daddy, *no*! Absolutely no question of my letting Alain take the wheel while we're driving through Switzerland! He's too absent-minded. And besides, he doesn't really like driving. I know him!'

'She knows me,' Alain echoed in his own mind. 'Perhaps she really thinks she does. Over and over again, I've said to her too: "I know you, my girl." Saha knows her too. Where is that Saha?'

His eyes searched round for the cat. Then, starting limb by limb, first one shoulder, then the other, he unglued himself from the armchair and went lazily down the five steps into the garden.

The garden was very large and surrounded by other

gardens. It breathed out into the night the heavy smell of well-manured earth given over to producing flowers and constantly forced into fertility. Since Alain's birth, the house had hardly changed at all. 'An only son's house,' Camille said jeeringly. She did not hide her contempt for the high-pitched roof with the top-storey windows set in the slates and for certain modest mouldings which framed the french windows on the ground floor.

The garden, like Camille, also seemed to despise the house. Huge trees, which showered down the black, calcined twigs which fall from elms in their old age, protected it from neighbours and passers-by. A little farther on, in a property for sale and in the playground of a school, stood isolated pairs of similar old elms, relics of a princely avenue which had formed part of a park which the new Neuilly was fast destroying.

'Where are you, Alain?'

Camille was calling him from the top of the steps but, on an impulse, he refused to answer. Deliberately, he made for the safer refuge of the shadows, feeling his way along the edge of the shaven lawn with his foot. High in the sky a hazy moon held court, looking larger than usual through the mist of the first warm days. A single tree – a poplar with newly opened glossy leaves – caught the moonlight and trickled with as many sparkles as a waterfall. A silver shadow leapt out of a clump of bushes and glided like a fish against Alain's ankles.

'Ah! There you are, Saha! I was looking for you. Why didn't you appear at table tonight?'

'Me – rrou – wa,' answered the cat, 'me-rrou-wa.'

'What, me-rrou-wa? And why me-rrou-wa? Do you really mean it?'

'Me-rrou-wa,' insisted the cat, 'me-rrou-wa.'

He stroked her, tenderly groping his way down the long spine that was softer than a hare's fur. Then he felt under his hand the small, cold nostrils dilated by her violent purring. 'She's my cat. My very own cat.'

'Me-rrou-wa,' said the cat very softly. 'R . . . rrou-wa.'

Camille called once more from the house and Saha vanished under a clipped euonymus hedge, black-green like the night.

'Alain! We're going!'

He ran to the steps, while Camille watched him with a welcoming smile.

'I can see your hair running,' she called out. 'It's crazy to be as fair as all that!'

He ran quicker still, strode up the five steps in one bound, and found Camille alone in the drawing-room.

'Where are the others?' he asked under his breath.

'Cloakroom,' she whispered back. 'Cloakroom and visit to "work in progress". General gloom. "It's not getting on! It'll never be finished!" What the hell do we care! If one was smart, one could hold on to Patrick's studio for keeps. Patrick could find himself another. I'll fix it, if you like.'

'But Patrick would only leave the "Wedge" as a special favour to please *you*.'

'Of course. One will take advantage of that.'

Her face sparkled with that peculiarly feminine unscrupulousness which Alain could not bring himself to accept as a matter of course. But he remonstrated only on her habit of saying 'one' for 'we', and she took this as a reproach.

'I'll soon get into the way of saying "we".'

So that he should want to kiss her, she turned out the ceiling light as if by accident. The one lamp left alight on a table threw a tall, sharply defined shadow behind the girl.

With her arms raised and her hands clasped on the nape of her neck, Camille gave him an inviting look. But he had eyes only for the shadow. 'How beautiful she is on the wall! Just fine-drawn enough, just as I should like her to be.'

He sat down to compare the one with the other. Flattered, Camille arched herself, thrusting out her breasts and her hips like a nautch-girl, but the shadow was better at that game than she was. Unclasping her hands, the girl walked across the room, preceded by the ideal shadow. Arrived at the open french window, the shadow leapt on one side and fled out into the garden along the pink gravel of a path, embracing the moon-spangled poplar between its two long arms as it went. 'What a pity!' sighed Alain. Then he feebly reproached himself for his inclination to love in Camille herself some perfected or motionless image of Camille. This shadow, for example, or a portrait or the vivid memory she left him of certain moments, certain dresses.

'What's the matter with you tonight? Come and help me put on my cape, at least.'

He was shocked at what that 'at least' secretly implied and also because Camille, as she passed before him through the door leading to the cloakroom and pantry, had almost imperceptibly shrugged her shoulders. 'She doesn't need to shrug her shoulders. Nature and habit do that for her anyway. When she's not careful, her neck makes her look dumpy. Ever, ever so slightly dumpy.'

In the cloakroom they found Alain's mother and Camille's parents stamping as if with cold and leaving footmarks the colour of dirty snow on the matting. The cat, seated on the window-sill outside, watched them inhospitably but with no animosity. Alain imitated her patience and endured the ritual of pessimistic lamentations.

'It's the same old thing.'

'It's hardly any farther on than it was a week ago.'

'My dear, if you want to know what *I* think, it won't be a fortnight, it'll be a month. What am I talking about, a month? More likely two months before their nest . . .'

At the word 'nest', Camille flung herself into the peaceful fray so shrilly that Alain and Saha closed their eyes.

'But since we've already decided what to do! And since we're actually frightfully *pleased* at having Patrick's place! And since it suits Patrick down to the ground because he hasn't a bean – hasn't any money – sorry, Mummy. We'll just take our suitcases and – Alley Oop! – straight up to heaven on the ninth floor! Won't we, Alain?'

He opened his eyes again, smiled into the void, and put her light cape round her shoulders. In the mirror opposite them he met Camille's black, reproachful look but it did not soften his heart. 'I didn't kiss her on the lips when we were alone. All right, very well then, I didn't kiss her on the lips. She hasn't had her full ration of kisses-on-the-lips today. She had the quarter-to-twelve one in the Bois, she had the two o'clock one after coffee, she had the half-past-six one in the garden, but she's missed tonight's. Well, if she's not satisfied, she's only got to put it down on the account . . . What's the matter with me? I'm so sleepy, I'm going mad. This life's idiotic; we're seeing far too much of each other and yet we never see each other properly. On Monday I'll definitely go down to the shop and . . .'

In imagination, the chemical acidity of the bales of new silk assailed his nostrils. But the inscrutable smile of M. Veuillet appeared to him as in a dream and, as in a dream, he heard words which, at twenty-four, he had still not learnt to hear without dread. 'No, no, my young friend. Will a new adding-machine that costs seventeen thousand francs pay back its initial outlay within the year? It all depends on that. Allow your poor father's oldest partner . . .' Catching sight again in the looking-glass of the vindictive image and handsome dark eyes which were watching him, he folded Camille in both his arms.

'Well, Alain?'

'Oh, my dear, let him alone! These poor infants . . .'

Camille blushed and disengaged herself. Then she held up her cheek to Alain in such a boyish brotherly grace that he nearly put his head on her shoulder. 'Oh, to lie down and go to sleep! Oh, good Lord! Just to lie down and sleep!'

From the garden came the voice of the cat.

'Me-rrou-wa . . . Rrr-rrouwa.'

'Hark at the cat! She must be hunting,' said Camille calmly. 'Saha! Saha!'

The cat was silent.

'Hunting?' protested Alain. 'Whatever makes you think that? To begin with, we're in May. And then she's saying: "Me-rrou-wa!"'

'So what?'

'She wouldn't be saying "Me-rrou-wa" if she were hunting! What she's saying there – and it's really rather strange – means a warning. It's almost the cry calling her little ones together.'

'Good Lord!' cried Camille, flinging up her arms. 'If Alain's going to start interpreting the cat, we shall be here all night!'

She ran down the steps and, at the touch of old Emile's shaking hand, two old-fashioned gas-globes, like huge mauve planets, illuminated the garden.

Alain walked ahead with Camille. At the entrance gate, he kissed her under her ear, breathed in, under a perfume too old for her, a good smell of bread and dark hair, and squeezed the girl's bare elbows under her cape. When she seated herself at the steering-wheel, with her parents in the back, he felt suddenly wide awake and gay.

'Saha! Saha!'

The cat sprang out of the shadow, almost under his feet. When he began to run, she ran too, leaping ahead of him with long bounds. He guessed she was there without seeing her; she burst before him into the hall and came back to wait for him at the top of the steps. With her frill standing out and her ears low, she watched him running towards her, urging him on with her yellow eyes. Those deep-set eyes were proud and suspicious, completely masters of themselves.

'Saha! Saha!'

Pronounced in a certain way, under his breath, with

the 'h' strongly aspirated, her name sent her crazy. She lashed her tail, bounded into the middle of the poker-table and, with her two cat's hands spread wide open, she scattered the playing-cards.

'That cat, that cat!' said his mother's voice. 'She hasn't the faintest notion of hospitality! Look how delighted she is that our friends have gone!'

Alain let out a spurt of childish laughter, the laugh he kept for home and the close intimacy which did not extend beyond the screen of elms or the black, wrought-iron gate. Then he gave a frantic yawn.

'Good heavens, how tired you look! Is it possible to look as tired as that when one's happy? There's still some orangeade. No? We can go up then. Don't bother, Emile will turn out the lights.'

'Mother's talking to me as if I were getting over an illness or as if I were starting up paratyphoid again.'

'Saha! Saha! What a demon! Alain, you couldn't persuade that cat? . . .'

By a vertical path known to herself, marked on the worn brocade, the cat had almost reached the ceiling. One moment she imitated a grey lizard, flattening against the wall with her paws spread out; then she pretended to be giddy and tried an affected little cry of appeal. Alain obediently came and stood below and Saha slid down, glued to the wall like a raindrop sliding down a pane. She came to rest on Alain's shoulder and the two of them went up together to their bedroom.

A long hanging cluster of laburnum, black outside the open window, became a long pale yellow cluster when Alain turned on the ceiling light and the bedside lamp. He poured the cat off on to the bed by inclining his shoulder, then wandered aimlessly to and from between his room and the bathroom like a man who is too tired to go to bed.

He leaned out over the garden, looked with a hostile eye

for the white mass of the 'alterations'. Then he opened and shut several drawers and boxes in which reposed his real secrets: a gold dollar, a signet ring, an agate charm attached to his father's watch chain, some red and black seeds from an exotic canna plant, a First Communicant's mother-of-pearl rosary and a thin broken bracelet, the souvenir of a tempestuous young mistress who had passed swiftly and noisily out of his life. The rest of his worldly goods consisted merely of some paper-covered books he had had rebound and some letters and autographs.

Dreamily he turned over these little scraps of wreckage, bright and worthless as the coloured stones one finds in the nests of pilfering birds. 'Should I throw all this away . . . or leave it here? It means nothing to me. Or does it mean something?' Being an only child, he was attached to everything which he had never shared with anyone else and for whose possession he had never had to fight.

He saw his face in the glass and became suddenly irritated with himself. 'Why can't you go to bed? You look a wreck. Positively disgraceful!' he said to the handsome fair young man. 'People only think me handsome because I'm fair. If I were dark, I'd be hideous.' For the hundredth time, he criticized his long cheeks and his slightly equine nose. But, for the hundredth time, he smiled so as to display his teeth to himself and admiringly touched the natural wave in his fair, over-thick hair. Once again he was pleased with the colour of his eyes, greenish-grey between dark lashes. Two dints hollowed his cheeks on either side of the smile, his eyes receded, circled with mauve shadows. He had shaved that morning but already a pale, stubbly bristle coarsened his upper lip. 'What a mug! I pity myself. No, I repel myself. Is *that* a face for a wedding night?' In the depths of the mirror, Saha gravely watched him from the distance.

'I'm coming, I'm coming.'

He flung himself on the cool expanse of the sheets, humouring the cat. Rapidly, he went through certain ritual litanies dedicated to the particular graces and virtues of a small, perfect, pure-bred Russian Blue.

'My little bear with the big cheeks. Exquisite, exquisite, exquisite cat. My blue pigeon. Pearl-coloured demon.'

As soon as he turned out the light, the cat began to trample delicately on her friend's chest. Each time she pressed down her feet, one single claw pierced the silk of the pyjamas, catching the skin just enough for Alain to feel an uneasy pleasure.

'Seven more days, Saha,' he sighed.

In seven days and seven nights he would begin a new life in new surroundings with an amorous and untamed young woman. He stroked the cat's fur, warm and cool at the same time and smelling of clipped box, thuya and lush grass. She was purring full-throatedly and, in the darkness, she gave him a cat's kiss, laying her damp nose for a second under Alain's nose between his nostrils and his lip. A swift, immaterial kiss which she rarely accorded him.

'Ah! Saha. Our nights . . .'

The headlights of a car in the nearest avenue pierced the leaves with two-revolving white beams. Over the wall of the room passed the enlarged shadow of the laburnum and of a tulip-tree which stood alone in the middle of a lawn. Above his own face Alain saw Saha's face illuminated for a moment. Before it was eclipsed again, he had seen that her eyes were hard.

'Don't frighten me!' he implored.

For, when Alain was sleepy, he became once more weak and fanciful, caught in the mesh of a sweet and interminable adolescence.

He shut his eyes while Saha kept vigil, watching all the invisible signs which hover over sleeping human beings when the light is put out.

He always dreamed a great deal and descended into his dreams by definite stages. When he woke up, he did not talk about his adventures of the night. He was jealous of a realm which had been enlarged by a delicate and ill-governed childhood; by long sojourns in bed during his swift growth into a tall frail slender boy.

He loved his dreams and cultivated them. Not for anything in the world would he have revealed the successive stages which awaited him. At the first stopping-place, while he could still hear the motor-horns in the avenue, he met an eddy of faces, familiar yet distorted, which he passed through as he might have passed through a friendly crowd, geeting one here and there. Eddying, bulbous, the faces approached Alain, growing larger and larger. Light against a dark background, they became lighter still as if they received their illumination from the sleeper himself. Each was furnished with one great eye and they circled round in an effortless gyration. But a submerged electric current shot them far away as soon as they touched an invisible barrier. In the humid gaze of a circular monster, in the eye of a plump moon or that of a wild archangel with rays of light for hair, Alain could recognize the same expression, the same intention which none of them had put into words and which Alain of the dream noted with a sense of security: 'They'll tell it me tomorrow.'

Sometimes they disappeared by exploding into scattered, faintly luminous fragments. At other times, they only continued as a hand, an arm, a forehead, an eyeball full of thoughts or as a starry dust of chins and noses. But always there remained that prominent, convex eye which, just at the moment of making itself clear, turned round and exposed only its other, black surface.

The sleeping Alain pursued, under Saha's watchful care, his nightly shipwreck. He passed beyond the world of convex faces and eyes and descended through a zone of darkness where he was conscious of nothing but a powerful, positive blackness, indescribably varied and, as it were, composed of submerged colours. On the confines of this, he launched into the real, complete, fully formed dream.

He came up violently against a barrier which gave a great clang like the prolonged, splintering clash of a cymbal. And then he found himself in the dream city, among the passers-by, the inhabitants standing in their doorways, the gold-crowned guardians of the square and the stage crowd posted along the path of an Alain who was completely naked and armed with a walking-stick. This Alain was extremely lucid and sagacious: 'If I walk rather fast, after tying my tie in a special way, and particularly if I whistle, there's every chance that no one will notice I am naked.' So he tied his tie in a heart-shaped knot and whistled. 'That's not whistling, what I'm doing. It's purring. Whistling's like this . . .' But he still continued to purr. 'I'm not at the end of my tether yet. All I've got to do . . . it's perfectly simple . . . is to cross this sun-drenched open space and go round the bandstand where the military band is playing. Child's play. I run, making perilous jumps to distract attention, and I come out in the zone of shadow . . .'

But he was paralysed by the warm, dangerous look of a dark man in the stage crowd; a young man with a Greek profile perforated by a great eye like a carp's. 'The zone of shadow . . . the zone of *the* shadow . . .' Two long shadowy arms, graceful and rustling with poplar leaves, appeared at the word 'shadow' and carried Alain away. During the most ambiguous hour of the short night, he rested in that provisional tomb where the living exile sighs, weeps, fights, and succumbs, and from which he rises, unremembering, with the day.

TWO

THE high sun was edging the window when Alain awoke. The newly-opened cluster of laburnum hung, translucid, above the head of Saha; a blue, diurnal Saha, innocently engaged in washing herself.

'Saha!'

'Me-rrang!' answered the cat aggressively.

'Is it my fault if you're hungry? You only had to go downstairs and ask for your milk if you're in a hurry.'

She softened at her friend's voice and repeated the same word less emphatically, showing her red mouth planted with white teeth. That look of loyal and exclusive love alarmed Alain: 'Oh heavens, this cat! What to do with this cat? I'd forgotten I was getting married. And that we've got to live in Patrick's place.'

He turned towards the photograph in the chromium frame where Camille gleamed as if covered in oil; a great splash of reflected light on her hair, her painted mouth vitrified in inky black, her eyes enormous between two palisades of eyelashes.

'Fine piece of studio portraiture,' muttered Alain.

He had quite forgotten that he himself had chosen this photograph for his room; a photograph which bore no resemblance to Camille or to anyone at all. 'That eye . . . I've seen that eye.'

He took a pencil and lightly retouched the eye, toning down the excess of white. All he succeeded in doing was to spoil the print.

'Mouek, mouek, mouek. Ma-a-a-a . . . Ma-a-a-a,' said Saha, addressing a little moth imprisoned between the window-pane and the net curtain.

Her leonine chin was trembling; she coveted it so much that she stammered. Alain caught the moth with two fingers and offered it to the cat.

'Hors-d'oeuvre, Saha!'

In the garden, a rake was lazily combing the gravel. Alain could see in his mind the hand that guided the rake; the hand of an ageing woman; a mechanical, obstinate hand in a huge white glove like a policeman's.

'Good morning, Mother!' he called.

A distant voice answered him, a voice whose words he

did not try to catch; the affectionate, insignificant murmur was all that he needed. He ran downstairs, the cat at his heels. In broad daylight, she knew how to change herself into a kind of blustering dog. She would hurtle noisily down the stairs and rush into the garden with tomboyish jumps that had no magic about them. She seated herself on the little breakfast table, among the medallions of sunlight, beside Alain's plate. The rake, which had stopped, slowly resumed its task.

Alain poured out Saha's milk, stirred a pinch of salt and a pinch of sugar into it, then gravely helped himself. When he breakfasted alone, he did not have to blush for certain gestures elaborated by the unconscious wishes of the maniac age between six and seven. He was free to blind all the 'eyes' in his bread with butter and to frown when the coffee in his cup rose above the water-line marked by a certain gilt arabesque. A second thin slice had to follow the first thick slice, whereas the second cup demanded an extra lump of sugar. In fact a very small Alain, hidden in the depths of a tall, fair, handsome young man, was impatiently waiting for breakfast to be over so that he could lick both sides of the honey spoon; an old ivory spoon, blackened and flexible with age.

'Camille, at this moment, is eating her breakfast standing up. She's biting at one and the same time into a slice of lean ham squeezed between two rusks and into an American apple. And she keeps putting down a cup of tea without sugar in it on various bits of furniture and forgetting it.'

He raised his eyes and contemplated his domain; the domain of a privileged child which he cherished and whose every inch he knew. Over his head the old, severely pollarded elms stirred only the tips of their young leaves. A cushiony mass of pink silene, fringed with forget-me-nots, dominated one lawn. Dangling like a scarf from the dead tree's scraggy elbow, a trail of polygonum intertwined with the four-petalled purple clematis fluttered in every breath of wind. One of the standard sprinklers spread a white peacock tail shot with a shifting rainbow as it revolved over the turf.

'Such a beautiful garden . . . such a beautiful garden,' said Alain under his breath. He stared disgustedly at the silent heaps of rubbish, timber, and bags of plaster which defaced the west side of the house. 'Ah! It's Sunday, so they're not working. It's been Sunday all the week for me.' Though young and capricious, and pampered, he now lived according to the commercial rhythm of a six-day week and felt Sunday in his bones.

A white pigeon moved furtively behind the weigela and the pink clusters of the deutzias. 'It's not a pigeon; it's mother's hand in her gardening glove.' The big white glove moved just above ground, raising a drooping stalk, weeding out the blades of grass that sprang up overnight. Two greenfinches came hopping along the gravel path to pick up the breakfast crumbs, and Saha followed them with her eye without getting excited. But a tomtit, hanging upside down in an elm above the table, chirped at the cat out of bravado. Sitting there with her paws folded, her head thrown back, and the frill of fur under her chin displayed like a pretty woman's jabot, Saha tried hard to restrain herself; but her cheeks swelled with fury and her little nostrils moistened.

'As beautiful as a fiend! More beautiful than a fiend!' Alain told her.

He wanted to stroke the broad skull in which lodged ferocious thoughts, and the cat bit him sharply to relieve her anger. He looked at the two little beads of blood on his palm with the irascibility of a man whose woman has bitten him at the height of her pleasure.

'Bad girl! Bad girl! Look what you've done to me!'

She lowered her head, sniffed the blood, and timidly questioned her friend's face. She knew how to amuse him and charm him back to good humour. She scooped up a rusk from the table and held it between her paws like a squirrel.

The May breeze passed over them, bending a yellow rose-bush which smelt of flowering reeds. Between the cat, the rose-bush, the pairs of tomtits, and the last cock-chafers, Alain had one of those moments when he slipped out of time and felt the anguished illusion of being once more back in his childhood. The elms suddenly became enormous, the path grew wider and longer and vanished under the arches of a pergola that no longer existed. Like the hag-ridden dreamer who falls off a tower, Alain returned violently to the consciousness of being nearly twenty-four.

'I ought to have slept another hour. It's only half-past nine. It's Sunday. Yesterday was Sunday for me too. Too many Sundays. But tomorrow . . .'

He smiled at Saha as though she were an accomplice. 'Tomorrow, Saha, there's the final trying-on of the white dress. Without me. It's a surprise. Camille's dark enough to look her best in white. During that time, I'll go and look at the car. It's a bit cheese-paring, a bit mingy, as Camille would say, a roadster. That's what you get for being "such a young married couple".'

With a vertical bound, rising in the air like a fish leaping to the surface of the water, the cat caught a black-veined cabbage-white. She ate it, coughed, spat out one wing, and licked herself affectionately. The sun played on her fur, mauve and bluish like the breast of a woodpigeon.

'Saha!'

She turned her head and smiled at him.

'My little puma! Beloved cat! Creature of the tree-tops! How will you live if we're separated? Would you like us to enter an Order? Would you like? . . . oh, I don't know what . . .'

She listened to him, watching him with a tender, absent expression. But when the friendly voice began to tremble, she looked away.

'To begin with, you'll come with us. You don't hate cars. If we take the saloon instead of the roadster, behind the seats there's a ledge . . .'

He broke off and became gloomy at the recent memory of a girl's vigorous voice, ideally pitched for shouting in the open air, trumpeting the numerous merits of the roadster. 'And then, when you put down the windscreen, Alain, its *mar*vellous. When she's all out, you can feel the skin of your cheeks shrinking right back to your *ears*.'

'Shrinking right back to your ears. Can you imagine anything more frightful, Saha?'

He compressed his lips and made a long face like an obstinate child planning to get its own way by guile.

'It's not settled yet. Suppose I prefer the saloon? I suppose I've got *some* say in the matter?'

He glared at the yellow rose-bush as if it were the young girl with the resonant voice. Promptly the path widened, the elms grew taller, and the non-existent pergola reappeared. Cowering among the skirts of two or three female relatives, a childish Alain surveyed another compact family among whose opaque block gleamed a very dark little girl whose big eyes and black ringlets rivalled each other in a hostile, jetty brilliance. 'Say "How d'you do . . ." Why don't you want to say "How d'you do?"' It was a faint voice from other days, preserved through years of childhood, adolescence, college, the boredom of military service, false seriousness, false business competence. Camille did not want to say 'How d'you do?' She sucked the inside of her cheek and stiffly sketched the brief curtsey expected of little girls. 'Now she calls that a "twist-your-ankle" curtsey. But when she's in a temper, she still bites the inside of her cheek. It's a funny thing, but at those moments she doesn't look ugly.'

He smiled and felt an honest glow of warmth for his fiancée. After all, he was quite glad that she should be healthy and slightly commonplace in her sensuality. Defying the innocent morning, he called up images designed now to excite her vanity and impatience, now to engender anxiety, even confusion. Emerging from these disturbing fancies, he found the sun too white and the wind dry. The cat had disappeared but, as soon as he stood up, she was at his side and accompanied him, walking with a long, deer-like step and avoiding the round pebbles in the pinkish gravel. They went together as far as the 'alterations' and inspected with equal hostility the pile of rubbish, a new french window, devoid of panes, inserted in a wall, various bathroom appliances, and some porcelain tiles.

Equally offended, they calculated the damage done to their past and their present. An old yew had been torn up and was very slowly dying upside down, with its roots in the air. 'I ought never, never to have allowed that,' muttered Alain. 'It's a disgrace. You've only known it for three years, Saha, that yew. But I . . .'

At the bottom of the hole left by the yew, Saha sensed a mole whose image, or rather whose smell went to her head. For a minute she forgot herself to the point of frenzy, scratching like a fox-terrier and rolling over like a lizard. She jumped on all four paws like a frog, clutched a ball of earth between her thighs as a fieldmouse does with the egg it has stolen; escaped from the hole by a series of miracles, and found herself sitting on the grass, cold and prudish and recovering her breath.

Alain stood gravely by, not moving. He knew how to keep a straight face when Saha's demons possessed her beyond her control. The admiration and understanding of cats was innate in him. Those inborn rudiments made it easy for him, later on, to read Saha's thoughts. He had read her like some masterpiece from the day, when on his return from a cat-show, Alain had put down a little five-months old she-cat on the smooth lawn at Neuilly. He had brought her because of her perfect face, her precocious dignity, and her modesty that hoped for nothing behind the bars of a cage.

'Why didn't you buy a Persian instead?' asked Camille.

'That was long before we were engaged,' thought Alain. 'It wasn't only a little she-cat I bought. It was the nobility of all cats, their infinite disinterestedness, their knowledge of how to live, their affinities with the highest type of humans.' He blushed and mentally excused himself. 'The highest, Saha, is the one that understands *you* best.'

He had not yet got to the point of thinking 'likeness' instead of 'understanding' because he belonged to that class of human beings which refuses to recognize or even to imagine its animal affinities. But at the age when he might have coveted a car, a journey abroad, a rare binding, a pair of skis, Alain nevertheless remained the young-man-who-has-bought-a-little-cat. His narrow world resounded with it. The staff of Amparat et Fils in the Rue des Petits Champs were astonished and M. Veuillet inquired after the 'little beastie'.

'Before I chose you, Saha, I don't believe I'd ever realized that one *could* choose. As for all the rest . . . My marriage pleases everyone, including Camille. There are moments when it pleases me too, but . . .'

He got up from the green bench and assumed the important smile of the heir of Amparat Silks who is condescendingly marrying the daughter of Malmert Mangles, 'a girl who's not *quite* our type', as Mme Amparat said. But Alain was well aware that, when Malmert Mangles spoke about Amparat Silks among themselves, they did not forget to mention, sticking up their chins: 'The Amparats aren't in silk any more. The mother and son have only kept their shares in the business and the son's not the real director, only a figurehead.'

Cured of her madness, her eyes gentle and golden, the cat seemed to be waiting for the return of mental trust, of that telepathic murmur for which her silver-fringed ears were straining.

'You're not just a pure and sparkling spirit of a cat either,' went on Alain. 'What about your first seducer, the white tom without a tail? Do you remember that, my ugly one, my trollop in the rain, my shameless one?'

'What a bad mother your cat is!' exclaimed Camille indignantly. 'She doesn't even give a thought to her kittens, now they've been taken away from her.'

'But that was just what a young girl would say,' Alain went on defiantly. 'Young girls are always admirable mothers before they're married.'

The full, deep note of a bell sounded on the tranquil air. Alain leapt up with a guilty start at the sound of wheels crushing the gravel.

'Camille! It's half-past eleven . . . Good Heavens!'

He pulled his pyjama jacket together and retied the cord so hastily and nervously that he scolded himself. 'Come, come, what's the matter with me? I shall be seeing plenty more of them in a week. Saha, are you coming to meet them?'

But Saha had vanished and Camille was already stamping across the lawn with reckless heels. 'Ah! She really does look attractive.' His blood pulsed pleasurably in his throat and flushed his cheeks. He was entirely absorbed in the spectacle of Camille in white, with a little lock of well-tapered hair on either temple and a tiny red scarf which matched her lipstick. Made-up with skill and restraint, her youth was not obvious at the first glance. Then it revealed itself in the cheek that was white under the ochre powder; in the smooth, unwrinkled eyelids under the light dusting of beige powder round the great eyes that were almost black. The brand-new diamond on her left hand broke the light into a thousand coloured splinters.

'Oh!' she cried. 'You're not ready! On a lovely day like this!'

But she stopped at the sight of the rough, dishevelled fair hair, of the naked chest under the pyjamas and Alain's flushed confusion. Her young girl's face so clearly expressed a woman's warm indulgence that Alain no longer dared to give her the quarter-to-twelve kiss of the Bois.

'Kiss me,' she implored, very low, as if she were asking him for help.

Gauche, uneasy and ill-protected by his thin pyjamas, he made a gesture towards the pink flowering shrubs from whence came the sound of the shears and the rake. Camille did not dare throw herself on his neck. She lowered her eyes, plucked a leaf, and pulled her shining locks of hair forward on her cheeks. But, from the movement of her nostrils, Alain saw she was searching in the air, with a certain primitive wildness, for the fragrance of a fair-skinned, barely covered body. In his heart he secretly condemned her for not being sufficiently afraid of it.

THREE

When he woke up, he did not sit up in bed at one bound. Haunted in his sleep by the unfamiliar room, he half-opened his eyes and realized that cunning and constraint had not entirely left him during his sleep, for his left arm, flung out across a desert of linen sheet, lay ready to recognize, but ready, also, to repel . . . But all the wide expanse of bed to his left was empty and cool once more. If there had been nothing in front of the bed but the barely rounded corner of the triangular room and the unaccustomed green gloom, split by a rod of bright yellow light which separated two curtains of solid shadow, Alain would have gone to sleep again lulled by the sound of someone humming a little Negro song.

He turned his head cautiously and opened his eyes a trifle wider. He saw someone moving about, now white, now pale blue according to whether she was in the narrow strip of sunlight or the shadow. It was a naked young woman with a comb in her hand and a cigarette between her lips, wandering about the room and humming. 'What impudence,' he thought. 'Completely naked! Where does she think she is?'

He recognized the lovely legs with which he had long been familiar, but the stomach, shortened by a navel placed rather low, surprised him. An impersonal youthfulness justified the muscular buttocks and the breasts were small above the visible ribs. 'Has she got thinner, then?' The solidity of her back, which was as wide as her chest, shocked Alain. 'She's got a common back.' At that moment, Camille leaned her elbow on one of the window-sills, arched her back, and hunched up her shoulders. 'She's got a back like a charwoman.' But suddenly she stood upright again, took a couple of dancing steps and made a charming gesture of embracing the empty air. 'No, I'm wrong. She's beautiful. But what a . . . what brazenness; Does she think I'm dead? Or does it seem perfectly natural to her to wander about stark naked? Oh, but that will change!'

As she turned towards the bed, he closed his eyes again. When he opened them, Camille had seated herself at the dressing-table they called the 'invisible dressing-table', a transparent sheet of beautiful thick glass laid on a black metal frame. She powdered her face, touched her cheeks and chin with the tips of her fingers, and suddenly smiled, turning her eyes from the glass with a gravity and a weariness which disarmed Alain. 'Is she happy then? Happy about what? *I* certainly don't deserve it. But why is she naked?'

'Camille,' he called out.

He thought she would rush towards the bathroom, hastily covering herself with some hastily snatched-up undergarment. Instead, she ran to the bed and bent over the young man who lay there, overwhelming him with her strong brunette's smell.

'Darling! Have you slept well?'

'Stark naked!' he scolded.

She opened her big eyes comically.

'What about you?'

Bare to his waist, he did not know what to reply. She paraded for him, so proudly and so completely devoid of modesty that he rather rudely flung her the crumpled pyjama-jacket which lay on the bed.

'Quick, put that on. Personally, I'm hungry.'

'Old mother Buque's at her post. Everything's in working order and functioning.'

She disappeared and Alain wanted to get up and dress and smooth his rumpled hair. But Camille returned, girded in a big bathrobe that was new and too long for her, and gaily carrying a loaded tray.

'What a mess, my dears! There's a kitchen bowl and a pyrex cup and the sugar's in the lid of a tin. I'll get it all straightened out in a day or two. My ham's dry. These anaemic peaches are left-overs from lunch. Mother Buque's a bit lost in her electric kitchen. I'll teach her how to manage the various switches. Then I've put some water in the ice compartments of the fridge. It's a good thing I'm here! Monsieur has his coffee very hot and his milk boiling and his butter hard. No, that's my tea, don't touch! What are you looking for?'

'Nothing.'

Because of the smell of coffee, he was looking for Saha.

'What's the time?'

'At last a tender word!' cried Camille. 'Very early, my husband. It was a quarter-past eight by the kitchen alarm-clock.'

As they ate, they laughed a good deal and spoke little. By the increasing smell of the green oilcloth curtains, Alain could guess the strength of the sun which warmed them. He could not take his mind off that sun outside, the unfamiliar horizon, the nine vertiginous storeys, and the bizarre architecture of the 'Wedge' which was their temporary home.

He listened to Camille as attentively as he could,

touched at her pretending to have forgotten what had passed between them in the night. He was touched, too, by her pretending to be perfectly at home in their haphazard lodging and by her unselfconsciousness, as if she had been married at least a week. Now that she had something on, he tried to find a way of showing his gratitude. 'She doesn't resent either what I've done to her or what I haven't, poor child. After all, the most tiresome part is over. Is it always like this the first night? This bruised, unsatisfactory feeling? This half-success, half-disaster?'

He threw his arm cordially round her neck and kissed her.

'Oh! You're nice!'

She had said it so loud and with so much feeling that she blushed and he saw her eyes fill with tears. But she bravely fought down her emotion and jumped off the bed on the pretext of removing the tray. She ran towards the windows, tripped over her long bathrobe, let out a great oath, and hauled on a ship's rope. The oilcloth curtains slid back. Paris, with its suburbs, bluish and unbounded like the desert, dotted with still-fresh verdure and flashes of shining panes, entered at one bound into the triangular room which had only one cement wall, the other two being half glass.

'It's beautiful,' said Alain softly.

But he was half lying and his head sought the support of a young shoulder from which the bathrobe had slipped. 'It's not a place for human beings to live. All this horizon right on top of one, right in one's bed. And what about stormy days. Abandoned on the top of a lighthouse among the albatrosses.'

Camille was lying beside him on the bed now. Her arm was round his neck and she looked fearlessly, now at the giddy horizons of Paris, now at the fair, dishevelled head. This new pride of hers which seemed to draw strength ahead from the coming night and the days that would follow, was no doubt satisfied with her newly acquired rights. She was licensed to share his bed, to prop up a young man's naked body against her thigh and shoulder, to become acquainted with its colour and curves and defects. She was free to contemplate boldly and at length the small dry nipples, the loins she envied, and the strange design of the capricious sex.

They bit into the same tasteless peach and laughed, showing each other their splendid, glistening teeth and the gums which were a little pale, like tired children's.

'That day yesterday!' sighed Camille. 'When you think that there are people who get married so often!'

Her vanity returned and she added: 'All the same, it went off very well. Not a single hitch. It did go off well, didn't it?'

'Yes,' said Alain feebly.

'Oh, *you* . . . You're just like your mother. I mean, as long as your lawn isn't ruined and people don't throw cigarette-ends on your gravel, you think everything's fine. Isn't that a fact? All the same, our wedding would have been prettier at Neuilly. Only that would have disturbed the sacred cat! Tell me, you bad boy, what do you keep looking at all round you?'

'Nothing,' he said sincerely, 'because there's nothing to look at. I've seen the dressing-table. I've seen the chair – we've seen the bed . . .'

'Couldn't you live here? I'd love to. Just think . . . three rooms and three balconies! If only one could stay here!'

'Doesn't one say: "If only *we* could stay here"?'

'Then why do *you* say: "One says"? Yes, if only one could stay here, as *we* say.'

'But Patrick will be back from his cruise in three months.'

'Who cares? He'll come back. And we'll explain that we want to stay on. And we'll chuck him out.'

'Oh! You'd actually do that?'

She shook her black mop affirmatively, with a radiant, feminine assurance in dishonesty. Alain wanted to give her a severe look but, under his eyes, Camille changed and became as nervous as he felt himself. Hastily he kissed her on the mouth.

Silent and eager, she returned his kiss, feeling for the hollow of the bed with a movement of her loins. At the same time her free hand, which was holding a peach-stone, groped in the air for an empty cup or ashtray.

Leaning over her, he caressed her lightly, waiting for her to open her eyes again.

She was pressing her eyelashes down over two small, glittering tears which she was trying to stop from flowing. He respected this restraint and this pride. They had done their best, the two of them, aided by the morning warmth and their two odorous, facile bodies.

Alain remembered Camille's quickened breathing and her warm docility. She had shown an untimely eagerness which was very charming. She reminded him of no other woman; in possessing her for the second time, he had thought only of the careful handling she deserved. She lay against him, her legs and arms relaxed, her hands half-closed, cat-like for the first time. 'Where is Saha?'

Mechanically he gave Camille the ghost of a caress 'for Saha', drawing his nails slowly and delicately all the way down her stomach. She cried out with shock and stiffened her arms. One of them hit Alain who nearly hit her back. She sat up, with her hair on end and her eyes hostile and threatening.

'Are you vicious, by any chance?'

He had expected nothing like this and burst out laughing.

'There's nothing to laugh about!' cried Camille. 'I've always been told that men who tickle women are vicious. They may even be sadists!'

He got off the bed so as to be able to laugh more freely, quite forgetting he was naked. Camille stopped talking so suddenly that he turned round and surprised her lit-up, dazed face staring at the body of the young man whom one night of marriage had made hers.

'D'you mind if I steal the bathroom for ten minutes?'

He opened the glass door let into one end of the longest wall which they called the hypotenuse.

'And then I'll go over to my mother's for a moment.'

'Yes . . . Don't you want me to come with you?'

He looked shocked and she blushed for the first time that day.

'I'll see if the alterations . . .'

'Oh! the alterations! Don't tell me you're interested in those alterations! Admit' – she folded her arms like a tragic actress – 'admit that you're going to see my rival!'

'Saha's not your rival,' said Alain simply.

'How can she be your rival,' he went on to himself. 'You can only have rivals in what's impure.'

'I don't need *such* a serious protestation, darling. Hurry up! You haven't forgotten that we're lunching together on our own at Père Léopold's? On our own at last, just the two of us! You'll come back soon? You haven't forgotten we're going for a drive? Are you taking in what I'm saying?'

What he took in very clearly was that the words 'come back' had acquired a new and preposterous significance and he looked at Camille askance. She was flaunting her newly married bride's tiredness, drawing his attention to the faint swelling of her lower lids under the corners of her great eyes. 'Will you always have such enormous eyes the moment you wake up, whatever time of day or night? Don't you know how to keep your eyes half-closed? It gives me a headache to see eyes as wide open as all that.'

He felt a dishonest pleasure, an evasive comfort in calling her to account in his mind. 'After all, it's less ungracious than being frank.' He hurried to reach the square bathroom, the hot water, and a solitude propitious to thought. But, as the glass door inserted in the hypotenuse reflected him from head to foot, Alain opened it with complacent slowness and was in no haste to shut it again.

When he was leaving the flat an hour later, he opened the wrong door on one of the balconies which ran along every side of the Wedge. Like the sharp down-stroke of a fan, the east wind which was turning Paris blue, blowing away the smoke and scouring the distant Sacré Coeur, caught him full in the face. On the cement parapet, five or six pots, put there by well-meaning hands, contained white roses and hydrangeas and lilies sullied by their pollen. 'Last night's dessert is never attractive.' Nevertheless, before he went down, he sheltered the ill-treated flowers from the wind.

FOUR

He stole into the garden like a boy in his teens who has stayed out all night. The air was full of the heady scent of beds being watered, of the secret exhalation of the filth which nourishes fleshy, expensive flowers and of spray blown on the breeze. In the very act of drawing a deep breath to inhale it all, he suddenly discovered he needed comforting.

'Saha! Saha!'

She did not come for a moment or two, and at first he did not recognize that bewildered, incredulous face which seemed clouded by a bad dream.

'Saha darling!'

He took her on his chest, smoothing the soft flanks which seemed to him a trifle hollow, and removed cobwebs, pine needles, and elm twigs from the neglected fur. She pulled herself together quickly and resumed her familiar expression and her cat's dignity. Her face, her pure golden eyes looked again as he had known them. Under his thumb, Alain could feel the palpitations of a hard, irregular little heart and also the beginnings of a faint, uncertain purr. He put her down on an iron table and stroked her head. But at the moment of thrusting her head into Alain's hand, wildly and as if for life in the way she had, she sniffed that hand and stepped back a pace.

His eyes sought the white pigeon, the gloved hand behind the pink flowering shrubs, behind the flaming rhododendrons. He rejoiced that yesterday's 'ceremony' had respected the beautiful garden and only ravaged Camille's home.

'Imagine those people here! And those four bridesmaids in pink paper! And the flowers they'd have picked, and the deutzias sacrificed to adorn fat women's bosoms! And Saha!'

He called in the direction of the house: 'Has Saha had anything to eat or drink? She looks awfully queer. I'm here, Mother.'

A heavy white shape appeared in the doorway of the hall and answered from the distance: 'No. Just fancy, she had no supper and wouldn't drink her milk this morning. I think she was waiting for you. Are you all right, dear?'

He stood at the foot of the steps, deferential in his mother's presence. He noticed that she did not offer him her cheek as usual and that she kept her hands clasped together at her waist. He understood and shared this motherly sense of decency with a mixture of embarrassment and gratitude. 'Saha hasn't kissed me either.'

'After all, the cat's often seen you go away. She made allowances for your going off sometimes.'

'But I didn't go so far,' he thought.

Near him, on the iron table, Saha drank her milk avidly like an animal that has walked far and slept little.

'Alain, wouldn't you like a cup of warm milk too? Some bread and butter?'

'I've had breakfast, Mother. *We've* had breakfast.'

'Not much of a breakfast, I imagine. In such a glory-hole!'

With the eye of an exile, Alain contemplated the cup with the gilt arabesque beside Saha's saucer; then his mother's heavy face, amiable under the mass of wavy, prematurely white hair.

'I haven't asked you whether my new daughter is satisfied.' She was frightened he would misunderstand her and added hurriedly: 'I mean, whether she's in good health.'

'Excellent, Mother. We're going out to Rambouillet for lunch in the forest. I've got to run the car in.' He corrected himself: '*We've* got to run the car in, I mean.'

They remained alone together in the garden, he and Saha, both torpid with silence and weariness and overcome with longing to sleep.

The cat fell asleep suddenly on her side, her chin up and her teeth bared like a dead animal. Feathery panicles from the Venetian sumach and clematis petals rained down on her without her so much as twitching in the depths of the dream in which, no doubt, she was enjoying the security of her friend's inalienable presence. Her defeated attitude, the pale, drawn corners of her periwinkle-grey lips gave evidence of a night of miserable watching.

Above the withered stump draped with climbing plants, a flight of bees over the ivy-flowers gave out a solemn cymbal note, the identical note of so many summers. 'To go to sleep out here, on the grass, between the yellow rose-bush and the cat. Camille won't come till dinner-time, that will be very pleasant. And the cat, good heavens, the cat . . .' Over by the 'alterations' could be heard the rasp of a plane shaving a beam, the clang of an iron hammer on a metal girder, and Alain promptly embarked on a dream about a village peopled with mysterious blacksmiths. As eleven sounded from the belfry of the school near by, he got up and fled without daring to wake the cat.

FIVE

June came with its longer days, its night skies devoid of mystery which the late glow of the sunset and the early glimmer of dawn over the east of Paris kept from being wholly dark. But June is cruel only to city-dwellers who have no car and are caged up in hot stone and forced to live elbow to elbow. A never-still breeze played round the Wedge, rippling the yellow awnings. It blew through the triangular room and the studio, broke against the prow of the building, and dried up the little hedges of privet that stood in boxes on the balconies. With the help of their daily drives, Alain and Camille lived pleasantly enough. The warm weather and their sensual life combined to make them drowsy and less exacting with each other.

'Why did I call her an untamed girl?' Alain asked himself in surprise. Camille swore less when she was driving the car and had lost certain crudities of speech. She had also lost her passion for night-clubs with female gipsy singers who had nostrils like horses.

She spent much time eating and sleeping, opened her now much gentler eyes very wide, gave up a dozen summer projects, and became interested in the 'alterations' which she visited daily. Often she lingered long in the garden at Neuilly, where Alain, when he came back from the dark offices of Amparat Fils in the Rue des Petits Champs, would find her idle, ready to prolong the afternoon and drive along the hot roads.

Then his mood would darken. He would listen to her giving orders to the singing painters and the distant electricians. She would question him in a general, peremptory way as if, as soon as he was there, it was her duty to renounce her new gentleness.

'Business going all right? Crisis still expected? Have you managed to put over the spotted foulard on the big dress-houses?'

She did not even respect old Emile, whom she shook

until he let fall certain formulas pregnant with oracular imbecility.

'What do you think of our shanty, Emile? Have you ever seen the house looking so nice?'

Between his whiskers, the old butler muttered answers as shallow and colourless as himself.

'You wouldn't know the place any more. Had anyone told me, in the old days, that this house would be divided up into little compartments . . . There's certainly a difference. It will be very nice being so near each other, very gay.'

Or else, drop by drop, he poured a stream of blessings over Alain, blessings in which there was an undercurrent of hostility.

'Monsieur Alain's young lady is beginning to look ever so well. What a fine voice she has. When she's speaking loud, the neighbours can hear every word. You can't deny she has a splendid voice but . . . The young lady speaks her mind all right. She told the gardener that the bed of pink silene and forget-me-not looked cuckoo. I still have to laugh when I think of it.'

And he raised his pale, oyster-coloured eyes, which had never laughed in their life, to the pure sky. Alain did not laugh either. He was worried about Saha. She was getting thinner and seemed to have given up a hope; undoubtedly the hope of seeing Alain every day again – and alone. She no longer ran away when Camille arrived. But she did not escort Alain to the gate and, when he sat by her, she looked at him with a profound and bitter wisdom. 'Her look when she was a little cat behind the bars. The same, same look.' He called her very softly: 'Saha . . . Saha . . .' strongly aspirating the h's. But she did not jump or flatten her ears and it was days since she had given her insistent: 'Me-rrang'! or the 'Mouek-mouek-mouek' of good humour and greed.

One day, when he and Camille had been summoned to Neuilly to be informed that the enormous, heavy, new sunk bath would cave in the tiled platform supporting it, he heard his wife sigh: 'It'll never be finished!'

'But,' he said, surprised, 'I thought you really much preferred the Wedge with its petrels and cormorants.'

'Yes. But all the same . . . And after all it's your house here, your real house. *Our* house.'

She leaned on his arm, rather limp and unusually hesitant. The bluish whites of her eyes, almost as blue as her light summer dress; the unnecessary but admirable make-up of her cheeks and mouth and eyelids did not move him in the least.

Nevertheless, it seemed to him that, for the first time, she was asking his advice without speaking. 'Camille here with me. So soon! Camille in pyjamas under the rose trellis.' One of the oldest climbing roses carried its load of flowers, which faded as soon as they opened, as high as his head and their oriental scent dominated the garden in the evening; he could smell it where they stood by the steps. 'Camille in a bathrobe under the screen of elms. Wouldn't it be better, all things considered, to keep her shut away in the little gazebo of the Wedge? Not here, not here . . . not yet.'

The June evening, drenched with light, was reluctant to give way to darkness. Some empty glasses on a wicker table were still attracting the big orange bumble-bees but, under all the trees except the pines, an area of impalpable damp was growing, bringing a promise of coolness. Neither the rose geraniums, so prodigal of their southern scent upon the air, nor the fiery poppies suffered from the fierce onslaught of summer. 'Not here, not here,' Alain repeated to the rhythm of his own footsteps. He was looking for Saha and did not want to call her out loud. He found her lying on the little low wall which buttressed a blue knoll covered with lobelias. She was asleep, or appeared to be asleep, curled up in a ball. 'Curled up in a ball? At this time and in this weather? Sleeping curled up like that is a winter position!'

'Saha darling!'

She did not quiver as he picked her up and held her in the air. She only opened two hollow eyes, very beautiful and almost indifferent.

'Heavens, how light you are! But you're ill, my little puma!'

He carried her off and ran back to his mother and Camille.

'But, Mother, Saha's ill! Her coat's shocking – she weighs next to nothing – and you never told me!'

'It's because she eats nothing,' said Mme Amparat. 'She refuses to eat.'

'She doesn't eat? And what else?'

He cradled the cat against his chest and Saha abandoned herself to him. Her breathing was shallow and her nostrils dry. Mme Amparat's eyes, under the thick white waves, glanced intelligently at Camille.

'Nothing else,' she said.

'She's bored with you,' said Camille. 'After all she's your cat, isn't she?'

He thought she was laughing at him and raised his head defiantly. But Camille's face had not changed and she was seriously examining Saha, who shut her eyes again as soon as touched by her.

'Feel her ears,' said Alain sharply. 'They're burning.'

In an instant, his mind was made up.

'Right. I'm taking her with me. Mother, get them to fetch me her basket, will you? And a sack of sand for the tray. We've got everything else she needs. You understand I simply couldn't bear . . . This cat believes . . .'

He broke off and turned belatedly to his wife.

'It won't worry you, Camille, if I take Saha while we're waiting to come back here?'

'What a question! But where do you propose to put her at night?' she added so naïvely that Alain blushed because of his mother's presence and answered acridly: 'That's for her to decide.'

They left in a little procession; Alain carrying Saha, mute in her travelling-basket. Old Emile was bowed under the sack full of sand and Camille brought up the rear, bearing an old frayed kasha travelling rug which Alain called the Kashasaha.

SIX

'No, I never thought a cat would get acclimatized so quickly.'

'A cat's merely a cat. But Saha's Saha.'

Alain was proudly doing the honours of Saha. He himself had never kept her so close at hand, imprisoned in twenty-five square metres and visible at all hours. For her feline meditation, for her craving for solitude and shadow, she was reduced to withdrawing under the giant armchairs scattered about the studio or into the miniature hall or into one of the built-in wardrobes camouflaged with mirrors.

But Saha was determined to triumph over all obstacles. She accepted the uncertain times of meals and of getting up and going to bed. She choose the bathroom with its cork-topped stool to sleep in and she explored the Wedge with no affectation of wildness or disgust. In the kitchen, she condescended to listen to the lazy voice of Mme Buque summoning 'the pussy' to raw liver. When Alain and Camille went out, she installed herself on the giddy parapet and gazed into the abysses of air, following the flying backs of swallows and sparrows below her with a calm, untroubled eye. Her impassiveness on the edge of a sheer drop of nine storeys and the habit she had of washing herself at length on the parapet, terrified Camille.

'Stop her,' she yelled to Alain. 'She makes my heart turn over and gives me cramp in my calves.'

Alain gave an unperturbed smile and admired his cat who had recovered her taste for food and life.

It was not that she was blooming or particularly gay. She did not recover the iridescence of her fur that had gleamed like a pigeon's mauve plumage. But she was more alive; she waited for the dull 'poum' of the lift which brought up Alain and accepted extra attentions from Camille, such as a tiny saucer of milk at five o'clock or a small chicken bone offered high up, as if to a dog who was expected to jump for it.

'Not like that! Not like that!' scolded Alain.

And he would lay the bone on a bath-mat or simply on the thick-piled beige carpet.

'Really . . . on Patrick's carpet!' Camille scolded in turn.

'But a cat can't eat a bone or any solid food on a polished surface. When a cat takes a bone off a plate and puts it down on the carpet before eating it, she's told she's dirty. But the cat needs to hold it down with her paw while she crunches and tears it and she can only do it on bare earth or on a carpet. People don't know that.'

Amazed, Camille broke in: 'And how do *you* know?'

He had never asked himself that and got out of it by a joke: 'Hush! It's because I'm extremely intelligent. Don't tell a soul. M. Veuillet hasn't a notion of it.'

He taught her all the ways and habits of the cat, like a foreign language over-rich in subtle shades of meaning. In spite of himself, he spoke with emphatic authority as he taught. Camille observed him narrowly and asked him any number of questions which he answered unreservedly.

'Why does the cat play with a piece of string when she's frightened of the big ship's rope?'

'Because the ship's rope is the snake. It's the thickness of a snake. She's afraid of snakes.'

'Has she ever seen a snake?'

Alain looked at his wife with the grey-green, black-lashed eyes she found so beautiful . . . 'So treacherous' she said.

'No . . . certainly not. Where could she have seen one?'

'Well, then?'

'Well, then she invents one. She creates one. You'd be frightened of snakes too, even if you'd never seen one.'

'Yes, but I've been told about them. I've seen them in pictures. I know they exist.'

'So does Saha.'

'But how?'

He gave her a haughty smile.

'How? But by her birth, like persons of quality.'

'So I'm not a person of quality?'

He softened, but only out of compassion.

'Good Heavens, no. Console yourself: I'm not either. Don't you believe what I tell you?'

Camille, sitting at her husband's feet, contemplated him with her wildest eyes, the eyes of the little girl of other days who did not want to say 'How d'you do?'

'I'd better believe it,' she said gravely.

They took to dining at home nearly every night, because of the heat, said Alain, 'and because of Saha' insinuated Camille. One evening after dinner, Saha was sitting on her friend's knee.

'What about me?' said Camille.

'I've two knees,' Alain retorted.

Nevertheless, the cat did not use her privilege for long. Some mysterious warning made her return to the polished ebony table where she seated herself on her own bluish reflection immersed in a dusky pool. There was nothing unusual about her behaviour except the fixed attention she gave to the invisible things straight in front of her in the air.

'What's she looking at?' asked Camille.

She was pretty every evening at that particular hour; wearing white pyjamas, her hair half loosened on her forehead and her cheeks very brown under the layers of powder she had been superimposing since the morning. Alain sometimes kept on his summer suit, without a waistcoat, but Camille laid impatient hands on him, taking off his jacket and tie, opening his collar and rolling up his shirt-sleeves, seeking and displaying the bare skin. He treated her as a hussy, letting her do as she wished. She laughed a little unhappily as she contained her feelings. And it was he who lowered his eyes with an anxiety that was not entirely voluptuous. 'What ravages of desire on that face! Her mouth is quite distorted with it. A young wife who's so *very* young. Who taught her to forestall me like that?'

The round table, flanked by a little trolley on rubber wheels, gathered the three of them together at the entrance to the studio, near the open bay window. Three tall old poplars, relics of a beautiful garden that had been destroyed, waved their tops at the height of the balcony and the great setting sun of Paris, dark red and smothered in mists, was going down behind their lean heads from which the sap was retreating.

Mme Buque's dinner – she cooked food well and served it badly – enlivened the hour. Refreshed, Alain forgot his day and the Amparat office and the tutelage of M. Veuillet. His two captives in the glass tower made a fuss of him. 'Were you waiting for me?' he murmured in Saha's ear.

'I heard you coming!' cried Camille. 'One can hear every sound from here!'

'Have you been bored?' he asked her one evening, fearing that she was going to complain. But she shook her black mop in denial.

'Not the least bit in the world. I went over to Mummy's. She's presented me with the treasure.'

'What treasure?'

'The little woman who'll be my maid over there. Provided old Emile doesn't give her a baby. She's quite attractive.'

She laughed as she rolled up her white crêpe sleeves over her bare arms before she cut open the red-fleshed melon round which Saha was tiptoeing. But Alain did not laugh: he was too taken up with the horror of imagining a new maid in his house.

'Yes? But do you remember,' he brought out, 'my mother's never changed her servants since I was a child.'

'That's obvious,' said Camille trenchantly. 'What a museum of old crocks!'

She was biting into a crescent of melon as she spoke and laughing, with her face to the setting sun. Alain admired, in a detached way, how vivid a certain cannibal radiance could be in those glittering eyes and on the glittering teeth in the narrow mouth. There was something Italian about her regular features. He made one more effort to be considerate.

'You never see your girl friends nowadays, it seems to me. Mightn't you perhaps . . .'

She took him up fiercely.

'And what girl friends, may I ask? Is this your way of telling me I'm a burden on you? So that I shall give you a little breathing space. That's it, isn't it?'

He raised his eyebrows and clicked his tongue 'tst . . . tst'. She yielded at once with a plebeian respect for the man's disdain.

'It's quite true. I never had any friends when I was a little girl. And now . . . can you see me with a girl who's not married. Either I'd have to treat her as a child or I'd have to answer all her dirty questions: "And what does one do *here* and how does he do *that* to you!" Girls,' she explained with some bitterness, 'girls don't stick together decently. There's no solidarity. It's not like all you men.'

'Forgive me! I'm not one of "all-you-men"!'

'Oh, I know that all right,' she said sadly. 'Sometimes I wonder if I wouldn't rather . . .'

She was very rarely sad and, when she was, it was because of some secret reticence or some doubt that she did not express.

'*You* haven't any friends either,' she went on. 'Except Patrick and he's away. And even Patrick, you don't really care a damn about him.'

She broke off at a gesture from Alain.

'Don't let's talk about these things,' she said intelligently. 'There'll only be a quarrel.'

The long-drawn-out cries of children rose from the ground level and blended with the airy whistling of the swallows. Saha's beautiful yellow eyes, in which the great nocturnal pupil was slowly invading the iris, stared into space, picking out moving, floating, invisible points.

'Tell me, whatever's the cat looking at? Are you sure there's nothing, over there where she's staring?'

'Nothing . . . for us.'

Alain evoked with regret the faint shiver, the seductive fear that his cat friend used to communicate to him in the days when she slept on his chest at night.

'She doesn't make you frightened, I hope?' he said condescendingly.

Camille burst out laughing, as if the insulting word were just what she had been waiting for.

'Frightened? There aren't many things that frighten *me*, you know!'

'That's the statement of a silly little fool,' said Alain angrily.

Let's say you're feeling the storm coming, shall we?' said Camille, shrugging her shoulders.

She pointed to the wall, purpled with clouds which were coming up with the night.

'And you're like Saha,' she added. 'You don't like storms.'

'No one like storms.'

'I don't hate them,' said Camille judicially. 'Anyway, I'm not the slightest bit afraid of them.'

'The whole world is afraid of storms,' said Alain, hostile.

'All right, I'm not the whole world, that's all.'

'You are for me,' he said with a sudden, artificial grace which did not deceive her.

'Oh!' she scolded under her breath. 'I shall hit you.'

He bent his fair head towards her over the table and showed his white teeth.

'All right, hit me!'

But she deprived herself of the pleasure of rumpling that golden hair and offering her bare arm to those shining teeth.

'You've got a crooked nose,' she flung at him fiercely.

'It's the storm,' he said, laughing.

This subtlety was not at all to Camille's taste, but the first low rumblings of the thunder distracted her attention. She threw down her napkin to run out on the balcony.

'Come along! There'll be some marvellous lightning.'

'No,' said Alain, without moving. 'Come along, yourself.'

'Where to?'

He jerked his chin in the direction of their room. Camille's face assumed the obstinate expression, the dull-witted greed he knew so well. Nevertheless, she hesitated.

'But couldn't we look at the lightning first?'

He made a sign of refusal.

'Why not, horrid?'

'Because *I'm* frightened of storms. Choose. The storm or . . . me.'

'What do you think!'

She ran to their room with an eagerness which flattered Alain's vanity. But, when he joined her there, he found she had deliberately lighted a luminous glass cube near the vast bed. He deliberately turned it out.

The rain came in through the open bay-windows as they lay calm again, warm and tingling, breathing in the ozone that filled the room with freshness. Lying in Alain's arms, Camille made him understand that, while the storm raged, she would have liked him once again to forget his terror of it with her. But he was nervously counting the great sheets of lightning and the tall dazzling trees silhouetted against the cloud and he moved away from Camille. She resigned herself, raised herself on her elbow and combed her husband's crackling hair with one hand. In the pulsations of the lightning-flashes their two blue plaster faces rose out of the night and were swallowed up in it again.

'We'll wait till the storm's over,' she consented.

'And *that,*' said Alain to himself, '*that's* what she finds to say after an encounter that really means something. She might at least have kept quiet. As Emile says, the young lady speaks her mind straight out.'

A flickering flash, long as a dream, was reflected in a blade of fire in the thick slab of glass on the invisible dressing-table. Camille clutched Alain against her bare leg.

'Is that to reassure me? We know you're not frightened of lightning.'

He raised his voice so as to be heard above the hollow rumbling and the rain cascading on the flat roof. He felt tired and on edge, tempted to be unjust yet frightened to say openly that nowadays he was never alone. In his mind he returned violently to his old room with its white wallpaper patterned with stiff conventional flowers, a room which no one had ever tried to make prettier or uglier. His longing for it was so fierce that the murmur of the inefficient old radiator came back with the memory of the pale flowers on the wallpaper. The wheezy mutter that came from the hollow space below its copper pipes seemed to be part of the murmurs of the whole house; of the whispering of the worn old servants, half-buried in their basement, who no longer cared to go out even into the garden. . . . 'They used to say "She" when they talked about my mother but I've been "Monsieur Alain" since I first went into knickerbockers.'

A dry crackle of thunder roused him from the brief doze into which he had fallen. His young wife, leaning over him, propped on her elbow, had not stirred.

'I like you so much when you're asleep,' she said. 'The storm's going off.'

He took this as a demand and sat up.

'I'm following its example,' he said. 'How hot and sticky it is! I'm going to sleep on the waiting-room bench.'

The 'waiting-room bench' was their name for the narrow divan which was the solitary piece of furniture in a tiny room, a mere strip of glass-walled passage which Patrick used for sunbathing.

'Oh, no! Oh, no!' implored Camille. 'Do stay.'

But he had already slipped out of the bed. The great flashes in the clouds revealed Camille's hard, offended face.

'Pooh! Baby boy!'

At this, which he was not expecting, she pulled his nose. With an instinctive reflex of his arm, which he could not control and did not regret, he beat down the disrespectful hand. A sudden lull in the wind and rain left them alone in the silence, as if struck dumb. Camille massaged her hand.

'But . . .' she said at last, 'But . . . you're a brute.'

'Possibly,' said Alain. 'I don't like having my face touched. Isn't the rest of me enough for you? Never touch my face.'

'But you *are* . . . you really *are* a brute,' Camille repeated slowly.

'Don't keep on saying it. Apart from that, I've nothing against you. Just mind you don't do it again.'

He lifted his bare leg back on to the bed.

'You see that big grey square on the carpet? It's nearly daybreak. Shall we go to sleep?'

'Yes . . . let's . . .' said the same, hesitant voice.

'Come on, then!'

He stretched out his left arm so that she could rest

her head on it. She did so submissively and with a circumspect politeness. Pleased with himself, Alain gave her a friendly jostle and pulled her towards him by her shoulder. But he bent his knees a little to keep her at a safe distance and fell asleep almost at once. Camille lay awake, breathing carefully, and watched the grey patch on the carpet growing lighter. She listened to the sparrows celebrating the end of the storm in the three poplars whose rustling sounded like the faint continuation of the rain. When Alain, changing his position, withdrew his arm, he gave her an unconscious caress. Three times his hand slid lightly over her head as if accustomed to stroking fur that was even softer than her soft black hair.

SEVEN

It was towards the end of June that incompatibility became established between them like a new season of the year. Like a season, it had its surprises and even its pleasures. To Alain, it was like a harsh, chilly spring inserted in the heart of summer. He was incessantly and increasingly aware of his repugnance at the idea of making a place for this young woman, this outsider, in his own home. He nursed this resentment and fed it with secret soliloquies and the sullen contemplation of their new dwelling. Camille, exhausted with the heat, called out from the high and now windless balcony: 'Oh, let's chuck everything. Let's take the old scooter and go somewhere where we can bathe. Shall we, Alain?'

'All right by me,' he answered with wily promptitude. 'Where shall we go?'

There was a peaceful interlude while Camille enumerated beaches and names of hotels. With his eye on Saha who lay flat and prostrated, Alain had the leisure to think and to conclude: 'I don't want to go away with her I . . .

I daren't. I'm quite willing to go for a drive, as we used to, and come back in the evening or late at night. But that's all. I don't want evenings in hotels and nights in a casino, evenings of . . .' He shuddered: 'I need time. I realize that I take a long time to get used to things, that I'm a difficult character, that . . . But I don't want to go off with *her*.' He felt a pang of shame as he realized that he had mentally said '*her*' just like Emile and Adèle when they were discussing 'Madame' in undertones.

Camille bought road-maps and they played at travelling through a France spread in quarters over the polished ebony table which reflected their two blurred, inverted faces.

They added up the mileage, ran down their car, cursed each other affably and felt revived, even rehabilitated by a comradeship they had forgotten. But tropical showers unaccompanied by gales drowned the last days of June and the balconies of the Wedge. Sheltering behind the closed panes, Saha watched the level rivulets, which Camille mopped up by stamping on table-napkins, winding across the inlaid tiles. The horizon; the city; the shower itself; all took on the colour of clouds loaded with inexhaustible rain.

'Would you rather we took the train?' suggested Alain suavely.

He had foreseen that Camille would fly out at the detested word. Fly out she did indeed – and blasphemously.

'I'm afraid,' he went on, 'that you're getting bored. All those trips we'd promised ourselves.'

'All those summer hotels. All those restaurants full of flies. All those seas full of people bathing,' she railed plaintively. 'Look here, you and I are quite used to driving around. But what we're good at is just going for drives. We're quite lost when it comes to a real journey.'

He saw that she was slightly depressed and gave her a brotherly kiss. But she turned round and bit him on his mouth and under his ear. Once again, they fell into the diversion which shortens the hours and makes the body attain its pleasure easily. It was beginning to make Alain tired. When he dined at his mother's with Camille and had to stifle his yawns, Mme Amparat lowered her eyes and Camille invariably gave a little, swaggering laugh. For she was proudly conscious of the habit Alain had acquired of making love to her hurriedly and almost peevishly, flinging her away the moment it was over to return to the cool side of the uncovered bed.

Ingenuously, she would rejoin him there and he did not forgive her for that although, silently, he would yield again. After that he felt at liberty to probe at leisure into the sources of what he called their incompatibility. He was wise enough to put these outside their frequent love-making. Clear-headed, helped by the very fact of his sexual exhaustion, he returned to those retreats where the hostility of man to woman keeps its unageing freshness. Sometimes she revealed herself to him in some commonplace realm where she slept in broad sunshine, like an innocent creature. Sometimes he was astonished, even scandalized, that she should be so dark. Lying in bed behind her, he surveyed the short hairs on her shaved neck, ranged like the prickles of a sea-urchin and drawn on the skin like the hatching on a map. The shortest of them were blue and visible under the fine skin before each one emerged through a small blackened pore.

'Have I never really had a dark woman?' he wondered. 'Two or three little black-haired things haven't left me any impression of *such* darkness.' And he held his own arm up to the light. It was yellowish-white; a typical fair man's arm with green-gold down and jade-coloured veins. His own hair seemed to him like a forest with violet shadows, whereas Camille's showed the strange whiteness of the skin between the exotic abundance of those ranks of black, slightly crinkled stalks.

The sight of a fine, very black hair stuck to the side of a

basin made him feel sick. Then the little neurosis changed and, abandoning the detail, he concentrated on her whole body. Holding that young, appeased body in his arms in the night which hid its contours he began to be annoyed that a creative spirit, in moulding Camille, had shown a strict reasonableness like that of his English nurse. 'Not more prunes than rice, my boy,' she used to say. 'Not more rice than chicken.' That spirit had modelled Camille adequately but with no concessions to lavishness or fantasy. He carried his annoyances and regrets into the antechamber of his dreams during that incalculable moment reserved for the black landscape peopled with bulbous eyes, fish with Greek noses, moons and chins. There he desired a big-hipped charmer of the 1900 type, liberally developed above a tiny waist, to compensate for the acid smallness of Camille's breasts. At other times, half asleep, he compromised and preferred a top-heavy bosom; two quivering, monstrous hillocks of flesh with sensitive tips. Such feverish desires, which were born of the sexual act and survived it, never affronted the light of day nor even complete wakefulness. They merely peopled a narrow isthmus between nightmare and voluptuous dream.

When the flesh was warm, the 'foreigner' smelt of wood licked by tongues of flame; birch, violets . . . a whole bouquet of sweet, dark tenacious scents which clung long to the palms. These fragrances produced in Alain a kind of perverse excitement but did not always arouse his desire.

'You're like the smell of roses,' he said one day to Camille, 'you take away one's appetite.'

She looked at him dubiously and assumed the slightly gauche, downcast expression with which she received double-edged compliments.

'How awfully eighteen-thirty you are,' she murmured.

'You're much more so,' replied Alain. 'Oh, ever so much more so. I know who you're like.'

'Marie Dubas, the actress. I've been told that before.'

'Hopelessly wrong, my girl! Minus the bandeau, you're like all those girls who weep on the tops of towers on the works of Loïsa Puget. You can see them weeping on the cover of his romantic songs, with *your* great, prominent Greek eyes and those thick rims to the lower lid that makes the tears jump down on to the cheeks . . .'

One after another, Alain's senses took advantage of him to condemn Camille. He had to admit, at least, that she stood up admirably to certain remarks he fired her point-blank. They were provocative rather than grateful remarks that burst out of him at the times when, lying on the floor, he measured her with narrowed eyes and appraised her new merits without indulgence or regard for her feelings. He judged her particular aptitudes; he noted how that sensual ardour of hers, that slightly monotonous passion, had already developed an enlightened self-interest remarkable in so young a married woman. Those were moments of frankness and certainty and Camille did all she could to prolong their half-silent atmosphere of conflict; their tension like that of a tight-rope on which balance was precarious and dangerous.

Having no deep-seated malice in herself, Camille never suspected that Alain was only half taken in by deliberate challenges, pathetic appeals and even by a cool Polynesian cynicism, and that each time he possessed his wife, he meant it to be the last. He mastered her as he might have put a hand on her mouth to stop her from screaming or as he might have murdered her.

When she was dressed again and sitting upright beside him in their roadster, he could look at her closely without rediscovering what it was that had made her his worst enemy. As soon as he regained his breath, listening to his decreasing heartbeats, he ceased to be the dramatic young man who stripped himself naked before wrestling with his companion and overthrowing her. The brief routine of pleasure; the controlled expert movements, the real or stimulated gratitude were relegated to the ranks of what is over, of what will probably never happen again. Then his greatest preoccupation would return, the one which he accepted as natural and honourable, the question which reassumed the first place it had so long deserved: 'How to stop Camille from living in *my* house?'

Once this period of hostility towards the 'alterations' had passed, he had genuinely put his faith in the return to the home of his childhood, in the tranquillizing influence of a life on ground level; a life in contact with the earth and everything the earth brings forth. 'Here, I'm suffering from living up in the air. Oh, to see branches and birds from *underneath* again!' he sighed. But he concluded severely, 'Pastoral life is no solution,' and once more had recourse to his indispensable ally, the lie.

On a blazing afternoon which melted the asphalt he went to his domain. All about it, Neuilly was a desert of the empty roads and empty tramways of July; the gardens were abandoned except for a few yawning dogs. Before leaving Camille, he had installed Saha on the coolest balcony of the Wedge. He was vaguely worried every time he left his two females alone together.

The garden and the house were asleep and the little iron gate did not creak as he opened it. Overblown roses, red poppies, the first ruby-throated Canna lilies and dark snapdragons burned in isolated clumps on the lawns. At the side of the house gaped the new doorway and two new windows in a freshly painted little one-storey building. 'It's all finished,' Alain realized. He walked carefully, as he did in his dreams, and trod only on the grass.

Hearing the murmur of a voice rising from the basement, he stopped and absent-mindedly listened. It was only the old well-known voices of servility and ritual grumbling, the old voices of which used to say 'She' and 'Monsieur Alain'. Once upon a time they had flattered the fragile, fair-haired little boy and his childish pride . . . 'I was a king, once,' Alain said to himself, smiling sadly.

'Well, so *she'll* soon be coming to sleep here, I suppose?' one of the old voices asked audibly.

'That's Adèle,' thought Alain. Leaning against the wall, he listened without the least scruple.

'Of course she will,' bleated Emile. 'That flat's shockingly badly built.

The housemaid, a greying Basque woman with a hairy face, broke in: 'You're right there. From their bathroom you can hear everything that goes on in the water-closet. Monsieur Alain won't like *that*.'

'*She* said, the last time *she* came that *she* didn't need curtains in her little drawing-room because there are no neighbours on the garden side.'

'No neighbours? What about us when we go to the wash-house? What's one going to see when *she's* with Monsieur Alain?'

Alain could guess the smothered laughter and the ancient Emile continued: 'Oh, perhaps one won't see as much as all *that*. *She*'ll be put in her place, all right. Monsieur Alain's not the sort to let himself go on a sofa at any time of day or night.'

There was a silence during which Alain could hear nothing but the sound of a knife on the grindstone. But he stayed listening, with his back against the hot wall and his eyes vaguely searching between a flaming geranium and the acid green of the turf as if he half-expected to see Saha's moonstone-coloured fur.

'As for me,' said Adèle, 'I think it's oppressive, that scent *she* puts on.'

'And her frocks,' supplemented Juliette, the Basque woman. 'The way she dresses isn't really good style. *She* looks more like an actress. Behaves like one too, with that brazen way of hers. And now what's she going to land us with in the way of a lady's maid? Some creature out of an orphanage, I believe, or worse.'

A fanlight slammed and the voices were cut off. Alain felt weak and trembling. He breathed like a man who has just been spared by a gang of murderers. He was neither surprised nor indignant. There was not much difference between his own opinion of Camille and that of the harsh judges in the basement. But his heart was beating fast because he had meanly eavesdropped without being punished for it and because he had been listening to prejudiced witnesses and unsought accomplices. He wiped his face and took a deep breath as if inhaling this gust of misogyny, this pagan incense offered exclusively to the male principle, had anaesthetized him. His mother, who had just wakened from her siesta and was putting back the shutters of her room, saw him standing there, with his cheek still leant against the wall.

She called softly, like a wise mother.

'Ah! my boy . . . Is anything the matter?'

He took her hands over the window-sill, like a lover.

'Nothing at all. I was out for a walk and just thought I'd look in.'

'A very good idea.'

She did not believe him but they smiled at each other, perfectly aware that neither was telling the truth.

'Mother, could I ask you to do me a little favour?'

'A little favour in the way of money, isn't that it? I know you're none too well off this year, my poor children.'

'No, Mother. Please, would you mind not telling Camille that I came here today? As I didn't come here for any special reason, I mean with no special reason except just to look in and give you a kiss. I'd rather . . . Actually, that's not all. I want you to give me some advice. Strictly between the two of us, you know.'

Mme Amparat lowered her eyes, ran her hand through her wavy white hair, and tried to avert the confidence.

'I'm not much of a talker, as you know. You've caught me all untidy. I look like an old gipsy. Won't you come inside into the cool?'

'No, Mother. Do you think there's any way . . . it's an idea I can't get out of my head . . . a polite way, of course . . . something that wouldn't offend anyone . . . but some way of stopping Camille from living here?'

He seized his mother's hands, expecting them to tremble or to draw away. But they stayed, cold and soft, between his own.

'These are just a young husband's ideas,' she said, embarrassed.

'What do you mean?'

'With young married couples, things go too well or they go too badly. I don't know which works out best in the end. But they never go straightforwardly, just of their own accord.'

'But, Mother, that's not what I'm asking you. I'm asking you whether there isn't any way . . .'

For the first time, he was unable to look his mother in the face. She gave him no help and he turned away irritably.

'You're talking like a child. You run about the streets in this frightful heat and you come to me after a quarrel and ask me impossible questions. *I* don't know. Questions whose only answer is divorce. Or moving house. Or heaven knows what.'

She got breathless whenever she talked and Alain only reproached himself for making her flush and pant even at saying so little. 'That's enough for today,' he thought prudently.

'We haven't had a quarrel, Mother. It's only I who can't get used to the idea . . . who doesn't want to see . . .'

With a wide, embarrassed gesture, he indicated the garden that surrounded them: the green lake of the lawn; the bed of fallen petals under the rose arches; a swarm of bees over the flowering ivy; the ugly, revered house.

The hand he had kept in one of his clenched and hardened into a little fist and he suddenly kissed that sensitive hand: 'Enough, that's enough for today.'

'I'm off now, Mother. Monsieur Veuillet's telephoning you at eight tomorrow about this business of the shares going down. Do I look better now, Mother?'

He raised his eyes that looked greener in the shade of the tulip-tree and threw back his face which from habit, affection and diplomacy he had forced into his old childish expression. A flutter of the lids to brighten the eye, the seductive smile, a little pout of the lips. His mother's hand unclenched again and reached over the sill to feel Alain's well-known weak spots; his shoulder-blades, his Adam's apple, the top of his arm. She did all this before replying.

'A little better. Yes, really, quite a lot better.'

'I've pleased her by asking her to keep something secret from Camille.' At the remembrance of his mother's last caress, he tightened his belt under his jacket. 'I've got thinner, I'm getting thinner. No more physical culture – no physical culture other than making love.'

He went off with a light step, in his summer clothes, and the cooling breeze dried his sweat and blew the acrid smell of it ahead of him. He left his native castle inviolate, his subterranean cohort intact, and the rest of the day would pass easily enough. Until midnight, no doubt, sitting in the car beside an inoffensive Camille, he would drink in the evening air, now sylvan as they drove between oak plantations edged with muddy ditches, now dry and smelling of wheatstraw. 'And I'll bring back some fresh couch-grass for Saha.'

Vehemently, he reproached himself for the lot of his cat who lived so soundlessly at the top of their glass tower. 'She's like her own chrysalis, and it's my fault.' At the hour of their conjugal games she banished herself so rigorously that Alain had never seen her in the triangular room. She ate just sufficient to keep alive; she had lost her varied language and given up all her demands, seeming to prefer her long waiting to everything else.

'Once again, she's waiting behind bars. She's waiting for me.'

Camille's shattering voice came through the closed door as he reached the landing.

'It's that filthy bloody swine of an animal! I wish it were dead! What? No, Madame Buque, I don't care what you say. To hell with it! To hell with it!'

He made out a few more violent expressions. Very softly he turned the key in the lock but, once over his own threshold, he could not consent to listen without being seen. 'A filthy bloody swine of an animal? But what animal? An animal in the house?'

In the studio Camille, wearing a little sleeveless pull-over and a knitted beret miraculously balanced on her skull, was furiously pulling a pair of gauntlet gloves over her bare hands. She seemed stupefied at the sight of her husband.

'It's you! Where have you sprung from?'

'I haven't sprung from anywhere. I've simply arrived home. Who are you so furious with?'

She avoided the trap and neatly turned the attack on Alain.

'You're very cutting, the first time you get home punctually. *I'm* ready. I've been waiting for you.'

'You haven't been waiting for me since I'm punctual to the minute. Who were you so angry with? I heard "filthy bloody swine of an animal?" What animal?'

She squinted very slightly but sustained Alain's look.

'The dog!' she cried. 'That damned dog downstairs, the dog that barks morning, noon and night. It's started again! Can't you hear it barking? Listen!'

She raised her finger to make him keep quiet and Alain had time to notice that the gloved finger was shaking. He yielded to a naïve need to make sure.

'Just fancy, I thought you were talking about Saha.'

'Me?' cried Camille. 'Me speak about Saha in that tone?

Why I wouldn't dare! The heavens would fall if I did! For goodness' sake, are you coming?'

'Go and get the car out, I'll join you down below. I've just got to get a handkerchief and a pullover.'

His first thought was to find the cat. On the coolest balcony, near the deck-chair in which Camille occasionally slept in the afternoon, he could see nothing but some fragments of broken glass. He stared at them blankly.

'The cat's with me, Monsieur,' came the fluting voice of Mme Buque. 'She's very fond of my wicker stool. She sharpens her claws on it.'

'In the kitchen,' thought Alain painfully. 'My little puma, my cat of the garden, my cat of the lilacs and the butterflies, in the kitchen! Ah! All that's going to change!'

He kissed Saha on the forehead and chanted some ritual praises, very low. He promised her couch-grass and sweet acacia flowers. But he found both the cat and Mme Buque artificial and constrained; Mme Buque in particular.

'We may be back to dinner and we may not, Madame Buque. Has the cat everything she needs?'

'Yes, Monsieur. Oh yes, indeed, Monsieur,' said Mme Buque hurriedly. 'I do everything I possibly can, really I do, Monsieur!'

The big, fat woman was red in the face and seemed on the verge of tears. She ran a friendly, clumsy hand over the cat's back. Saha arched her back and proffered a little 'm'hain', the mew of a poor timid cat which made her friend's heart swell with sadness.

The drive was more peaceful than he had hoped. Sitting at the wheel, her eyes alert, her feet and hands perfectly synchronized, Camille drove him as far as the slope of Montfort-l'Amaurey.

'Shall we have dinner out of doors, Alain? Shall we, Alain, darling?'

She smiled at him in profile, beautiful as she always

was in the twilight; her cheek brown and transparent, her teeth and the corner of her eye the same glittering white. In the forest of Rambouillet, she put down the windscreen and the wind filled Alain's ears with a sound of leaves and running water.

'A little rabbit! . . .' cried Camille. 'A pheasant!'

'It's still a rabbit . . . One moment more and I . . .'

'He doesn't know his luck, that chap!'

'You've got a dimple in your cheek like you have in your photos as a child,' said Alain, beginning to come to life.

'Don't talk about it! I'm getting enormous!' she said, shaking her shoulders.

He watched for the return of the laugh and the dimple, and his eyes wandered down to the robust neck, free of any trace of the 'girdle of Venus', the round, inflexible neck of a handsome white Negress. 'Yes, she really has got fatter. And in the most seductive way. For her breasts, those too . . .' He withdrew into himself once more and came up, morosely, against the age-old male grievance. 'She's getting fat from making love. She's battening on *me*.' He slipped a jealous hand under his jacket, felt his ribs, and ceased to admire the childish dimple in her cheeks.

But he felt a certain gratified vanity when they sat down a little later at a famous inn and the neighbouring diners stopped talking and eating to stare at Camille. And he exchanged with his wife the smiles, the movements of the chin and all the rituals of coquetry suitable to a 'handsome couple'.

However, it was only for him that Camille lowered her voice and displayed a certain languor and certain charming attentions which were not in the least for show. In revenge, Alain snatched out of her hand the dish of raw tomatoes and the basket of strawberries, insisted that she ate chicken with a cream sauce, and poured her out a wine which she did not care for but which she drank fast.

'You know perfectly well I don't like wine,' she repeated each time she emptied her glass.

The sun had set but the sky was still almost white, dappled with small deep-pink clouds. But night and coolness seemed to be rising as one from the forest which loomed, massive, beyond the tables of the inn. Camille laid her hand on Alain's.

'What is it? What is it? What's the matter?' he said in terror.

Astonished, she withdrew her hand. The little wine she had drunk gleamed gaily in her eyes in which shone the tiny, quivering image of the pink balloons hung from the pergola.

'Nothing's the matter, silly. You're as nervous as a cat! Is it forbidden for me to put my hand on yours?'

'I thought,' he admitted weakly, 'I thought you wanted to tell me something . . . something serious . . . I thought,' he burst out with it, 'you were going to tell me you were pregnant.'

Camille's shrill little laugh attracted the attention of the men at the near-by tables.

'And you were as overcome as all that? With joy or . . . fed-up-ness?'

'I don't exactly know. What about you? Would you be pleased or not pleased? We've hardly thought about it . . . at least, *I* haven't. But what are you laughing at?'

'Your face! All of a sudden, a face as if you were just going to be hanged. It's too funny. You'll make my eye-black come unstuck.'

With her two forefingers, she lifted up either eyelid.

'It isn't funny, it's serious,' said Alain, glad to put her in the wrong. 'But why was I so terrified?' he thought.

'It's only serious,' said Camille, 'for people who've got nowhere to live or who've only got two rooms. But people like us . . .'

Serene, lulled into optimism by the treacherous wine,

she smoked and talked as if she were by herself, her thigh against the table and her legs crossed.

'Pull down your skirt, Camille.'

She did not hear him and went on: 'We've got all the essentials a child needs. A garden – and what a garden! And a dream of a room with its own bathroom.'

'A room?'

'Your old room. We'd have it repainted. And it would be very nice of you not to insist on a frieze of little ducks and fir trees on a sky-blue background. That would ruin the taste of our offspring.'

He restrained himself from stopping her. She was talking at random, her cheeks flushed, as she stared into the distance, seeing all she was building up. He had never seen her so beautiful. He was fascinated by the base of her neck, like the smooth unwrinkled bole of a tree, and by the nostrils which were blowing out smoke. 'When I give her pleasure and she tightens her lips, she opens her nostrils like a little horse as she breathes.

He heard such crazy predictions fall from the reddened scornful lips that they ceased to alarm him: Camille was calmly proceeding with her woman's life among the wreckage of Alain's past. 'Good Lord,' he thought. 'How she's got it all organized. I'm certainly learning something!' A tennis-court was to replace the great, useless lawn. The kitchen and the pantries . . .

'Haven't you ever realized how inconvenient they are? And think of all that wasted space. It's like the garage. I'm only saying all this, darling, so as you should know I think a lot about our real setting up house. Above all, we must be tactful with your mother. She's so awfully sweet . . . we mustn't do anything she wouldn't approve of. Must we?'

He put in haphazard 'Yesses' and 'Noes' as he picked up some wild strawberries scattered on the cloth. After hearing her say 'your old room', he had been immunized by a provisional calm, a foretaste of indifference.

'Only one thing may make things awkward for us,' Camille went on. 'Patrick's last postcard dated from the Balearic Isles. Do pay attention! It'll take less time for Patrick to get back from the Balearics than for our decorator to get everything finished. I hope he comes to a violent end, that son of Penelope by a male tortoise! But I shall put on my siren voice: "Patrick, my pet . . ." You know my siren voice makes a tremendous impression on Patrick.'

'From the Balearic Isles . . .' broke in Alain thoughtfully. 'From the Balearic Isles.'

'Otherwise practically from next door. Where are you off to? Do you want us to go? It was so nice here.'

Her brief intoxication was over. She stood up shivering and yawning with sleepiness.

'I'll drive,' said Alain. 'Put on the old coat that's under the cushion. And go to sleep.'

A flak of flying insects, bright silver moths and stag-beetles hard as pebbles, whirled in front of the headlights and the car drove back the wing-laden air like a wave. Camille did indeed go to sleep, sitting perfectly upright. She was trained not to encumber the driver's arm and shoulder, even in her sleep. She merely gave a little forward jerk of her head at every jolt in the road.

'From the Balearic Isles,' Alain kept repeating to himself. The dark air, the white fires which caught and repulsed and decimated the flying creatures took him back to the populous threshold of his dreams; the sky with its stardust of exploded faces, the great hostile eyes which put off till tomorrow a reckoning, a password or a significant figure. He was so deep in that world that he forgot to take the short cut between Pontchartrain and the Versailles toll-gate and Camille scolded him in her sleep. 'Bravo!' applauded Alain. 'Good reflex action! Good little faithful, vigilant senses. Ah, how much I like you, how well we get on, when you're asleep and I'm awake.'

*

Their sleeves and their unprotected hair were wet with dew when they set foot in their newly built street, empty in the moonlight. Alain looked up; nine storeys up, in the middle of the almost round moon, the little horned shadow of a cat was leaning forward, waiting.

'Look! Look how she's waiting!'

'You've got good eyes,' said Camille, yawning.

'If she were to fall! Whatever you do, don't call her!'

'You needn't worry,' said Camille. 'If I did call her, she wouldn't come.'

'For good reason,' said Alain unpleasantly.

As soon as he had said it, he was angry with himself. 'Too soon, too soon! And what a bad moment to choose!' Camille dropped the hand that was just about to push the bell.

'For good reason? For what good reason? Come on, out with it. I've been lacking in respect to the sacred animal again? The cat's complained of me?'

'I've gone too far,' thought Alain, as he closed the garage door. He crossed the street again and rejoined his wife who was waiting for him in battle order. 'Either I give in for the sake of a quiet night, or I stop the discussion by giving her a good, hard slap . . . or . . . It's too soon.'

'Well! I'm talking to you!'

'Let's go up first,' said Alain.

They did not speak as they went up, squeezed side by side in the narrow lift. As soon as they reached the studio, Camille tore off her beret and gloves and threw them across the room as if to show she had not given up the quarrel. Alain busied himself with Saha, inviting her to quit her perilous post. Patient, determined not to displease him, the cat followed him into the bathroom.

'If it's because of what you heard before dinner, when you came in,' began Camille shrilly the moment he reappeared.

Alain had decided on his line and interrupted her wearily: 'My dear, what are we going to say to each other?

Nothing that we don't know already. That you can't bear the cat, that you blew up Mother Buque because the cat broke a vase – or a glass – I saw the pieces. I shall answer that I'm extremely fond of Saha and that you'd be just as jealous if I'd kept a warm affection for some friend of my childhood. And so it'll go on all night. I'd prefer to sleep, thanks very much. Look here, the next time, I advise you to take the initiative and have a little dog.'

Startled, embarrassed by having nothing for her temper to fasten on, Camille stared at him with raised eyebrows.

'The next time? What next time? What do you mean? What initiative?'

As Alain merely shrugged his shoulders, she flushed, her face suddenly became very young again and the extreme brightness of her eyes presaged tears. 'Oh, how bored I am!' groaned Alain inwardly. 'She's going to admit it. She's going to tell me I was right. How boring!'

'Listen, Alain.'

With an effort, he feigned anger and assumed a false air of authority.

'No, my dear. No, no, no! You're not going to force me to finish off this charming evening with a barren discussion. You're not going to make a drama out of a piece of childish nonsense any more than you're going to stop me being fond of animals.'

A kind of bitter gaiety came into Camille's eyes but she said nothing. 'Perhaps I was a little hard. "Childish nonsense," was unnecessary. And as to being fond of animals, what do I know about that?' A small, shadowy blue shape, outlined like a cloud with a hem of silver, sitting on the dizzy edge of the night, absorbed his thoughts and removed him from that soulless place where, inch by inch, he was defending his chance of solitude, his egotism, his poetry . . .

'Come along, my little enemy,' he said with disloyal charm, 'let's go and rest.'

She opened the door of the bathroom where Saha, installed for the night on the cork-seated stool, appeared to take only the faintest notice of her.

'But why, but why? Why did you say "the next time"?'

The noise of running water drowned Camille's voice. Alain did not attempt to answer. When he rejoined her in the huge bed, he wished her good-night and kissed her carelessly on her unpowdered nose, while Camille's mouth clung to his chin with a small greedy sound.

Waking early, he went off quietly to lie down on the 'waiting-room bench', the narrow divan squeezed between two walls of glass panes.

It was there that, during the following nights, he finished off his sleep. He closed the opaque oilcloth curtains on either side; they were almost new but already half destroyed by the sun. He breathed on his body the very perfume of his solitude, the sharp feline smell of rest-harrow and flowering box. One arm extended, the other folded on his chest, he resumed the relaxed, lordly attitude of his childhood sleep. Suspended from the narrow top of the three-cornered house, he encouraged with all his might the return of his old dreams which the lover's exhaustion had dispersed.

He escaped more easily than Camille could have wished, constrained as he was to fly on the very spot. Escape no longer meant a staircase descended on tiptoe, the slamming of a taxi door, a brief farewell note. None of his mistresses had prepared him for Camille and her young girl's eagerness; Camille and her reckless desire. Neither had they prepared him for Camille's stoical behaviour as an offended partner. She made it a point of honour not to complain.

Having escaped and lain down again on the waiting-room bench, Alain strained an uneasy ear toward the room he had just left, as his head felt for the hard little cushion he preferred to all the others. But Camille never reopened the door. Left alone, she pulled the crumpled sheet and the silk eiderdown over her, gnawed her bent finger in resentful regret, and snapped off the chromium strip-light which threw a narrow white beam across the bed. Alain never knew whether she had slept in the empty bed or whether she was learning so young that a solitary night imposes an armed vigil. It was impossible to tell, since she reappeared fresh and rather carefully dressed instead of in the bathrobe and pyjamas of the night before. But she could not understand that a man's sensuality is brief and seasonal and that its unpredictable return is never a new beginning.

Lying alone, bathed in the night air, measuring the height and the silence of his tower-top by the faintness of the hoots from the boats on the near-by Seine, the unfaithful husband delayed going to sleep till the apparition of Saha. She came to him, a shadow bluer than the shadows, along the ledge outside the open glass pane. There she stayed on the watch and would not come down on to Alain's chest although he implored her with the words that she knew: 'Come, my little puma, come along . . . My cat of the tree-tops, my cat of the lilacs. Saha, Saha, Saha.'

She resisted, sitting there above him on the window-sill. He could see nothing of her but her cat's shape against the sky, her chin down and her ears passionately orientated towards him. He could never catch the expression of her look.

Sometimes the dry dawn, the dawn before the wind got up, found the two of them sitting on the east side balcony. Cheek by cheek they watched the sky pale and the flight of white pigeons leaving the beautiful cedar of the Folie-Saint-James one by one. Together they felt the same surprise at being so high above the earth, so alone and so far from being happy. With the ardent, sinuous movement of a huntress, Saha followed the pigeons' flight and uttered an occasional 'ek . . . ek . . .' the faint echo of the 'mouek . . . mouek . . .' of excitement, greed and violent games.

'Our room,' Alain said in her ear. 'Our garden, our house.'

She was getting thin again and Alain found her light and enchanting. But he suffered at seeing her so gentle and patient. Her patience was that of all those who are wearied out and sustained by a promise.

Sleep overcame Alain again as soon as daylight had begun to shorten the shadows. Rayless at first and looming larger through the mist of Paris, the sun swiftly shrank and lightened. As it rose, already burning hot, it awoke a twittering of sparrows in the gardens. The growing light revealed all the untidiness of a hot night on balconies and window-sills and in little yards where captive shrubs languished – a garment forgotten on a deck-chair, empty glasses on a metal table, a pair of sandals. Alain hated the indecency of small dwellings oppressed by summer and regained his bed with one bound through a yawning panel in the glass. At the foot of the nine-storeyed building, a gardener lifted his head and saw this white young man leap through the transparent wall like a burglar.

Saha did not follow him. Sometimes she strained her ears in the direction of the triangular room; sometimes she dispassionately watched the awakening of the distant world on ground level. Someone let out a dog from a small decrepit house. The dog leapt forward without a bark, rushed round and round the tiny garden, and did not recover its voice until it had finished its aimless run. Women appeared at the windows; a maid furiously slammed doors and shook out orange cushions on a flat roof; men, waking regretfully, lit the first bitter cigarette. At last, in the fireless kitchen of the Wedge, the automatic, whistling coffee-pot and the electric teapot clashed against each other; through the porthole window of the bathroom there emerged Camille's perfume and her noisy yawning. Saha resignedly folded her paws beneath her and pretended to sleep.

EIGHT

ONE evening in July, when the two of them were waiting for Alain's return, Camille and the cat were resting on the same parapet; the cat crouched on all four paws, Camille leaning on her folded arms. Camille did not like this balcony-terrace, reserved for the cat and shut in by two cement partitions which cut off both the wind and all communication with the balcony on the prow.

They exchanged a glance of sheer mutual investigation and Camille did not say a word to Saha. Propped on her elbows, she leant over as if to count the storeys by the orange awnings that flapped from top to bottom of the dizzy façade, she brushed against the cat who got up to make room for her, stretched, and lay down a little farther off.

When Camille was alone, she looked very much like the little girl who did not want to say 'how d'you do?' Her face returned to childhood because it wore that expression of inhuman innocence, of angelic hardness which ennobles children's faces. Her gaze wandered over Paris, over the sky from which the light drained a little earlier each day, with an impartial severity which possibly condemned nothing. She yawned nervously, stood upright, and took a few absent-minded steps. Then she leant over again, forcing the cat to jump down. Saha stalked away with dignity and would have preferred to go back into the room. But the door in the hypotenuse had been shut and Saha patiently sat down. The next moment she had to get out of Camille's way for she was pacing from one partition to the other with long, jerky strides. The cat jumped back on to the parapet. As if in play, Camille dislodged her as she leant on her elbows and once again Saha took refuge against the closed door.

Motionless, her eyes far away, Camille stood with her back to her. Nevertheless the cat was looking at Camille's back and her breath came faster. She got up, turned two or three times on her own axis and looked questioningly at the closed door. Camille had not moved. Saha inflated her nostrils and showed a distress which was almost like nausea. A long, desolate mew escaped from her, the wretched reply to a silent imminent threat. Camille faced round abruptly.

She was a trifle pale; that is to say, her rouge stood out in two oval moons on her cheeks. She affected an air of absent-mindedness as she would if a human eye had been staring at her. She even began to sing under her breath and resumed her pacing from one partition to the other, pacing to the rhythm of her song, but her voice failed her. She forced the cat, whom her foot was about to kick, to regain her narrow observation post with one bound, then to flatten herself against the door.

Saha had regained her self-control and would have died rather than utter a second cry. Tracking the cat down, without appearing to see her, Camille paced to and fro in silence. Saha did not jump on the parapet till Camille's feet were right on top of her and she only leapt down again on to the floor of the balcony to avoid the outstretched arm which would have hurled her from the height of the nine storeys.

She fled methodically and jumped carefully, keeping her eyes fixed on her adversary and condescending neither to fury nor to supplication. The most violent emotion of all, the terror of dying, soaked the sensitive soles of her paws with sweat so that they left flower-like prints on the stucco balcony.

Camille seemed the first to weaken and to lose her criminal strength. She made the mistake of noticing that the sun was going down, gave a glance at her wrist watch, and was aware of the clink of glasses inside. A moment or two more and her resolution would have deserted her as sleep deserts the somnambulist, leaving her guiltless and exhausted. Saha felt her enemy's firmness waver, hesitated on the parapet and Camille, stretching out both arms, pushed her into space.

She had time to hear the grating of claws on the rough-cast wall, to see Saha's blue body, twisted into an S, clutching the air with the force of a rising trout; then she shrank away, with her back to the wall.

She felt no temptation to look down into the little kitchen garden edged with new rubble. Back in the room, she put her hands over her ears, withdrew them, and shook her head as if she could hear the hum of a mosquito. Then she sat down and nearly fell asleep. But the oncoming night brought her to her feet again. She drove away the twilight by lighting up glass bricks, luminous tubes and blinding mushrooms of lamps. She also lit up the long chromium eye which poured the opaline beam of its glance across the bed.

She walked about with supple movements, handling objects with light, adroit, dreaming hands.

'It's as if I'd got thinner,' she said out loud.

She changed her clothes and dressed herself in white.

'My fly in the milk,' she said, imitating Alain's voice. Her cheeks regained their colour at a sudden sensual memory which brought her back to reality and she waited for Alain's arrival.

She bent her head in the direction of the buzzing lift and shivered at every noise; those dull knockings, those metallic clangs, those sounds as of a boat grinding at anchor, those muffled bursts of music, which echo the discordant life of a new block of flats. But she was not surprised when the hollow tinkle of the bell in the hall replaced the fumbling of a key in the lock. She ran and opened the door herself.

'Shut the door,' Alain ordered. 'I must see first of all

whether she hasn't hurt herself. Come and hold the lamp for me.'

He carried Saha alive in his arms. He went straight to the bedroom, pushed aside the things on the invisible dressing-table, and gently put the cat on the slab of glass. She held herself upright and firm on her paws but her deep-set eyes wandered all about her as they would have done in a strange house.

'Saha!' called Alain in a whisper. 'If there's nothing the matter with her, it's a miracle. Saha!'

She raised her head, as if to reassure her friend, and leant her cheek against his hand.

'Walk a little, Saha. Look, she's walking! Good Lord! Falling six storeys. It was the awning of the chap on the second floor that broke the fall. From there she bounced off on to the concierge's little lawn – the concierge saw her pass in the air. He said: "I thought it was an umbrella falling." What's she got on her ear? No, it's some white off the wall. Wait till I listen to her heart.'

He laid the cat on her side and listened to the beating ribs, the tiny disordered mechanism. With his fair hair spread out and his eyes closed, he seemed to be sleeping on Saha's flank and to wake with a sigh only to see Camille standing there silent and apart, watching the close-knit group they made.

'Can you believe it? There's nothing wrong. At least I can't find anything wrong with her except a terribly agitated heart. But a cat's heart is usually agitated. But however could it have happened! I'm asking you as if you could possibly know, my poor pet! She fell from this side,' he said, looking at the open french window. 'Jump down on the ground, Saha, if you can.'

After hesitating, she jumped but lay down again on the carpet. She was breathing fast and went on looking all round the room with the same uncertain look.

'I think I'll phone Chéron. Still, look, she's washing

herself. She wouldn't wash herself if she'd been injured internally. Oh, good Lord!'

He stretched, threw his jacket on the bed, and came over to Camille.

'What a fright. How pretty you look, all in white. Kiss me, my fly in the milk!'

She let herself fall into the arms which had remembered her at last and could not hold back some broken sobs.

'No? You're actually crying?'

He was upset himself and hid his forehead in the soft, black hair.

'I . . . I didn't know that you were kind.'

She had the courage not to draw away from him at that. However, Alain quickly returned to Saha whom he wanted to take out on the balcony because of the heat. But the cat resisted and contented herself with lying near the open door, turned towards the evening, blue as herself. From time to time, she gave a brief shudder and looked anxiously into the triangular room behind her.

'It's the shock,' explained Alain. 'I wanted her to go and sit outside.'

'Leave her alone,' said Camille faintly, 'since she doesn't want to.'

'Her wishes are orders. Today, of all days! Is there likely to be anything eatable left over at this hour? It's half-past nine!'

Mother Buque wheeled the table out on to the balcony and they dined looking over the east side of Paris where the most lights glimmered. Alain talked a lot, drank water with a little wine in it, and accused Saha of clumsiness, impudence, and 'cat's sins'.

'"Cat's sins" are the kind of playful mistakes and lapses of judgement which can be put down to their having been civilized and domesticated. They've nothing in common with the clumsiness and carelessness that are almost deliberate.'

But Camille no longer asked him: 'How do you know that?' After dinner, he carried Saha and drew Camille into the studio where the cat consented to drink the milk she had refused. As she drank, she shivered all over as cats do when they are given something too cold to drink.

'It's the shock,' Alain repeated. 'All the same, I shall ask Chéron to look in and see her tomorrow morning. Oh, I'm forgetting everything!' he cried gaily. 'Will you phone the concierge? I've left that roll of plans down in his lodge. The one that Massart, our precious furnishing chap, deposited there.'

Camille obeyed while Alain, tired and relaxed after the strain, dropped into one of the scattered armchairs and closed his eyes.

'Hallo!' said Camille at the telephone. 'Yes . . . That must be it. A big roll . . . Thanks so much.'

He laughed with his eyes still closed. She had returned to his side and stood there, watching him laugh.

'That absurd little voice you put on! What is this new little voice? "A big roll . . . Thanks so much",' he mimicked. 'Do you keep that extremely small voice for the concierge? Come here, it needs the two of us to face Massart's latest creations.'

He unrolled a sheet of thick drawing-paper, on the ebony table. Saha, who loved all kinds of paper, promptly leapt on the tinted drawing.

'Isn't she sweet!' exclaimed Alain. 'It's to show me she's not in the least hurt. O my miraculously escaped one! Hasn't she a bump on her head? Camille, feel her head. No, she hasn't a bump. Feel her head all the same, Camille.'

A poor little murderess meekly tried to emerge from her banishment, stretched out her hand, and touched the cat's head with humble hatred.

Her gesture was received with the most savage snarl, a scream and an epileptic leap. Camille shrieked 'Ha!' as if she had been burned. Standing on the unrolled drawing the cat covered the young woman with a flaming stare of accusation, the fur on her back erect, her teeth bared and the dry red of her open jaw showing.

Alain had sprang up, ready to protect Saha and Camille from each other.

'Take care! She's . . . perhaps she's mad . . . Saha!'

She stared at him angrily but with a lucidity that proved she had not lost her reason.

'What happened? Where did you touch her?'

'I didn't touch her at all.'

They were both speaking low, hardly moving their lips.

'Then, why this?' said Alain. 'I don't understand. Put your hand out again.'

'No, I don't want to!' protested Camille. 'Perhaps she's gone wild,' she added.

Alain took the risk of stroking Saha. She flattened her erect fur and yielded to the friendly palm but glared once more at Camille with brilliant, accusing eyes.

'Why *this*?' Alain repeated slowly. 'Look, she's got a scratch on her nose. I hadn't seen it. It's dried blood. Saha, Saha, good now,' he said, seeing the fury growing in the yellow eyes.

Because her cheeks were swelled out and her whiskers stiffly thrust forward as if she were hunting, the furious cat seemed to be laughing. The joy of battle stretched the mauve corners of her mouth and tautened the mobile, muscular chin. The whole of her feline face was striving towards a universal language, towards a word forgotten by men.

'Whatever's *that*?' said Alain suddenly.

'Whatever's *what*?'

Under the cat's stare Camille was recovering her courage and the instinct of self-defence. Leaning over the drawing, Alain could make out damp prints in groups of four little spots round a central, irregular patch.

'Her paws . . . wet?' muttered Alain.

'She must have walked in some water,' said Camille. 'You're making a fuss about nothing.'

Alain raised her head towards the dry blue night.

'In water? What water?'

He turned again to his wife. He looked at her with round eyes which made him look suddenly extraordinarily ugly. 'Don't you know what those footprints mean?' he said harshly. 'No, *you* wouldn't know. Fear, d'you understand, *fear*. The sweat of fear. Cat's sweat, the only time cats *do* sweat. So she was frightened.'

Delicately, he lifted one of Saha's front paws and dried the sweat on the fleshy pad. Then he pulled back the living white sheath into which the claws had been drawn back.

'She's got all her claws broken,' he said, talking to himself. 'She must have held on . . . clutching. She scratched the stone trying to save herself. She . . .'

He broke off his monologue and, without another word, took the cat under his arm and carried her off to the bathroom.

Alone, unmoving, Camille strained her ears. She kept her hands knotted together; free as she was, she seemed to be loaded with fetters.

'Madame Buque,' said Alain's voice, 'have you any milk?'

'Yes, Monsieur. In the fridge.'

'Then it's ice-cold?'

'But I can warm it on the stove. It won't take a second. It is for the cat? She's not ill, is she?'

'No, she's . . .'

Alain's voice stopped short and changed its tone: 'She's a little off meat in this heat. Thank you, Madame Buque. Yes, you can go now. See you in the morning.'

Camille heard her husband moving to and fro and turning on a tap. She knew that he was giving the cat food and fresh water. A diffused shadow, above the metal lampshade, came up as high as her face which was as still as a mask except for the slow movement of the great eyes.

Alain returned, carelessly tightening his leather belt, and sat down again at the ebony table. But he did not summon Camille back to sit beside him and she was forced to speak first.

'You've sent old Mother Buque off?'

'Yes. Shouldn't I have?'

He lit a cigarette and squinted at the flame of the lighter.

'I wanted her to bring something tomorrow morning.'

'Oh, it doesn't matter a bit . . . don't apologize.'

'But I'm not apologizing. Though, actually, I ought to.'

He went over to the open bay window, drawn by the blue of the night. He was studying a certain tremor in himself, a tremor which did not come from his recent emotion, but which was more like the tremolo of an orchestra, muffled and foreboding. From the Folie-Saint-James a rocket shot up, burst into luminous petals that withered one by one as they fell, and the blue of the night recovered its peace and its powdery depth. In the amusement park, a grotto, a colonnade, and a waterfall were suddenly lit up with incandescent white; Camille came nearer to him.

'Are they having a gala night? Let's wait for the fireworks. Do you hear the guitars?'

Absorbed in his inner tremor, he did not answer her. His wrists and hands were tingling, his loins were weak and felt as if a thousand insects were crawling over them. His state reminded him of the hateful lassitude, the fatigue he used to feel after the school sports. After running and rowing he would emerge vindictive, throbbing and exhausted and equally contemptuous of his victory or defeat. Now, he was at peace only in that part of himself which was no longer anxious about Saha. For several minutes – or perhaps for very few – ever since the discovery of the broken claws, ever since Saha's furious terror, he had lost all sense of time.

'It's not fireworks,' he said. 'Probably just some dances.'

From the movement Camille made beside him in the shadow, he realized that she had given up expecting him to answer her. He felt her coming closer without apprehension. He saw the outline of the white dress; a bare arm; a half face lit by the yellow light from the lamps indoors and a half face that shadowed blue in the clear night. The two halves were divided by the small straight nose and each was provided with a large, almost unblinking eye.

'Yes, of course, it's dances,' she agreed. 'They're mandolines, not guitars. Listen . . . "*Les donneurs . . . de sé-é-réna . . . des, Et les bel-les é-écou-teu . . .*'

Her voice cracked on the highest note and she coughed to excuse her failure.

'But what a tiny voice . . .' thought Alain, astonished. 'What has she done with her voice that's as big and open as her eyes?' She's singing in a little girl's voice. Hoarse, too.'

The mandolines stopped and the breeze brought a faint human noise of clapping and applause. A moment later, a rocket shot up, burst into an umbrella of mauve rays in which hung tears of living fire.

'Oh!' cried Camille.

Both of them had emerged from the darkness like two statues; Camille in lilac marble; Alain whiter, with his hair greenish and his eyes almost colourless. When the rocket had gone out, Camille sighed.

'It never lasts long enough,' she said plaintively.

The distant music started again. But the capricious wind deadened the sound of the stringed instruments into a vague shrill buzzing and carried the blasts of the accompanying brass, on two notes, loudly and insistently right into their ears.

'What a shame,' said Camille. 'They've probably got

a frightfully good jazz band. That's "Love in the Night" they're playing.'

She hummed the tune in a high, shaky, almost inaudible voice, as if she had just been crying. This new voice of hers acutely increased Alain's disquiet. It induced in him a need for revelation, a desire to break down whatever it was that – a long time ago or only a moment ago? – had risen between himself and Camille. It was something to which he could not yet give a name but which was growing fast; something which prevented him from putting his arm round her neck like a boy; something which kept him motionless at her side, alert and expectant, against the wall still warm from the heat of the day. Turning impatient, he said, 'Go on singing.'

A long red, white, and blue shower, falling like the branches of a weeping willow, streaked the sky over the park and showed Alain a Camille startled and already defiant: 'Singing what?'

'"Love in the Night" or anything else. It doesn't matter what.'

She hesitated, then refused.

'Let me listen to the jazz . . . even from here you can hear it's simply marvellous.'

He did not insist. He restrained his impatience and mastered the tingling which had now spread over his entire body.

A swarm of gay little suns, revolving brightly against the darkness, took flight. Alain secretly confronted them with the constellations of his favourite dreams.

'Those are the ones to remember. I'll try and take them with me down there,' he noted gravely. 'I've neglected my dreams too much.' At last, in the sky over the Folie, there rose and expanded a kind of straying pink and yellow dawn which burst into vermilion discs and fiery ferns and ribbons of blinding metal.

The shouts of children on the lower balconies greeted this miraculous display. By its light, Alain saw Camille absent and remote, absorbed in other lights in her own mind.

As soon as the night closed in again, his hesitation vanished and he slipped his own bare arm under Camille's. As he touched that bare arm, he fancied he could see it; its whiteness hardly tinged by the summer and clothed in a fine down that lay flat on the skin, reddish-brown on the forearm, paler near the shoulder.

'You're cold,' he murmured. 'You're not feeling ill?'

She began to cry very quietly and so promptly that Alain suspected she had been preparing her tears.

'No. It's you. It's you who . . . who don't love me.'

He leant back against the wall and drew Camille against his hip. He could feel her trembling, and cold from her shoulders to her knees, bare above her rolled stockings. She clung to him faithfully, leaning all her weight on him.

'Aha, so I don't love you. Right! Is this another jealousy scene on account of Saha?'

He felt a muscular tremor run through the whole of the body he was supporting, a renewal of energy and self-defence. Encouraged by the moment, by a kind of indescribable opportunism, he insisted: 'Instead of adopting this charming animal, like me. Are we the only young couple who have a cat or a dog? Would you like a parrot or a marmoset – a pair of doves – a dog, to make me very jealous in my turn?'

She shook her shoulders, protesting with annoyance through closed lips. With his head high, Alain carefully controlled his own voice and egged himself on. 'Go on, a few more bits of nonsense; fill her up and we'll get somewhere. She's like a jar that I've got to turn upside down to empty. Go on. Go on.'

'Would you like a little lion . . . or a baby crocodile of barely fifty? No? Come on, you'd much better adopt Saha. If you'd just take the least bit of trouble, you'd soon see . . .'

Camille wrenched herself out of his arms so violently that he staggered.

'No!' she cried. '*That*, never! Do you hear me? *Never*!'

'Ah, now we've got it!' Alain said to himself with delight. He pushed Camille into the room, pulled down the outer blind, lit up the rectangle of glass in the ceiling, and shut the window. With an animal movement, Camille rushed over to the window and Alain opened it again.

'On condition you don't scream,' he said.

He wheeled the only armchair up to Camille and sat astride on the solitary chair at the foot of the wide, turned-down bed with its new, clean sheets. The oilcloth curtains, drawn for the night, gave a greenish cast to Camille's pale face and her creased white dress.

'Well?' began Alain. 'No compromise possible? Appalling story? Either her or me?'

She answered with a brief nod and Alain realized that he must drop his bantering tone.

'What do you want me to say?' he went on, after a silence. 'The only thing I don't want to say to you? You know very well I'll never give up this cat. I should be ashamed to. Ashamed in myself and ashamed before her.'

'I know,' said Camille.

'And before you,' Alan finished.

'Oh, *me*!' said Camille, raising her hand.

'You count too,' said Alain hardly. 'Tell me. Is it only me you've anything against? You've no reproach against Saha except her affection for me?'

She answered only with a troubled, hesitant look and he was irritated at having to go on questioning her. He had thought that a short violent scene would force all the issues; he had relied on this easy way out. But, after her one cry, Camille had stiffened defensively and was furnishing no fuel for a quarrel. He resorted to patience: 'Tell me, my dear. What is it? Mustn't I call you my dear? Tell me, if it were a question of another cat and not Saha, would you be so intolerant?'

'Of course I wouldn't,' she said very quickly. 'You wouldn't love it as much as that one.'

'Quite true,' said Alain with loyal accuracy.

'Even a woman,' went on Camille, beginning to get heated, 'you probably wouldn't love a *woman* as much as that.'

'Quite true,' said Alain.

'You're not like most people who are fond of animals. No, you're *not*. Patrick's fond of animals. He takes big dogs by the scruff of their necks and rolls them over. He imitates cats to see the faces they make – he whistles to the birds.'

'Quite. In other words, he's not difficult,' said Alain.

'But you're quite different. You *love* Saha.'

'I've never pretended not to. But I wasn't lying to you, either, when I said to you: "Saha's not your rival."'

He broke off and lowered his eyelids over his secret which was a secret of purity.

'There are rivals *and* rivals,' said Camille sarcastically.

Suddenly she reddened. Flushed with sudden intoxication, she advanced to Alain.

'I saw the two of you!' she almost shrieked. 'In the morning, when you spend the night on your little divan. Before daybreak. I've seen you, both of you.'

She pointed a shaking hand towards the balcony.

'Sitting there, the two of you . . . you didn't even hear me! You were like that, cheek to cheek.'

She went over to the window, recovered her breath and marched down on Alain again.

'It's for you to say honestly whether I'm wrong in being jealous of this cat and wrong in suffering.'

He kept silence so long that she became angry again.

'Do speak! Do *say* something! At the point we've got to . . . What are you waiting for?'

'The sequel,' said Alain. 'The rest.'

He stood up quietly, bent over his wife, and lowered

his voice as he indicated the french window: 'It was you, wasn't it? You threw her over?'

With a swift movement she put the bed between herself and him but she did not deny it. He watched her escape with a kind of smile: 'You threw her over,' he said dreamily. 'I felt very definitely that you'd changed everything between us. You threw her over . . . she broke her claws trying to clutch on to the wall.'

He lowered his head, imagining the attempted murder.

'But *how* did you throw her over? By holding her by the skin of her neck? By taking advantage of her being asleep on the parapet? Had you been planning this for a long time? You hadn't had a fight with each other first?'

He raised his head and stared at Camille's hands and arms.

'No, you've no marks. She accused you well and truly, didn't she, when I made you touch her. She was magnificent.'

His eyes left Camille and embraced the night, the dust of stars, the tops of the three poplars which the lights in the room lit up.

'Very well,' he said simply, 'I'm going away.'

'Oh listen . . . do *listen* . . .' Camille implored wildly, almost in a whisper.

Nevertheless, she let him go out of the room. He opened cupboards, talked to the cat in the bathroom. The sound of his footsteps warned Camille that he had changed into his outdoor shoes and she looked, automatically, at the time. He came in again, carrying Saha in a bulging basket which Mme Buque used for shopping. Hurriedly dressed, with his hair dishevelled and a scarf round his neck, his untidiness so much suggested that of a lover that Camille's eyelids pricked. But she heard Saha moving in the basket and tightened her lips.

'As you see, I'm going away,' repeated Alain. He lowered his eyes, lifted the basket a trifle, and corrected himself with calculated cruelty. '*We're* going away.'

He secured the wicker lid, explaining as he did so: 'This was all I could find in the kitchen.'

'You're going to your home?' inquired Camille, forcing herself to imitate Alain's calm.

'But of course.'

'Are you . . . can I count on seeing you during the next few days?'

'Why, certainly.'

Surprise made her weaken again. She had to make an immense effort not to plead, not to weep.

'What about you?'said Alain. 'Will you stay here alone tonight? You won't be frightened? If you insisted, I'd stay, but . . .'

He turned his head towards the balcony.

'But, frankly, I'm not keen on it. What do you propose to say to your family?'

Hurt at his sending her, by implication, home to her people, Camille pulled herself together.

'I've nothing to say to them. These are things which only concern *me*, I presume. I've no inclination for family councils.'

'I entirely agree with you . . . provisionally.'

'Anyway, we can decide as from tomorrow.'

He raised his free hand to ward off this threat of a future.

'No. Not tomorrow. Today there isn't any tomorrow.'

In the doorway, he turned back.

'In the bathroom, you'll find my key and all the money we've got here.'

She interrupted with irony: 'Why not a hamper of provisions and a compass?'

She was putting on a brave act and surveyed him with one hand on her hip and her head erect on her handsome neck. 'She's building up my exit,' thought Alain. He wanted to reply with some similar last-minute coquetry, to toss his hair over his forehead and give her that narrowed look between his lashes which seemed to disdain what it rested on. But he renounced a pantomime which would look absurd when he was carrying a shopping-basket and confined himself to a vague bow in Camille's direction.

She kept up her expression of bravado and her theatrical stance. But before he went out, he could see more clearly, at a distance, the dark circles round her eyes and the moisture which covered her temples and her smooth, unlined neck.

Downstairs, he crossed the street automatically, the key of the garage in his hand. 'I can't do that,' he thought and he retraced his steps towards the avenue some way off where cruising taxis could be picked up at night. Saha mewed two or three times and he calmed her with his voice. 'I can't do that. But it really would be much pleasanter to take the car. Neuilly is impossible at night.' He was surprised, having counted on a blessed sense of release, to find himself losing his composure as soon as he was alone. Walking did not restore his calm. When, at last, he found a stray taxi, the five-minute drive seemed almost interminable.

He shivered in the warm night under the gas-jet, waiting for the gate to be opened. Saha, who had recognized the smell of the garden, was giving short sharp mews in the basket which he had put down on the pavement.

The scent of the wistarias in their second flowering came across the air and Alain shivered more violently, stamping from one foot to the other as if it were bitterly cold. He rang again but the house gave no sign of life in spite of the solemn, scandalous clamour of the big bell. At last a light appeared in the little buildings by the garage and he heard old Emile's dragging feet on the gravel.

'It's me, Emile,' he said when the colourless face of the old valet peered through the bars.

'Monsieur Alain?' said Emile, exaggerating his quavering voice. 'Monsieur Alain's young lady isn't indisposed? The summer is so treacherous. Monsieur Alain has some luggage, I see.'

'No, it's Saha. Leave her, I'll carry her. No, don't turn up the gas-lamps, the light might wake Madame. Just open the front door for me and go back to bed.'

'Madame is awake – it was she who rang for me. I hadn't heard the big bell. In my first sleep, you see.'

Alain hurried ahead to escape Emile's chatter and the sound of his shaky footsteps following him. He did not stumble at the turnings of the paths though there was no moon that night. The great lawn, paler than the flower-beds, guided him. The dead, draped tree in the middle of the grass looked like a huge standing man with his coat over his arm. The smell of watered geraniums made Alain's throat tighten and he stopped. He bent down, opened the basket with groping fingers, and released the cat.

'Saha, our garden.'

He felt her glide out of the basket and, from pure tenderness, took no more notice of her. Like an offering, he gave her back the night, her liberty, the soft spongy earth, the wakeful insects, and the sleeping birds.

Behind the shutters on the ground floor, a lighted lamp was waiting and Alain's spirits fell again. 'To have to talk again, to have to explain to my mother . . . explain what? It's so simple. It's so difficult.'

All he longed for was silence, the room with the faded flowers on the wallpaper, his bed, and, above all, for vehement tears; great sobs as raucous as coughs that would be his secret, guilty compensation.

'Come in, darling, come in.'

He seldom went into his mother's room. His selfish aversion to medicine bottles and droppers, boxes of digitalis pills and homoeopathic remedies dated from childhood and was as acute as ever. But he could not resist the sight of the narrow, unadorned bed and of the woman with the thick white hair who was heaving herself up on her wrists.

'You know, Mother, there's nothing extraordinary about all this.'

He accompanied this idiotic statement with a smile of which he was promptly ashamed; a horizontal, stiff-cheeked smile. His tiredness had overwhelmed him in the sudden rush, making him do and say the exact opposite of what he meant to. He sat down by his mother's bedside and loosened his scarf.

'Forgive my appearance. I came just as I was. I arrive at preposterous times without giving you warning.'

'But you did give me warning,' said Mme Amparat.

She glanced at Alain's dusty shoes.

'Your shoes look like a tramp's.'

'I've only come from my place, Mother. But it was a long time before I could find a taxi. I was carrying the cat.'

'Ah,' said Mme Amparat, with an understanding look. 'You've brought back the cat?'

'Yes, of course. If you knew . . .'

He stopped, restrained by an odd discretion. 'These are things one doesn't tell. These stories aren't for parents.'

'Camille's not very fond of Saha, Mother.'

'I know,' said Mme Amparat.

She forced herself to smile and shook her wavy hair.

'That's extremely serious!'

'Yes. For Camille,' said Alain spitefully.

He got up and paced about among the furniture. It had white covers on it for the summer like the furniture in houses in the provinces. Having made up his mind not to denounce Camille, he could find nothing more to say.

'You know, Mother, there haven't been any screams or smashing of crockery. The glass dressing-table's still intact and the neighbours haven't come rushing up. Only I just need a little . . . a little time to be by myself . . . to rest. I won't hide it from you. I'm at the end of my tether,' he said, seating himself on the bed.

'No. You don't hide it from me,' said Mme Amparat. She laid a hand on Alain's forehead, turning up the young face, on which the pale stubble was beginning to show, towards the light. He complained, turning his changeable eyes away, and succeeded in holding off a little longer the storm of tears he had promised himself.

'If there aren't any sheets on my old bed, Mother, I'll wrap myself up in any old thing.'

'There are sheets on your bed,' said Mme Amparat.

At that, he threw his arms round his mother and kissed her blindly on her eyes and cheeks and hair. He thrust his face into her neck, stammered 'Good-night' and went out of the room, sniffing.

In the hall, he pulled himself together and did not go upstairs at once. The night which was ending called to him and so did Saha. But he did not go far. The steps down into the garden were far enough. He sat down on one of them in the darkness and his outstretched hand encountered the fur, the sensitive antennae-like whiskers and the cool nostrils of Saha.

She turned round and round on one spot according to the ritual of wild creatures when they caress. She seemed very small to him and light as a kitten. Because he was hungry himself, he thought she must be needing food.

'We'll eat tomorrow . . . quite soon now . . . it's almost daylight.'

Already she smelt of mint and geranium and box. He held her there, trusting and perishable, promised, perhaps, ten years of life. And he suffered at the thought of the briefness of so great a love.

'After you, probably anyone can have me who wants me. A woman, many women. But never another cat.'

A blackbird whistled four notes that rang through the whole garden. But the sparrows had heard it and answered. On the lawn and the massed flowerbeds, faint ghosts of colour began to appear. Alain could make out a sickly white, a dull red more melancholy than black itself, a yellow smeared on the surrounding green, a round yellow flower which began to revolve and become more yellow and was followed by eyes and moons. Staggering, dropping with sleep, Alain reached his room, threw off his clothes, uncovered the bed, and was unconscious almost as soon as he had slipped between the cool sheets.

Lying on his back with one arm flung out and the cat, silent and concentrated, kneading his shoulder, he was falling straight like a plummet into the very depths of sleep when a start brought him back to the daylight, the swaying of the awakened trees, and the blessed clanging of the distant trams.

'What's the matter with me? I wanted . . . Ah, yes! I wanted to cry.' He smiled and fell asleep again.

His sleep was feverish and crowded with dreams. Two or three times he thought he had woken up and was becoming conscious of where he was, but each time he was undeceived by the expression of the walls of his room. They were angrily watching the fluttering of a winged eye.

'But I'm asleep . . . of course, I'm asleep.'

'I'm asleep . . .' he answered again to the crunching gravel. 'I'm asleep, I tell you,' he called to two dragging feet that brushed against the door. The feet went away and the sleeper congratulated himself in his dream. But the dream had come to a head under the repeated solicitings and Alain opened his eyes.

The sun he had left on the window-sill in May had become an August sun and reached no farther than the satiny trunk of the tulip-tree opposite the house. 'How the summer has aged,' Alain said to himself. He got up, naked, looked for something to wear and found some pyjamas, too short and too tight in the sleeves and a faded dressing-gown which he joyfully pulled on. The window summoned him but he was stopped by Camille's photograph which he had left, forgotten, by his bed. Curiously, he examined the inaccurate, retouched little portrait; whitened here, blackened there. 'It's more like her than I supposed,' he thought. 'How was it I didn't notice it? Four months ago I used to say "Oh, she's entirely different from that. Much more subtle, not nearly so hard." But I was wrong.'

The long, steady breeze ran through the trees with a murmur like a river's. Dazed and quite painfully hungry, Alain lay back on his pillows. 'How delightful it is, a convalescence.' To complete the illusion a knuckle tapped on the door and the bearded Basque woman entered, carrying a tray.

'But I'd have had breakfast in the garden, Juliette!'

A kind of smile appeared among the grey hairs on her face.

'I thought as much. Would Monsieur Alain like me to take the tray down?'

'No, no, I'm too hungry. Leave that there. Saha'll come in by the window.'

He called the cat who rose from some invisible retreat as if she had come into existence at his call. She bounded up the vertical path of climbing plants and fell back again – she had forgotten her broken claws.

'Wait, I'm coming!'

He brought her back in his arms and they gorged themselves, she on milk and rusks, he on slices of bread and butter and scalding hot coffee. On one corner of the tray, a little rose adorned the lid of the honey-pot.

'It's not one of my mother's roses,' Alain decided. It was an ill-made, stunted little rose, picked from a low branch, that gave out the queer smell of a yellow rose. 'It's a little homage from the Basque.'

Saha, radiant, seemed to have grown plumper overnight. Her shirt-frill erect, her four darker stripes well marked between her ears, she stared at the garden with the eyes of a happy despot.

'How simple it all is, isn't it, Saha? For you, at any rate.'

Old Emile entered in his turn and insisted on removing Alain's shoes.

'There's one of the laces got very worn. Monsieur Alain hasn't another? It doesn't matter, I'll put one of my own laces in,' he bleated with emotion.

'Decidedly, it's my gala-day,' said Alain to himself. The word drove him back by contrast to all the things that only yesterday had been daily bothers; time to get up and dress, time to go to the Amparat office, time to come back to lunch with Camille.

'But I've nothing on earth to put on!' he cried.

In the bathroom he recognized the slightly rusty razor, the worn cake of pink soap and the old toothbrush, and used them with the delight of a man who has got shipwrecked for fun. But he had to come down in the outgrown pyjamas as the Basque woman had carried off his clothes.

'Come Saha, Saha.'

She went ahead and he ran after her uncertainly in a pair of frayed raffia sandals that kept threatening to slip off. He stretched out his shoulders to feel the cape of the mild sun fall on them and half closed his eyes that had grown unaccustomed to the green reverberations of the lawns and the hot colours which blazed above a serried block of crimson love-lies-bleeding and a tuft of red salvias bordered with heliotrope.

'Oh, the same, the very same salvias!'

Alain had always known that little heart-shaped bed as red and invariably bordered with heliotrope. It was shaded by a lean, ancient cherry-tree which occasionally produced a few cherries in September.

'I can see six . . . seven. Seven green cherries!'

He was talking to the cat who, with empty, golden

eyes, had her mouth half open, almost overcome by the excessive scent of the heliotropes. Her face had the look of almost sickened ecstasy animals assume when confronted with an overpowering smell.

She ate a blade of grass to recover herself, listened to various voices, and rubbed her nose against the hard twigs of the privet hedge. But she did not display any exuberance, any irresponsible gaiety and she walked nobly, surrounded by the tiny silver halo which outlined all her body.

'Thrown, from a height of nine storeys,' Alain thought as he watched her. 'Grabbed . . . or pushed. Perhaps she defended herself . . . perhaps she escaped to be caught again and thrown over. Assassinated.'

He tried by such conjectures to arouse his just anger, but he did not succeed. 'If I truly, deeply loved Camille, how furious I should be.' Around him shone his kingdom, threatened like all kingdoms. 'My mother assures me that in less than twenty years no one will be able to keep on houses and gardens like this. She's probably right. I'm quite willing to lose them. I don't want to let *them* come into them.'

He was shaken by the sound of a telephone ringing in the house. 'Come, come now! I'm not frightened, am I? Camille's not so stupid as to telephone me. To do her justice, I've never known a young woman so restrained in using that instrument.'

But he could not stop himself from running awkwardly towards the house, losing his sandals and tripping over pebbles, and calling out: 'Mother! Who's that on the phone?'

The thick white dressing-gown appeared on the steps and Alain felt ashamed of having called out.

'How I love your big white dressing-gown, Mother! Always the same, always the same.'

'Thank you very much on behalf of my dressing-gown,' said Mme Amparat.

She kept Alain waiting a moment before she said: 'It was Monsieur Veuillet. It's half-past nine. Have you forgotten the ways of the house?'

She combed her son's hair with her fingers and buttoned up the too-tight pyjama jacket.

'You're a pretty sight. I suppose you don't intend to spend the rest of your life as a ragamuffin?'

Alain was grateful to her for questioning him so adroitly.

'No question of that, Mother. In a moment, I'll get busy about all that.'

Mme Amparat tenderly interrupted his vague, wide gesture.

'Tonight . . . where will you be?'

'Here!' he cried, and the tears welled up in his eyes.

'Good gracious, what a child!' said Mme Amparat and he took up the word with the earnestness of a boy scout.

'Perhaps I am a child, Mother. That's why I want to think over what I ought to do to get out of this childishness.'

'Get out of it how? By a divorce? That's a door that makes a lot of noise.'

'But which lets in some air,' he dared to retort sharply.

'Wouldn't a separation . . . a temporary one, give just as good results? What about a thorough rest or a little travel, perhaps?'

He threw up his arms indignantly.

'My poor dear Mother, you've no idea. You're a thousand miles from imagining.'

He was going to bring it all out and tell her about the attempted murder.

'Very well then, leave me a thousand miles! Such things don't concern me. Have a little . . . a little reserve,' said Mme Amparat hastily and Alain took advantage of a misunderstanding which was due to her innate modesty.

'Now, Mother, there's still all the tiresome side to be thought of. I mean the family point of view which is all mixed up with the business side. From the Malmerts' point of view, my divorce will be quite indefensible, no matter how much Camille may be partly responsible. A bride of three and a half months! I can hear it all.'

'Where do you get the idea that there's a business side involved? You and the little Malmert girl aren't running a firm together. A married couple is not a pair of business partners.'

'I know, Mother. But if things turn out as I expect, there's bound to be a horrible period of formalities and interviews and so on. It's never as simple as everyone says, a divorce.'

She listened to her son with gentle forbearance. She knew that certain causes produce unexpected results and that, all through his life, a man has to be born many times with no other assistance than that of chance, of bruises, of mistakes.

'It's never simple to leave anything we've wanted to attach to ourselves,' said Mme Amparat. 'She's not so bad, that little Malmert. A little . . . coarse, a little lacking in manners. No, not so bad. At least, that's my way of seeing it. I don't want to impose it on you. We've plenty of time to think it over.'

'I've taken care of that,' said Alain with harsh politeness. 'And, at the moment, I prefer to keep a certain story to myself.'

His face suddenly lit up in a laugh that restored it to childhood. Standing up on her hind legs, Saha, using her paw as a spoon, was fishing drowned ants out of a brimming watering-can.

'Look at her, Mother! Isn't she a miraculous cat?'

'Yes,' sighed Mme Amparat. 'She's your chimera.'

He was always surprised when his mother employed an unusual word. He greeted this one with a kiss on her prematurely aged hand with its swollen veins and the little brown flecks which Juliette lugubriously called 'earth-stains'.

At the sound of the bell ringing at the gate, he jerked himself upright.

'Run and hide,' said Mme Amparat. 'We're right in the way of the tradesmen. Go and dress yourself. Do you want the butcher's little boy to catch you in that extraordinary get-up?'

But they both knew perfectly well that it was not the butcher's little boy ringing at the visitor's gate. Mme Amparat had already turned her back and was hurrying up the steps, holding up her dressing-gown in both hands. Behind the clipped hedge Alain could see the Basque woman retreating in disorder, her black silk apron flying in the wind, while a slither of slippers on the gravel announced the flight of old Emile. Alain cut off his escape.

'You have at least opened the gate?'

'Yes, Monsieur Alain. The young lady's behind her car.'

He lifted terrified eyes to the sky, hunched up his shoulders, as if he were in a hailstorm, and vanished.

'Well, that's certainly something like a picnic! I wish I'd had time to get dressed. Gracious, she's got a new suit!'

Camille had seen him and came straight up to him without overmuch haste. In one of those moments of almost hilarious anxiety that crop up on dramatic occasions, he thought confusedly: 'Perhaps she's come to lunch.'

Carefully and lightly made-up as she was, armed with black lashes and beautiful parted lips and shining teeth, she seemed all the same to lose her self-assurance when Alain came forward to meet her. For he was approaching without breaking away from the shelter of his protective atmosphere. He was treading his native lawn under the rich patronage of the trees, and Camille looked at him with the eyes of a poor person.

'Forgive me, I look like a schoolboy who's suddenly shot up out of all knowledge. We didn't arrange to meet this morning, did we?'

'No. I've brought you your big suitcase. It's packed full.'

'But you shouldn't have done that!' he expostulated. 'I'd have sent Emile round today to fetch it.'

'Don't talk to me about Emile. I wanted to give him your case but the old idiot rushed off as if I'd got the plague. The case is down there by the gate.'

She flushed with humiliation, biting the inside of her cheek. 'It's beginning well,' said Alain to himself.

'I'm terribly sorry. You know what Emile's like. Listen,' he decided, 'let's go on the lawn inside the yew hedges. We'll be quieter there than in the house.'

He promptly repented his choice, for that clearing, enclosed in clipped yews and furnished with wicker chairs, had been the scene of their secret kisses in the old days.

'Wait while I dust the twigs off. You mustn't spoil the pretty suit. Incidentally, I don't know it, do I?'

'It's new,' said Camille in a tone of profound sadness, as if she had said: 'It's dead.'

She sat sideways, looking about her. Two arched arcades, one opposite the other, broke the circle of greenery. Alain remembered something Camille had once confided to him: 'You've no idea how your beautiful garden used to frighten me. I used to come here like the little girl from the village who comes to play with the son of the grand people at the château, in their park. And yet, when you come to think of it . . .' She had spoiled everything by that last remark. That 'when you come to think of it' implied the prosperity of Malmert Mangles compared with the declining house of Amparat.

He observed that Camille kept her gloves on. 'That's a precaution that defeats its own ends. Without those gloves it's possible I mightn't have thought about her hands, about what they've done. Ah, at last a little . . . just a little anger,' he said to himself, listening to his heartbeats. 'I've taken enough time about it.'

'Well,' said Camille sadly, 'well, what are you going to do? Perhaps you haven't decided yet.'

'Oh yes. I've decided,' said Alain.

'Ah!'

'Yes. I can't come back.'

'I quite understand that there's no question of your coming back today.'

'I don't want to come back.'

'Not at all? Ever?'

He shrugged his shoulders:

'What does that mean, ever? I don't want to come back. Not now. I don't want to.'

She watched him closely, trying to distinguish the false from the true, the deliberate irritation from the authentic shudder. He returned her suspicion for suspicion. 'She's small, this morning. She looks rather like a pretty shop-girl. She's lost in all this green. We've already exchanged a fair number of useless remarks.'

In the distance, through one of the arched arcades, Camille caught sight of traces of the 'alterations' on one side of the face of the house; a new window, some freshly painted shutters. Bravely she threw herself into the path of danger: 'Suppose I'd said nothing yesterday?' she suggested abruptly. 'Suppose you'd known nothing?'

'What a superb woman's idea,' he sneered. 'It does you honour.'

'Oh,' said Camille, shaking her head. 'Honour, honour. It wouldn't be the first time that the happiness of two married people depended on something that couldn't be owned up to . . . or wasn't owned up to. But I've got the idea that by *not* telling you, I'd only have made things worse than ever for myself. I didn't feel you were . . . I don't know how to put it.'

Hunting for the word, she mimed it by clenching her

hands together. 'She's wrong to draw attention to her hands.' thought Alain vindictively. 'Those hands that have sent someone to their death.'

'After all, you're so awfully little on my side,' said Camille. 'That's true, isn't it?'

That struck him. He had to admit, mentally, that she was right. He said nothing and Camille insisted plaintively in a voice he knew all too well.

'Isn't it true, you hateful man?'

'But, good God!' he burst out. 'That's not the question. The only thing that can possibly interest me – interest me in *you* – is to know whether you regret what you've done, whether you can't stop thinking about it, whether it makes you sick to think of it. Remorse, good heavens, remorse! There does exist such a thing as remorse!'

Carried away he got up and strode round the circular lawn, wiping his brow on his sleeve.

'Ah!' said Camille with a contrite, affected expression. 'Naturally, of course. I'd a million times rather *not* have done it. I must have lost my head.'

'You're lying,' he cried, trying not to shout. 'All you regret is that you didn't bring it off! One's only got to listen to you, to look at you with your little hat on one side and your gloves and your new suit – everything you've so carefully arranged to charm me. If you really had any regret, I'd see it in your face. I'd feel it!'

He was shouting now, in a low grating voice, and was no longer quite master of the rage he had fostered. The worn stuff of his pyjamas burst at the elbow and he tore off nearly the whole of his sleeve and flung it on a bush.

At first Camille had eyes only for the gesticulating arm, extraordinarily white against the dark block of the yew hedge.

He put his hands over his eyes and forced himself to speak lower.

'A little blameless creature, blue as the loveliest dreams.

A little soul. Faithful, capable of quietly, delicately dying if what she has chosen fails her. You held *that* in your hands, over empty space . . . and you opened your hands. You're a monster. I don't wish to live with a monster.'

He uncovered his damp face and came nearer to Camille, trying to find words which would overwhelm her. Her breath came short and her eyes went from the white naked arm to the bloodless face which was no less white.

'An animal!' she cried indignantly. 'You're sacrificing me to an animal. I'm your wife, all the same! You're leaving me for an animal!'

'An animal? Yes, an animal.'

Apparently calm now, he hid behind a mysteriously informed smile. 'I'm perfectly willing to admit that Saha's an animal. If she's really one, what is there higher than this animal and how can I make Camille understand that? She makes me laugh, this barefaced little criminal, all virtue and indignation, who pretends to know what an animal is.' He was prevented from going further by the sound of Camille's voice.

'*You're* the monster!'

'Pardon?'

'Yes, you. Unfortunately I can't exactly explain why. But I assure you I'm right. *I* wanted to get rid of Saha. That wasn't at all admirable. But to kill something that gets in her way, that makes her suffer – it's the first idea that comes into a woman's head, especially a jealous woman's. It's perfectly normal. What's abnormal, what's monstrous, is you. It's . . .'

She was struggling to make herself understood and, at the same time, pointing to certain accidental things about Alain which did indeed suggest a kind of delirium: the torn-off sleeve; the trembling,insulting mouth; the cheek from which all the blood had retreated; the wild crest of dishevelled fair hair. He made no protest and did not deign to defend himself. He seemed lost in some exploration from which there was no return.

'If I'd killed . . . or wanted to kill . . . a woman out of jealousy, you'd probably forgive me. But since I raised my hand against the cat, you're through with me. And yet you don't want me to treat you as a monster.'

'Have I said I didn't want you to?' he broke in haughtily.

She looked at him with terrified eyes and made a gesture of impotence. Sombre and detached, he watched the young, execrable gloved hand every time it moved.

'Now for the future, what are we going to do? What's going to happen to us, Alain?'

He was so brimming over with intolerance that he nearly groaned. He wanted to cry out: 'We separate, we keep silent, we sleep, we breathe without the other always there! I'll withdraw far, far away – under this cherry-tree for example, under the wing of that magpie. Or into the peacock tail of the hose-jet. Or into my cold room under the protection of a little golden dollar, a handful of relics and a Russian Blue cat.'

He mastered himself and deliberately lied:

'But nothing, at the moment. It's too soon to make a . . . a decision. Later on, we'll see.'

This final effort to be reasonable and sociable exhausted him. He tottered as soon as he took the first steps when he got up to accompany Camille. She accepted this vague conciliation with hungry hope.

'Yes, of course. It's much too soon. A little later on. Stay where you are, don't bother to come with me to the gate. With your sleeve, people will think we've been fighting. Listen, perhaps I'll go and get a little swimming at Ploumanach with Patrick's brother and sister-in-law. Because the mere idea of living with my family at this moment . . .'

'Yes, do that. Take the roadster,' proposed Alain.

She flushed and thanked him too effusively.

'I'll give it you back, you know, the minute I get back to Paris. You may need it. Don't hesitate to ask me for it back. Anyway, I'll let you know when I'm going and when I get back.'

'Already she's organizing it all. Already she's throwing out the strands of her web, throwing out bridges. Already she's picking up the fabric, darning it, weaving the threads together again. It's horrifying. Is that what my mother admires in her? Perhaps, after all, it's very fine. I don't feel any more capable of understanding her than of making things up with her. How completely at ease she is in everything I find insupportable. If she'd only go now, if she'd only go away!'

She was going away, carefully avoiding holding out her hand to him. But, under the arcade of clipped trees, she dared vainly to brush against him with her ripening breasts. Left alone, he collapsed into a chair and near him, on the wicker table, suddenly, like a miracle, appeared the cat.

A bend in the path and a gap in the leaves allowed Camille to see Alain and the cat once more from the distance. She stopped short and made a movement as if to retrace her steps. But she swayed only for an instant and then walked away faster than ever. For a while Saha, on guard, was following Camille's departure as intently as a human being. Alain was half-lying on his side, ignoring it. With one hand hollowed into a paw, he was playing deftly with the first green, prickly August chestnuts.

Anita Desai

extract from

Clear Light of Day

Tara returns from abroad to a family reunion in Delhi and finds that old antagonisms between herself and her sister are still unresolved.

The koels began to call before daylight. Their voices rang out from the dark trees like an arrangement of bells, calling and echoing each other's calls, mocking and enticing each other into ever higher and shriller calls. More and more joined in as the sun rose and when Tara could no longer bear the querulous demand in their voices, she got up and went out on to the veranda to find the blank white glare of the summer sun thrusting in between the round pillars and the purple bougainvillaea. Wincing, she shielded her eyes as she searched for the birds that had clamoured for her appearance, but saw nothing. The cane chairs on the veranda stood empty. A silent line of ants filed past her feet and down the steps into the garden. Then she saw her sister's figure in white, slowly meandering along what as children they had called 'the rose walk'.

Dropping her hands to pick up the hem of her long nightdress, Tara ran down the steps, bowing her head to the morning sun that came slicing down like a blade of steel on to the back of her neck, and crossed the dry crackling grass of the lawn to join her sister, who stood watching, smiling.

The rose walk was a strip of grass, still streaked green and grey, between two long beds of roses at the far end of the lawn where a line of trees fringed the garden – fig and silver oak, mulberry and eucalyptus. Here there was still shade and, it seemed to Tara, the only bit of cultivation left; everything else, even the papaya and lemon trees, the bushes of hibiscus and oleander, the beds of canna lilies, seemed abandoned to dust and neglect, to struggle as they could against the heat and sun of summer.

But the rose walk had been maintained almost as it was. Or had it? It seemed to Tara that there had been far more roses in it when she was a child – luscious shaggy pink ones, small crisp white ones tinged with green, silky yellow ones that smelt of tea – and not just these small negligible crimson heads that lolled weakly on their thin stems. Tara had grown to know them on those mornings when she had trailed up and down after her mother, who was expecting her youngest child and had been advised by her doctor to take some exercise. Her mother had not liked exercise, perhaps not the new baby either, and had paced up and down with her arms folded and her head sunk in thought while the koels mocked and screamed and dive-bombed the trees. Tara had danced and skipped after her, chattering, till she spied something flashing from under a pile of fallen rose petals – a pearl, or a silver ring? – and swooped upon it with a cry that broke into her mother's reverie and made her stop and frown. Tara had excitedly swept aside the petals and uncovered – a small, blanched snail. Her face wrinkling with disgust, her mother turned and paced on without a word, leaving Tara on her knees to contemplate the quality of disillusion.

But here was Bim. Bim, grey and heavy now and not so unlike their mother in appearance, only awake, watchful, gazing at her with her fullest attention and appraisal. Bim laughed when she saw Tara panting slightly in her eagerness.

Tara laughed back. 'Bim, the old rose walk is still here.'

'Of course,' said Bim, 'only the roses grow smaller and sicker every year,' and she bent to shake a long spindly branch from which a fully bloomed rose dangled. It came apart instantly, revealing a small naked centre and a few pathetic stamens clinging to the bald head while the petals fell in a bunch to the chocolate earth below.

Tara's mouth opened in dismay at the destruction of a rose in full bloom – she would never have done what Bim did – and then she saw the petals that had clung together in a bunch in their fall part and scatter themselves. As she stared, a petal rose and tumbled on to its back and she saw uncovered the gleam of a – a pearl? a silver ring? Something that gleamed, something that flashed, then flowed – and she saw it was her childhood snail slowly, resignedly making its way from under the flower up a clod of earth only to tumble off the top on to its side – an eternal, miniature Sisyphus. She brought her hands together in a clap and cried, 'Look, a snail!'

Bim watched her sister in surprise and amusement. Was Tara, grown woman, mother of grown daughters, still child enough to play with a snail? Would she go down on her knees to scoop it up on a leaf and watch it draw its albuminous trail, lift its tiny antennae, gaze about it with protruding eyes and then, the instant before the leaf dipped and it slid downwards, draw itself into its pale pod?

As Tara performed the rites of childhood over the handy creature, Bim stood with lowered head, tugging at the hair that hung loosely about her face as she had done when she had sat beside her brother's bed that summer that he was ill, with her forehead lowered to the wooden edge of the bed, a book of poetry open on her lap, reading aloud the lines:

> Now sleeps the crimson petal, now the white;
> Nor waves the cypress in the palace walk;
> Nor winks the gold fin in the porphyry font:
> The firefly wakens . . .

Her lips moved to the lines she had forgotten she remembered till she saw the crimson petals fall in a heap on the snail in the mud, but she would not say them aloud to

Tara. She had no wish to use the lines as an incantation to revive that year, that summer when he had been ill and she had nursed him and so much had happened in a rush. To bury it all again, she put out her toe and scattered the petals evenly over the damp soil.

Now Tara's hand trembled, the leaf she held dipped and the doomed creature slid soundlessly back to earth.

They both stood staring as it lay there, shocked and still.

Tara murmured, 'You looked so like Mama from a distance, Bim – I mean, it's so – the sun –' for she realized at once that Bim would not like the comparison.

But Bim did not seem to hear, or care. 'Did you sleep at all?' she asked instead, for last night on arriving from the airport Tara had laughed and chattered and claimed to be too excited to sleep.

'How could I?' cried Tara, laughing, and talked of the koels in the morning, and the dog barking in the night, and the mosquitoes singing and stinging in the dark, as they walked together up the grassy path, Tara in her elegant pale blue nylon nightgown and elegant silver slippers and Bim in a curious shapeless hand-made garment that Tara could see she had fashioned out of an old cotton sari by sewing it up at both sides, leaving enough room for her arms to come through and cutting out a wide scoop for her neck. At the feet a border of blue and green peacocks redeemed the dress from total shabbiness and was – Tara laughed lightly – original. 'How he barks,' she repeated. 'Don't the neighbours complain?'

'I think they've grown used to him at last, or else they've realized it does no good to complain – I never will chain him up and, as I tell them when they do protest, he has such a beautiful voice, it's a pleasure to hear him. Not like the yipping and yapping of other people's little lap dogs,' she said with a toss of her grey head.

Although they spoke softly, no louder than a pair of birds to each other, the dog must have heard his name or realized he was being discussed. When Tara had come out on to the veranda he had been asleep under the wooden divan, hidden from her by the striped cotton rug with which it was covered, and he had only twitched his whiskers when he heard her pass by. Now he was suddenly out there on the grass walk with them, standing with his four legs very wide apart, his nose diving down into the clods of earth where the snail still lay futilely struggling to upright itself. As it finally flipped on to its edge, he gave a thunderous sneeze.

'Badshah!' cried Bim, delighted with his theatrical performance, and his one eye gleamed at the approval in her voice while the other followed the snail. But it disappeared under the rose petals once more and he came lolloping towards them, stubbed his moist nose into their legs, scuffed his dirty claws into their heels, salivated over their feet and then rushed past them in a show of leadership.

'He does like to be first always,' Bim explained.

'Is he nine now, Bim, or ten?'

'Twelve,' exclaimed Bim. 'See his old whiskers all white,' she said, diving forwards at his head and catching him by the ears, making him stand still with his head against her thigh. He closed his eyes and smiled a foolish smile of pleasure at her attention, then drew away with a long line of saliva dribbling from his jaws on to the grass, more copious and irregular than the fluent snail's. 'He is Begum's son, you know, and she lived to be – fourteen?'

Tara lifted her hair from the back of her neck and let it fall again, luxuriantly, with a sigh. 'How everything goes on and on here, and never changes,' she said. 'I used to think about it all,' and she waved her arm in a circular swoop to encompass the dripping tap at the end of the grass walk, the trees that quivered and shook with birds, the loping dog, the roses – 'and it is all exactly the same, whenever we come home.'

'Does that disappoint you?' Bim asked drily, giving her

a quick sideways look. 'Would you like to come back and find it changed?'

Tara's face was suddenly wound up tightly in a frown as if such a thought had never struck her before and she found it confusing. 'Changed? How? You mean the house newly painted, the garden newly planted, new people coming and going? Oh no, how could I, Bim?' and she seemed truly shocked by the possibility.

'But you wouldn't want to return to life as it used to be, would you?' Bim continued to tease her in that dry voice. 'All that dullness, boredom, waiting. Would you care to live that over again? Of course not. Do you know anyone who would – secretly, sincerely, in his innermost self – *really* prefer to return to childhood?'

Still frowning, Tara murmured meaninglessly, 'Prefer to what?'

'Oh, to going on – to growing up – leaving – going away – into the world – something wider, freer – brighter,' Bim laughed. 'Brighter! Brighter!' she called, shading her eyes against the brightness.

Tara's head sank low, her frown deepened. She could not trust Bim to be quite serious: in her experience, the elder sister did not take the younger seriously – and so all she said was a murmured, 'But you didn't, Bim.'

'I?' said Bim flatly, with her eyes still shaded against the light that streamed across the parched lawn and pressed against the trees at the fringe. 'Oh, I never go anywhere. It must seem strange to you and Bakul who have travelled so much – to come back and find people like Baba and me who have never travelled at all. And if we still had Mira-*masi* with us, wouldn't that complete the picture? This faded old picture in its petrified frame?' She stopped to pluck the dead heads off a rose bush dusted grey with disease. 'Mira-*masi* swigging secretly from her brandy bottle. Baba winding up his gramophone. And Raja, if Raja were here, playing Lord Byron on his death-bed. I, reading to him. That is what you might have come back to, Tara. How would you have liked that?'

Tara stood staring at her silver toes, at the clods of upturned earth in the beds and the scattered dead heads, and felt a prickle of distrust in Bim. Was Bim being cruel again? There could be no other motive. There could be no reply. She made none and Bim swung away and marched on, striding beside Badshah.

'That is the risk of coming home to Old Delhi,' she announced in the hard voice that had started up the prickle of distrust that ran over the tips of the hairs on Tara's arms, rippling them. 'Old Delhi does not change. It only decays. My students tell me it is a great cemetery, every house a tomb. Nothing but sleeping graves. Now *New* Delhi, they say is different. That is where things happen. The way they describe it, it sounds like a nest of fleas. So much happens there, it must be a jumping place. I never go. Baba never goes. And here, here nothing happens at all. Whatever happened, happened long ago – in the time of the Tughlaqs, the Khiljis, the Sultanate, the Moghuls – that lot.' She snapped her fingers in time to her words, smartly. 'And then the British built New Delhi and moved everything out. Here we are left rocking on the backwaters, getting duller and greyer, I suppose. Anyone who isn't dull and grey goes away – to New Delhi, to England, to Canada, the Middle East. They don't come back.'

'I must be peculiar then,' Tara's voice rose bravely. 'I keep coming back. And Bakul.'

'They pay your fare, don't they?' her sister said.

'But we *like* to come, Bim. We *must* come – if we are not to lose touch, I with all of you, with home, and he with the country. He's been planning this trip for months. When the girls arrive, and we go to Hyderabad for the wedding, Bakul wants to go on from there and do a tour of the whole country. He did it ten years ago and he says it is time to do it again, to make sure –'

'Of what?'

The question was sarcastic but Tara gave her head a toss of assurance and pride. Her voice too had taken on the strength and sureness that Bim noticed it usually did when she spoke of her husband. She told Bim evenly, 'That he hasn't forgotten, or lost touch with the way things are here. If you lose touch, then you can't represent your country, can you?' she ended, on an artificial note.

Bim of course detected that. She grunted, 'Hmph. I don't know. If that is what they tell you in the diplomatic service then that is what you must say.'

'But it's true,' Tara exclaimed, immediately dropping artificiality and sounding earnest. 'One has to come back, every few years, to find out and make sure again. I'd like to travel with him really. But there's the wedding in Raja's house, I suppose that will be enough to keep us busy. Are you coming, Bim? You and Baba? Couldn't we all go together? Then it will be a proper family reunion. Say you'll come! You have your summer vacation now. What will you do alone in Delhi, in the heat? Say you'll come!'

Bim said nothing. In the small silence a flock of mynahs suddenly burst out of the green domes of the trees and, in a loud commotion of yellow beaks and brown wings, disappeared into the sun. While their shrieks and cackles still rang in the air, they heard another sound, one that made Bim stop and stare and the dog lift his head, prick up his ears and then charge madly across to the eucalyptus trees that grew in a cluster by the wall. Rearing up on his hind legs, he tore long strips of blue and mauve bark off the silken pink tree-trunks and, throwing back his head, bellowed in that magnificent voice that Bim admired so much and that soured – or spiced – her relations with the neighbours.

'What is it?' called Tara as Bim ran forwards, lifting the peacock-edged nightie in order to hurry.

It was her cat, crouched in the fork of the blue and pink

tree, black and bitter at being stranded where she could not make her way down. Discovered first by the mynahs and then by Badshah, she felt disgraced.

Bim stood below her, stretching out her arms and calling, imploring her to jump. Badshah warned her not to do anything of the sort in a series of excited barks and whines. Tara waited, laughing, while the cat turned her angry face from one to the other, wondering whom to trust. At last Bim coaxed her down and she came slithering along the satiny bark, growling and grumbling with petulance and complaint at her undignified descent. Then she was in Bim's arms, safely cradled and shielded from Badshah's boisterous bumps and jumps, cuddled and cushioned and petted with such an extravagance of affection that Tara could not help raising her eyebrows in embarrassment and wonder.

Although Bim was rubbing her chin on the cat's flat-topped head and kissing the cold tips of her ears, she seemed to notice Tara's expression. 'I know what you're thinking,' she said. 'You're thinking how old spinsters go ga-ga over their pets because they haven't children. Children are the *real* thing, you think.'

Tara's look of surprise changed to guilt. 'What makes you say that? Actually, I was thinking about the girls. I was wondering –'

'Exactly. That's what I said. You think animals take the place of babies for us love-starved spinsters,' Bim said with a certain satisfaction and lowered the rumpled cat to the gravel walk as they came up to the house. 'But you're wrong,' she said, striding across the sun-slashed drive. 'You can't possibly feel for them what I do about these wretched animals of mine.'

'Oh Bim,' protested Tara, recognizing the moment when Bim went too far with which all their encounters had ended throughout their childhood, but she was prevented from explaining herself by the approach of a monstrous body of noise that seemed to be pushing its way out through a tight tunnel, rustily grinding through, and then emerged into full brassy volume, making the pigeons that lived on the ledge under the veranda ceiling throw up their wings and depart as if at a shot. It was not Bakul who was responsible for the cacophony. He was sitting – flabbily, flaccidly – in one of the cane chairs on the veranda with the tea tray in front of him, waiting for someone to come and pour. The noise beat and thrummed in one of the curtained rooms behind him. 'Sm-o-oke gets in your eyes,' moaned an agonized voice, and Tara sighed, and her shoulders drooped by a visible inch or two.

'Baba still plays the same old records?' she asked as they went slowly up the wide stairs between the massed pots of spider lilies and asparagus fern to the veranda.

'He never stops,' said Bim, smiling. 'Not for a day.'

'Don't you mind the noise?'

'Not any more,' said Bim, the lightness of her tone carefully contrived. 'I don't hear it any more.'

'It's loud,' complained Tara in a distressed voice. 'I used to look for records to send Baba – I thought he'd like some new ones – but they don't make 78s any more.'

'Oh he doesn't want any new records,' said Bim. 'He wouldn't play them. He loves his old ones.'

'Isn't it strange,' said Tara, wincing at the unmodulated roar that swept across the still, shady veranda in an almost visible onslaught of destruction.

'We *are* strange, I *told* you,' laughed Bim, striding across the tiled floor to the cane chairs and the tea tray. 'Oh, Bakul – *bhai*, you're up. Did you sleep?' she asked carelessly, sitting down in front of the tray. But instead of pouring out the tea she only lifted the milk jug and, bending down, filled a saucer for the cat who crouched before it and began to lap even before Bim had finished pouring so that some drops fell on her ears and on her whiskers, a sight that made Bim laugh as she held the jug, waiting for the cat to finish the milk. Then she bent and refilled the saucer. Tara, who had poured out a cup of tea for Bakul, waited for her to surrender the milk jug. When she did, there was very little left in it for Bakul's tea. Tara shook it to bring out a few reluctant drops.

'Is that enough?' she asked uneasily, even guiltily, handing the cup to Bakul.

He shrugged, making no reply, his lower lip thrust out in the beginning of a sulk. It may not have been the lack of milk, though, it might have been the din that stood about them like sheets of corrugated iron, making conversation impossible. As he stirred his tea thoughtfully with a little spoon, the song rose to its raucous crescendo as though the singer had a dagger plunged into his breast and were letting fly the heartfelt notes of his last plaint on earth. Then at last the rusty needle ground to a halt in the felt-embedded groove of the antique record and they all sighed, simultaneously, and sank back in their chairs, exhausted.

The pigeons that had retreated to the roof came fluttering back to their nests and settled down with small complaining sounds, guttural and comfortable. The bamboo screen in the doorway lifted and Baba came out for his tea.

He did not look as if he could be held responsible for any degree of noise whatsoever. Coming out into the veranda, he blinked as if the sun surprised him. He was in his pyjamas – an old pair with frayed ends, over which he wore a grey bush-shirt worn and washed almost to translucency. His face, too, was blanched, like a plant grown underground or in deepest shade, and his hair was quite white, giving his young, fine face a ghostly look that made people start whenever he appeared.

But no one on the veranda started. Instead, they turned on him their most careful smiles, trying to make their smiles express feelings that were comforting, reassuring, not startling.

Then Bim began to bustle. Now she called out for more

milk and a freshly refilled jug appeared from the pantry, full to the brim, before Bakul's widened eyes. Baba's cup was filled not with tea at all but with milk that had seemed so short a moment ago. Then, to top it, a spoonful of sugar was poured in as well and all stirred up with a tremendous clatter and handed, generously slopping, to Baba who took it without any expression of distaste or embarrassment and sat down on his little cane stool to sip it. Even the cat was transfixed by the spectacle and sat back on her haunches, staring at him with eyes that were circles of sharp green glass.

Only Bim seemed to notice nothing odd. Nor did she seem to think it necessary to speak to or be spoken to by Baba. She said, 'Look at her. You'd think I had given her enough but no, if we take any ourselves, she feels it's come out of her share.'

After a minute Tara realized she was speaking of the cat. Tara had lost the childhood habit of including animals in the family once she had married and begun the perpetual travels and moves that precluded the keeping of pets. It was with a small effort that she tore her eyes away from her brother and regarded the reproachful cat.

'She's too fat,' she said, thinking pet-owners generally liked such remarks. It was not a truthful one: the cat was thin as a string.

Bim put out her toe and scratched the creature under her ear but the cat turned angrily away, refusing such advances, and kept her eyes riveted on Baba till he had sipped the last drop of milk and put the cup back on the saucer with an unmistakably empty ring. Then she dropped sulkily on to the tiles and lay there noisily tearing at her fur with a sandpapered tongue of an angry red.

While the two women sat upright and tense and seethed with unspoken speech, the two men seemed dehydrated, emptied out, with not a word to say about anything. Only the pigeons cooed on and on, too lazy even to open their beaks, content to mutter in their throats rather than sing or call. The dog, stretched out at Bim's feet, writhed and coiled, now catching his tail between his teeth, now scrabbling with his paws, then bit at fleas and chewed his hair, weaving a thick mat of sound together with the cat who was busy with herself.

Bakul could bear it no longer. When his expression had grown so thin and so sour that it was about to split, he said, in a voice meant to be sonorous, 'Our first morning in Delhi.' To Bim's wonder and astonishment, Tara smiled at this radiantly as though he had made a profound remark on which he was to be congratulated. He gave her a small, confidential smile in return. 'What shall we do with it?'

Bim suddenly scratched her head as if the dog had started up something there. 'I don't know about you,' she said, 'but I have some of my students coming over this morning.'

'Students? But Bim, I thought your summer vacation had begun.'

'Yes, yes, but I wanted to give them some reading lists so they don't waste all their time walking up and down the Mall in Simla or going to the pictures. Then they reminded me I had missed a tutorial and had to see some of their papers. You see, it isn't just I who make them work – they make me work, too. So I asked them to come down here – they love to come, I don't know why. I'll go and get ready – I'm late. And you? You two? What will you do?'

Tara gazed at her husband for answer till he finally lowered his eyes by careful inches from the plaster moulding under the ceiling where the pigeons strutted and squatted and puffed themselves, and said, 'Perhaps I could ask my uncle to send us a car. Then we could go and call on some of my relations in New Delhi. They will be expecting us.'

'I'll get ready,' said Tara, instantly getting to her feet as if in relief.

Bim, who remembered her as a languid little girl, listless, a dawdler, noted her quick movements, her efficient briskness, with some surprise, but said nothing. Instead, she turned to Baba and drawled, slowly, 'And Baba,' as she bent forward and started stacking the cups on to the wooden tray. The others got up and stretched and walked about the veranda except for Baba, who sat calmly with his long white hands dangling loosely on either side of him. When Bim said 'Baba' again, he smiled gently at the floor. 'Baba,' she said again in a very low voice so that Bakul, standing on the steps and scrutinizing the bougainvillaea at the pillars, would not hear her, 'do you think you might go to the office today?'

Tara, who was at the door at the end of the veranda, about to lift the bamboo curtain and go in, paused. Somehow she had heard. Even in her rush to get dressed and be ready for anything her husband might suggest, she paused in shock to find that Bim still made attempts to send Baba to the office. Considering their futility, she thought they must have been given up long ago. She could not help stopping and turning round to see Bim piling up the tea tray and Baba seated on his small child's stool, smiling, his hands helplessly dangling, the busy dog licking, scratching, while the morning took another stride forward and stood with its feet planted on the tiled floor.

'Won't you go today, Baba?' Bim asked softly, not looking at him, looking at the tea cups. 'Do go. You could catch a bus. It'll make a change. We'll all be busy. Then come home to lunch. Or stay if you find it interesting.'

Baba smiled at the bare tiles. His hands swung as if loose in their sockets, as if in a light breeze. But there was no breeze: the heat dropped out of the sky and stood before them like a sheet of foil.

Then Bim got up and lifted the tray and went barefoot down the other end of the veranda to the pantry. Tara could hear her talking to the cook in her normal speaking voice. She turned and went into the room herself, unable to face the sight of Baba alone and hopeless on the veranda. But Baba did not stay either. He must have gone back to his room, too, for in another minute or two she heard that ominous roar pushing its way through the tunnel and emerging as the maudlin clamour of 'Lilli Marlene'.

'Now this is precisely what I told you,' Bakul said, bustling into the bedroom after making his phone call. 'I pointed out to you how much more convenient it would be to stay with my uncle and aunt, right in the centre of town, on Aurangzeb Road, how it would save us all the trouble of finding a car to travel up and down in . . .'

Tara, who was bending over the bed, laying out his clothes, straightened and said in a strained voice, 'But I had not meant to go anywhere. I only wanted to stay at home.'

He flicked his silk dressing gown open and said impatiently, 'You know you can't do that when there's so much to do – relations to visit, colleagues to look up, all that shopping you had planned to do –'

'I'll wait till the girls come. I'll go shopping with them,' said Tara with an unaccustomed stubbornness. She held up a cluster of ties and waited, a bit sullenly, for him to choose one.

He put out his hand and picked one of broadly striped raw silk and said, 'You surely don't mean that. You can't just sit about with your brother and sister all day, doing nothing.'

'But it's what I want – just to be at home again, with them. And of course there are the neighbours – I'll see them. But I don't want to go anywhere today, and I don't want to go to New Delhi at all.'

'Of course you will come,' Bakul said quite sharply,

going towards the bathroom with an immense towel he had picked up. 'There's no question about that.'

When the bathroom door had shut, Tara went out on to the veranda again. The veranda ran all around the house and every room opened out on to it. This room had been hers and Bim's when they were girls. It opened on to the dense grove of guava trees that separated the back of the house from the row of servants' quarters. Bright morning sounds of activity came from them – a water tap running, a child crying, a cock crowing, a bicycle bell ringing – but the house was separated from them by the thick screen of low, dusty guava trees in which invisible parrots screamed and quarrelled over the fruit. Now and then one fell to the ground with a soft thud. Tara could see some lying in the dust with chunks bitten out by the parrots. If she had been younger – no, if she had been sure Bakul would not look out and see – she would have run down the veranda steps and searched for one that was whole. Her mouth tingled with longing to bite into that hard astringent flesh under the green rind. She wondered if her girls would do it when they arrived to spend their holidays here. No, they would not. Much travelled, brought up in embassies, fluent in several languages, they were far too sophisticated for such rustic pleasures, she knew, and felt guilty over her own lack of that desirable quality. She had fooled Bakul into believing that she had acquired it, that he had shown her how to acquire it. But it was all just dust thrown into his eyes, dust.

Further up the veranda was Baba's room and from behind the light bamboo curtain that hung in the doorway came the guttural rattling of 'Don't Fence Me In'. For a while Tara leant her head against a pillar, listening. It was not unfamiliar, yet it disturbed.

A part of her was sinking languidly down into the passive pleasure of having returned to the familiar – like a pebble, she had been picked up and hurled back into the pond, and sunk down through the layer of green scum, through the secret cool depths to the soft rich mud at the bottom, sending up a line of bubbles of relief and joy. A part of her twitched, stirred like a fin in resentment: why was the pond so muddy and stagnant? Why had nothing changed? She had changed – why did it not keep up with her?

Why did Bim allow nothing to change? Surely Baba ought to begin to grow and develop at last, to unfold and reach out and stretch. But whenever she saw them, at intervals of three or five years, all was exactly as before.

Drawing away from the pillar, she moved towards his room, propelled by her disturbance, by her resentment at this petrified state in which her family lived. Bakul was right to criticize it, disapprove of it. Yes, he was right, she told herself and, lifting the dusty bamboo curtain, slipped into Baba's room.

He was sitting on his bed, a string cot spread with a cotton rug and an old sheet, that stood in the centre of the room under the slowly revolving electric fan. He was crouched low, listening raptly to the last of 'Don't Fence Me In' unwinding itself on the old HMV gramophone on a small bamboo table beside his bed. The records, not so very many of them – there must have been breakages after all – were stacked on a shelf beneath the table in their tattered yellow sleeves. The string cot, the table, the HMV gramophone, a canvas chair and a wardrobe – nothing else. It was a large room and looked bare. Once it had been Aunt Mira's room, and crowded. Baba looked up at her.

Tara stood staring, made speechless by his fine, serene face, the shapeliness of his long fingers, his hands that either moved lightly as if in a breeze or rested calmly at his sides. He was an angel, she told herself, catching her lip between her teeth – an angel descended to earth, unsoiled by any of it.

But then why did he spend his days and years listening to this appalling noise? Her daughters could not live through a day without their record-player either; they, too, kept it heaped with records that slipped down on to the turntable in a regular sequence, keeping them supplied with an almost uninterrupted flow of music to which they worked and danced with equal ease. But, she wanted to explain to him, theirs was an ever-growing, ever-changing collection, their interest in it was lively, fresh, developing all the time. Also, she knew they would outgrow their need of it. Already Maya had friends who took her to concerts from which she returned with a sheen of uplifting pleasure spread across her face and talked of learning to play the flute. Soon it would be behind her – this need for an elemental, primitive rhythm automatically supplied. But Baba would never leave his behind, he would never move on.

Her anguish and impatience made her say, very quickly and loudly, as the record ground to a halt and before Baba could turn it over, 'Are you going out this morning, Baba? We've sent for a car – can we give you a lift?'

Baba lifted the smoothly curving metal arm off the record and sat with his hand resting on it, protectively. It was clear he would have liked to turn over the record but he hesitated, politely, his eyes cast down, flickering slightly as if with fear or guilt.

Tara too began to squirm with guilt at having caused him this panic. 'Are you, Baba?'

He glanced at her very quickly, with a kind of pleading, and then looked away and shook his head very slightly.

This made her cry out, 'But don't you go to the office in the mornings?'

He kept his head lowered, smiling slightly, sadly.

'Never?'

The room rang with her voice, then with silence. In the shaded darkness, silence had the quality of a looming dragon. It seemed to roar and the roar to reverberate, to dominate. To escape from it would require a burst of recklessness, even cruelty. Was it to keep it at bay that Baba played those records so endlessly, so obsessively? But it was not right. She herself had been taught, by her husband and by her daughters, to answer questions, to make statements, to be frank and to be precise. They would have none of these silences and shadows. Here things were left unsaid and undone. It was what they called 'Old Delhi decadence'. She knotted her fingers together in an effort to break it.

'Do you think you will go to the office today?' she persisted, beads of perspiration welling out of her upper lip.

Now Baba took his hand off the gramophone arm, relinquishing it sadly, and his hands hung loosely at his sides, as helplessly as a dead man's. His head, too, sank lower and lower.

Tara was furious with herself for causing him this shame, this distress. She hated her probing, her questioning with which she was punishing him. Punishing him for what? For his birth – and for that he was not responsible. Yet it was wrong to leave things as they were – she knew Bakul would say so, and her girls, too. It was all quite lunatic. Yet there was no alternative, no solution. Surely they would see there was none. Sighing, she said in a tone of defeat, 'I'll ask Bim.'

She had said the right thing at last. Quite inadvertently, even out of cowardice. It made Baba raise his head and smile, sweetly and gently as he used to do. He even nodded, faintly, in agreement. Yes, Bim, he seemed to say, Bim will decide. Bim can, Bim will. Go to Bim. Tara could not help smiling back at his look of relief, his happy dependence. She turned to leave the room and heard him lift the record and turn it over. As she escaped down the veranda she heard Bing Crosby's voice bloating luxuriantly out into 'Ah-h'm dream-in' of a wha-ite Christmas . . .'

*

But now something had gone wrong. The needle stuck in a groove. 'Dream-in', dream-in', dream-in" hacked the singer, his voice growing more and more officious. Shocked, Baba's long hands moved with speed to release it from the imprisoning groove. Then he found the needle grown so blunt and rusty that, as he peered at it from every angle and turned it over and over with a melancholy finger, he accepted it would do no longer. He sighed and dropped it into the little compartment that slid out of the green leather side of the gramophone and the sight of all the other obsolete needles that lay in that concealed grave seemed to place a weight on his heart. He felt defeated and infinitely depressed. Too depressed to open the little one-inch square tin with the picture of the dog on it, and pick out a clean needle to insert in the metal head. It remained empty, toothless. The music had come to a halt. Out in the garden a koel called its wild, brazen call. It was not answered so it repeated the call, more demandingly.

For a while Baba paced about the room, his head hanging so low that one would have thought it unnatural, physically impossible. Now and then he lifted his hands to his head and ran his long bony fingers nervously through his white hair so that it was grooved and furrowed like the lines of an aged face. The silence of the room, usually so loud with the rollicking music of the forties, seemed to admit those other sounds that did not soothe or protect him but, on the contrary, startled him and drove him into a panic – the koel calling, calling out in the tall trees, a child crying in the servants' quarters, a bicycle dashing past, its bell jangling. Baba began to pace up and down faster and faster as if he were running away from it. Then, when he could bear it no longer, he went to the cupboard and pulled open its door, searched frantically for clothes to wear, pulled out whatever seemed to him appropriate, and began to dress hurriedly, dropping his pyjamas on to the floor, flinging others on to the sagging canvas chair by the bed, hurriedly buttoning and lacing and pulling on and off till he felt sufficiently clothed.

Without a glance into the mirror on the cupboard door or an attempt to tidy the room, he fled from it.

Tara, still sitting on the steps with an arm around the veranda pillar, waiting for Bakul to emerge so that she could go in and dress, saw a pale elongated shape lurching and blundering down the veranda and on to the drive, bent almost double as if in pain or in fear – or perhaps because of the sun beating down with white-hot blows. She stood up in fright and it took her a minute to realize it was Baba.

By then he was already at the gate and had turned out of it into the road. Tara hurried down the steps on to the drive, shading her eyes, her mouth open to call him, but she stopped herself. How old was Baba now? If he wanted to go out, ought he at his age to be called back and asked to explain?

If she had, Baba would have been grateful. If anything, anyone had stopped him now, he would have collapsed with relief and come crawling home like a thirsty dog to its water bowl. Once, when he had ventured out, a bicycle had dashed against him as he stood hesitating at the edge of the road, wondering whether to cross. The bicyclist had fallen and cursed him, his voice rising to a shrill peak and then breaking on Baba's head like eggs, or slivers of glass. Another time, he had walked as far as the bus stop but when the bus had arrived there was such a scuffle between those trying to get off and those trying to get on that people were pushed and bumped and shoved and when one man was somehow expelled from the knotted mob, Baba saw his sleeve torn off his shirt, hanging limply as if he had no arm, were an amputee. Baba thought of the man's face, of the ruined shirt. He heard all those shouts again, the shouts that had been flung at his head, knocking into him till he was giddy with blows.

He was small. He was standing on the dunes. There was nothing here but the silver sand and the grey river and the white sky. But out of that lunar stillness a man loomed up, military in a khaki uniform and towering scarlet turban, and roughly pushed past him shouting '*Hato! Hato!*' to make way for a white horse that plunged up out of the dunes and galloped past Baba, crouching on his knees in the sand, the terror of the horse hooves beating through his head, the sand flying back into his face and the voice still commanding '*Hato! Hato!*'

His knees trembled in anticipation, knowing he would be forced down, or flung down if he continued down the road. But it was as if Tara had given him a push down a steep incline. She had said he was to go. Bim had said he was to go. Bim and Tara, both of them, wanted him to go. He was going.

His feet in their unfastened sandals scuffed through the dust of Bela Road. Sharp gravel kept slipping into them, prodding him. His arms swung wildly, propelling him along. His head bobbed, his white hair flopped. His eyes strained and saw black instead of white. Was he going to faint? Would he fall? Should he stop? Could he? Or would they drive him on? '*Hato! Hato!*'

Then he heard the crash he knew would come. Instantly he flinched and flung up his arm to protect his face. But it was not he who had crashed. It was a cart carrying a load of planks that had tipped forwards as the horse that drew it fell first on to its knees, then on to its nose and lay squirming in the middle of the road. Baba shrank back, against the wall, and held his arm before his eyes but still he saw what happened: the driver, a dark man with a red rag tied about his head, leapt down from the mound of planks and raised his arm, and a switch or a whip, and brought it down with all his force on the horse's back. The horse gave a neighing scream, reared up its head with the wet, wringing mane streaming from it, and then stretched out on the stones, a shiver running up and down its legs so that it twitched and shook. Again the man raised the whip, again it came down on the horse's back, neck, head, legs – again and again. Baba heard screams but it was the man who screamed as he whipped and slashed and beat, screamed abuse at the animal who did not move but seemed to sink lower and lower into the dust. 'Swine! Son of a swine!' the man panted, red eyes straining out of the dark face. '*Suar! Sala! Suar ka bachcha!*' All the time his arm rose up in the air and came down, cutting and slashing the horse's flesh til black stuff oozed on to the white dust and ran and spread, black and thick, out of the horse.

Baba raise both his arms, wrapped them about his head, his ears and eyes, tightly, and, blind, turned and stumbled, almost fell but ran on back up the road to the house, to the gate. His shoulder hit the white gate-post so that he lurched and fell to his knees, then he rose and stumbled, his arms still doubled over his eyes so that he should not see and about his ears so that he should not hear.

Tara saw him as he came climbing up the steps on his knees and ran forwards to help him to his feet. Tugging at his arms to drag them away from his face, she cried, 'Are you hurt? Baba, Baba, say – are you hurt? Has someone hurt you?' Pulling his arms away, she uncovered his face and saw his eyes rolling in their sockets like a wild horse's, his lips drawn back from his teeth as if he were racing, and the blue-black shadows that always lay under his eyes spreading over his face like a bruise, wet with his tears. Then she stopped demanding that he should speak, and helped him to his room, on to his bed, rushed out and down the veranda in search of Bim, in search of water. There was no one on the veranda or in the kitchen. The cook had gone out to market. She tilted the earthen water jar to fill a tumbler and hurried back with it, her legs cutting into her nightgown and the water spilling in splashes on to the tiles as she hurried, thinking of Baba's face. She lifted his head to help him drink but most of it ran down his chin into his shirt. When she lowered his head, he shrank into a heap, shivering, and she stayed a while, smoothing his hair and patting his cheek till she thought he was quieter, nearly asleep, then went to find Bim.

But Bakul stepped out of their room, his tie in one hand and his shoes in another, to ask, 'Aren't you getting ready, Tara? We'll be late. The car will be here any minute and you know Uncle is very punctual. We mustn't keep him waiting.' He went back to finish dressing without having seen Tara's face or anything there to stop him.

He noticed nothing – a missing shoe-horn and frayed laces having presented him with a problem meanwhile – till she came in, her shoulders sloping, her hair hanging, and sat down on the foot of the bed instead of going in to dress. Then he spoke more sharply. 'Why aren't you getting ready?'

'I don't think I'll come after all,' she mumbled. She always mumbled when she was afraid, as if she hoped not to be heard.

She expected him to explode of course. But even for Bakul it was too hot, the atmosphere of the old house too turgid and heavy to push or manipulate. Bending down to tie two perfect bows, he merely sighed, 'So, I only have to bring you home for a day, Tara, and you go back to being the hopeless person you were before I married you.'

'Yes,' she muttered, 'hopeless.' Like Baba's, her face looked bruised.

'And you won't let me help you. I thought I had taught you a different life, a different way of living. Taught you to execute your will. Be strong. Face challenges. Be decisive. But no, the day you enter your old home, you are as weak-willed and helpless and defeatist as ever.' He stood up and looked down to see if his shoes were bright enough to reflect his face. Nothing less would do. Yes,

yes. He shrugged his shoulders inside his shirtsleeves. 'What should I do with you? I ought to take you away immediately. Let us go and stay with my uncle in New Delhi.'

'No.' She shook her head. 'Leave me here.'

'You're not happy here,' he said, and the unexpectedness of these words made her look up at him, questioning. 'Look at your face – so sad, so worried.' He even came close to her and touched her cheek, very lightly, as if he could hardly bear the unpleasant contact but forced himself to do it out of compassion. 'If only you would come with me, I would show you how to be happy. How to be active and busy – and then you would be happy. If you came.'

But she shook her head. She felt she had followed him enough, it had been such an enormous strain, always pushing against her grain, it had drained her of too much strength, now she could only collapse, inevitably collapse.

Bakul had married her when she was eighteen. He knew her. He left her, saying, 'Then I'll tell Uncle you are busy with your own family and will come another time,' and went out to wait for the car.

He passed Bim as he went through the drawing room. Bim was holding court there – seated on the divan with her legs drawn up under her – like Tara, she had not dressed yet and was still in her nightdress – and on the carpet below sat the students, a brightly coloured bunch of young girls in jeans and in *salwar-kameez*, laughing and eyeing each other and him as he went through. He raised his eyebrows at Bim and gave her a significant look as if to say, '*This* – your history lesson?'

Bim nodded and laughed and wriggled her toes and waggled her pencil, completely at ease and without the least sense of guilt. 'No, no, you won't,' he heard her say as he went out on to the veranda, 'you won't get me started on the empress Razia – nor on the empress

Nur Jehan. I refuse. We must be serious. We are going to discuss the war between Shivaji and Aurangzeb – no empresses.'

The girls groaned exaggeratedly. 'Please, miss,' he heard them beg as he sat down on a creaking cane chair to wait, 'please let's talk about something interesting, miss. You will enjoy it too, miss.'

'Enjoy? You rascals, I haven't asked you here to enjoy yourselves. Come on, Keya, please begin – I'm listening –' and then there was some semblance of order and of a tutorial going on that Bakul could almost recognize and approve. He wondered, placing one leg over the other reflectively, as he had sometimes wondered when he had first started coming to this house, as a young man who had just entered the foreign service and was in a position to look around for a suitable wife, if Bim were not, for all her plainness and brusqueness, the superior of the two sisters, if she had not those qualities – decision, firmness, resolve – that he admired and tried to instil in his wife who lacked them so deplorably. If only Bim had not that rather coarse laugh and way of sitting with her legs up . . . now Tara would never . . . and if her nose were not so large unlike Tara's which was small . . . and Tara was gentler, more tender . . . He sighed a bit, shifting his bottom on the broken rattan seat of the chair. Things were as they were and had to be made the most of, he always said. At least in this country, he sighed, and just then his uncle's car appeared at the gate, slowly turned in, its windshield flooded by the sun, and came up the drive to park beneath the bougainvillea.

Bim did get Tara to smile before the morning was over, however. Tara was leaning against the veranda pillar, watching the parrots quarrel in the guava trees, listening for a sound from Baba's room, hoping to hear a record played, when Bim came out with her band of girls and suddenly shouted, 'Ice-cream! Caryhom Ice-cream-wallah!' and, before Tara's startled eyes, a bicycle with a small painted van attached to it that had been rolling down the empty, blazing road stopped and turned in at the gate with its Sikh driver beaming broadly at the laughing girls and their professor.

Seeing Tara, Bim called out, 'Look at these babies, Tara. When they hear the Caryhom ice-cream man going by they just stop paying any attention to my lecture. I can't do anything till I've handed each of them a cone. I suppose strawberry cones are what you all want, you babies? Strawberry cones for all of them, *Sardar-ji*,' she ordered and stood laughing on the steps as she watched him fill the cones with large helpings of pink ice-cream and hand them to the girls, who were giggling, Tara realized, as much at their professor as at this childish diversion.

Bim noticed nothing. Swinging her arms about, she saw to it that each girl got her cone and then had one of them, a pretty child dressed in *salwar-kameez* patterned with pink and green parrots, carry a dripping cone down the veranda to Tara. 'Tara,' she called, 'that's for you. *Sardar-ji* made it specially for you,' she laughed, smiling at the ice-cream man who had a slightly embarrassed look, Tara thought. Embarrassed herself, she took the slopping cone from the girl and licked it to please Bim, her tongue recoiling at the synthetic sweetness. 'Oh Bim, if my daughters were to see me now – or Bakul,' she murmured, as Bim walked past holding like a cornucopia a specially heaped and specially pink ice-cream cone into Baba's room. Tara stopped licking, stared, trying to probe the bamboo screen into the room where there had been silence and shadows all morning. She heard Bim's voice, loud and gay, and although Baba made no audible answer, she saw Bim come out without the cone and knew Baba was eating it, perhaps quite happily. There was something magnetic about the icy pink sweetness, the synthetic sweet pinkness, she reflected, licking.

Now Bim let out a shout and began to scold. One of the girls had tipped the remains of her cone on to the veranda steps for the dog to lick – she had seen him standing by, watching, his tongue lolling and leaking. 'You silly, don't you know dogs shouldn't eat anything sweet? His hair will fall out – he'll get worms – it'll be your fault – he'll be spoilt – he won't eat his bread and soup now.'

'Let him enjoy himself, miss,' said the girl, smirking at the others because they all knew perfectly well how pleased Bim was to see them spoil her dog.

Tara narrowed her eyes at the spectacle of Bim scolding her students and smiling with pleasure because of the attention they had paid her dog, who had now licked up all the ice-cream and was continuing to lick and lick the floor as if it might have absorbed some of the delicious stuff. Remembering how Bim used to scold her for not disciplining her little daughters and making them eat up everything on their plates or go to bed on time, she shook her head slightly.

But the ice-cream did have, she had to admit, a beneficial effect all round: in a little while, as the students began to leave the house, prettily covering their heads against the sun with coloured veils and squealing as the heat of the earth burnt through their slippers, the gramophone in Baba's room stirred and rumbled into life again. Tara was grateful for it. She wished Bakul could see them now – her family.

When Bakul did come, late in the afternoon, almost comatose from the heat and the heavy lunch he had eaten, to fall on to his bed and sleep, this passage of lightness was over, or overcome again by the spirit of the house.

Tara, upright in a chair, tried first to write a letter to her daughters, then decided it was too soon, she would wait till she had more to say to them, and put the letter away in her case and tried to read instead, a book from the drawing-room bookshelf that had been there even when she was a child – Jawaharlal Nehru's *Letters To A Daughter* in a green cloth binding – and sitting on the stuffed chair, spongy and clammy to touch, she felt that heavy spirit come and weigh down her eyelids and the back of her neck so that she was pinned down under it, motionless.

It seemed to her that the dullness and the boredom of her childhood, her youth, were stored here in the room under the worn dusty red rugs, in the bloated brassware, amongst the dried grasses in the swollen vases, behind the yellowed photographs in the oval frames – everything, everything that she had so hated as a child and that was still preserved here as if this were the store-room of some dull, uninviting provincial museum.

She stared sullenly, without lifting her head, at a watercolour above the plaster mantelpiece – red cannas painted with some watery fluid that had trickled weakly down the brown paper: who could have painted that? Why was it hung here? How could Bim bear to look at it for all of her life? Had she developed no taste of her own, no likings that made her wish to sweep the old house of all its rubbish and place in it things of her own choice? Tara thought with longing of the neat, china-white flat in Washington, its cleanliness, its floweriness. She wished she had the will to get to her feet and escape from this room – where to? Even the veranda would be better, with the pigeons cooing soothingly, expressing their individual genius for combining complaint and contentment in one tone, and the spiky bougainvillaeas scraping the outer walls and scattering their papery magenta flowers in the hot, sulphur-yellow wind. She actually got up and went to the door and lifted the bamboo screen that hung there, but the blank white glare of afternoon slanted in and slashed at her with its flashing knives so that she quickly dropped the screen. It creaked into place, releasing a noseful of dust. On the wall a gecko clucked loudly and disapprovingly at this untoward disturbance. She went back to the chair. If she could sleep, she might forget where she was, but it was not possible to sleep with the sweat trickling down one's face in rivulets and the heat enclosing one in its ring of fire.

Bakul said one could rise above the climate, that one could ignore it if one filled one's mind with so many thoughts and activities that there was no room for it. 'Look at me,' he had said the winter that they froze in Moscow. 'I don't let the cold immobilize me, do I?' and she and the girls, swaddled in all their warm clothing and the quilts and blankets off their beds, had had to agree that he did not. And gradually he had trained her and made her into an active, organized woman who looked up her engagement book every morning, made plans and programmes for the day ahead and then walked her way through them to retire to her room at night, tired with the triumphant tiredness of the virtuous and the dutiful. Now the engagement book lay at the bottom of her trunk. Bim had said nothing of engagements and, really, she could not bear to have any in this heat. The day stretched out like a sheet of glass that reflected the sun – too bare, too exposed to be faced.

Out in the garden only the coppersmiths were awake, clinging to the tree-trunks, beating out their mechanical call – tonk-tonk-tonk. Tonk-tonk-tonk.

Here in the house it was not just the empty, hopeless atmosphere of childhood, but the very spirits of her parents that brooded on – here they still sat, crouched about the little green baize folding table that was now shoved into a corner with a pile of old *Illustrated Weeklies* and a brass pot full of red and yellow spotted canna lilies on it as if to hold it firmly down, keep it from opening up with a snap and spilling out those stacks of cards, those long note-books and thin pencils with which her parents had sat, day after day and year after year till their deaths, playing bridge with friends like themselves, mostly silent, heads bent so that the knobs in their necks protruded, soft stained hands shuffling the cards, now and then speaking those names and numbers that remained a mystery to the children, who were not allowed within the room while a game was in progress, who had sometimes folded themselves into the dusty curtains and stood peeping out, wondering at this strange, all-absorbing occupation that kept their parents sucked down into the silent centre of a deep, shadowy vortex while they floated on the surface, staring down into the underworld, their eyes popping with incomprehension.

Raja used to swear that one day he would leap up on to the table in a lion-mask, brandishing a torch, and set fire to this paper-world of theirs, while Bim flashed her sewing scissors in the sunlight and declared she would creep in secretly at night and snip all the cards into bits. But Tara simply sucked her finger and retreated down the veranda to Aunt Mira's room where she could always tuck herself up in the plum-coloured quilt that smelt so comfortingly of the aged relation and her ginger cat, lay her head down beside that purring creature and feel such a warmth, such a softness of comfort and protection as not to feel the need to wreck her parents' occupation or divert their attention. It would have frightened her a bit if they had come away, followed her and tried to communicate with her.

And now she stirred uneasily in her chair although it held her damply as if with suckers, almost afraid that they would rise from their seats, drop their cards on the table and come towards her with papery faces, softly shuffling fingers, smoky breath, and welcome her back, welcome her home.

Once her father had risen, padded quietly to her mother's bedroom behind that closed door, and Tara had slipped in behind him, folded herself silently into the faded curtain and watched. She had seen him lean over her mother's bed and quickly, smoothly press a little shining syringe into her mother's arm that lay crookedly on the blue cover, press it in very hard so that she tilted her head back with a quick gasp of shock, or pain – Tara saw her chin rising up into the air and the grey head sinking back into the pillow and heard a long, whimpering sigh like an air-bag minutely punctured so that Tara had fled, trembling, because she was sure she had seen her father kill her mother.

All her life Tara had experienced that fear – her father had killed her mother. Even after Aunt Mira and Bim and Raja had explained to her what it was he did, what he kept on doing daily, Tara could not rid herself of the feel of that original stab of suspicion. Sometimes, edging up close to her mother, she would study the flabby, floury skin punctured with a hundred minute needle-holes, and catch her breath in an effort not to cry out. Surely these were the signs of death, she felt, not of healing?

Now she stared fixedly at the door in the wall, varnished a bright hideous brown with the varnish swelling into blisters or cracking into spidery patterns in the heat, and felt the same morbid, uncontrollable fear of it opening and death stalking out in the form of a pair of dreadfully familiar ghosts that gave out a sound of paper and filled her nostrils with white insidious dust.

In the sleeping garden the coppersmiths beat on and on monotonously like mechanics at work on a metal sheet – tonk-tonk-tonk. Tonk-tonk-tonk.

To look at Bim one would not think she had lived through the same childhood, the same experiences as Tara. She led the way so briskly up the stairs on the outside of the house to the flat rooftop where, as children, they had flown kites and hidden secrets, that it was clear she feared no ghosts to meet her there. Now they leant upon the stucco balustrade and looked down at the garden patterned with the light and shade of early evening. The heat of the day and the heavy dust were being sluiced and washed away by the garden hose as the gardener trained it now on the jasmines, now on the palms, bringing out the green scent of watered earth and refreshed plants. Flocks of parrots came winging in, a lurid, shrieking green, to settle on the sunflowers and rip their black-seeded centres to bits, while mynahs hopped up and down on the lawn, quarrelling over insects. Bim's cat, jet-black, picked her way carefully between the puddles left by the gardener's generously splashing, spraying hose, and twitched her whiskers and went 'meh-meh-meh' with annoyance when the mynahs shrieked at the sight of her and came to swoop over and dive-bomb her till she retreated under the hedge. A pair of hoopoes promenaded sedately up and down the lawn, furling and unfurling the striped fans on their heads. A scent of spider lilies rose from the flowerpots massed on the veranda steps as soon as they were watered, like ladies newly bathed, powdered and scented for the evening.

On either side of their garden were more gardens, neighbours' houses, as still and faded and shabby as theirs, the gardens as overgrown and neglected and teeming with wild, uncontrolled life. From the rooftop they could see the pink and yellow and grey stucco walls, peeling and spotted, or an occasional *gol mohur* tree scarlet with summer blossom.

Outside the sagging garden gate the road led down to the Jumna river. It had shrunk now to a mere rivulet of mud that Tara could barely make out in the huge flat expanse of sand that stretched out to the furry yellow horizon like some sleeping lion, shabby and old. There were no boats on the river except for a flat-bottomed ferry boat that idled slowly back and forth. There was no sign of life beyond an occasional washerman picking his washing off the sand dunes and loading it on to his donkey, and a few hairless *pai* dogs that slunk about the mud flats, nosing about for a dead fish or a frog to devour. A fisherman strode out into the river, flung out his net with a wave of his wrists and then drew in an empty net.

Tara could tell it was empty because he did not bend to pick up anything. There was nothing. 'Imagine,' she said, with wonder, for she could not believe the long-remembered, always-remembered childhood had had a backdrop as drab as this, 'we used to *like* playing there – in that dust and mud. What could we have seen in it – in that muddy little trickle? Why, it's hardly a river – it's nothing, just nothing.'

'Now Tara, your travels have made you very snobbish,' Bim protested, but lazily, good-naturedly. She was leaning heavily on her elbows, letting her grey-streaked hair tumble in whatever bit of breeze came off the river up to them, and now she turned to lean back against the balustrade and look up at the sky that was no longer flat and white-hot but patterned and wrinkled with pale brush-strokes of blue and grey and mauve. A flock of white egrets rose from the river bed and stitched their way slowly and evenly across this faded cloth. 'Nothing?' she repeated Tara's judgement. 'The holy river Jumna? On whose banks Krishna played his flute and Radha danced?'

'Oh Bim, it is nothing of the sort,' Tara dared to say, sure she was being teased. 'It's a little trickle of mud with banks of dust on either side.

'It's where my ashes will be thrown after I am dead and burnt,' Bim said unexpectedly and abruptly. 'It is where Mira-*masi*'s ashes were thrown. Then they go down into the sea.' Seeing Tara start and quiver, she added more lightly, 'It's where we played as children – ran races on the dunes and dug holes to bury ourselves in and bullied the ferryman into giving us free rides to the melon fields. Don't you remember the melons baking in the hot sand and splitting them open and eating them all warm and red and pouring with pink juice?'

'That was you and Raja,' Tara reminded her. 'I never dared get into that boat, and of course Baba stayed at home. It was you and Raja who used to play there, Bim.'

'I and Raja,' Bim mused, continuing to look up at the sky till the egrets pierced through the soft cloth of it and disappeared into the dusk like so many needles lost. 'I and Raja,' she said, 'I and Raja.' Then, 'And the white horse and Hyder Ali Sahib going for his evening ride?' she asked Tara almost roughly, trying to shake out of her some corroboration as if she were unsure if this image were real or only imagined. It had the making of a legend, with the merest seed of truth. 'Can you remember playing on the sand late in the evening and the white horse riding by, Hyder Ali Sahib up on it, high above us, and his peon running in front of him, shouting, and his dog behind him, barking?' She laughed quite excitedly, seeing it again, this half-remembered picture. 'We stood up to watch them go past and he wouldn't even look at us. The peon shouted to us to get out of the way. I think Hyder Ali Sahib used to think of himself as some kind of prince, a nawab. And Raja *loved* that.' Her eyes gleamed as much with malice as with remembrance. 'Raja stood up straight and stared and stared and I'm sure he longed to ride on a white horse with a dog to run behind him just as old Hyder Ali did. Hyder Ali Sahib was always Raja's ideal, wasn't he?' she ended up.

Her words had cut a deep furrow through Tara's forehead. She too pressed down on her elbows, feeling the balustrade cut into her flesh as she tried to remember. Did she really remember or was it only Bim's picture that she saw, in shades of white and black and scarlet, out there on the shadowy sand-bank? To cover up a confusion she failed to resolve, she said 'Yes, and d'you remember Raja marching up and down here on the roof, swinging his arms and reciting his poems to us while we sat here on the balustrade, swinging our legs and listening? I used to feel like crying, it was so beautiful – those poems about death, and love, and wine, and flames.'

'They weren't. They were terrible,' Bim said icily, tossing her head with a stubborn air, like a bad-tempered mare's. '*Terrible* verses he wrote.'

'Oh Bim,' Tara exclaimed in dismay, widening her eyes in horror at such sacrilege. It was a family dictum that Raja was a poet and wrote great poetry. Now Bim, his favourite sister, was denying this doctrine. What had happened?

'Of course it was, Tara – terrible, terrible,' Bim insisted. 'We're not fifteen and ten years old any more – you and I. Have you tried reading it recently? It's *nauseating*. Can you remember any two lines of it that wouldn't make you sick with embarrassment now?'

Tara was too astounded, and too stricken to speak. Throughout her childhood, she had always stood on the outside of that enclosed world of love and admiration in which Bim and Raja moved, watching them, sucking her finger, excluded. Now here was Bim, cruelly and wilfully smashing up that charmed world with her cynicism, her criticism. She stood dismayed.

Bim was fierce. She no longer leant on the balustrade, drooping with reminiscences. She walked up and down agitatedly, swinging her arms in agitation, as Raja had done when quoting poetry in those days when he was a poet, at least to them. 'If you'll just come to my room,' she said, suddenly stopping, 'I'll show you some of those poems – I think they must be still lying around although I don't know why I haven't torn them all up.'

'Of course you wouldn't!' Tara exclaimed.

'Why not?' Bim flung at her. 'Come and see, tell me if you think it worth keeping,' and she swept down the stairs with a martial step, looking back once to shout at Tara, '*And*, apart from poetry recitals, Tara, this terrace is where I cut your hair for you and made you cry. What an uproar there was.' She gave her head a quick, jerky toss. 'And here you are, with your hair grown long again, and it's mine that's cut short. Only no one cared when I cut *mine*.'

Tara hung back. She had been perfectly content to pace the terrace in the faint breeze, watch the evening darken, wait for the stars to come out and talk about the old days. Even if it was about the haircut, painful as that had been. But Bim was clattering down the stone stairs, the bells of the pink-spired temple at the bend of the river were suddenly clanging loudly and discordantly, the sky had turned a deep green with a wide purple channel through it for the night to come flowing in, and there was nothing for it but to follow Bim down the stairs, into the house, now unbearably warm and stuffy after the freshness and cool of the terrace, and then into Bim's cluttered, untidy room.

It had been their father's office room and the furniture in it was still office furniture – steel cupboards to hold safes and files, metal slotted shelves piled with registers and books, and the roll-top desk towards which Bim marched as Tara hesitated unwillingly by the door. Throwing down the lid, Bim started pulling out papers from the pigeon-holes and opening drawers and rifling through files and tutorial papers and college registers. Out of this mass of paper she separated some sheets and held them out to Tara with an absent-minded air.

Tara, glancing down at them, saw that they were in Urdu, a language she had not learnt. It was quite useless her holding these sheets in her hand and pretending to read the verses that Raja had once recited to them and that had thrilled her then with their Persian glamour. But Bim did not notice her predicament, she was still occupied with the contents of the rifled desk. Finally she found what she was looking for and handed that, too, to Tara with a grim set of her mouth that made Tara quake.

'What is this, Bim?' she asked, looking down and seeing it was in Raja's English handwriting.

'A letter Raja wrote – read it. Read it,' she repeated as Tara hesitated, and walked across to the window and stood there staring out silently, compelling Tara to read while she tensely waited.

Tara read – unwillingly, unbelievingly.

Raja had written it years ago, she saw, and tried to link the written date with some event in their family history that might provide it with a context.

> You will have got our wire with the news of Hyder Ali Sahib's death. I know you will have been as saddened by it as we are. Perhaps you are also a bit worried about the future. But you must remember that when I left you, I promised I would always look after you, Bim. When Hyder Ali Sahib was ill and making out his will, Benazir herself spoke to him about the house and asked him to allow you to keep it at the same rent we used to pay him when father and mother were alive. He agreed – you know he never cared for money, only for friendship – and I want to assure you that now that he is dead and has left all his property to us, you may continue to have it at the same rent, I shall never think of raising it or of selling the house as long as you and Baba need it. If you have any worries, Bim, you have only to tell – Raja.

It took Tara some minutes to think out all the implications of this letter. To begin with, she studied the date and tried to recall when Hyder Ali had died. Instead a series of pictures of the Hyder Ali family flickered in the half-dark of the room. There was Hyder Ali, once their neighbour and their landlord, as handsome and stately as a commissioned oil painting hung over a mantelpiece, all in silver and grey and scarlet as he had been on the white horse on which he rode along the river bank in the evenings while the children stood and watched. He had cultivated the best roses in Old Delhi and given parties to which poets and musicians came. Their parents were not amongst his friends. Then there was his daughter Benazir, a very young girl, plump and pretty, a veil thrown over her head as she hurried into the closed carriage that took her to school, and the Begum whom they seldom saw, she lived in the closed quarters of the house, but at Id sent them, and their other tenant-neighbours, rich sweets covered with fine silver foil on a tray decked with embroidered napkins. They had lived in the tall stucco house across the road, distinguished from all the others by its wealth of decorative touches like the coloured fanlight above the front door, the china tiles along the veranda walls and the coloured glass chandeliers and lamps. They had owned half the houses on that road. When they left Delhi during the partition riots of 1947, they sold most of these houses to their Hindu tenants for a song – all except for Bim's house which she did not try to buy and which he continued to let to her at the same rent as before. It was to this that Raja, his only son-in-law and inheritor of his considerable property, referred in his letter. It was a very old letter.

Still confused, she said slowly, 'But, Bim, it's a very old letter – years old.'

'But I still have it,' Bim said sharply, staring out of the window as if she too saw pictures in the dark. 'I still keep it in my desk – to remind me. Whenever I begin to wish to see Raja again or wish he would come and see us, then I take out that letter and read it again. Oh, I can tell you, I could write him such an answer, he wouldn't forget it for many years either!' She gave a short laugh and ended it with a kind of a choke, saying, 'You say I should come to Hyderabad with you for his daughter's wedding. How can I? How can I enter his house – my landlord's house? I, such a poor tenant? Because of me, he can't raise the rent or sell the house and make a profit – imagine that. The sacrifice!'

'Oh Bim,' Tara said helplessly. Whenever she saw a tangle, an emotional tangle of this kind, rise up before her, she wanted only to turn and flee into that neat, sanitary, disinfected land in which she lived with Bakul, with its set of rules and regulations, its neatness and orderliness. And seemliness too – seemliness. She sat down weakly on the edge of Bim's bed, putting the letter down on the bedside table beside a pile of history books. She turned the pages of Sir Mortimer Wheeler's *Early India and Pakistan* and thought how relevant such a title was to the situation in their family, their brother's marriage to Hyder Ali's daughter. She wished she dared lighten the atmosphere by suggesting this to Bim, but Bim stood with her back arched, martial and defiant. 'Why let this go on and on?' she sighed instead. 'Why not end it now by going to Moyna's wedding, and then forget it all?'

'I have ended it already,' Bim said stubbornly, 'by not going to see them and not having them here either. It is ended. But I don't forget, no.'

'I wouldn't ever have believed – no one would ever have believed that you and Raja who were so close – so close – could be against each other ever. It's just unbelievable, Bim, and so – unnecessary, too,' she ended in a wail.

'Yes?' said Bim with scorn, turning around to stare at her sister. 'I don't think so. I don't think it is unnecessary to take offence when you are insulted. What was he trying to say to me? Was he trying to make me thank him – go down on my knees and thank him for this house in which we all grew up? Was he trying to threaten me with eviction and warn me what might happen if I ever stopped praising him and admiring him?'

'Of course not, Bim. How silly. He simply didn't know quite what he was writing. I suppose he was in a state – his father-in-law having just died, and you know how he always felt about him – and then having to take over Benazir's family business and all that. He just didn't know what he was writing.'

'A poet – not knowing what he was writing?' Bim laughed sarcastically as she came and picked up the letter and put it back in the desk. It seemed to have a pigeon-hole all to itself as if it were a holy relic like fingernails or a crooked yellow tooth.

'Do tear it up,' cried Tara, jumping up. 'Don't put it back there to take out and look at and hold against Raja. Tear it up, Bim, throw it away,' she urged.

Bim put the lid up with a harsh set to her mouth. 'I will keep it. I must look at it and remind myself every now and then. Whenever you come here and ask why I don't go to Hyderabad and visit him and see my little nieces and nephews – well then, I feel I have to explain to you, prove to you . . .' She stammered a bit and faltered to a stop.

'*Why*, Bim?'

But Bim would not tell her why she needed this bitterness and insult and anger. She picked up an old grey hairbrush that had lost half its bristles and was so matted with tangles of hair that Tara shuddered at the sight of it, and began to brush her hair with short, hard strokes. 'Come, let's go and visit the Misras. They've been asking about you, they want to see you. Ask Bakul to come, too – he must be getting bored. And he knows the Misras. You *met* him at their house – I'd nearly forgotten,' she laughed, a bit distractedly.

Tara followed her out, relieved to be in the open again, out of the dense musty web of Bim's room, Bim's entanglements, and to see the evening light and the garden. A bush of green flowers beside the veranda shook out its night scent as they came out and covered them with its powdery billows. Badshah rushed up, whining with expectation.

The sound of a 1940s foxtrot on Baba's gramophone

followed them down the drive to the gate as if a mechanical bird had replaced the koels and pigeons of daylight. Here Bim stopped and told Badshah firmly to sit. They stood watching, waiting for him to obey. He made protesting sounds, turned around in circles, pawed Bim's feet with his claws, even whined a bit under his breath. Finally he yawned in resignation and sank on to his haunches. Then they turned out of the gate and ceased to hear the tinny rattle of the wartime foxtrot.

Walking up the Misras' driveway, they could hear instead the sounds of the music and dance lessons that the Misra sisters gave in the evenings after their little nursery school had closed for the day, for it seemed that they never ceased to toil and the pursuit of a living was unending. Out on the dusty lawn cane chairs were set in a circle and here the Misra brothers sat taking their rest – which they also never ceased to do – dressed in summer clothes of fine muslin, drinking iced drinks and discussing the day, which meant very little since the day for them had been as blank and unblemished as an empty glass.

They immediately rose to welcome their neighbours but Bim stood apart, feeling a half-malicious desire to go into the house and watch the two grey-haired, spectacled, middle-aged women – once married but both rejected by their husbands soon after their marriage – giving themselves up to demonstrations of ecstatic song and dance, the songs always Radha's in praise of Krishna, the dance always of Radha pining for Krishna. She hadn't the heart after all and instead of joining the men on the lawn, she went up the steps to the veranda where the old father half-sat, half-reclined against the bolsters on a wooden divan, a glass of soda water in his hand, looking out and listening to his sons and occasionally shouting a command at them that went unheard, then sadly, meditatively burping. Tara and Bakul sat down with the brothers on the lawn and talked and listened to the voices of pupils and teachers mournfully rising and falling down the scales played on a lugubrious harmonium and tried, while talking of Delhi and Washington, politics and travel, to imagine the improbable scene indoors. Eventually the little pupils came out, drooping and perspiring, and rushed off down the drive to the gate where their ayahs waited for them, chatting and chewing betel leaves. After a while, the teachers, too, emerged on to the veranda. They too drooped and perspired and were grey with fatigue. There was nothing remotely amusing about them.

'Bim, Bim, why must you sit here with Papa? Come into the garden and have a drink,' they cried at once, together.

But Bim would not listen. She tucked up her feet under her to make it plain she was not getting up. 'No, no, I want to listen to Uncle,' she said, not wishing to add that she had no liking for his sons' company. 'Uncle is telling me how he was sent to England to study law but somehow landed up in Burma and made a fortune instead. I want to hear the whole story. And you must go and meet Tara and Bakul. They've come.'

'Tara and Bakul?' cried the two sisters and, straightening their spectacles and smoothing down their hair and their saris, they rushed down into the garden while Bim stayed by the sick old man.

'But Uncle, is it a true story?' she teased him. 'I never know with you.'

'Can't you see the proof?' he asked, waving his glass of soda water so that it spilt and frothed and sizzled down his arm. 'Now if I had gone north and had to work in a cold climate, learnt to wear a tie and button a jacket and keep my shoes laced and polished, I would have returned a proper person, a disciplined man. Instead, as you see, I went east, in order to fulfil a *swami's* prophecy, and there I could make money without working, and had to undress to keep cool, and sleep all afternoon, and drink all evening – and so I came back with money and no discipline and no degree,' he laughed, deliberately spilling some more soda water as if in a gesture of fatalism.

'What, all to satisfy a *swami*?'

'Yes, yes, it is true, Bimla. My father used to go to this *swami-ji*, no great man, just one of those common little *swamis* who sit outside the railway station and catch those people who come from the village to make their fortunes in the city. "*Swami-ji, swami-ji*, will I have luck?" they ask, and he puts his hand on their heads in blessing and says, "Yes, son, if you first put five rupees in my pocket." That sort of man. My father went to him to buy a blessing for me – I was leaving for England next day. My trunk was packed, my passage booked, my mother was already weeping. But perhaps my father didn't give the *swami-ji* enough money. He said, "Your son go to England? To Vilayat? Certainly not. He will never go north. He will go east." "No, no," said my father, "his passage is already booked on a P & O boat, he is leaving for Bombay tomorrow to catch it, he is going to study law in a great college in England." But *swami-ji* only shook his head and refused to say another word. So, as my father was walking home, very slowly and thoughtfully, who should bump into him, outside the Kashmere Gate post office, but an old friend of his who had been in school with him and then gone to Burma to set up in the teak business. And this man, this scoundrel, may he perish – oh, I forgot! He perished long ago, Bimla, leaving me all his money – he clasped my father in his arms and said, "You are like a brother to me. Your son is my son. Send him to me, let him work for me and I will make a man of him." And so my passage was cancelled, I gave up my studies and went east, to Burma.' He gulped down half a glass of soda water suddenly, thirstily. 'That *swami-ji*,' he burped.

'And do you think if the *swami-ji* had not made that prophecy, your father would not have accepted his friend's offer?' asked Bim, filled with curiosity.

'Who can tell?' groaned the old man, shifting about in search of a more comfortable position. 'Fate – they talk about Fate. What is it?' He struck his head dramatically. 'This fate?'

'What is it, uncle? Does it pain?' Bim asked because his face, normally as smooth and bland as butter was furrowed and gleaming with sweat.

He sank back, sighing, 'Nothing, nothing, Bimla, my daughter, it is only old age. Just fate and old age and none of us escapes from either. You won't. You don't know, you don't think – and then suddenly it is there, it has come. When it comes, you too will know.'

Bim laughed, helping herself to some of the betel leaves in the silver box at his side. As she smeared them with lime and sprinkled them with aniseed and cardamoms, she said, 'You think one doesn't know pain when one is young, uncle? You should sit down some day with ninety examination papers to correct and try and make out ninety different kinds of handwriting, all illegible, and see that your class has presented you with ninety different versions of what you taught them – all wrong!' She laughed and rolled up the betel leaf and packed it into her mouth. 'That is what I have been doing all day and it has given me a fine pain, too.' She grasped her head theatrically and the old man laughed. Bim had always made him laugh, even when she was a little girl and did tricks on her bicycle going round the drive while his two daughters screamed, 'Bim, you'll fall!'

'You work too hard,' he said. 'You don't know how to enjoy life. You and my two girls – you are too alike – you work and let the brothers enjoy. Look at my sons there –' he waved his arm at them, the muslin sleeve of his shirt falling back to reveal an amulet tied to his arm with a black thread running through the thick growth of white hair. 'Look at them – fat, lazy slobs, drinking whisky. Drinking whisky all day that their sisters have to pay for – did you ever hear of such a thing? In my day, our sisters used to tie coloured threads on our wrists on Rakhibandhan day, begging for our protection, and we gave them gifts and promised to protect them and take care of them, and even if it was only a custom, an annual festival, we at least meant it. When my sister's husband died, I brought her to live here with us. She has lived here for years, she and her children. Perhaps she is still here, I don't know, I haven't seen her,' he trailed off vaguely, then ended up with a forceful, 'but *they* – they let their sisters do the same ceremony, and they just don't care what it means as long as they can get their whisky and have the time to sit on their backsides, drinking it. Useless rubbish, my sons. Everything they ever did has failed . . .'

'What, not the new business as well? The real estate business that Brij started? Has that failed already?'

'Of course,' cried the old man, almost with delight. 'Of course it has. Can it succeed when Brij, the manager, cannot go to the office because he thinks it is degrading and refuses to speak to his clients because they are Punjabis, from Pakistan, and don't belong to the old families of Delhi? What is one to do with a fool like that? Am I to kick him out of the house and flog him down the road to the office? And look at Mulk – our great musician – all he does is wave his hand in the air and look at the stars in the daytime sky, and sing. Sing! He only wants to sing. Why? For whom? Who asked him to sing? Nobody. He just wants to, that is all. He doesn't think anyone should ask him to work or earn money – they should only ask him to sing.'

Out on the lawn there was a burst of laughter.

'And what about the old business they ran – the ice factory and soda water business? They had a good manager to run that.'

'Good manager – ho, yes! Very good manager. Had them eating out of his hand. They thought he was an angel on earth – a *farishtha* – slaving for their sakes, to fill their coffers with gold – till one day they went to the office to open the coffer for some gold – they must have needed it for those Grant Road women they go to, those song-and-dance women – and they found it empty, and the money gone.'

'And the manager?'

'Gone! He took care of money – the money went – he went with it.' The old man roared, slapping his thigh so that a fold of his *dhoti* fell aside, revealing the grey-haired stretch of old, slack flesh. Straightening it casually, he added, 'What did they think? Someone else will work so that they can eat?'

'I didn't know about that,' said Bim, concerned. She had thought the Misras had at least one secure business behind them, as her own family still had their father's insurance business that still existed quietly and unspectacularly without their aid and kept them housed and fed. If the manager made more money than he ought to, Bim did not grudge him that. She earned her own living to supplement that unearned income, and it was really only Baba who needed to be supported. But the Misra boys – fat, hairy brutes – why should others look after them? The poor Misra girls, so grey and bony and needle-faced, still prancing through their Radha-Krishna dances and impersonating lovelorn maidens in order to earn their living . . . Bim shook her head.

'Fools,' the old man was still muttering as he fumbled about, looking for something under the pillows and bolsters and not finding it. Bim knew it was the hookah he was no longer allowed to smoke. 'Ugh,' he cried, the corners of his mouth turned down as though he were about to cry, like a baby. 'Not even my hookah any more. The doctor has said no, and the girls listen to the doctor, not to their father. What it is to be a father, to live without a smoke, or drink . . .'

Out on the lawn they were laughing again, their laughter spiralling up, up in the dark, as light as smoke.

'Laugh, laugh,' said the old man. 'Yes, laugh now – before it is all up with you and you are like me – washed up. But never mind, never mind,' he said to Bim, straightening his head and folding his arms so that he looked composed again, like a piece of stone sculpture. 'When I was young, when I was their age – do you think I was any better?' He winked suddenly at the surprised Bim. 'Was *I* a saint?' he laughed. 'I can tell you, I was just as fat, as greedy, as stupid, as wicked as *any* of them,' he suddenly roared, flinging out an arm as if to push them out of his way in contempt. 'A boozer, a womanizer, a bankrupt – running after drink, women, money – that was all I did, just like them, *worse* than them, any of them . . .' he chuckled and now his head wobbled on his neck as if something had come loose. '*Much* worse than any of them,' he repeated with desperate pride.

Bim, red-faced in the dark shadows, let down her feet cautiously and searched for her slippers.

And here was Jaya coming up the steps to fetch her. 'Bim, come and join us,' she called. 'Tara is telling us about Washington – it is such fun – and Papa should eat his dinner and go to sleep. Papa, I'm sending the cook with your dinner –' and she rushed off towards the kitchen while Bim went down the steps into the garden. The old man had sunk back against the bolsters and shut his eyes. She even thought he might have fallen asleep, he was so still, but a little later she heard him call, 'The pickle, Jaya – don't forget the black lemon pickle – let me have a little of it, will you?'

Out on the lawn the talk was more sober, more predictable in spite of the whisky that accompanied it. Someone brought Bim a tall glass that chattered with ice. Could it be from their factory, Bim wondered, sipping, stretching her bare feet in the grass and feeling its dry tickle.

'Bakul-*bhai*, tell me,' said the older brother, rolling the ice cubes around in his glass, 'as a diplomat in an Indian embassy, how do you explain the situation to foreigners? Now when the foreign press asks you, perhaps you just say "No comment", but when you meet friends at a party, and they ask you what is going on here – how can a Prime Minister behave as ours does – how can ministers get away with all they do here – what is being done about the problems of this country – who is going to solve them – how, why is it like this? – then what do you say to them, Bakul-*bhai*?'

Bim, who was lighting herself a cigarette, stopped to watch her brother-in-law cope with this interrogation. It was quite dark on the lawn and although a light had been switched on in the veranda so that the old father could see to eat his dinner, it only threw a pale rectangle of light across the beds of cannas close to the house, and did not illuminate Bakul's face. He kept them all waiting in silence as he considered and then began his measured and diplomatic reply.

Elegantly holding his cigarette in its holder at arm's length, Bakul told them in his ripest, roundest tones, 'What I feel is my duty, my vocation, when I am abroad, is to be my country's ambassador. All of us abroad are, in varying degrees, ambassadors. I refuse to talk about famine or drought or caste wars or – or political disputes. I refuse – I *refuse* to discuss such things. "No comment" is the answer if I am asked. I can discuss such things here, with you, but not with foreigners, not in a foreign land. There I am an ambassador and I choose to show them and inform them only of the best, the finest.'

'The Taj Mahal?' asked Bim, blowing out a spume of smoke that wavered in the darkness, and avoiding Tara's eye, watchful and wary.

'Yes, exactly,' said Bakul promptly. 'The Taj Mahal – the Bhagavad Gita – Indian philosophy – music – art – the great, immortal values of ancient India. But why talk of local politics, party disputes, election malpractices, Nehru, his daughter, his grandson – such matters as will soon pass into oblivion? *These* aren't important when compared with India, eternal India –'

'Yes, it does help to live abroad if you feel that way,' mused Bim, while her foot played with the hem of her sari and she looked carefully away from Tara who watched. 'If you lived here, and particularly if you served the Government here, I think you would be obliged to notice such things: you would see their importance. I'm not sure if you could ignore bribery and corruption, red-tapism, famine, caste warfare and all that. In fact, living here, working here, you might easily forget the Taj Mahal and the message of the Gita –'

'Never,' interrupted Bakul firmly, ripely. 'A part of me lives here, the deepest part of me, always –'

'Ah,' Bim in turn interrupted him. 'Then it is definitely important to live abroad. In all the comfort and luxury of the embassy, it must be much easier, *very* easy to concentrate on the Taj, or the Emperor Akbar. Over here I'm afraid you would be too busy queueing up for your rations and juggling with your budget, making ends meet –'

'Oh Bim,' Tara burst out in protest, 'you *do* exaggerate. I don't see you queueing up for your rations – or even for a *bus*!'

Bim burst out laughing, delighted at having provoked Tara, and agreed there was some exaggeration in what she said. This annoyed Bakul, who had taken it all so perfectly seriously, and he tapped his cigarette holder on the arm of his chair with the air of a judge tapping a gavel at a meeting grown unruly.

Tara cast her eyes around, looking for an escape. But Bim had thrown back her head in laughter, all the men beside her were laughing. Then she leant forward, a cigarette in her mouth, and Bakul leant towards her to light it. Seeing the match flare, the cigarette catch fire with a little throb, Tara was pricked with the realization that although it was she who was the pretty sister, had always been, so that in their youth the young men had come flocking about her like inquisitive, hopeful, sanguine bees in search of some nectar that they sniffed on the air, it was Bim who was attractive. Bim who, when young, had been too tall and square-shouldered to be thought pretty, now that she was grey – and a good deal grey, observed Tara – had arrived at an age when she could be called handsome. All the men seemed to acknowledge this and to respond. There was that little sensual quiver in the air as they laughed at what she said, and a kind of quiet triumph in the way in which she drew in her cheeks to make the cigarette catch fire and then threw herself back into her chair, giving her head a toss and holding the cigarette away so that a curl of smoke circled languidly about her hand. Tara thought how attractive a woman who smokes is: there is some link formed between the man who leans forward with a match and the woman who bends her head towards that light, as Bakul and Bim did.

Tara did not smoke and no one offered her a light. Or was it just that Tara, having married, had rescinded the right to flirt, while Bim, who had not married, had not rescinded? No, it was not, for Bim could not be said to flirt. Slapping hard at a mosquito that had lighted on her arm, she was saying to Manu who had offered to fetch a Flit-gun, 'That's too much of a bother – don't.' Bim never bothered.

The Misra brothers and sisters were not interested in the subtleties underlying such exchanges. One brother wanted to know, 'What is the price of good whisky in Washington? Not that terrible thing called bourbon but scotch – can you get scotch?' and the sisters asked Tara where she had bought her chiffon sari and her leather bag, and for how much. Bim listened to Tara giving them shoppers' information glibly but a little too fast, making her sound unreliable. It amused Bim to see, through a haze of cigarette smoke, Tara's not quite assimilated cosmopolitanism that sat on her oddly, as if a child had dressed up in its mother's high-heeled shoes – taller, certainly, but wobbling. Then the sisters' heads drew closer still to Tara, their voices dropped an octave, and they murmured, one from the left and one from the right, 'But how much longer can you keep your girls abroad? Mustn't they come home to marry now?'

Tara cowered back in her basket chair. 'They are only sixteen and seventeen,' she said plaintively.

'Time to marry – better to marry – time, time,' they cried, and Tara rubbed her mosquito-bitten toe in the grass in pained embarrassment, and Bim, overhearing them, lifted her eyebrows in horror and turned to Mulk, the younger brother who was silent, for sympathy.

Mulk had already drunk more glasses of whisky than anyone could count and sat ignoring the company, beating one hand on his knee, singing in little snatches in his hoarse, cracked voice, swaying his head joyfully to music that was audible only to him. Even since she had last seen him, he seemed to have deteriorated – his jaws prickled with several days' growth of beard, he wore a shirt with several buttons missing and a sleeve irremediably stained with betel juice, the slippers on his unwashed feet needed mending. He rolled his eyes in their sockets like a dog howling at the moon and hummed to himself. '*Zindagi*, O *Zindagi*,' he sang, tunelessly, and refreshed himself with another gulp of whisky.

Then suddenly the scene split, with a tearing sound. It was only whisky pouring out of an overturned glass and Mulk struggling to get out of the canvas chair, too tight for his heavy frame. As they all stopped talking to stare at him, he gestured widely and shouted dramatically, 'Where is my *tabla*-player? My harmonium player? My accompanists? Where are they? *Chotu-mia! Bare-mia!*' Standing, swaying on his thick legs, he roared at the lighted house and the scurrying figures on the veranda.

'Shh, Mulk-*bhai*,' cried Jaya and Sarla, their faces shrinking into small dark knots. 'You will wake Papa. Why are you shouting? You know they aren't there.'

'Yes, I know they aren't there,' he blasted them, turning around and staggering towards them so that Bim and Tara had to hastily draw up their feet or he would have tripped over them. 'I know who turned them out – you two – you two turned them out –'

'Mulk, Mulk,' murmured his brothers.

Suddenly Mulk was clutching his hands to his chest like two puffy little birds and his voice rose in shrill, grotesque mimicry. '"It is a waste of money. How can we afford to keep them? We have to feed ourselves. Tell them to go, they must go – go – go –"' and he pushed out the two birds so that they fluttered away and fell at his sides. 'That is all I hear from them – these two –'

'Mulk, Mulk,' rose the pacifying croon from the pigeons in the chairs.

Mulk swung around to face Bim and Tara and Bakul now. 'They have got rid of my musicians,' he nearly wept. 'Sent them away. How am I to sing without accompaniment?'

'Mulk-*bhai*, we only pointed out that we haven't the money to pay them and we could not keep feeding them on kebabs and pilaos and kormas as you expected us to. Is it our fault if they went away once we stopped serving such food?'

'Food! It wasn't food they wanted. You are insulting them. You are insulting my *guru*. He does not want food, or money. He wants respect. Regard. That is what we must pay to a *guru*. But you have no respect, no regard. You think only of money – money – money. That is what you think about, you two –'

'Mulk, Mul-lk.'

'They have minds full of money, *dirty* minds. They don't understand the artist, how the artist lives for his art. They don't know how it is only music –' here he clasped his chest with a moist, sweating paw – 'only music that keeps me alive. Not food. Not money. Music: what can it mean to those who only think of money? If I say, "I must have accompaniment for my singing," they say, "Oh there is no money!" If I say, "I want my friends to come tonight so I can sing for them, cook dinner for them please," they cry, "Oh we have no money!" Do you need money to make music?' he roared, lifting his arm so that the torn sleeve showed his armpit and the bush of grey hair in it. He stood, swaying, with the arm uplifted, the torn sleeve drooping, as he faced his visitors. 'Do you?' he roared, and they could see spit flying from his mouth and spraying them where they sat, helpless. 'Tell me – do you?'

The visitors were frozen. The family seethed. Then the sisters cracked like old dry pods from which the black seeds of protest and indignation spilt, infertile. Money, they were both saying, where were they to find money to pay for concerts and dinners?

'Don't I give you money?' shouted Mulk, lowering his head and swaying it from side to side threateningly. 'Where is all the money I give you – hey? Tell me. Tell me. Where is that five hundred rupee note I gave you – hey? Where is it? Show it to me. I want to see it. I want it.'

He began to plunge his legs up and down in the grass like a beast going methodically out of control. One of the small bamboo tables was knocked down, a glass spilt. Now at last Bakul acted. Rising to his feet casually, elegantly, he took Mulk by the arm, murmured to him in his most discreet voice, began to lead him away towards the house. They heard Mulk crying something about 'My *guru* – his birthday – I want to give – they won't let me – for my *guru* –' and then some sobbing intakes of breath, gasps for reason and control, and then only the flow of Bakul's voice, slipping and spreading as smoothly and evenly as oil, and then silence in which they became aware of Badshah barking fiercely out on the road.

Bim rose at last, brushing her sari as if there were crumbs, saying, 'Listen to Badshah – he's saying we must get back. Come, Tara, if we don't go home at once, the cook will fall asleep and we'll have no dinner and Baba will go to bed without any.'

Now the Misra sisters too were released from their shell-shocked postures and rose gratefully, chattering once more. 'But why don't you stay to dinner, Bim?' 'Tara, have pot luck with us. We can't throw a dinner party as we would have in the old days – but pot luck . . .' and the brothers shouted, 'Let's call Baba. Tell him we'll have music that will make him forget that rubbish he listens to – we'll get Mulk to sing!' Strangely enough, and much to Bim's and Tara's astonishment, Brij and Manu began to laugh, thumping each other like schoolboys. One even wiped his eyes of tears as he repeated 'Get Mulk to sing – Mulk to sing for us –' as if it were a family joke that only needed to be mentioned to set them off uncontrollably.

The sisters, a little more circumspect, edged closer to Tara, saying, 'Mulk gets that way when he has had too much to drink. He doesn't mean it – he will forget about it – we'll give him his dinner – and, oh stay for pot luck, Tara!'

But Bim would not listen. The last time she had accepted an invitation to 'pot luck' she had been distressed to see the two Misra sisters halving and sharing a *chapati* between them, and jars of pickles had had to be opened to make up for the lack of meat and vegetables. It would not do. 'No, that won't do,' she said firmly. 'Can you hear Badshah calling? Listen to that bark – he'll have all the neighbours up, and your father, too,' and she swept up the veranda to say good night to the old man who lay supine on the divan, his two white, knobbed feet sticking out at the end of the sheet that covered him, saw that he was asleep and then went down to herd Tara and Bakul down the drive.

The sisters came to the gate with them, lingering by the jasmine bush to pick some for Tara. Giving her a handful, Jaya said, 'Oh, Tara, these flowers make me think of that picnic – so many years ago now – do you remember, too? It was springtime – the flowers in Lodi Gardens –'

'And bees!' cried Sarla suddenly, catching Tara by the wrist so that a few of the jasmines fell. 'How those bees attacked Bim – oh don't you remember?'

But Tara withdrew her hand, dropping the remaining jasmine as she did so. She shook her head, refusing to remember any more. Bim, smiling faintly, covered up her ears with her hands and said, 'How that dog barks – he has a voice like a trumpet,' and led Tara and Bakul across the road to their own gate where Badshah waited.

As they crossed the dusty road, Bakul cast a look at the tall dark house behind the hedge and asked, 'What has happened to the Hyder Alis' house? Doesn't anyone live there?'

'No. I mean, only a poor relation of theirs. He must have been a nuisance to Raja in Hyderabad so they sent him here as caretaker. He takes opium – he just lies around – and the house is falling down about his ears. No one's replaced a brick or painted a wall there for years.'

'Oh what a shame – it was a lovely house, you know, Bakul,' said Tara.

Badshah's barks grew so urgent they could not speak to each other any more.

Baba was already asleep on his bed in the veranda when the sisters slipped quietly past, only glancing to see him lying on his side, one leg stretched out and the other slightly bent at the knee as if he were running, half-flying through the sky, one hand folded under his chin and the other uncurled beside it, palm upwards and fingers curved in – a finely composed piece of sculpture in white. Marble. Or milk. Or less: a spider's web, faint and shadowy, or just some moonlight spilt across the bed. There was something unsubstantial about his long slimness in the light white clothes, such a total absence of being, of character, of clamouring traits and characteristics. He was no more and no less than a white flower or harmless garden spider, the sisters thought, as if, when he was born, his parents, late in their lives, had no vitality and no personality left to hand down to him, having given it away in thoughtless handfuls to the children born earlier. Lying there in the dark, dressed in white, breathing quite imperceptibly, he might have been a creature without blood in his veins, without flesh on his bones, the sisters thought as they tiptoed past him, down the steps to the lawn to stroll.

The whole neighbourhood was silent now, asleep. The sound of traffic on the highway was distant, smothered by dust and darkness. At last one became aware of the presence of stars, the scent of night-flowering plants. The sisters, sleepless, rustled through the grass, up and down beside the long hedge. The black cat, pacing sedately beside them to begin with, suddenly leapt up into the air, darted sideways and disappeared.

Hands behind her back as she paced, Bim murmured, 'Do you know, for a long time after Mira-*masi* died – for a long, long time – I used to keep seeing her, just here by the hedge –'

'Bim,' Tara cried incredulously.

'Yes, yes, I used to *feel* I was seeing her – just out of the corner of my eye, never directly before me, you know – just slipping past this hedge here –' she put out her hand and touched the white-flowering *chandni* – 'quite white and naked, as she was when she – when she –'

'Then – at that time,' Tara helped, pained.

'– small, like a thin little dog, a white one, just slipping along quietly – I felt as if towards the well at the back – that well –'

'That the cow drowned in?'

'And she used to say she would drown herself in but because she didn't, because she died, after all, in bed, I felt she was still trying to get there. A person needs to choose his death. But if I turned my head very quickly – then she would vanish – just disappear into the hedge –' and Bim touched it again, to remember, and had the back of her hand scratched by a thorn and heard some small creature skitter away into the leaves. 'I felt like one of those Antarctic explorers T.S. Eliot wrote about in his notes to *The Waste Land*, to that verse, do you know it, Tara?

Who is the third who walks always beside you?
When I count, there are only you and I together
But when I look ahead up the white road
There is always another one walking beside you
Gliding wrapt in a brown mantle, hooded
I do not know whether a man or a woman
– But who is that on the other side of you?

They were silent as they scraped through the catching grasses at their feet, and had their heads bowed, not looking. Tara gave a small sigh that she disguised as a yawn: she had listened so often to Bim and Raja quoting poetry – the two of them had always had so much poetry that they carried in their heads. As a little girl, tongue-tied and shy, too diffident to attempt reciting or even memorizing a poem – there had been that wretched episode in school when she was made to stand up and recite 'The Boy Stood On the Burning Deck' and it was found she could not proceed beyond the title – Tara was always struck dumb with wonder at their ability to memorize and quote. It was another of those games they shared and she did not. She felt herself shrink into that small miserable wretch of twenty years ago, both admiring and resenting her tall, striding sister who was acquainted with Byron, with Iqbal, even with T.S. Eliot.

Bim was calmly unaware of any of her sister's agonies, past or present. 'Only I was not at any extremity like those explorers in the icy wastes who used to see ghost figures,' she continued. 'I was not frozen or hungry or mad. Or even quite alone. I had Baba. After you married, and Raja went to Hyderabad, and Mira-*masi* died, I still had Baba. And that summer I got my job at the college and felt so pleased to be earning my living –'

She stopped abruptly as though there were a stone in the grass that she had stumbled on. Tara walked on, distracted, till she noticed Bim was not with her, then stopped to look back, fearfully. But Bim did not revive her tirade against Raja although Tara had feared they were beginning to slip into it again.

'Really, I was not mad in the least,' said Bim, strolling on. 'So then I thought there might be something in what the Tibetans say about the dead – how their souls linger on on earth and don't really leave till the forty-ninth day when a big feast is given and the last prayers are said and a final farewell given to the departed. It takes forty-nine days, they say in their Bardol Thodol, to travel through the three Bardos of death and all their stages. I felt Mira-*masi* was lingering on, in the garden, not able to leave because she hadn't been seen through all the stages with the relevant prayers and ceremonies. But then, who is?' Bim said more loudly, tossing her head, 'except for the Buddhist monks and nuns who die peacefully in their monasteries in the Himalayas? *We* were anything but peaceful that summer.'

'Yes, *what* a summer,' Tara murmured.

'Isn't it strange how life won't *flow*, like a river, but moves in jumps, as if it were held back by locks that are opened now and then to let it jump forwards in a kind of flood? There are these long still stretches –

nothing happens – each day is exactly like the other – plodding, uneventful – and then suddenly there is a crash – mighty deeds take place – momentous events – even if one doesn't know it at the time – and then life subsides again into the backwaters till the next push, the next flood? That summer was certainly one of them – the summer of '47 –'

'For everyone in India,' Tara reminded primly. 'For every Hindu and Muslim. In India and in Pakistan.'

Bim laughed. 'Sometimes you sound exactly like Bakul.'

Tara stopped, hurt. Bim had always had this faculty of cutting her short, hurting her, and not even knowing.

But this time, it seemed, she did know. She touched Tara's elbow lightly. 'Of course you must – occasionally – when you've been married so long,' she explained good-humouredly and even apologetically.

'But wouldn't you agree?' Tara said coldly.

'Yes, yes, you are perfectly right, Tara – it was so for all of us – for the whole family, and for everyone we knew, here in this neighbourhood. Nineteen forty-seven. That summer. We could see the fires burning in the city every night –'

Tara shuddered. 'I hate to think about it.'

'Why? It was the great event of our lives – of our youth. What would our youth have been without it to round it off in such a definite and dramatic way?'

'I was glad when it was over,' Tara's voice trembled with the passion she was always obliged to conceal. 'I'm so glad it is over and we can never be young again.'

'Young?' said Bim wonderingly, and as they were now near the veranda, she sank down on the steps where the quisqualis creeper threw its bunches of inky shadow on the white-washed steps, and sat there hugging her knees. Tara leaned against the pillar beside her, staring out and up at the stars that seemed to be swinging lower and lower as the night grew stiller. They made her deeply uneasy – they seemed so many milestones to mark the long distances, the dark distances that stretched and stretched beyond human knowledge and beyond human imagination. She huddled against the pillar, hugging it with one arm, like a child.

'Youth?' said Bim, her head sinking as if with sleep, or sorrow. 'Yes, I am glad, too, it is over – I never wish it back. Terrible, what it does to one – what it did to us – and one is too young to know how to cope, how to deal with that first terrible flood of life. One just goes under – it sweeps one along – and how many years and years it is before one can stand up to it, make a stand against it –' she shook her head sleepily. 'I never wish it back. I would never be young again for anything.'

An invisible cricket by her feet at that moment began to weep inconsolably.

Margaret Drabble

extract from

The Millstone

Rosamund Stacey, Cambridge arts graduate in her twenties, has survived the distant hostilities of her family, the demands of her predatory flat-mate and the attentions of Roger and George, neither of whom she really loves. Then the unexpected happens. She discovers that she is pregnant and allows her deepest emotions to surface for the first time.

My baby was due in early March: I amused myself by trying to finish my thesis before my baby. It was in fact somewhat of a hopeless task, as I was not even expected to finish it before the following Christmas, but I have always been a quick worker and now I had very little else to distract me. As the winter wore on, and spring set in, I felt less and less like going out, even as far as to the British Museum, and I organized myself so that I could do a good deal of work at home. It was less entertaining than working in the library, but I could at least get on with it. It was all shaping up quite nicely: my director of studies, a don in Cambridge, had approved my synopsis, rough draft, first chapter, and other indications of the final product, and had been most encouraging. I felt happy about it; I had got it all into shape in my head and knew more or less exactly what I was going to say and what ground I had to cover. Then, towards the end of January, I began to flag. Although I would not admit it, I felt at times too tired to read. I ate more and more iron pills but they did not seem to have much effect. In the end I decided that I had merely got stale through too much concentration on too few things, and that I ought to branch out a little. It was, however, impossible to find anything amusing to do; I did not enjoy walking any more, public transport was a continual trial, I could not sit comfortably through a full-length picture, and I could not eat anything interesting without suffering for it afterwards. I felt thoroughly annoyed; I could understand, in this condition, why women are, as they certainly are, such perpetual complaining bores. I was discussing my problem with Lydia one evening; she suggested all sorts of occupations, like knitting, or rug-making, or basket-work, or weaving, but I rejected all these pseudo-useful employments with contempt. Then she said, finally, why don't you do jigsaw puzzles; and they were what I took up.

One can, if one tries, buy extremely complicated jigsaw puzzles with a thousand interlocking pieces, and pictures by old masters, or of ships at sea, and heaven knows what: also puzzles in the shape of maps of Europe, square puzzles, circular puzzles, star-shaped puzzles, reversible puzzles, anything one can imagine in the way of puzzles. I became addicted and would spend hours over them; it was a soothing, time-consuming process, and when I went to bed I would dream not of George, nor of babies locked away from me where I couldn't feed them, nor even of childbirth, but of pieces of blue sky edged with bits of tree, or small blue irregular shapes composing the cloak of the Virgin Mary. Lydia had an irritating habit of coming in at the end of an evening, just when I had mastered the most difficult part of a puzzle, and putting in all the easy obvious middle pieces; I got very annoyed with her. As a therapy, it worked extremely well; I found I could write my book and do a puzzle for alternate hours without getting unduly bored by either.

I suppose the end of anyone's first pregnancy is frightening. I cannot quite remember how frightened I was, because it is one of the horrible tricks of nature to make one forget instantly after childbirth all that one had feared and suffered, presumably so that one will carry on gaily with the next. In the same way one will protect with the utmost care an unborn child which one does not want and would prefer to lose, and which indeed as in my case may even have taken some steps, however feeble and ill-informed, towards losing; in January, after a party, I slipped on the stairs going down from a friend's flat and would certainly have fallen had I been in anything like my normal state of balance: but as it was I clutched and hung on to the banisters like grim death and got away with a mere twisted ankle. And thus, unwillingly, I have forgotten how worried I must have been, because it now seems so long ago and to have so little importance. I was worried partly through ignorance, as I had deliberately found nothing out about the subject at all, and had steered clear of all natural childbirth classes, film strips of deliveries, and helpful diagrams, convinced that I had only to go near a natural childbirth class in order to call down upon myself the most phenomenally unnatural birth of all time. There was no point in tempting providence, I thought; one might as well expect the worst as one would probably get it anyway.

I remember, however, the night before it was born with some clarity. It was not due for another week so I was not particularly worried; I boiled myself a couple of eggs, then went to eat them in the sitting-room at about half past eight, and got out my typewriter at the same time in order to read over the last page of thesis that I had left inside it. When I opened the typewriter, however, it was not a page of discussion on Drayton's use of irony that met my eyes, but a page of something quite different, and not written by me at all. I knocked the top off my egg and started to read it, assuming, and rightly, that it was something of Lydia's; she had been complaining for weeks that her machine was going wrong. It was indeed something of Lydia's; it was a page from her next novel, which she had started shortly after moving in with me and which she had been working on, intermittently, ever since. I read the page with fascinated alarm; it was in the first person, and it was about a girl having an illegitimate baby. When I had finished the page, I abandoned my eggs and went into Lydia's bedroom to look for more. I found it, in a heap of loose leaves by her bed, and carried it back with me and sat down on the settee and started to read it.

I read the whole lot straight off, or what there was of it; it was not finished. It was nothing more nor less than my life story, with a few minor alterations here and there, and a few interesting false assumptions amongst the alterations. Clearly Lydia, for instance, had always assumed that Joe was the father of the child; there was an interesting though cleverly concealed portrait of Joe, and an absorbing scene in which the character that was me quarrelled violently with him and left him for ever. Her motives for this I thought a little far-fetched; she had apparently discovered that he was still sleeping with his mislaid wife, whom she had had the privilege of meeting, which was more than I had. This discovery had enraged her to such an extent that she had broken with him and refused any financial assistance from him. She had been planning to have the child only on the assumption that she and the Joe-character would live together and bring it up between them. Far-fetched as the theory seemed with regard to me, who did not know what the word jealousy meant, and indeed suffered from its opposite, if it has one, it certainly explained a possible line of conduct: it amused me to think of Lydia sitting there racking her brains trying to work out why I was having the child, and why I hadn't got rid of it. She had been inefficient enough on that score herself, by her own account, but then one never suspects that others share one's own degree of incompetence in such matters.

At first, for the first few chapters, I flattered myself that I emerged rather well – independent, strong-willed, and very worldly and *au fait* with sexual problems. An attractive girl, I thought. But then, as the chapters wore on, I began to have my doubts. Like myself, the character was engaged in academic research, an activity which Lydia appeared to regard with thorough contempt: she had invented for me a peculiarly meaningless and abstruse research subject, in fact none less than the ill-famed Henryson. I remembered I had told Lydia about my

Indian in some detail and she had laughed with me about him. I could not, however, be too indignant as I have always been aware that the Elizabethans, except for Shakespeare, are somewhat of a luxury subject, unlike nineteenth-century novelists or prolific Augustan poets. However, I did object very strongly to the way, subtle enough technically, that she hinted that the Rosamund character's obsession with scholarly detail and discovery was nothing more nor less than an escape route, an attempt to evade the personal crises of her life and the realities of life in general. She drew a very persuasive picture of the academic ivory tower; whenever anything unpleasant happened to this character, as in the course of the extant ten chapters was too frequently the case, she would retire to bed or the British Museum with a pile of books, as others retire perhaps with a bottle of gin. There was also a long discussion on this very topic between the girl and a friend of hers, who presumably represented vitality, modernity, honesty and so on; I was not malicious enough to consider this a self-portrait of Lydia, for it clearly was not, as the girlfriend in question was not like anyone I have ever met. She accused the me-character of having a jigsaw puzzle mind, a nasty crack in the circumstances I thought; she herself was busy frittering her life away in vital pursuits like serving in a theatre bar, working on a magazine, and having an affair with a television producer.

All in all, by the time I had finished this work I was both annoyed and upset. I did not think this view of scholarship at all justifiable; I could not produce my reasons for believing in its value, but in a way I was all the surer for that, for I knew it for a fact. Scholarship is a skill and I am good at it, and even if one rated it no higher than that it is still worth doing. Whether I used it as an escape or not was a different matter, and did not seem to me to be as relevant. It was work, and I did it, and reasons did not come into it; *il faut cultiver notre jardin,* as Voltaire so admirably said. Apart, however, from being annoyed by this attack on my livelihood, I was also very annoyed by the thought that Lydia had been living in my house for nothing and writing all this about me without saying a word. She had compared herself once to a spider, an image not wholly new, drawing material from its own entrails, but this seemed to me to be a somewhat more parasitic pursuit.

After re-reading certain passages, I put the whole lot back by her bed, including the sheet that had been in my typewriter; I had no intention of saying anything to her but I thought it possible she might remember where she had left it and suffer from her own conclusions. Then I went back and sat down by the fire and switched on the radio, just in time to hear George talking about next Sunday's concert. I thought how odd it was that I had bumped into Clare at Selfridge's but had not even set eyes in the last eight months on George. I switched off again when he had finished announcing as my thoughts kept reverting to Lydia, with decreasing anger. After all, I thought, she had been making herself very useful recently, doing all the heavy shopping, even the odd few minutes' Hoovering, and had, moreover, acquired through a friend of hers a woman who had volunteered to come in and mind the baby two days a week when I was well enough to go out. In fact, lately I had even come to think myself slightly in her debt, despite the disadvantageous rent situation: and here, at least, in those pages of typescript had been proof that I was still the donor, she still the recipient. More than ever now I had the upper hand; she had got her money's worth out of me. Do not think I resented this: on the contrary, looking at our relationship in this light, I felt much happier, for I saw that we had maintained a basis of mutual profit. Having arrived at this conclusion, I thought I would go to bed, and when I got up I found I was suffering from distinct pains in the back.

Once I noticed that I was feeling them, I realized that

I had been feeling them for quite a long time without paying them much attention. I instantly took them to be what, in fact, they were and was overcome with panic as it seemed such an inconvenient time to have to disturb hospital and ambulance men. It was a quarter past eleven, a time for all good citizens to be asleep. I was in a dilemma: the pains were not yet at all bad and I could clearly hang on at home for some time, but on the other hand the longer I waited the more inconvenient would grow the hour and the more irritable the nurses, midwives and ambulance people that I would have to encounter. I went to the bedroom and got out my little leaflet of instructions which told me to time the contractions and to ring the hospital when they became regular and more frequent than once every quarter of an hour. So I started to time them, and found to my alarm that they were perfectly regular and occurring once every three minutes. At half past eleven I rang the hospital, who told me to take an aspirin or two and ring the ambulance. So I did. Then I got out my suitcase, prepacked to order, put on my coat and waited. The men arrived within ten minutes, at exactly the same moment as Lydia who was returning home rather gay after a party. When she discovered my state and destination, she flung her arms around me, kissed me several times, and accompanied me downstairs in the lift, telling me en route about the party and how she had met Joe Hurt there, and how they had talked about me, and he had yet another book finished, and how fond of me he was, and how concerned, and how perhaps she quite liked him after all, and she would let him know instantly about the baby, whatever it turned out to be: the ambulance men and I listened to her story in solid quiet, but I was glad to have her there to stop my having to say things like It's a fine night, isn't it, or Sorry to disturb you at this hour, to these two silent men. Lydia looked rather weird, as her hair was coming down and she had lipstick all over one cheek: also she was wearing a strange long green lace dress and over it her usual grey mackintosh. She had no other coat. Her preoccupation with the subject of Joe I found illuminating, and I was glad to be able to put together, on new evidence, an attitude of hers that I had never understood.

I was glad too to be going from so good an address. I felt that by it alone I had bought a little deference and, sure enough, at the bottom of the stairs one of the men turned to Lydia and said, 'Would you like to come along, Miss, to see your friend in?' He was rather taken by her, I could see, and her eyes too lit up at the prospect of so strange an excursion, but I said firmly that I would be better off on my own, it was only just down the road, I couldn't dream of disturbing her; what she needed was a good sleep. I did not fancy the idea of the details of my labour becoming available to her professional curiosity: she could have a baby herself, I thought, if she really wanted to know what it was like. She stood on the pavement and waved goodbye, shouting good luck after me as the ambulance drew away; she was an odd and charming sight in her strangely tiered garments.

On the way to the hospital I thought how unnerving it is, suddenly to see oneself for a moment as others see one, like a glimpse of unexpected profile in an unfamiliar combination of mirrors. I think I know myself better than anyone can know me, and I think this even in cold blood, for too much knowing is my vice; and yet one cannot account for the angles of others. Once at a party I met a boy whom I had known at school, and not seen since; we both had known that the other would be present and I had recognized him at once, but when we met and talked he confessed that when looking out for me he had taken another girl to be me. I asked him which, and he had pointed through the crowd at a tall, skinny girl with too-neat hair and a shut, frightened face: I was amazed and oddly hurt by his near-mistake, for she was so utterly unlike me, so devoid of any of my qualities or defects. And yet she was the same height, the same colouring, and, looking back, I could see that there was enough in me at sixteen that could have developed that way and that in six years sixteen-year-old Rosamund Stacey might well have been her and not me.

When we arrived at the hospital, I thought with some relief that this would be my last visit, and that at the least the clinic was over with all its eroding grind. I climbed out of the ambulance and started off down the corridor, but one of the men stopped me and said that I had to go in a wheelchair. What do you mean, I said, I can walk.

'You're not allowed to walk,' he said.

'Why ever not?' I asked, not because I objected to going in a wheelchair, but because I couldn't see why not. 'I walked at the other end,' I said.

'Ah yes,' said the man, 'but at this end you're not allowed to. Come along now, you're our responsibility now, we can't allow you to walk, I'm afraid.'

So I sat down, succumbing to his threat that he would lose his job if I didn't, and they wheeled me off down countless corridors, up in a lift, down a floor in another one, and into a large room where I was told to get up and go and sign a list. Here, it seemed, I was allowed to walk. I had been expecting to see a few familiar faces, such as the thin little Yorkshire nurse, the fat Irish one, or even the smart red-haired midwife; I had, luckily in the event, no grandiose expectations of seeing any doctors or gynaecologists. But there was not a face I recognized in sight: a whole new army of people appeared to have taken over, who presumably came out only at night. I was a little disappointed; the other faces had become almost endeared by familiarity. I signed my name on the relevant register; the nurse in charge of it looked up and said, 'Well, you're the only one in tonight, we *were* having a quiet night,' and I smiled feebly, unsure whether she was expressing pleasure or annoyance at having something to do.

Then they took me off to another room and took away all my clothes and put me in a hospital nightgown and asked me how often my contractions were. When I told them, they said Nonsense, but when they investigated they naturally enough found me to be right. Then they did various other unpleasant and compulsory things, found me my book when I asked for it, and left me to it, telling me to ring if I wanted anything. I lay there on this hard high bed for half an hour, trying to read, and then I rang the bell and asked if they couldn't do something about it. Not yet, they said, and off they went. I lay there for another ten minutes and then a quite different nurse came in and said I had to move, somebody else had to have my bed. I lay there and looked at her and said how. Don't you feel like walking, she said, and I said Oh, all right, as she seemed to expect me to, and I heaved myself down off this mountainously high iron bedstead and followed her down a corridor and into another room, where she helped me on to an equally high identical bed. Then I asked once more, politely, if they couldn't do something about it, and she said Oh yes, of course, wasn't it time I had some pethidine, and she would go and find someone to give me an injection.

A quarter of an hour later about five nurses arrived with the pethidine, which they administered; then they all sat in a row in the corridor outside and started to talk about their boyfriends. I listened to their conversation, trying to distract myself from sensations that did not seem quite reasonable or endurable, and after a while the drug began to work: the pain did not diminish but my resistance to it disappeared, and every two minutes regularly it flowed through me as though I were some other person, and as though I myself, what was left of me, was watching this swell and ebb from many miles away. It was no longer personal and therefore bearable; I just lay there and let it happen, and the voices of the five girls came to me very clearly and purely, the syntax and connections of their dialogue illuminated by a strange pale warm light. One of them started off by telling the others about some character called Frank, against whom the others had apparently been warning her for some time, for when she described the way in which he had squeezed her knee in the cinema, the others began to exclaim with predestined admiring indignation.

'Honestly, I *told* you what he was like,' one of them said. 'I *told* you what he'd be up to, didn't I? You should have heard what Elaine said about him after the Christmas Ball.'

'Elaine asks for it,' said another voice, and they all giggled, and somebody else said, 'Well, you don't exactly go out of your way to avoid it yourself, do you? I mean to say, what *about* that dress you had on the other day? If that wasn't a topless dress, I'd like to know what is.'

'Do you know *what*,' said the owner of the dress, 'happened to me last time I was wearing it? I had to dash home, it was a Thursday and I hadn't got a late leave, and I *just* got to the corner of Charles Street at eleven-thirty, and I had to run like anything, and anyway I just got to the door as Bessie was locking up and I got in all right, but who do you think I met on the other side but Mrs Sammy Spillikins, all in her dressing-gown and slippers, and she gave me such a look and said in that voice of hers, you know what she sounds like, Well, well, well, Miss Ellis, she said, you do cut things rather fine, don't you? Are you in the habit of leaving things to the last moment like this? Mean old cow, I'd like to know what it's got to do with her. And she said she wanted a word, and she followed me all the way up to my room, just on the pretext of asking me some question about what Dr Cohen asked Gillian to do about the new radiator in the waiting room, and she stayed so long I had to take my coat off, and she kept looking and looking at me, and when she left do you know what she said? She said, In my day, with a dress like that, we used to wear modesty vests.'

Once more they all giggled merrily, and then someone volunteered the information that however old Sammy Spillikins looked, she was really only forty-two, which she had on the best of authority, and somebody else described, though as a matter of fact inaccurately, what a modesty vest was, when one of the gathering claimed not to know.

'How *disgusting*,' the ignorant one said vehemently when enlightened.

They then told some more anecdotes about their evidently circumscribed love lives before moving on to discuss their trade. They began mildly enough by inquiring how many had been born the night before, and what had happened to the little premature one that was failing earlier in the evening, but after a while the tone really became too extreme for my possible comfort; they described cases of women who had lain in labour for unbelievable lengths of time, of one who had screamed solidly for three hours, of a black woman who had scratched a nurse's face when she tried to give her an enema, of a white woman who had sworn at one of the black nurses and told her to get out, she wasn't having her filthy hands on her nice clean new baby. One of them said *en passant*, 'I'll be really glad to get out of this ward. I don't really mind the babies, but the mothers are enough to give anyone the creeps.' Then one of them started to recount in vivid detail the story of a woman whose labour she had attended a month earlier, who had died because they discovered at the last moment that this that and the other hadn't been properly dealt with; 'it was awful,' this girl said, 'the way they kept on telling her it was all fine, and I could see them getting bluer and bluer, you know how they look when anything really bad starts up.' At this I could take it no longer, and I heard my voice yell, from a long way away, 'Oh, for God's sake, pack it in, can't you?'

I don't think they caught what I said despite my

unnatural loudness of tone, but two of them came bustling in and said, 'What was that, did you call, how are you getting on?'

'I think this drug thing must be wearing off,' I said mildly, 'because it seems to be getting worse and worse, can you give me something else please, quick?'

'Oh no!' they said, 'not yet, you've a long time to go yet, we have to leave something to give you later on.'

'Oh,' I said feebly, 'what a pity.'

'Never mind,' they said, 'you're coming along nicely,' and they turned and went back to their row of seats outside and had just resumed their conversation, though in more muffled tones, when I heard myself start to moan rather violently, and they all came rushing back and within five minutes my child was born.

Right up to the very last minute, through sensations which though unbelievably violent were now no longer painful but indeed almost a promise of pleasure, I could hear them arguing among themselves, all of them; one had been dispatched for the midwife, one was looking for the gas and air, one was asking the others why they hadn't believed what I said, and another, while delivering the baby, had taken upon herself the task of calmer and soother of my nerves.

'That's all right,' she kept saying, 'that's fine, you're coming along fine. Oh, do try not to push.'

There was more panic in her smooth tones than in me; I felt all right now, I felt fine. The child was born in a great rush and hurry, quite uncontrolled and undelivered; they told me afterwards that they only just caught her, and I felt her fall from me and instantly sat up and opened my eyes, and they said, 'It's a girl, it's a lovely little girl.'

They told me to lie down again, and I lay down, asking if the baby was all right, expecting suddenly I don't know what, missing arms and fingers, and they said she was all right; so I lay there, happy that it was over, not expecting they would let me see her, and then I heard her cry, a strange loud sobbing cry. The midwife had by now arrived, all smiles and starch, and actually apologized for not having been there. 'It was quite a case,' she said, 'of too many cooks spoil the broth, you know, but you certainly managed to do all right without me, didn't you?' All the nurses too were suddenly humanized; they clustered round, helping to wash me and straighten me out, and telling me how unbelievably quick I'd been, and how I should have made more fuss, and that it was only half past two, and what was I going to call the baby. This last question was hastily silenced by the midwife, who presumably assumed the child would not be mine for long, but I did not care. I felt remarkably well, a usual reaction I believe on such occasions, and I could have got up and walked away. After ten minutes or so, when I had been returned to my own nightdress, a garment covered in Mexican embroidery which Beatrice had sent specially for the occasion, and which drew screams of admiration from the girls, the midwife asked me if I would like to see the child. 'Please,' I said gratefully, and she went away and came back with my daughter wrapped up in a small grey bloodstained blanket, and with a ticket saying Stacey round her ankle. She put her in my arms and I sat there looking at her, and her great wide blue eyes looked at me with seeming recognition, and what I felt it is pointless to try to describe. Love, I suppose one might call it, and the first of my life.

Daphne Du Maurier

The Birds

On December the third the wind changed overnight and it was winter. Until then the autumn had been mellow, soft. The leaves had lingered on the trees, golden red, and the hedgerows were still green. The earth was rich where the plough had turned it.

Nat Hocken, because of a wartime disability, had a pension and did not work full-time at the farm. He worked three days a week, and they gave him the lighter jobs: hedging, thatching, repairs to the farm buildings.

Although he was married, with children, his was a solitary disposition; he liked best to work alone. It pleased him when he was given a bank to build up, or a gate to mend at the far end of the peninsula, where the sea surrounded the farm land on either side. Then, at midday, he would pause and eat the pasty that his wife had baked for him, and sitting on the cliff's edge would watch the birds. Autumn was best for this, better than spring. In spring the birds flew inland, purposeful, intent; they knew where they were bound, the rhythm and ritual of their life brooked no delay. In autumn those that had not migrated overseas but remained to pass the winter were caught up in the same driving urge, but because migration was denied them followed a pattern of their own. Great flocks of them came to the peninsula, restless, uneasy, spending themselves in motion; now wheeling, circling in the sky, now settling to feed on the rich new-turned soil, but even when they fed it was as though they did so without hunger, without desire. Restlessness drove them to the skies again.

Black and white, jackdaw and gull, mingled in strange partnership, seeking some sort of liberation, never satisfied, never still. Flocks of starlings, rustling like silk, flew to fresh pasture, driven by the same necessity of movement, and the smaller birds, the finches and the larks, scattered from tree to hedge as if compelled.

Nat watched them, and he watched the sea-birds too. Down in the bay they waited for the tide. They had more patience. Oyster-catchers, redshank, sanderling and curlew watched by the water's edge; as the slow sea sucked at the shore and then withdrew, leaving the strip of seaweed bare and the shingle churned, the sea-birds raced and ran upon the beaches. Then that same impulse to flight seized upon them too. Crying, whistling, calling, they skimmed the placid sea and left the shore. Make haste, make speed, hurry and begone; yet where, and to what purpose? The restless urge of autumn, unsatisfying, sad, had put a spell upon them and they must flock, and wheel, and cry; they must spill themselves of motion before winter came.

Perhaps, thought Nat, munching his pasty by the cliff's edge, a message comes to the birds in autumn, like a warning. Winter is coming. Many of them perish. And like people who, apprehensive of death before their time, drive themselves to work or folly, the birds do likewise.

The birds had been more restless than ever this fall of the year, the agitation more marked because the days were still. As the tractor traced its path up and down the western hills, the figure of the farmer silhouetted on the driving-seat, the whole machine and the man upon it would be lost momentarily in the great cloud of wheeling, crying birds. There were many more than usual, Nat was sure of this. Always, in autumn, they followed the plough, but not in great flocks like these, nor with such clamour.

Nat remarked upon it, when hedging was finished for

the day. 'Yes,' said the farmer, 'there are more birds about than usual; I've noticed it too. And daring some of them, taking no notice of the tractor. One or two gulls came so close to my head this afternoon I thought they'd knock my cap off! As it was, I could scarcely see what I was doing, when they were overhead and I had the sun in my eyes. I have a notion the weather will change. It will be a hard winter. That's why the birds are restless.'

Nat, tramping home across the fields and down the lane to his cottage, saw the birds still flocking over the western hills, in the last glow of the sun. No wind, and the grey sea calm and full. Campion in bloom yet in the hedges, and the air mild. The farmer was right, though, and it was that night the weather turned. Nat's bedroom faced east. He woke just after two and heard the wind in the chimney. Not the storm and bluster of a sou' westerly gale, bringing the rain, but east wind, cold and dry. It sounded hollow in the chimney, and a loose slate rattled on the roof. Nat listened, and he could hear the sea roaring in the bay. Even the air in the small bedroom had turned chill: a draught came under the skirting of the door, blowing upon the bed. Nat drew the blanket round him, leant closer to the back of his sleeping wife, and stayed wakeful, watchful, aware of misgiving without cause.

Then he heard the tapping on the window. There was no creeper on the cottage walls to break loose and scratch upon the pane. He listened, and the tapping continued until, irritated by the sound, Nat got out of bed and went to the window. He opened it, and as he did so something brushed his hand, jabbing at his knuckles, grazing the skin. Then he saw the flutter of the wings and it was gone, over the roof, behind the cottage.

It was a bird, what kind of bird he could not tell. The wind must have driven it to shelter on the sill.

He shut the window and went back to bed, but feeling his knuckles wet put his mouth to the scratch. The bird had drawn blood. Frightened, he supposed, and bewildered, the bird, seeking shelter, had stabbed at him in the darkness. Once more he settled himself to sleep.

Presently the tapping came again, this time more forceful, more insistent, and now his wife woke at the sound, and turning in the bed said to him, 'See to the window, Nat, it's rattling.'

'I've already seen to it,' he told her, 'there's some bird there, trying to get in. Can't you hear the wind? It's blowing from the east, driving the birds to shelter.'

'Send them away,' she said, 'I can't sleep with that noise.'

He went to the window for the second time, and now when he opened it there was not one bird upon the sill but half a dozen; they flew straight into his face, attacking him.

He shouted, striking out at them with his arms, scattering them; like the first one, they flew over the roof and disappeared. Quickly he let the window fall and latched it.

'Did you hear that?' he said. 'They went for me. Tried to peck my eyes.' He stood by the window, peering into the darkness, and could see nothing. His wife, heavy with sleep, murmured from the bed.

'I'm not making it up,' he said, angry at her suggestion. 'I tell you the birds were on the sill, trying to get into the room.'

Suddenly a frightened cry came from the room across the passage where the children slept.

'It's Jill,' said his wife, roused at the sound, sitting up in bed. 'Go to her, see what's the matter.'

Nat lit the candle, but when he opened the bedroom door to cross the passage the draught blew out the flame.

There came a second cry of terror, this time from both children, and stumbling into their room he felt the beating of wings about him in the darkness. The window was wide open. Through it came the birds, hitting first the ceiling and the walls, then swerving in mid-flight, turning to the children in their beds.

'It's all right, I'm here,' shouted Nat, and the children flung themselves, screaming, upon him, while in the darkness the birds rose and dived and came for him again.

'What is it, Nat, what's happened?' his wife called from the further bedroom, and swiftly he pushed the children through the door to the passage and shut it upon them, so that he was alone now, in their bedroom, with the birds.

He seized a blanket from the nearest bed, and using it as a weapon flung it to right and left about him in the air. He felt the thud of bodies, heard the fluttering of wings, but they were not yet defeated, for again and again they returned to the assault, jabbing his hands, his head, the little stabbing beaks sharp as a pointed fork. The blanket became a weapon of defence; he wound it about his head, and then in greater darkness beat at the birds with his bare hands. He dared not stumble to the door and open it, lest in doing so the birds should follow him.

How long he fought with them in the darkness he could not tell, but at last the beating of the wings about him lessened and then withdrew, and through the density of the blanket he was aware of light. He waited, listened; there was no sound except the fretful crying of one of the children from the bedroom beyond. The fluttering, the whirring of the wings had ceased.

He took the blanket from his head and stared about him. The cold grey morning light exposed the room. Dawn, and the open window, had called the living birds; the dead lay on the floor. Nat gazed at the little corpses, shocked and horrified. They were all small birds, none of any size; there must have been fifty of them lying there upon the floor. There were robins, finches, sparrows, blue tits, larks and bramblings, birds that by nature's law kept to their own flock and their own territory, and now, joining one with another in their urge for battle, had destroyed themselves against the bedroom walls, or in the strife had been destroyed by him. Some had lost feathers in the fight, others had blood, his blood, upon their beaks.

Sickened, Nat went to the window and stared out across his patch of garden to the fields.

It was bitter cold, and the ground had all the hard black look of frost. Not white frost, to shine in the morning sun, but the black frost that the east wind brings. The sea, fiercer now with the turning tide, white-capped and steep, broke harshly in the bay. Of the birds there was no sign. Not a sparrow chattered in the hedge beyond the garden gate, no early missel-thrush or blackbird pecked on the grass for worms. There was no sound at all but the east wind and the sea.

Nat shut the window and the door of the small bedroom, and went back across the passage to his own. His wife sat up in bed, one child asleep beside her, the smaller in her arms, his face bandaged. The curtains were tightly drawn across the window, the candles lit. Her face looked garish in the yellow light. She shook her head for silence.

'He's sleeping now,' she whispered, 'but only just. Something must have cut him, there was blood at the corner of his eyes. Jill said it was the birds. She said she woke up, and the birds were in the room.'

His wife looked up at Nat, searching his face for confirmation. She looked terrified, bewildered, and he did not want her to know that he was also shaken, dazed almost, by the events of the past few hours.

'There are birds in there,' he said, 'dead birds, nearly fifty of them. Robins, wrens, all the little birds from hereabouts. It's as though a madness seized them, with the east wind.' He sat down on the bed beside his wife, and held her hand. 'It's the weather,' he said, 'it must be that, it's the hard weather. They aren't the birds, maybe, from here around. They've been driven down, from up country.'

'But Nat,' whispered his wife, 'it's only this night that

the weather turned. There's been no snow to drive them. And they can't be hungry yet. There's food for them, out there, in the fields.'

'It's the weather,' repeated Nat. 'I tell you, it's the weather.'

His face too was drawn and tired, like hers. They stared at one another for a while without speaking.

'I'll go downstairs and make a cup of tea,' he said.

The sight of the kitchen reassured him. The cups and saucers, neatly stacked upon the dresser, the table and chairs, his wife's roll of knitting on her basket chair, the children's toys in a corner cupboard.

He knelt down, raked out the old embers and relit the fire. The glowing sticks brought normality, the steaming kettle and the brown teapot comfort and security. He drank his tea, carried a cup up to his wife. Then he washed in the scullery, and, putting on his boots, opened the back door.

The sky was hard and leaden, and the brown hills that had gleamed in the sun the day before looked dark and bare. The east wind, like a razor, stripped the trees, and the leaves, crackling and dry, shivered and scattered with the wind's blast. Nat stubbed the earth with his boot. It was frozen hard. He had never known a change so swift and sudden. Black winter had descended in a single night.

The children were awake now. Jill was chattering upstairs and young Johnny crying once again. Nat heard his wife's voice, soothing, comforting. Presently they came down. He had breakfast ready for them, and the routine of the day began.

'Did you drive away the birds?' asked Jill, restored to calm because of the kitchen fire, because of day, because of breakfast.

'Yes, they've all gone now,' said Nat. 'It was the east wind brought them in. They were frightened and lost, they wanted shelter.'

'They tried to peck us,' said Jill. 'They went for Johnny's eyes.'

'Fright made them do that,' said Nat. 'They didn't know where they were, in the dark bedroom.'

'I hope they won't come again,' said Jill. 'Perhaps if we put bread for them outside the window they will eat that and fly away.'

She finished her breakfast and then went for her coat and hood, her school books and her satchel. Nat said nothing, but his wife looked at him across the table. A silent message passed between them.

'I'll walk with her to the bus,' he said. 'I don't go to the farm today.'

And while the child was washing in the scullery he said to his wife, 'Keep all the windows closed, and the doors too. Just to be on the safe side. I'll go to the farm. Find out if they heard anything in the night.' Then he walked with his small daughter up the lane. She seemed to have forgotten her experience of the night before. She danced ahead of him, chasing the leaves, her face whipped with the cold and rosy under the pixie hood.

'Is it going to snow, Dad?' she said. 'It's cold enough.'

He glanced up at the bleak sky, felt the wind tear at his shoulders.

'No,' he said, 'it's not going to snow. This is a black winter, not a white one.'

All the while he searched the hedgerows for the birds, glanced over the top of them to the fields beyond, looked to the small wood above the farm where the rooks and jackdaws gathered. He saw none.

The other children waited by the bus stop, muffled, hooded like Jill, the faces white and pinched with cold.

Jill ran to them, waving. 'My dad says it won't snow,' she called, 'it's going to be a black winter.'

She said nothing of the birds. She began to push and struggle with another little girl. The bus came ambling up the hill. Nat saw her on to it, then turned and walked back towards the farm. It was not his day for work, but he wanted to satisfy himself that all was well. Jim, the cowman, was clattering in the yard.

'Boss around?' asked Nat.

'Gone to market,' said Jim. 'It's Tuesday, isn't it?'

He clumped off round the corner of a shed. He had no time for Nat. Nat was said to be superior. Read books, and the like. Nat had forgotten it was Tuesday. This showed how the events of the preceding night had shaken him. He went to the back door of the farmhouse and heard Mrs Trigg singing in the kitchen, the wireless making a background to her song.

'Are you there, missus?' called out Nat.

She came to the door, beaming, broad, a good-tempered woman.

'Hullo, Mr Hocken,' she said. 'Can you tell me where this cold is coming from? Is it Russia? I've never seen such a change. And it's going on, the wireless says. Something to do with the Arctic circle.'

'We didn't turn on the wireless this morning,' said Nat. 'Fact is, we had trouble in the night.'

'Kiddies poorly?'

'No . . .' He hardly knew how to explain it. Now, in daylight, the battle of the birds would sound absurd.

He tried to tell Mrs Trigg what had happened, but he could see from her eyes that she thought his story was the result of a nightmare.

'Sure they were real birds,' she said, smiling, 'with proper feathers and all? Not the funny-shaped kind, that the men see after closing hours on a Saturday night?'

'Mrs Trigg,' he said, 'there are fifty dead birds, robins, wrens and such, lying low on the floor of the children's bedroom. They went for me; they tried to go for young Johnny's eyes.'

Mrs Trigg stared at him doubtfully.

'Well there, now,' she answered, 'I suppose the weather brought them. Once in the bedroom, they wouldn't know where they were to. Foreign birds maybe, from that Arctic circle.'

'No,' said Nat, 'they were the birds you see about here every day.'

'Funny thing,' said Mrs Trigg, 'no explaining it, really. You ought to write up and ask the *Guardian*. They'd have some answer for it. Well, I must be getting on.'

She nodded, smiled, and went back into the kitchen.

Nat, dissatisfied, turned to the farm-gate. Had it not been for those corpses on the bedroom floor, which he must now collect and bury somewhere, he would have considered the tale exaggeration too.

Jim was standing by the gate.

'Had any trouble with the birds?' asked Nat.

'Birds? What birds?'

'We got them up our place last night. Scores of them, came in the children's bedroom. Quite savage they were.'

'Oh?' It took time for anything to penetrate Jim's head. 'Never heard of birds acting savage,' he said at length. 'They get tame, like, sometimes. I've seen them come to the windows for crumbs.'

'These birds last night weren't tame.'

'No? Cold maybe. Hungry. You put out some crumbs.'

Jim was no more interested than Mrs Trigg had been. It was, Nat thought, like air-raids in the war. No one down this end of the country knew what the Plymouth folk had seen and suffered. You had to endure something yourself before it touched you. He walked back along the lane and crossed the stile to his cottage. He found his wife in the kitchen with young Johnnie.

'See anyone?' she asked.

'Mrs Trigg and Jim,' he answered. 'I don't think they believed me. Anyway, nothing wrong up there.'

'You might take the birds away,' she said. 'I daren't go into the room to make the beds until you do. I'm scared.'

'Nothing to scare you now,' said Nat. 'They're dead, aren't they?'

He went up with a sack and dropped the stiff bodies into it, one by one. Yes, there were fifty of them, all told. Just the ordinary common birds of the hedgerow, nothing as large even as a thrush. It must have been fright that made them act the way they did. Blue tits, wrens, it was incredible to think of the power of their small beaks, jabbing at his face and hands the night before. He took the sack out into the garden and was faced now with a fresh problem. The ground was too hard to dig. It was frozen solid, yet no snow had fallen, nothing had happened in the past hours but the coming of the east wind. It was unnatural, queer. The weather prophets must be right. The change was something connected with the Arctic circle.

The wind seemed to cut him to the bone as he stood there, uncertainly, holding the sack. He could see the white-capped seas breaking down under in the bay. He decided to take the birds to the shore and bury them.

When he reached the beach below the headland he could scarcely stand, the force of the east wind was so strong. It hurt to draw breath, and his bare hands were blue. Never had he known such cold, not in all the bad winters he could remember. It was low tide. He crunched his way over the shingle to the softer sand and then, his back to the wind, ground a pit in the sand with his heel. He meant to drop the birds into it, but as he opened up the sack the force of the wind carried them, lifted them, as though in flight again, and they were blown away from him along the beach, tossed like feathers, spread and scattered, the bodies of the fifty frozen birds. There was something ugly in the sight. He did not like it. The dead birds were swept away from him by the wind.

'The tide will take them when it turns,' he said to himself.

He looked out to sea and watched the crested breakers, combing green. They rose stiffly, curled, and broke again, and because it was ebb tide the roar was distant, more remote, lacking the sound and thunder of the flood.

Then he saw them. The gulls. Out there, riding the seas.

What he had thought at first to be the white caps of the waves were gulls. Hundreds, thousands, tens of thousands . . . They rose and fell in the trough of the seas, heads to the wind, like a mighty fleet at anchor, waiting on the tide. To eastward, and to the west, the gulls were there. They stretched as far as his eye could reach, in close formation, line upon line. Had the sea been still they would have covered the bay like a white cloud, head to head, body packed to body. Only the east wind, whipping the sea to breakers, hid them from the shore.

Nat turned, and leaving the beach climbed the steep path home. Someone should know of this. Someone should be told. Something was happening, because of the east wind and the weather, that he did not understand. He wondered if he should go to the call box by the bus stop and ring up the police. Yet what could they do? What could anyone do? Tens and thousands of gulls riding the sea there, in the bay, because of the storm, because of hunger. The police would think him mad, or drunk, or take the statement from him with great calm. 'Thank you. Yes, the matter has already been reported. The hard weather is driving the birds inland in great numbers.' Nat looked about him. Still no sign of any other bird. Perhaps the cold had sent them all from up country? As he drew near to the cottage his wife came to meet him, at the door. She called to him, excited. 'Nat,' she said, 'it's on the wireless. They've just read out a special news bulletin. I've written it down.'

'What's on the wireless?' he said.

'About the birds,' she said. 'It's not only here, it's everywhere. In London, all over the country. Something has happened to the birds.'

Together they went into the kitchen. He read the piece of paper lying on the table.

'Statement from the Home Office at eleven a.m. today.

Reports from all over the country are coming in hourly about the vast quantity of birds flocking above towns, villages and outlying districts, causing obstruction and damage and even attacking individuals. It is thought that the Arctic air stream, at present covering the British Isles, is causing birds to migrate south in immense numbers, and that intense hunger may drive these birds to attack human beings. Householders are warned to see to their windows, doors and chimneys, and to take reasonable precautions for the safety of their children. A further statement will be issued later.'

A kind of excitement seized Nat; he looked at his wife in triumph.

'There you are,' he said, 'let's hope they'll hear that at the farm. Mrs Trigg will know it wasn't any story. It's true. All over the country. I've been telling myself all morning there's something wrong. And just now, down on the beach, I looked out to sea and there are gulls, thousands of them, tens of thousands, you couldn't put a pin between their heads, and they're all out there, riding on the sea, waiting.'

'What are they waiting for, Nat?' she asked.

He stared at her, then looked down again at the piece of paper.

'I don't know,' he said slowly. 'It says here the birds are hungry.'

He went over to the drawer where he kept his hammer and tools.

'What are you going to do, Nat?'

'See to the windows and the chimneys too, like they tell you.'

'You think they would break in, with the windows shut? Those sparrows and robins and such? Why, how could they?'

He did not answer. He was not thinking of the robins and the sparrows. He was thinking of the gulls . . .

He went upstairs and worked there the rest of the

morning, boarding the windows of the bedrooms, filling up the chimney bases. Good job it was his free day and he was not working at the farm. It reminded him of the old days, at the beginning of the war. He was not married then, and he had made all the blackout boards for his mother's house in Plymouth. Made the shelter too. Not that it had been of any use, when the moment came. He wondered if they would take these precautions up at the farm. He doubted it. Too easy-going, Harry Trigg and his missus. Maybe they'd laugh at the whole thing. Go off to a dance or a whist drive.

'Dinner's ready.' She called him, from the kitchen.

'All right. Coming down.'

He was pleased with his handiwork. The frames fitted nicely over the little panes and at the base of the chimneys.

When dinner was over and his wife was washing up, Nat switched on the one o'clock news. The same announcement was repeated, the one which she had taken down during the morning, but the news bulletin enlarged upon it. 'The flocks of birds have caused dislocation in all areas,' read the announcer, 'and in London the sky was so dense at ten o'clock this morning that it seemed as if the city was covered by a vast black cloud.

'The birds settled on rooftops, on window ledges and on chimneys. The species included blackbird, thrush, the common house-sparrow, and, as might be expected in the metropolis, a vast quantity of pigeons and starlings, and that frequenter of the London river, the black-headed gull. The sight has been so unusual that traffic came to a standstill in many thoroughfares, work was abandoned in shops and offices, and the streets and pavements were crowded with people standing about to watch the birds.'

Various incidents were recounted, the suspected reason of cold and hunger stated again, and warnings to householders repeated. The announcer's voice was smooth and suave. Nat had the impression that this man, in particular, treated the whole business as he would an elaborate joke. There would be others like him, hundreds of them, who did not know what it was to struggle in darkness with a flock of birds. There would be parties tonight in London, like the ones they gave on election nights. People standing about, shouting and laughing, getting drunk. 'Come and watch the birds!'

Nat switched off the wireless. He got up and started work on the kitchen windows. His wife watched him, young Johnny at her heels.

'What, boards for down here too?' she said. 'Why, I'll have to light up before three o'clock. I see no call for boards down here.'

'Better be sure than sorry,' answered Nat. 'I'm not going to take any chances.'

'What they ought to do,' she said, 'is to call the army out and shoot the birds. That would soon scare them off.'

'Let them try,' said Nat. 'How'd they set about it?'

'They have the army to the docks,' she answered, 'when the dockers strike. The soldiers go down and unload the ships.'

'Yes,' said Nat, 'and the population of London is eight million or more. Think of all the buildings, all the flats, and houses. Do you think they've enough soldiers to go round shooting birds from every roof?'

'I don't know. But something should be done. They ought to do something.'

Nat thought to himself that 'they' were no doubt considering the problem at that very moment, but whatever 'they' decided to do in London and the big cities would not help the people here, three hundred miles away. Each householder must look after his own.

'How are we off for food?' he said.

'Now, Nat, whatever next?'

'Never mind. What have you got in the larder?'

'It's shopping day tomorrow, you know that. I don't keep uncooked food hanging about, it goes off. Butcher doesn't call till the day after. But I can bring back something when I go in tomorrow.'

Nat did not want to scare her. He thought it possible that she might not go to town tomorrow. He looked in the larder for himself, and in the cupboard where she kept her tins. They would do, for a couple of days. Bread was low.

'What about the baker?'

'He comes tomorrow too.'

He saw she had flour. If the baker did not call she had enough to bake one loaf.

'We'd be better off in old days,' he said, 'when the women baked twice a week, and had pilchards salted, and there was food for a family to last a siege, if need be.'

'I've tried the children with tinned fish, they don't like it,' she said.

Nat went on hammering the boards across the kitchen windows. Candles. They were low in candles too. That must be another thing she meant to buy tomorrow. Well, it could not be helped. They must go early to bed tonight. That was, if . . .

He got up and went out of the back door and stood in the garden, looking down towards the sea. There had been no sun all day, and now, at barely three o'clock, a kind of darkness had already come, the sky sullen, heavy, colourless like salt. He could hear the vicious sea drumming on the rocks. He walked down the path, half-way to the beach. And then he stopped. He could see the tide had turned. The rock that had shown in mid-morning was now covered, but it was not the sea that held his eyes. The gulls had risen. They were circling, hundreds of them, thousands of them, lifting their wings against the wind. It was the gulls that made the darkening of the sky. And they were silent. They made not a sound. They just went on soaring and circling, rising, falling, trying their strength against the wind.

Nat turned. He ran up the path, back to the cottage.

'I'm going for Jill,' he said. 'I'll wait for her, at the bus stop.'

'What's the matter?' asked his wife. 'You've gone quite white.'

'Keep Johnny inside,' he said. 'Keep the door shut. Light up now, and draw the curtains.'

'It's only just gone three,' she said.

'Never mind. Do what I tell you.'

He looked inside the toolshed, outside the back door. Nothing there of much use. A spade was too heavy, and a fork no good. He took the hoe. It was the only possible tool, and light enough to carry.

He started walking up the lane to the bus stop, and now and again glanced back over his shoulder.

The gulls had risen higher now, their circles were broader, wider, they were spreading out in huge formation across the sky.

He hurried on; although he knew the bus would not come to the top of the hill before four o'clock he had to hurry. He passed no one on the way. He was glad of this. No time to stop and chatter.

At the top of the hill he waited. He was much too soon. There was half an hour still to go. The east wind came whipping across the fields from the higher ground. He stamped his feet and blew upon his hands. In the distance he could see the clay hills, white and clean, against the heavy pallor of the sky. Something black rose from behind them, like a smudge at first, then widening, becoming deeper, and the smudge became a cloud, and the cloud divided again into five other clouds, spreading north, east, south and west, and they were not clouds at all; they were birds. He watched them travel across the sky, and as one section passed overhead, within two or three hundred feet of him, he knew, from their speed, they were bound inland, up country, they had no business with the people here on the peninsula. They were rooks, crows, jackdaws, magpies, jays, all birds that usually preyed upon the smaller species; but this afternoon they were bound on some other mission.

'They've been given the towns,' thought Nat, 'they know what they have to do. We don't matter so much here. The gulls will serve for us. The others go to the towns.'

He went to the call-box, stepped inside and lifted the receiver. The exchange would do. They would pass the message on.

'I'm speaking from Highway,' he said, 'by the bus stop. I want to report large formations of birds travelling up country. The gulls are also forming in the bay.'

'All right,' answered the voice, laconic, weary.

'You'll be sure and pass this message on to the proper quarter?'

'Yes . . . yes . . .' Impatient now, fed-up. The buzzing note resumed.

'She's another,' thought Nat, 'she doesn't care. Maybe she's had to answer calls all day. She hopes to go to the pictures tonight. She'll squeeze some fellow's hand, and point up at the sky, "Look at all them birds!" She doesn't care.'

The bus came lumbering up the hill. Jill climbed out and three or four other children. The bus went on towards the town.

'What's the hoe for, Dad?'

They crowded around him, laughing, pointing.

'I just brought it along,' he said. 'Come on now, let's get home. It's cold, no hanging about. Here, you. I'll watch you across the fields, see how fast you can run.'

He was speaking to Jill's companions who came from different families, living in the council houses. A short cut would take them to the cottages.

'We want to play a bit in the lane,' said one of them.

'No, you don't. You go off home, or I'll tell your mammy.'

They whispered to one another, round-eyed, then scuttled off across the fields. Jill stared at her father, her mouth sullen.

'We always play in the lane,' she said.

'Not tonight, you don't,' he said. 'Come on now, no dawdling.'

He could see the gulls now, circling the fields, coming in towards the land. Still silent. Still no sound.

'Look, Dad, look over there, look at all the gulls.'

'Yes. Hurry, now.'

'Where are they flying to? Where are they going?'

'Up country, I dare say. Where it's warmer.'

He seized her hand and dragged her after him along the lane.

'Don't go so fast. I can't keep up.'

The gulls were copying the rooks and crows. They were spreading out in formation across the sky. They headed, in bands of thousands, to the four compass points.

'Dad, what is it? What are the gulls doing?'

They were not intent upon their flight, as the crows, as the jackdaws had been. They still circled overhead. Nor did they fly so high. It was as though they waited upon some signal. As though some decision had yet to be given. The order was not clear.

'Do you want me to carry you, Jill? Here, come pick-a-back.'

This way he might put on speed; but he was wrong. Jill was heavy. She kept slipping. And she was crying too. His sense of urgency, of fear, had communicated itself to the child.

'I wish the gulls would go away. I don't like them. They're coming closer to the lane.'

He put her down again. He started running, swinging Jill after him. As they went past the farm turning he saw the farmer backing his car out of the garage. Nat called to him.

'Can you give us a lift?' he said.

'What's that?'

Mr Trigg turned in the driving seat and stared at them. Then a smile came to his cheerful, rubicund face.

'It looks as though we're in for some fun,' he said. 'Have you seen the gulls? Jim and I are going to take a crack at them. Everyone's gone bird crazy, talking of nothing else. I hear you were troubled in the night. Want a gun?'

Nat shook his head.

The small car was packed. There was just room for Jill, if she crouched on top of petrol tins on the back seat.

'I don't want a gun,' said Nat, 'but I'd be obliged if you'd run Jill home. She's scared of the birds.'

He spoke briefly. He did not want to talk in front of Jill.

'O.K.,' said the farmer, 'I'll take her home. Why don't you stop behind and join the shooting match? We'll make the feathers fly.'

Jill climbed in, and turning the car the driver sped up the lane. Nat followed after. Trigg must be crazy. What use was a gun against a sky of birds?

Now Nat was not responsible for Jill he had time to look about him. The birds were circling still, above the fields. Mostly herring gull, but the black-backed gull amongst them. Usually they kept apart. Now they were united. Some bond had brought them together. It was the black-backed gull that attacked the smaller birds, and even new-born lambs, so he'd heard. He'd never seen it done. He remembered this now, though, looking above him in the sky. They were coming in towards the farm. They were circling lower in the sky, and the black-backed gulls were to the front, the black-backed gulls were leading. The farm, then, was their target. They were making for the farm.

Nat increased his pace towards his own cottage. He saw the farmer's car turn and come back along the lane. It drew up beside him with a jerk.

'The kid has run inside,' said the farmer. 'Your wife was watching for her. Well, what do you make of it? They're saying in town the Russians have done it. The Russians have poisoned the birds.'

'How could they do that?' asked Nat.

'Don't ask me. You know how stories get around. Will you join my shooting match?'

'No, I'll get along home. The wife will be worried else.'

'My missus says if you could eat gull, there'd be some sense in it,' said Trigg, 'we'd have roast gull, baked gull, and pickle 'em into the bargain. You wait until I let off a few barrels into the brutes. That'll scare 'em.'

'Have you boarded your windows?' asked Nat.

'No. Lot of nonsense. They like to scare you on the wireless. I've had more to do today than to go round boarding up my windows.'

'I'd board them now, if I were you.'

'Garn. You're windy. Like to come to our place to sleep?'

'No, thanks all the same.'

'All right. See you in the morning. Give you a gull breakfast.'

The farmer grinned and turned his car to the farm entrance.

Nat hurried on. Past the little wood, past the old barn, and then across the stile to the remaining field.

As he jumped the stile he heard the whirr of wings. A black-backed gull dived down at him from the sky, missed, swerved in flight, and rose to dive again. In a moment it was joined by others, six, seven, a dozen, black-backed and herring mixed. Nat dropped his hoe. The hoe was useless. Covering his head with his arms he ran towards the cottage. They kept coming at him from the air, silent save for the beating wings. The terrible, fluttering wings. He could feel the blood on his hands, his wrists, his neck. Each stab of a swooping beak tore his flesh. If only he could keep them from his eyes. Nothing else mattered. He must keep them from his eyes. They had not learnt yet how to cling to a shoulder, how to rip clothing, how to dive in mass upon the head, upon the body. But with each dive, with each attack, they became bolder. And they had no thought for themselves. When they dived low and missed, they crashed, bruised and broken, on the ground. As Nat ran he stumbled, kicking their spent bodies in front of him.

He found the door, he hammered upon it with his bleeding hands. Because of the boarded windows no light shone. Everything was dark.

'Let me in,' he shouted, 'it's Nat. Let me in.'

He shouted loud to make himself heard above the whirr of the gull's wings.

Then he saw the gannet, poised for the dive, above him in the sky. The gulls circled, retired, soared, one with another, against the wind. Only the gannet remained. One single gannet, above him in the sky. The wings folded suddenly to its body. It dropped, like a stone. Nat screamed, and the door opened. He stumbled across the threshold, and his wife threw her weight against the door.

They heard the thud of the gannet as it fell.

His wife dressed his wounds. They were not deep. The backs of his hands had suffered most, and his wrists. Had he not worn a cap they would have reached his head. As to the gannet . . . the gannet could have split his skull.

The children were crying, of course. They had seen the blood on their father's hands.

'It's all right now,' he told them. 'I'm not hurt. Just a few scratches. You play with Johnny, Jill. Mammy will wash these cuts.'

He half shut the door to the scullery, so that they could not see. His wife was ashen. She began running water from the sink.

'I saw them overhead,' she whispered. 'They began collecting just as Jill ran in with Mr Trigg. I shut the door fast, and it jammed. That's why I couldn't open it at once, when you came.'

'Thank God they waited for me,' he said. 'Jill would have fallen at once. One bird alone would have done it.'

Furtively, so as not to alarm the children, they whispered together, as she bandaged his hands and the back of his neck.

'They're flying inland,' he said, 'thousands of them. Rooks, crows, all the bigger birds. I saw them from the bus stop. They're making for the towns.'

'But what can they do, Nat?'

'They'll attack. Go for everyone out in the streets. Then they'll try the windows, the chimneys.'

'Why don't the authorities do something? Why don't they get the army, get machine guns, anything?'

'There's been no time. Nobody's prepared. We'll hear what they have to say on the six o'clock news.'

Nat went back into the kitchen, followed by his wife. Johnny was playing quietly on the floor. Only Jill looked anxious.

'I can hear the birds,' she said. 'Listen, Dad.'

Nat listened. Muffled sounds came from the windows, from the door. Wings brushing the surface, sliding, scraping, seeking a way of entry. The sound of many bodies, pressed together, shuffling on the sills. Now and again came a thud, a crash, as some bird dived and fell. 'Some of them will kill themselves that way,' he thought, 'but not enough. Never enough.'

'All right,' he said aloud, 'I've got boards over the windows, Jill. The birds can't get in.'

He went and examined all the windows. His work had been thorough. Every gap was closed. He would make extra certain, however. He found wedges, pieces of old tin, strips of wood and metal, and fastened them at the sides to reinforce the boards. His hammering helped to deafen the sound of the birds, the shuffling, the tapping, and more ominous – he did not want his wife or the children to hear it – the splinter of cracked glass.

'Turn on the wireless,' he said, 'let's have the wireless.'

This would drown the sound also. He went upstairs to the bedrooms and reinforced the windows there. Now he could hear the birds on the roof, the scraping of claws, a sliding, jostling sound.

He decided they must sleep in the kitchen, keep up the fire, bring down the mattresses and lay them out on the floor. He was afraid of the bedroom chimneys. The boards he had placed at the chimney bases might give way. In the kitchen they would be safe, because of the fire. He would have to make a joke of it. Pretend to the children they were playing at camp. If the worst happened, and the birds forced an entry down the bedroom chimneys, it would be hours, days perhaps, before they could break down the doors. The birds would be imprisoned in the bedrooms. They could do no harm there. Crowded together, they would stifle and die.

He began to bring the mattresses downstairs. At sight of them his wife's eyes widened in apprehension. She thought the birds had already broken in upstairs.

'All right,' he said cheerfully, 'we'll all sleep together in the kitchen tonight. More cosy here by the fire. Then we shan't be worried by those silly old birds tapping at the windows.'

He made the children help him rearrange the furniture, and he took the precaution of moving the dresser, with his wife's help, across the window. It fitted well. It was an added safeguard. The mattresses could now be lain, one beside the other, against the wall where the dresser had stood.

'We're safe enough now,' he thought, 'we're snug and tight, like an air-raid shelter. We can hold out. It's just the food that worries me. Food, and coal for the fire.

We've enough for two or three days, not more. By that time . . .'

No use thinking ahead as far as that. And they'd be giving directions on the wireless. People would be told what to do. And now, in the midst of many problems, he realized that it was dance music only coming over the air. Not Children's Hour, as it should have been. He glanced at the dial. Yes, they were on the Home Service all right. Dance records. He switched to the Light programme. He knew the reason. The usual programmes had been abandoned. This only happened at exceptional times. Elections, and such. He tried to remember if it had happened in the war, during the heavy raids on London. But of course. The BBC was not stationed in London during the war. The programmes were broadcast from other, temporary quarters. 'We're better off here,' he thought, 'we're better off here in the kitchen, with the windows and the doors boarded, than they are up in the towns. Thank God we're not in the towns.'

At six o'clock the records ceased. The time signal was given. No matter if it scared the children, he must hear the news. There was a pause after the pips. Then the announcer spoke. His voice was solemn, grave. Quite different from midday.

'This is London,' he said. 'A National Emergency was proclaimed at four o'clock this afternoon. Measures are being taken to safeguard the lives and property of the population, but it must be understood that these are not easy to effect immediately, owing to the unforeseen and unparalleled nature of the present crisis. Every householder must take precautions to his own building, and where several people live together, as in flats and apartments, they must unite to do the utmost they can to prevent entry. It is absolutely imperative that every individual stays indoors tonight, and that no one at all remains on the streets, or roads, or anywhere without doors. The birds, in vast numbers, are attacking anyone on sight, and have already begun an assault upon buildings; but these, with due care, should be impenetrable. The population is asked to remain calm, and not to panic. Owing to the exceptional nature of the emergency, there will be no further transmission from any broadcasting station until seven a.m. tomorrow.'

They played the National Anthem. Nothing more happened. Nat switched off the set. He looked at his wife. She stared back at him.

'What's it mean?' said Jill. 'What did the news say?'

'There won't be any more programmes tonight,' said Nat. 'There's been a breakdown at the BBC.'

'Is it the birds?' asked Jill. 'Have the birds done it?'

'No,' said Nat, 'it's just that everyone's very busy, and then of course they have to get rid of the birds, messing everything up, in the towns. Well, we can manage without the wireless for one evening.'

'I wish we had a gramophone,' said Jill, 'that would be better than nothing.'

She had her face turned to the dresser, backed against the windows. Try as they did to ignore it, they were all aware of the shuffling, the stabbing, the persistent beating and sweeping of wings.

'We'll have supper early,' suggested Nat, 'something for a treat. Ask Mammy. Toasted cheese, eh? Something we all like?'

He winked and nodded at his wife. He wanted the look of dread, of apprehension, to go from Jill's face.

He helped with the supper, whistling, singing, making as much clatter as he could, and it seemed to him that the shuffling and the tapping were not so intense as they had been at first. Presently he went up to the bedrooms and listened, and he no longer heard the jostling for place upon the roof.

'They've got reasoning powers,' he thought, 'they know it's hard to break in here. They'll try elsewhere. They won't waste their time with us.'

Supper passed without incident, and then, when they were clearing away, they heard a new sound, droning, familiar, a sound they all knew and understood.

His wife looked up at him, her face alight. 'It's planes,' she said, 'they're sending out planes after the birds. That's what I said they ought to do, all along. That will get them. Isn't that gun-fire? Can't you hear guns?'

It might be gun-fire, out at sea. Nat could not tell. Big naval guns might have an effect upon the gulls out at sea, but the gulls were inland now. The guns couldn't shell the shore, because of the population.

'It's good, isn't it,' said his wife, 'to hear the planes?' And Jill, catching her enthusiasm, jumped up and down with Johnny. 'The planes will get the birds. The planes will shoot them.'

Just then they heard a crash about two miles distant, followed by a second, then a third. The droning became more distant, passed away out to sea.

'What was that?' asked his wife. 'Were they dropping bombs on the birds?'

'I don't know,' answered Nat, 'I don't think so.'

He did not want to tell her that the sound they had heard was the crashing of aircraft. It was, he had no doubt, a venture on the part of the authorities to send out reconnaissance forces, but they might have known the venture was suicidal. What could aircraft do against birds that flung themselves to death against propeller and fuselage, but hurtle to the ground themselves? This was being tried now, he supposed, over the whole country. And at a cost. Someone high up had lost his head.

'Where have the planes gone, Dad?' asked Jill.

'Back to base,' he said. 'Come on, now, time to tuck down for bed.'

It kept his wife occupied, undressing the children before the fire, seeing to the bedding, one thing and another, while he went round the cottage again, making sure that nothing had worked loose. There was no further drone of aircraft, and the naval guns had ceased. 'Waste of life and effort,' Nat said to himself. 'We can't destroy enough of them that way. Cost too heavy. There's always gas. Maybe they'll try spraying with gas, mustard gas. We'll be warned first, of course, if they do. There's one thing, the best brains of the country will be on to it tonight.'

Somehow the thought reassured him. He had a picture of scientists, naturalists, technicians, and all those chaps they called the back-room boys, summoned to a council; they'd be working on the problem now. This was not a job for the government, for the chiefs-of-staff – they would merely carry out the orders of the scientists.

'They'll have to be ruthless,' he thought. 'Where the trouble's worst they'll have to risk more lives, if they use gas. All the livestock, to, and the soil – all contaminated. As long as everyone doesn't panic. That's the trouble. People panicking, losing their heads. The BBC was right to warn us of that.'

Upstairs in the bedrooms all was quiet. No further scraping and stabbing at the windows. A lull in battle. Forces regrouping. Wasn't that what they called it, in the old wartime bulletins? The wind hadn't dropped, though. He could still hear it, roaring in the chimneys. And the sea breaking down on the shore. Then he remembered the tide. The tide would be on the turn. Maybe the lull in battle was because of the tide. There was some law the birds obeyed, and it was all to do with the east wind and the tide.

He glanced at his watch. Nearly eight o'clock. It must have gone high water an hour ago. That explained the lull: the birds attacked with the flood tide. It might not work that way inland, up country, but it seemed as if it was so this way on the coast. He reckoned the time limit in his head. They had six hours to go, without attack. When the tide turned again, around one-twenty in the morning, the birds would come back . . .

There were two things he could do. The first to rest,

with his wife and the children, and all of them snatch what sleep they could, until the small hours. The second to go out, see how they were faring at the farm, see if the telephone was still working there, so that they might get news from the exchange.

He called softly to his wife, who had just settled the children. She came halfway up the stairs and he whispered to her.

'You're not to go,' she said at once, 'you're not to go and leave me alone with the children. I can't stand it.'

Her voice rose hysterically. He hushed her, calmed her.

'All right,' he said, 'all right. I'll wait till morning. And we'll get the wireless bulletin then too, at seven. But in the morning, when the tide ebbs again, I'll try for the farm, and they may let us have bread and potatoes, and milk too.'

His mind was busy again, planning against emergency. They would not have milked, of course, this evening. The cows would be standing by the gate, waiting in the yard, with the household inside, battened behind boards, as they were here at the cottage. That is, if they had time to take precautions. He thought of the farmer, Trigg, smiling at him from the car. There would have been no shooting party, not tonight.

The children were asleep. His wife, still clothed, was sitting on her mattress. She watched him, her eyes nervous.

'What are you going to do?' she whispered.

He shook his head for silence. Softly, stealthily, he opened the back door and looked outside.

It was pitch dark. The wind was blowing harder than ever, coming in steady gusts, icy, from the sea. He kicked at the step outside the door. It was heaped with birds. There were dead birds everywhere. Under the windows, against the walls. These were the suicides, the divers, the ones with broken necks. Wherever he looked he saw dead birds. No trace of the living. The living had flown seaward with the turn of the tide. The gulls would be riding the seas now, as they had done in the forenoon.

In the far distance, on the hill where the tractor had been two days before, something was burning. One of the aircraft that had crashed; the fire, fanned by the wind, had set light to a stack.

He looked at the bodies of the birds, and he had a notion that if he heaped them, one upon the other, on the window sills they would make added protection for the next attack. Not much, perhaps, but something. The bodies would have to be clawed at, pecked, and dragged aside, before the living birds gained purchase on the sills and attacked the panes. He set to work in the darkness. It was queer; he hated touching them. The bodies were still warm and bloody. The blood matted their feathers. He felt his stomach turn, but he went on with his work. He noticed, grimly, that every window-pane was shattered. Only the boards had kept the birds from breaking in. He stuffed the cracked panes with the bleeding bodies of the birds.

When he had finished he went back into the cottage. He barricaded the kitchen door, made it doubly secure. He took off his bandages, sticky with the birds' blood, not with his own cuts, and put on fresh plaster.

His wife had made him cocoa and he drank it thirstily. He was very tired.

'All right,' he said, smiling, 'don't worry. We'll get through.'

He lay down on his mattress and closed his eyes. He slept at once. He dreamt uneasily, because through his dreams there ran a thread of something forgotten. Some piece of work, neglected, that he should have done. Some precaution that he had known well but had not taken, and he could not put a name to it in his dreams. It was connected in some way with the burning aircraft and the stack upon the hill. He went on sleeping, though; he did not awake. It was his wife shaking his shoulder that awoke him finally.

'They've begun,' she sobbed, 'they've started this last hour, I can't listen to it any longer, alone. There's something smelling bad too, something burning.'

Then he remembered. He had forgotten to make up the fire. It was smouldering, nearly out. He got up swiftly and lit the lamp. The hammering had started at the windows and the doors, but it was not that he minded now. It was the smell of singed feathers. The smell filled the kitchen. He knew at once what it was. The birds were coming down the chimney, squeezing their way down to the kitchen range.

He got sticks and paper and put them on the embers, then reached for the can of paraffin.

'Stand back,' he shouted to his wife, 'we've got to risk this.'

He threw the paraffin on to the fire. The flame roared up the pipe, and down upon the fire fell the scorched, blackened bodies of the birds.

The children woke, crying. 'What is it?' said Jill. 'What's happened?'

Nat had no time to answer. He was raking the bodies from the chimney, clawing them out on to the floor. The flames still roared, and the danger of the chimney catching fire was one he had to take. The flames would send away the living birds from the chimney top. The lower joint was the difficulty, though. This was choked with the smouldering helpless bodies of the birds caught by fire. He scarcely heeded the attack on the windows and the door: let them beat their wings, break their beaks, lose their lives, in the attempt to force an entry into his home. They would not break in. He thanked God he had one of the old cottages, with small windows, stout walls. Not like the new council houses. Heaven help them up the lane, in the new council houses.

'Stop crying,' he called to the children. 'There's nothing to be afraid of, stop crying.'

He went on raking at the burning, smouldering bodies as they fell into the fire.

'This'll fetch them,' he said to himself, 'the draught and the flames together. We're all right, as long as the chimney doesn't catch. I ought to be shot for this. It's all my fault. Last thing I should have made up the fire. I knew there was something.'

Amid the scratching and tearing at the window boards came the sudden homely striking of the kitchen clock. Three a.m. A little more than four hours yet to go. He could not be sure of the exact time of high water. He reckoned it would not turn much before half-past seven, twenty to eight.

'Light up the primus,' he said to his wife. 'Make us some tea, and the kids some cocoa. No use sitting around doing nothing.'

That was the line. Keep her busy, and the children too. Move about, eat, drink; always best to be on the go.

He waited by the range. The flames were dying. But no more blackened bodies fell from the chimney. He thrust his poker up as far as it could go and found nothing. It was clear. The chimney was clear. He wiped the sweat from his forehead.

'Come on now, Jill,' he said, 'bring me some more sticks. We'll have a good fire going directly.' She wouldn't come near him, though. She was staring at the heaped singed bodies of the birds.

'Never mind them,' he said, 'we'll put those in the passage when I've got the fire steady.'

The danger of the chimney was over. It could not happen again, not if the fire was kept burning day and night.

'I'll have to get more fuel from the farm tomorrow,' he thought. 'This will never last. I'll manage, though. I can do all that with the ebb tide. It can be worked, fetching what we need, when the tide's turned. We've just got to adapt ourselves, that's all.'

They drank tea and cocoa and ate slices of bread and Bovril. Only half a loaf left, Nat noticed. Never mind though, they'd get by.

'Stop it,' said young Johnny, pointing to the windows with his spoon, 'stop it, you old birds.'

'That's right,' said Nat, smiling, 'we don't want the old beggars, do we? Had enough of 'em.'

They began to cheer when they heard the thud of the suicide birds.

'There's another, Dad,' cried Jill, 'he's done for.'

'He's had it,' said Nat, 'there he goes, the blighter.'

This was the way to face up to it. This was the spirit. If they could keep this up, hang on like this until seven, when the first news bulletin came through, they would not have done too badly.

'Give us a fag,' he said to his wife. 'A bit of a smoke will clear away the smell of the scorched feathers.'

'There's only two left in the packet,' she said. 'I was going to buy you some from the Co-op.'

'I'll have one,' he said, 't'other will keep for a rainy day.'

No sense trying to make the children rest. There was no rest to be got while the tapping and the scratching went on at the windows. He sat with one arm round his wife and the other round Jill, with Johnny on his mother's lap and the blankets heaped about them on the mattress.

'You can't help admiring the beggars,' he said, 'they've got persistence. You'd think they'd tire of the game, but not a bit of it.'

Admiration was hard to sustain. The tapping went on and on and a new rasping note struck Nat's ear, as though a sharper beak than any hitherto had come to take over from its fellows. He tried to remember the names of birds, he tried to think which species would go for this particular job. It was not the tap of the woodpecker. That would be light and frequent. This was more serious, because if it continued long the wood would splinter as the glass had done. Then he remembered the hawks. Could the hawks have taken over from the gulls? Were there buzzards now upon the sills, using talons as well as beaks? Hawks, buzzards, kestrels, falcons – he had forgotten the birds of prey. He had forgotten the gripping power of the birds of prey. Three hours to go, and while they waited the sound of the splintering wood, the talons tearing at the wood.

Nat looked about him, seeing what furniture he could destroy to fortify the door. The windows were safe, because of the dresser. He was not certain of the door. He went upstairs, but when he reached the landing he paused and listened. There was a soft patter on the floor of the children's bedroom. The birds had broken through . . . He put his ear to the door. No mistake. He could hear the rustle of wings, and the light patter as they searched the floor. The other bedroom was still clear. He went into it and began bringing out the furniture, to pile at the head of the stairs should the door of the children's bedroom go. It was a preparation. It might never be needed. He could not stack the furniture against the door, because it opened inward. The only possible thing was to have it at the top of the stairs.

'Come down, Nat, what are you doing?' called his wife.

'I won't be long,' he shouted. 'Just making everything shipshape up here.'

He did not want her to come; he did not want her to hear the pattering of the feet in the children's bedroom, the brushing of those wings against the door.

At five-thirty he suggested breakfast, bacon and fried bread, if only to stop the growing look of panic in his wife's eyes and to calm the fretful children. She did not know about the birds upstairs. The bedroom, luckily, was not over the kitchen. Had it been so she could not have failed to hear the sound of them, up there, tapping the boards. And the silly, senseless thud of the suicide birds, the death and glory boys, who flew into the bedroom, smashing their heads against the walls. He knew them of old, the herring gulls. They had no brains. The black-backs were different, they knew what they were doing. So did the buzzards, the hawks . . .

He found himself watching the clock, gazing at the hands that went so slowly round the dial. If his theory was not correct, if the attack did not cease with the turn of the tide, he knew they were beaten. They could not continue through the long day without air, without rest, without more fuel without . . . his mind raced. He knew there were so many things they needed to withstand siege. They were not fully prepared. They were not ready. It might be that it would be safer in the towns after all. If he could get a message through, on the farm telephone, to his cousin, only a short journey by train up country, they might be able to hire a car. That would be quicker – hire a car between tides . . .

His wife's voice, calling his name, drove away the sudden, desperate desire for sleep.

'What is it? What now?' he said sharply.

'The wireless,' said his wife. 'I've been watching the clock. It's nearly seven.'

'Don't twist the knob,' he said, impatient for the first time, 'it's on the Home where it is. They'll speak from the Home.'

They waited. The kitchen clock struck seven. There was no sound. No chimes, no music. They waited until a quarter past, switching to the Light. The result was the same. No news bulletin came through.

'We've heard wrong,' he said, 'they won't be broadcasting until eight o'clock.'

They left it switched on, and Nat thought of the battery, wondered how much power was left in it. It was generally recharged when his wife went shopping in the town. If the battery failed they would not hear the instructions.

'It's getting light,' whispered his wife. 'I can't see it, but I can feel it. And the birds aren't hammering so loud.'

She was right. The rasping, tearing sound grew fainter every moment. So did the shuffling, the jostling for place upon the step, upon the sills. The tide was on the turn. By eight there was no sound at all. Only the wind. The children, lulled at last by the stillness, fell asleep. At half-past eight Nat switched the wireless off.

'What are you doing? We'll miss the news,' said his wife.

'There isn't going to be any news,' said Nat. 'We've got to depend upon ourselves.'

He went to the door and slowly pulled away the barricades. He drew the bolts, and kicking the bodies from the step outside the door breathed the cold air. He had six working hours before him, and he knew he must reserve his strength for the right things, not waste it in any way. Food, and light, and fuel; these were the necessary things. If he could get them in sufficiency, they could endure another night.

He stepped into the garden, and as he did so he saw the living birds. The gulls had gone to ride the sea, as they had done before; they sought sea food, and the buoyancy of the tide, before they returned to the attack. Not so the land birds. They waited and watched. Nat saw them, on the hedge-rows, on the soil, crowded in the trees, outside in the field, line upon line of birds, all still, doing nothing.

He went to the end of his small garden. The birds did not move. They went on watching him.

'I've got to get food,' said Nat to himself. 'I've got to go to the farm to find food.'

He went back to the cottage. He saw to the windows and the doors. He went upstairs and opened the children's bedroom. It was empty, except for the dead birds on the floor. The living were out there, in the garden, in the fields. He went downstairs.

'I'm going to the farm,' he said.

His wife clung to him. She had seen the living birds from the open door.

'Take us with you,' she begged, 'we can't stay here alone. I'd rather die than stay here alone.'

He considered the matter. He nodded.

'Come on, then,' he said, 'bring baskets, and Johnny's pram. We can load up the pram.'

They dressed against the biting wind, wore gloves and scarves. His wife put Johnny in the pram. Nat took Jill's hand.

'The birds,' she whimpered, 'they're all out there, in the fields.'

'They won't hurt us,' he said, 'not in the light.'

They started walking across the field towards the stile, and the birds did not move. They waited, their heads turned to the wind.

When they reached the turning to the farm, Nat stopped and told his wife to wait in the shelter of the hedge with the two children.

'But I want to see Mrs Trigg,' she protested. 'There are lots of things we can borrow, if they went to market yesterday; not only bread, and . . .'

'Wait here,' Nat interrupted. 'I'll be back in a moment.'

The cows were lowing, moving restlessly in the yard, and he could see a gap in the fence where the sheep had knocked their way through, to roam unchecked in the front garden before the farm-house. No smoke came from the chimneys. He was filled with misgiving. He did not want his wife or the children to go down to the farm.

'Don't gib now,' said Nat, harshly, 'do what I say.'

She withdrew with the pram into the hedge, screening herself and the children from the wind.

He went down alone to the farm. He pushed his way through the herd of bellowing cows, which turned this way and that, distressed, their udders full. He saw the car standing by the gate, not put away in the garage. The windows of the farm-house were smashed. There were many dead gulls lying in the yard and around the house. The living birds perched on the group of trees behind the farm and on the roof of the house. They were quite still. They watched him.

Jim's body lay in the yard . . . what was left of it. When the birds had finished, the cows had trampled him. His gun was beside him. The door of the house was shut and bolted, but as the windows were smashed it was easy to lift them and climb through. Trigg's body was close to the telephone. He must have been trying to get through to the exchange when the birds came for him. The receiver was hanging loose, the instrument torn from the wall. No sign of Mrs Trigg. She would be upstairs. Was it any use going up? Sickened, Nat knew what he would find.

'Thank God,' he said to himself, 'there were no children.'

He forced himself to climb the stairs, but halfway he turned and descended again. He could see her legs, protruding from the open bedroom door. Beside her were the bodies of the black-backed gulls, and an umbrella, broken.

'It's no use,' thought Nat, 'doing anything. I've only got five hours, less than that. The Triggs would understand. I must load up with what I can find.'

He tramped back to his wife and children.

'I'm going to fill up the car with stuff,' he said. 'I'll put coal in it, and paraffin for the primus. We'll take it home and return for a fresh load.'

'What about the Triggs?' asked his wife.

'They must have gone to friends,' he said.

'Shall I come and help you, then?'

'No; there's a mess down there. Cows and sheep all over the place. Wait, I'll get the car. You can sit in it.'

Clumsily he backed the car out of the yard and into the

lane. His wife and the children could not see Jim's body from there.

'Stay here,' he said, 'never mind the pram. The pram can be fetched later. I'm going to load the car.'

Her eyes watched his all the time. He believed she understood, otherwise she would have suggested helping him to find the bread and groceries.

They made three journeys altogether, backwards and forwards between their cottage and the farm, before he was satisfied they had everything they needed. It was surprising, once he started thinking, how many things were necessary. Almost the most important of all was planking for the windows. He had to go round searching for timber. He wanted to renew the boards on all the windows at the cottage. Candles, paraffin, nails, tinned stuff; the list was endless. Besides all that, he milked three of the cows. The rest, poor brutes, would have to go on bellowing.

On the final journey he drove the car to the bus stop, got out, and went to the telephone box. He waited a few minutes, jangling the receiver. No good, though. The line was dead. He climbed on to a bank and looked over the countryside, but there was no sign of life at all, nothing in the fields but the waiting, watching birds. Some of them slept – he could see the beaks tucked into the feathers.

'You'd think they'd be feeding,' he said to himself, 'not just standing in that way.'

Then he remembered. They were gorged with food. They had eaten their fill during the night. That was why they did not move this morning . . .

No smoke came from the chimneys of the council houses. He thought of the children who had run across the fields the night before.

'I should have known,' he thought. 'I ought to have taken them home with me.'

He lifted his face to the sky. It was colourless and grey. The bare trees on the landscape looked bent and blackened by the east wind. The cold did not affect the living birds, waiting out there in the fields.

'This is the time they ought to get them,' said Nat, 'they're a sitting target now. They must be doing this all over the country. Why don't our aircraft take off now and spray them with mustard gas? What are all our chaps doing? They must know, they must see for themselves.'

He went back to the car and got into the driver's seat.

'Go quickly past that second gate,' whispered his wife. 'The postman's lying there. I don't want Jill to see.'

He accelerated. The little Morris bumped and rattled along the lane. The children shrieked with laughter.

'Up-a-down, up-a-down,' shouted young Johnny.

It was a quarter to one by the time they reached the cottage. Only an hour to go.

'Better have cold dinner,' said Nat. 'Hot up something for yourself and the children, some of that soup. I've no time to eat now. I've got to unload all this stuff.'

He got everything inside the cottage. It could be sorted later. Give them all something to do during the long hours ahead. First he must see to the windows and the doors.

He went round the cottage methodically, testing every window, every door. He climbed on to the roof also, and fixed boards across every chimney, except the kitchen. The cold was so intense he could hardly bear it, but the job had to be done. Now and again he would look up, searching the sky for aircraft. None came. As he worked he cursed the inefficiency of the authorities.

'It's always the same,' he muttered, 'they always let us down. Muddle, muddle, from the start. No plan, no real organization. And we don't matter, down here. That's what it is. The people up country have priority. They're using gas up there, no doubt, and all the aircraft. We've got to wait and take what comes.'

He paused, his work on the bedroom chimney finished, and looked out to sea. Something was moving out there. Something grey and white amongst the breakers.

'Good old Navy,' he said, 'they never let us down. They're coming down channel, they're turning in the bay.'

He waited, straining, his eyes watering in the wind, towards the sea. He was wrong, though. It was not ships. The Navy was not there. The gulls were rising from the sea. The massed flocks in the fields, with ruffled feathers, rose in formation from the ground, and wing to wing soared upwards to the sky.

The tide had turned again.

Nat climbed down the ladder and went inside the kitchen. The family were at dinner. It was a little after two. He bolted the door, put up the barricade, and lit the lamp.

'It's night-time,' said young Johnny.

His wife had switched on the wireless once again, but no sound came from it.

'I've been all round the dial,' she said, 'foreign stations, and that lot. I can't get anything.'

'Maybe they have the same trouble,' he said, 'maybe it's the same right through Europe.'

She poured out a plateful of the Triggs' soup, cut him a large slice of the Triggs' bread, and spread their dripping upon it.

They ate in silence. A piece of the dripping ran down young Johnny's chin and fell on to the table.

'Manners, Johnny,' said Jill, 'you should learn to wipe your mouth.'

The tapping began at the windows, at the door. The rustling, the jostling, the pushing for position on the sills. The first thud of the suicide gulls upon the step.

'Won't America do something?' said his wife. 'They've always been our allies, haven't they? Surely America will do something?'

Nat did not answer. The boards were strong against the windows, and on the chimneys too. The cottage was filled with stores, with fuel, with all they needed for the next few days. When he had finished dinner he would put the stuff away, stack it neatly, get everything shipshape, handy-like. His wife could help him, and the children too. They'd tire themselves out, between now and a quarter to nine, when the tide would ebb; then he'd tuck them down on their mattresses, see that they slept good and sound until three in the morning.

He had a new scheme for the windows, which was to fix barbed wire in front of the boards. He had brought a great roll of it from the farm. The nuisance was, he'd have to work at this in the dark, when the lull came between nine and three. Pity he had not thought of it before. Still, as long as the wife slept, and the kids, that was the main thing.

The smaller birds were at the window now. He recognized the light tap-tapping of their beaks, and the soft brush of their wings. The hawks ignored the windows. They concentrated their attack upon the door. Nat listened to the tearing sound of splintering wood, and wondered how many million years of memory were stored in those little brains, behind the stabbing beaks, the piercing eyes, now giving them this instinct to destroy mankind with all the deft precision of machines.

'I'll smoke that last fag,' he said to his wife. 'Stupid of me, it was the one thing I forgot to bring back from the farm.'

He reached for it, switched on the silent wireless. He threw the empty packet on the fire, and watched it burn.

Marguerite Duras

extract from

The Lover

In her sixteenth year, the narrator finds herself responsible for acquiring money to help her impoverished mother. Dressed like a child prostitute, she journeys to school across her city, Saigon, a headmistress's daughter who is, nevertheless, up for sale. She quickly attracts an elegant Chinese lover, a rich man's son, and the intensity of their erotic exploration remains the central experience in both their lives.

So you see it wasn't in the bar at Réam, as I wrote, that I met the rich man with the black limousine, it was after we left the concession, two or three years after, on the ferry, the day I'm telling you about, in that light of haze and heat.

It's a year and a half after that meeting that my mother takes us back to France. She'll sell all her furniture. Then go one last time to the dyke. She'll sit on the veranda facing the setting sun, look towards Siam one last time as she never will again, not even when she leaves France again, changes her mind again and comes back once more to Indo-China and retires to Saigon. Never again will she go and see that mountain, that green and yellow sky above that forest.

Yes, I tell you, when she was already quite old she did it again. She opened a French language school, the Nouvelle Ecole Française, which made enough for her to help me with my studies and to provide for her elder son as long as she lived.

My younger brother died in three days, of bronchial pneumonia. His heart gave out. It was then that I left my mother. It was during the Japanese occupation. Everything came to an end that day. I never asked her any more questions about our childhood, about herself. She died, for me, of my younger brother's death. So did my elder brother. I never got over the horror they inspired in me then. They don't mean anything to me any more. I don't know any more about them since that day. I don't even know how she managed to pay off her debts to the *chettys*, the Indian moneylenders. One day they stopped coming. I can see them now. They're sitting in the little parlour in Sadec wearing white sarongs, they sit there without saying a word, for months, years. My mother can be heard weeping and insulting them, she's in her room and won't come out, she calls out to them to leave her alone, they're deaf, calm, smiling, they stay where they are. And then one day, gone. They're dead now, my mother and my two brothers. For memories too it's too late. Now I don't love them any more. I don't remember if I ever did. I've left them. In my head I no longer have the scent of her skin, nor in my eyes the colour of her eyes. I can't remember her voice, except sometimes when it grew soft with the weariness of evening. Her laughter I can't hear any more – neither her laughter nor her cries. It's over, I don't remember. That's why I can write about her so easily now, so long, so fully. She's become just something you write without difficulty, cursive writing.

She must have stayed on in Saigon from 1932 until 1949. It was in December 1942 that my younger brother died. She couldn't move any more. She stayed on – to be near the grave, she said. Then finally she came back to France. My son was two years old when we met again. It was too late for us to be reunited. We knew it at first glance. There was nothing left to reunite. Except for the elder son, all the rest was over. She went to live, and die, in the department of Loir-et-Cher, in the sham Louis XIV château. She lived there with Dô. She was still afraid at night. She bought a gun. Dô kept watch in the attics on the top floor. She also bought a place for her elder son near Amboise. With woods. He cut them down. Then went and gambled the money away in a baccarat club in Paris. The woods were lost in one night. The point at which my memory suddenly softens, and perhaps my brother brings tears to my eyes, is after the loss of the money from the woods. I know he's found lying in his car in Montparnasse, outside the Coupole, and that he wants to die. After that, I forget. What she did, my mother, with that château of hers, is simply unimaginable, still all for the sake of the elder son, the child of fifty incapable of earning any money. She buys some electric incubators and instals them in the main drawing-room. Suddenly she's got six hundred chicks, forty square metres of them. But she made a mistake with the infra-red rays, and none of the chicks can eat, all six hundred of them have beaks that don't meet or won't close, they all starve to death and she gives up. I came to the château while the chicks were hatching, there were great rejoicings. Afterwards the stench of the dead chicks and their food was so awful I couldn't eat in my mother's château without throwing up.

She died between Dô and him she called her child, in her big bedroom on the first floor, where during heavy frosts she used to put the sheep to sleep, five or six sheep all around her bed, for several winters, her last.

It's there, in that last house, the one on the Loire, when she finally gives up her ceaseless to-ing and fro-ing, that I see the madness clearly for the first time. I see my mother is clearly mad. I see that Dô and my brother have always had access to that madness. But that I, no, I've never seen it before. Never seen my mother in the state of being mad. Which she was. From birth. In the blood. She wasn't ill with it, for her it was like health, flanked by Dô and her elder son. No one else but they realized. She always had lots of friends, she kept the same friends for years and years and was always making new ones, often very young, among the officials from up-country, or later on among the people in Touraine, where there were some who'd retired from the French colonies. She always had people around her, all her life, because of what they called her lively intelligence, her cheerfulness, and her peerless, indefatigable poise.

I don't know who took the photo with the despair. The one in the courtyard of the house in Hanoi. Perhaps my father, one last time. A few months later he'd be sent back to France because of his health. Before that he'd go to a new job, in Phnom Penh. He was only there a few weeks. He died in less than a year. My mother wouldn't go back with him to France, she stayed where she was, stuck there. In Phnom Penh. In the fine house overlooking the Mekong, once the palace of the king of Cambodia, in the midst of those terrifying grounds, acres of them, where my mother's afraid. At night she makes us afraid too. All four of us sleep in the same bed. She says she's afraid of the dark. It's in this house she'll hear of my father's death. She'll know about it before the telegram comes, the night before, because of a sign only she saw and could understand, because of the bird that called in the middle of the night, frightened and lost in the office in the north front of the palace, my father's office. It's there, too, a few days after her husband's death, that my mother finds herself face to face with her own father. She switches the light on. There he is, standing by the table in the big octagonal drawing-room. Looking at her. I remember a shriek, a call. She woke us up, told us what had happened, how he was dressed, in his Sunday best, grey, how he stood, how he looked at her, straight at her. She said: I wasn't afraid. She ran towards the vanished image. Both of them died on the day and at the time of the bird or the image. Hence, no doubt, our admiration for our mother's knowledge, about everything, including all that had to do with death.

*

The elegant man has got out of the limousine and is smoking an English cigarette. He looks at the girl in the man's fedora and the gold shoes. He slowly comes over to her. He's obviously nervous. He doesn't smile to begin with. To begin with he offers her a cigarette. His hand's trembling. There's the difference of race, he's not white, he has to get the better of it, that's why he's trembling. She says she doesn't smoke, no thanks. She doesn't say anything else, doesn't say Leave me alone. So he's less afraid. He tells her he must be dreaming. She doesn't answer. There's no point in answering, what would she say? She waits. So he asks, But where did you spring from? She says she's the daughter of the headmistress of the girls' school in Sadec. He thinks for a moment, then says he's heard of the lady, her mother, of her bad luck with the concession they say she bought in Cambodia, is that right? Yes, that's right.

He says again how strange it is to see her on this ferry. So early in the morning, a pretty girl like that, you don't realize, it's very surprising, a white girl on a native bus.

He says the hat suits her, suits her extremely well, that it's very . . . original . . . a man's hat, and why not? She's so pretty she can do anything she likes.

She looks at him. Asks him who he is. He says he's just back from Paris where he was a student, that he lives in Sadec too, on this same river, the big house with the big terraces with blue-tiled balustrades. She asks him what he is. He says he's Chinese, that his family's from North China, from Fushun. Will you allow me to drive you where you want to go in Saigon? She says she will. He tells the chauffeur to get the girl's luggage off the bus and put it in the black car.

Chinese. He belongs to the small group of financiers of Chinese origin who own all the working-class housing in the colony. He's the one who was crossing the Mekong that day in the direction of Saigon.

*

She gets into the black car. The door shuts. A barely discernible distress suddenly seizes her, a weariness, the light over the river dims, but only slightly. Everywhere, too, there's a very slight deafness, or fog.

Never again shall I travel in a native bus. From now on I'll have a limousine to take me to the high school and back from there to the boarding school. I shall dine in the most elegant places in town. And I'll always have regrets for everything I do, everything I've gained, everything I've lost, good and bad, the bus, the bus-driver I used to laugh with, the old women chewing betel in the back seats, the children on the luggage racks, the family in Sadec, the awfulness of the family in Sadec, its inspired silence.

He talked. Said he missed Paris, the marvellous girls there, the riotous living, the binges, ooh là là, the Coupole, the Rotonde, personally I prefer the Rotonde, the night-clubs, the 'wonderful' life he'd led for two years. She listened, watching out for anything to do with his wealth, for indications as to how many millions he had. He went on. His own mother was dead, he was an only child. All he had left was his father, the one who owned the money. But you know how it is, for the last ten years he's been sitting staring at the river, glued to his opium pipe, he manages his money from his little iron cot. She says she sees.

He won't let his son marry the little white whore from Sadec.

The image starts long before he's come up to the white child by the rails, it starts when he got out of the black car, when he began to approach her, and when she knew, knew he was afraid.

From the first moment she knows more or less, knows

he's at her mercy. And therefore that others beside him may be at her mercy too if the occasion arises. She knows something else too, that the time has now probably come when she can no longer escape certain duties toward herself. And that her mother will know nothing of this, nor her brothers. She knows this now too. As soon as she got into the black car she knew: she's excluded from the family for the first time and for ever. From now on they will no longer know what becomes of her. Whether she's taken away from them, carried off, wounded, spoiled, they will no longer know. Neither her mother nor her brothers. That is their fate henceforth. It's already enough to make you weep, here in the black limousine.

Now the child will have to reckon only with this man, the first, the one who introduced himself on the ferry.

It happened very quickly that day, a Thursday. He'd come every day to pick her up at the high school and drive her back to the boarding school. Then one Thursday afternoon, the weekly half-holiday, he came to the boarding school and drove off with her in the black car.

It's in Cholon. Opposite the boulevards linking the Chinese part of the city to the centre of Saigon, the great American-style streets full of trams, rickshaws and buses. It's early in the afternoon. She's got out of the compulsory outing with the other girls.

It's a native housing estate to the south of the city. His place is modern, hastily furnished from the look of it, with furniture supposed to be ultra-modern. He says: I didn't choose the furniture. It's dark in the studio, but she doesn't ask him to open the shutters. She doesn't feel anything in particular, no hate, no repugnance either, so probably it's already desire. But she doesn't know it. She agreed to come as soon as he asked her the previous evening. She's where she has to be, placed here. She feels a tinge of fear. It's as if this must be not only what she expects, but also what had to happen especially to her.

She pays close attention to externals, to the light, to the noise of the city in which the room is immersed. He's trembling. At first he looks at her as though he expects her to speak, but she doesn't. So he doesn't do anything either, doesn't undress her, says he loves her madly, says it very softly. Then is silent. She doesn't answer. She could say she doesn't love him. She says nothing. Suddenly, all at once, she knows, knows that he doesn't understand her, that he never will, that he lacks the power to understand such perverseness. And that he can never move fast enough to catch her. It's up to her to know. And she does. Because of his ignorance she suddenly knows: she was attracted to him already on the ferry. She was attracted to him. It depended on her alone.

She says: I'd rather you didn't love me. But if you do, I'd like you to do as you usually do with women. He looks at her in horror, asks, Is that what you want? She says it is. He's started to suffer here in this room, for the first time, he's no longer lying about it. He says he knows already she'll never love him. She lets him say it. At first she says she doesn't know. Then she lets him say it.

He says he's lonely, horribly lonely because of this love he feels for her. She says she's lonely too. She doesn't say why. He says: You've come here with me as you might have gone anywhere with anyone. She says she can't say, so far she's never gone into a bedroom with anyone. She tells him she doesn't want him to talk, what she wants is for him to do as he usually does with the women he brings to his flat. She begs him to do that.

He's torn off the dress, he throws it down. He's torn off her little white cotton panties and carries her over like that, naked, to the bed. And there he turns away and weeps. And she, slow, patient, draws him to her and starts to undress him. With her eyes shut. Slowly. He makes as if to help her. She tells him to keep still. Let me do it. She says she wants to do it. And she does. Undresses him. When she tells him to, he moves his body in the bed, but carefully, gently, as if not to wake her.

The skin's sumptuously soft. The body. The body's thin, lacking in strength, in muscle, he may have been ill, may be convalescent, he's hairless, nothing masculine about him but his sex, he's weak, probably a helpless prey to insult, vulnerable. She doesn't look him in the face. Doesn't look at him at all. She touches him. Touches the softness of his sex, his skin, caresses his goldenness, the strange novelty. He moans, weeps. In dreadful love.

And, weeping, he makes love. At first, pain. And then the pain is possessed in its turn, changed, slowly drawn away, borne towards pleasure, clasped to it.

The sea, formless, simply beyond compare.

Buchi Emecheta

extract from

Second Class Citizen

Adah leaves her parents in Nigeria to live in London's Kentish Town. She finds her husband's traditional views of what a wife should be are easier to bear in a society which may have many disadvantages but also facilitates a degree of freedom.

POPULATION CONTROL

The snow melted from the pavements, from the gardens and from the roofs of houses. Spring was in the air and everything sprung up as if injected with new life by the gods. Even in a dark street, as dark as Willes Road in Kentish Town, one could hear the birds sing.

One Monday morning, when her family were still asleep, Adah got together her wash things to have her bath. There was no bathroom in the house in which they lived so she paid visits to the public baths in Prince of Wales Road several times in the week. It was on one of these visits, on a Monday, that she saw this bird; grey, small, solitary but contented in its solitude. Adah stood still on the other side of the road watching this grey bird, singing, singing, hopping from one window ledge to another, happy in its lonely freedom. Adah was intrigued by the creature. Fancy being moved this early in the morning by such a small thing as this grey bird, when less than a year before she had seen wilder birds, all gaudy in their colours, all wild in their songs. She never took notice of birds then, in the back yards of Lagos houses. Then she thought to herself: suppose there was never any winter, when every living thing seems to disappear from the face of the earth, the birds would always be around, they would become an everyday thing, and she wouldn't have noticed and admired it and listened to its watery song. Was that not what we need in Africa, to have a long, long winter, when there would be no sunshine, no birds, no wild flowers and no warmth?

That would make us a nation of introverts, maybe, and when eventually spring came, then we would be able to appreciate the songs of birds. What does that mean? Has Nature been too merciful to us, robbing us of the ability to wake ourselves up from our tropical slumber to know that a simple thing like the song of a grey bird on a wet Monday morning in spring can be inspiring? Was that why the early Europeans who came to Africa thought the black man was lazy because of his over-abundant environment which robbed him of the ability to think for himself? Well, Adah concluded, to cheer herself up, that may be so, but that happened years and years ago, before the birth of her Pa.

She was different. Her children were going to be different. They were all going to be black, they were going to enjoy being black, be proud of being black, a black of a different breed. That's what they were going to be. Had she not now learned to listen to the songs of birds? Was that not one of the natural happenings that inspired her favourite poet, Wordsworth? She might never be a famous poet like Wordsworth, because he was too great, but Adah was going to train herself to admire the songs of birds however riotous, to appreciate the beauty of flowers however extravagant their scent. She jolted herself to, reminding herself that she was the mother of three babies, and that she was supposed to be rushing for her Monday morning bath.

The women who cleaned the baths greeted her like an old friend. They knew she was always the first customer on Monday mornings, because Saturdays were usually too busy, and the baths too crowded. She preferred Mondays, when most people had gone to work and the ladies working at the baths would not have to hurry her up. The only snag was that on Monday mornings she seldom got very hot water, because the boiler, or whatever heated the water, had to be turned off over the weekend. It usually took a long time to heat up, but Adah did not mind the lukewarmness of the water, because that was the price she was paying for a long, quiet bath.

Her bath that Monday morning was particularly important, because she was going to the Family Planning Clinic. She had attended the week before and had been loaded with masses of literature. She had read about the jelly, the Pill, the cap and so many other things. She told Francis she was going, but Francis told her not to go because men knew how to control themselves better, the way it was done in the Bible. You hold the child and you don't give it to the woman, you pour it away. Adah considered this. It was not because she had stopped trusting her husband, but her husband could hurt her without meaning to, for wasn't that the way he had been brought up? She knelt and prayed to God to forgive her for making other plans behind her husband's back.

When it was time to take Bubu to the clinic to be weighed, she saw a motherly-looking nurse and told her, 'Please, could I have the Pill? You see, I am not twenty-one yet and if I had another child it would be my fourth, and I originally came here to study and bring up the two babies I brought from home. Can you help me? I need the Pill.'

The woman smiled and tickled Bubu on the cheek. They had a Family Planning Clinic in the evenings on Mondays. She would get the literature for Adah to read and she could decide with her husband which would suit them best. Well, how was Adah to tell the woman that Francis said that the best way to control the population was to pour it on the floor? Adah could not bring herself to tell the nurse that. The last nail in the coffin was when the woman brought a form which Adah's husband was supposed to sign to tell them that he was all for it, that he wanted his wife equipped with birth-control gear. There was going to be trouble over that, for Francis would never sign a thing like that, and he would raise hell if he realized that Adah got the literature without his permission. What was Adah going to do? Why was it necessary to have a husband brought into an issue like that? Could not the woman be given the opportunity of exercising her own will? Whatever happened, she was not going to have any more children. She did not care which way she achieved this, but she was having no more children. Two boys and a girl were enough for any mother-in-law. If her mother-in-law wanted another one, she could get her son another wife. Adah was not going to have any more. It was not going to be easy for her to forget the experience she had had recently having Bubu. That was a warning. She might not be so lucky next time.

Francis announced that he had read his two chapters scheduled for the day and that he was tired of reading and that he was going down to the Nobles to watch their television. Adah encouraged him to go. She wanted to read the birth-control literature in detail. Adah fished the now rumpled leaflets out from under Bubu's cot where she had hidden them. She read them again and again. Three facts stuck. One was that the Pill is the one you swallow just like aspirin. Secondly, the jelly is the one you allow to melt inside. The cap, which was the third thing, was the one you fitted in. Adah chuckled and was amused at it all. Fancy making a special cap for your other end instead of for your head. Well, these Europeans would stop at nothing. She was not going to choose the cap though, as it would be too messy, messing around with one's insides. No, she would go for the Pill, that was less complicated. The jelly? No, Francis would notice and ask questions.

But how was she to make Francis sign the form? The thought came to her that she could sign it for him. But that would be forgery. She imagined herself at a court and the magistrate sending her to jail for seven years for forging her husband's signature. But at the end of it she would be alive, and once alive, she might be allowed to look after her children. But if she did not forge the signature it might mean another child, another traumatic birth, another mouth to feed; and she was still not getting anywhere with her studies. The price she would have to pay for being an obedient and loyal wife would be too much. She forged the signature. She saved and scraped from the housekeeping money to pay for the first lot of pills. The money had been saved, the form signed, and, to add to her joy, she now had another library job waiting for her at the Chalk Farm Library. She was going to keep this job, no matter what. She was not going to allow herself to get pregnant again. Never.

But first she had to have this Monday bath, in case she had to strip herself to be examined or something. She had told Francis that Bubu was such a big baby, gaining weight every day, that the people at the clinic would like his photograph taken that Monday evening. It pained her, having to resort to the very method she had always used when she was little. That horrible tendency to twist the facts. But what else was there for her to do? She prayed to God again and again to forgive her.

She had to take Bubu with her, because if she had not, Francis would have said, 'I thought you told me that the people at the clinic were going to take his photo, because he was such a beautiful baby?' So she took Bubu with her.

At the clinic, she was shown into a waiting-room, where there were other women waiting. Two were undressed with their stockings rolled down round their ankles, just as you are when you are expecting, and the doctor wants to examine you. They reminded Adah of the pre-natal clinics. She was now used to that sort of thing – stripping yourself naked to be examined. It did not bother her any more. She asked herself, why should it worry me? I've only got what you've got. Why should I be ashamed of my body? It did not matter any more.

Three screens were set up in the middle of the square room. Women were to undress behind the screen and then sit down and wait to be called one by one into the doctor's room to be equipped with birth-control gear.

Adah saw a young West Indian mother and purposely went and sat down beside her. She wanted to be on home ground because she was frightened and because the young girl was the only woman there holding a baby. Adah could look after her baby for her when she went in to be equipped, and she could look after Adah's. That would be fair. With such noble thoughts in her mind, she greeted the West Indian girl with a friendly smile. The girl smiled back showing a golden tooth wedged in between her ordinary teeth.

They soon started to talk. She, the West Indian girl, was going to be trained as a nurse, so she needed some form of birth-control during her training. Her husband did not mind. So, months before, she was given the Pill. But, she cried to Adah, see what the Pill had done to her. She pulled up her sleeves and showed Adah a very fine rash. The rash was all over her face and neck. Even her skinny wrists had not been spared. She was covered with the kind of rash that reminded Adah of the rash caused by prickly heat in Africa.

'Do they make you scratch? I mean, do you feel scratchy all the time?'

'Yeah, man. That's the trouble now. I don't mind the appearance. But they itch all the time.'

Adah looked at her face again, and as she did so the girl started to scratch the back of her skirt. She was trying to hide it from the other women, trying to hide the fact that her bottom was itching. God have mercy! thought Adah. Her bottom as well? Then she asked the girl, 'Have you got the itch down there as well?'

The girl nodded. She had it all over her. Adah called to God to have mercy on her again. What was she to do now? She was not going on the Pill if she was going to end up looking like somebody with chicken-pox, or scratching like this girl as if she was covered with yaws. No, she was not going to have the Pill, and she was not going home empty-handed with no birth-control. She thought about the jelly and knew that it would only work when husband and wife are in agreement, for he would have to wait until it melted before coming on. So the jelly was out of the question for her. She could only go for the cap. That almighty cap which is specially made for one's inside. She had to think quickly. Francis might not know. The business was always done in the dark anyway. But suppose he felt it? Supposing he saw her fixing the cap in their one-room apartment with no bathroom and with the toilet as filthy as a rubbish dump? She could not fix the cap in the toilet, for what would happen if the cap fell? It would have collected enough germs to send her to her Maker in no time with cancer of the bottom. Adah was sure you could get cancer easily from under there. What was she going to do now? If only Francis would be reasonable. Whatever happened, she was going to risk it. A cap was better than nothing.

It came to her turn to go and see the doctor and the midwife who fixed you up with your own special size of cap. It was a messy job. They kept trying this and that and kept scolding Adah to relax otherwise she would go home with the wrong cap that would not fit her properly and *that* would mean another child. The fear of what Francis would say and what he would write to his mother and her relations loomed, full of doom, in her subconscious. Only she could feel it. The other two females, who were now tut-tutting at her and growing impatient and telling her to relax her legs, could not see the same picture that Adah was seeing. It was the picture of her mother-in-law when she heard that Adah went behind her husband's back to equip herself with something that would allow her to sleep around and not have any more children. She was sure they would interpret it that way, knowing the psychology of her people. The shame of it would kill her. Her children's name would be smeared as well. God, don't let Francis find out. In desperation, the two women, the doctor and the midwife gave her a size of cap that they thought should fit. If it did not fit, it was not their fault, because Adah did not help them at all because she was feeling so guilty of what she was doing. First she had forged her husband's signature, now she had got a cap which she was sure was going to cause a row if he found out. But suppose he did not find out and suppose it worked? That would mean no children and she would keep her new job and finish her course in librarianship. With that happy thought, she put the new equipment in Bubu's pram and went home.

But when she got home, she was faced with another problem. How was she to know what was going to happen on a particular night? Must she then wear the cap every night? That was the safest thing, but the cap was not very comfortable and Adah knew that it wobbled and she had to walk funnily to keep it in. And of course Francis would know. Oh, God, if only they had an extra room, then Francis would not have to see and watch and to make irritating remarks about her every move!

She ran down to their backyard toilet that had no electric light and fitted herself with her new cap. She could hear Titi and Vicky having their usual fight, and soon Francis would start calling for her to come and quieten her children. She fitted the cap in a hurry, almost going sick at the thought of it all. At that moment she felt really sorry for doctors and nurses. The amount of messing they have to do with people's insides! She dashed up, for Francis was already calling her and asking her what the hell it was she was doing down there in the toilet. Was she having another baby in there? Adah looked blank and said nothing. The fact that she was quiet made Francis suspicious. He then asked her what the matter was. Adah said that nothing was the matter.

He looked at her again and asked, 'Have you got a boil or something?'

Adah turned round from where she was tucking the kids into bed and asked, 'What boil?'

And Francis, still looking intensely at her, replied: 'Boil in the leg. You walk funny.'

Adah smiled, a wobbly, uncertain sort of smile, for her heart was beating so fast and so loudly, the noise was like a Nigerian housewife pounding yams in her *Odo*. Her heart was going 'gbim, gbim, gbim,' just like that. She was surprised and shocked to realize that Francis could not hear the guilty beating of that heart of hers. She thought everybody could hear it because it was so loud to her that it hurt her chest, making it difficult to breathe. But she managed a smile, that sort of lying smile. And it worked wonders.

Then she said, just to press home another point, 'You were calling me so loudly when I was down there in the backyard, that I ran up the stairs, and I bumped my toe on one of them, and it hurts a bit.'

Francis arched his brows but said nothing.

Soon it was midnight, and the row which Adah had dreaded flared up. Francis got the whole truth out of her. So, she a married woman, married in the name of God and again married in the name of the Oboshi, the goddess of Ibuza, came to London and became clever enough within a year to go behind his back and equip herself with a cap which he, Francis, was sure had been invented for harlots and single women. Did Adah not know the gravity of what she had done? It meant she could take other men behind his back, because how was he to know that she was not going to do just that if she could go and get the gear behind his back? Francis called all the other tenants to come and see and hear about this great issue – how the innocent Adah who came to London only a year previously had become so clever. Adah was happy when Pa Noble came, because at least it made Francis stop hitting her. She was dizzy with pain and her head throbbed. Her mouth was bleeding. And once or twice during the proceeding she felt tempted to run out and call the police. But she thought better of it. Where would she go after that? She had no friends and she had no relations in London.

Francis made it clear that he was writing to his mother and father. Adah was not surprised at this. But she was frightened, for despite everything she still respected her mother-in-law. But her son Francis was severing the ties of friendship that existed between Adah and his family. She knew that, after that, things were not going to be the same any more. She cried then. She was lonely again, just as she was when Pa died and Ma married again and she had to live in a relative's house.

Her marriage with Francis? It was finished as soon as Francis called in the Nobles and the other tenants. She told herself that she could not live with such a man. Now everybody knew she was being knocked about, only a few weeks after she had come out of hospital. Everybody now knew that the man she was working for and supporting was not only a fool, but that he was too much of a fool to know that he was acting foolishly. Pa Noble reminded Francis of Adah's health and God bless the old man, he sent all the inquisitive tenants away. There was nothing bad in Adah getting birth-control gear, Pa Noble said, but she should have told her husband.

What was the point of Adah telling them that she had told her husband and he had said you could control children by pouring them on the floor? But it did not matter. She was almost twenty-one. And, among her people, a girl of twenty-one was no longer a girl, but a woman who could make decisions. Let Francis write to her people and his people. If she liked, she would read their letters, if she did not she could throw them into the fire. The only person that mattered was her brother. She would write and tell him the truth. Boy had never liked Francis anyway. He knew even before Adah found out that Francis looked like those men who could live off women because of his good looks. Adah had just left school and was full of the religious idea that you could change anybody by your own personal example and by prayers. She was wrong and Boy her brother was right.

A few weeks later, Francis had his examination result, and it was another failure. Of course the fault was Adah's, especially as she managed to scrape through a part of her library examination. To explain his failures Francis wrote to his parents about the cap. But by the time their reply came, Adah was being eaten up by another problem. She was pregnant again.

THE COLLAPSE

Yes, Adah was pregnant again. This time she did not cry, she did not wring her hands, but behaved philosophically. If this pattern was going to be her lot in life she would do all she could do change it, but what was she going to do if all her efforts failed?

She went to her Indian doctor. She told him her whole story and that she wanted the pregnancy terminated. The Indian doctor was not a young man at all, but he had a certain way of saying things and was so small that one could easily take him for a young man. He had made good in London and had two sons who were both up at Cambridge; he had married a woman doctor he met when he was a student himself. He was very popular among the blacks living in that part of Kentish Town at the time. Adah guessed that if she appealed to him, being Indian and once a student in London, he would understand her predicament.

He understood, shook his head, sympathized and said, 'You should have come to us for the cap. The ones sold at the clinic are cheap ones and they go loose quickly. You should have told me about it.'

That was very nice. That was what Adah ought to have done if she had known. But how was she supposed to know? Smell it out like a witch doctor? Had he and his wife not put a notice in the waiting-room about the danger of smoking? Could they not have had a similar notice to say that birth control was available for the asking? It was too late now. She was pregnant, she knew it, but the doctor told her that it was too early for confirmation. He would give her some white pills. Adah was to take them and they would work.

Adah wondered what those pills were meant to do for her. But in her state of apathetic resignation, she did not ask questions. The pills were going to terminate the pregnancy. If the pregnancy was going to be terminated, what was the point of telling Francis? How did she know he would not misunderstand? Even if he did understand, how could she be sure he was not going to repeat it to the Nobles, to his parents and to everybody? Could she tell Francis and say, 'Look, I am telling you this under the seal of the confessional. You must not repeat it.' That would be impossible.

She now saw this situation as a challenge, a new challenge. When she was little and alone, the challenge had been that of educating herself, existing through it all, alone, all by herself. She had hoped that in marriage she could get herself involved in her man's life and he would share the same involvement in hers. She had gambled with marriage, just like most people, but she had gambled unluckily and had lost. Now she was alone again with this new challenge that included her children as well. She was going to live, to survive, to exist through it all. Some day, help would come from somewhere. She had been groping for that help as if she were in the dark. Some day her fingers would touch something solid that would help her pull herself out. She was becoming aware of that Presence again – the Presence that had directed her through childhood. She went nearer to It in her prayers. She never knelt down to pray in the orthodox way. But she talked to Him while stirring peppery African soup on her cooker; she talked to Him when she woke up in the morning; she talked to Him all the time, and Adah felt that He was always there.

There was no time to go to church and pray. Not in England. It took her years to erase the image of the Nigerian church which usually had a festive air. In England, especially in London, 'church' was a big grey building with stained-glass windows, high ornamental ceilings, very cold, full of rows and rows of empty chairs, with the voice of the vicar droning from the distant pulpit, crying like the voice of John the Baptist lost in the wilderness. In London, churches were cheerless.

She could not then go to any of them because it made her cry to see such beautiful places of worship empty when, in Nigeria, you could hardly get a seat if you came in late. You had to stand outside and follow the service through a microphone. But you were happy through it all, you were encouraged to bellow out the songs – that bellowing took away some of your sorrows. Because most of the hymns seem to be written by psychologists. One was always sure of singing or hearing something that would come near to the problem you had in mind before coming to church. In England you were robbed of such comfort.

London, having thus killed Adah's congregational God, created instead a personal God who loomed large and really alive. She did not have to go to church to see this One. He was always there, when she was shelving books in the library, when she was tucking her babies up to sleep, when she was doing anything. She grew nearer to Him, to the people with whom she worked, but away from Francis. The gulf between them which had grown with her stay in the hospital had been made deeper by the cap incident, and now this new child would make it greater still. But she was not going to tell Francis and she did not feel guilty about it. Francis would not be of any help.

She concentrated on working and enjoying her new job.

It was at the Chalk Farm Library that she met Peggy, the Irish girl with a funny hair style, who was heartbroken because her Italian summer-holiday boyfriend did not fulfil his promises. Peggy had gone on holiday the summer before, just to enjoy the Italian sun and the Roman scenery. She got involved with this handsome Italian youth, surprisingly tall for an Italian, but Peggy said he was Italian. It was love at first sight, and many promises were made. Peggy was a library assistant and the young man was reading Engineering in a university, the name of which Adah had forgotten. The young man seemed to have forgotten the promises he had made Peggy, and she was threatening to go to the address he gave her to find him and give him a piece of her mind. The talk was always of this young man and what Peggy was going to do to him, and how she was going to get her own back. Peggy never really told Adah what it was she had given him that pained her so much. But she let Adah know that she gave so much that she would regret it all her life. She was twenty-three, not very beautiful but small and fun to be with.

Then there was the big boss, Mr Barking. He was thin and bad-tempered, but without a touch of malice. His daughter had married a worthless fellow and he was determined to squash that marriage if it cost him his life. That daughter was ill because of the mental cruelty being inflicted on her by this no-good husband. Mr Barking never talked about his wife; he had got so used to her being there, in his home, that she was never discussed. That wife of his made good chicken sandwiches. Adah had seen Mr Barking munching and munching away at lots of chicken sandwiches in the staff room, and sometimes they made her feel like having one.

Bill was a big handsome Canadian; Adah did not know why he had come to England in the first place, because he looked down on anything English. He used the word 'Britisher' for the English, just like the Americans do.

Even his Christmas cake was flown out from Canada. His mother sent him clothes, food, everything. He would not study for the British Library Association Examinations because he did not trust the British system of education. He had married the children's librarian the year before. Her name was Eileen and she was tall and beautiful, a more perfect match you could never imagine. But Bill knew a little about everything. He liked black writers. Adah did not know any black writers apart from the few Nigerian ones, like Chinua Achebe and Flora Nwapa, and she did not know that there were any other black writers. Bill tut-tutted at her and told her what a shame it was that an intelligent black girl like her should know so little about her own black people. Adah thought about it and realized that Bill was right. He was an intelligent man, that Canadian, and Adah liked him a lot. During the staff break he would talk and expand about authors and their new books. He would then request it and the Camden Borough would buy it, and he would read it first; then he would pass it on to Adah and she would pass it to Peggy. Peggy would pass it to any other members of the staff who were in the mood to read books. It was through Bill that Adah knew of James Baldwin. She came to believe, through reading Baldwin, that black was beautiful. She asked Bill about it and he said, did she not know that black was beautiful.

Bill was the first real friend she had had outside her family. She had a tendency to trust men more because her Pa never let her down. She had already cultivated the taste for wide reading, and Bill, whose wife was expecting a second child within two years of their marriage, was always in the mood for literary talk. Adah was fascinated. She even started reading Marx and was often quoting to herself that if the worst came to the very worst she would leave Francis with her children since she had nothing to lose but her chains.

She got into the light-hearted atmosphere in which the

library staff did their work. There was another girl, a half-caste West Indian, one of the people who found it difficult to claim to be black. She liked Adah because Adah was at that stage forcing everybody to like her. The people at that library made her forget her troubles. Everybody seemed to have troubles then. Bill's wife was having another baby and their flat was very small. He was toying with the idea of going back to his old job, for he had been a radio news-caster in Canada. Why did he come here in the first place? Adah had wondered. He gave the hint, very tentatively, that he was running away from his mother who seemed to have organized a girl she wanted him to marry. He came to England to escape, but then he had met Eileen. Poor man, he was too handsome to be left alone. He was a six footer. Peggy's problem was money to take her to Italy, where she hoped to get a working holiday in order to look for the young Italian who had lied to her. Mr Barking seldom joined in their light-hearted talk, but they all knew he was thinking of his daughter. Fay did not like to associate herself with the black people because she was too white, a mulatto. So, to press home this point, when she qualified as a librarian, she got engaged to this English man who was away in Cambridge reading Law. Adah never saw this man, but she saw Fay's car which was so smashed that it was going to cost Fay a fortune to repair. Fay said her boyfriend had smashed it. Adah was sorry for her, particularly as, although she was very beautiful in a film-star type of way with smooth, glossy skin, a perfect figure and thick beautiful hair, she was at least thirty. And thirty seemed an enormous age to Adah at the time. A woman of thirty and not married was to her an outrage then.

When everybody started talking about their problems, Adah would start laughing.

Peggy would say, 'What the bloody hell are you laughing for?'

Then Bill would reply for her: 'She has no problems.

She's happily married to a brilliant husband who is reading to be a Cost and Works accountant, and she is already going through all her library examinations . . .'

Adah would not contradict him. Was the world not too full of sadness? What was the point of telling them all her woes. Yes, they all believed she had no problems because she wanted them all to believe that.

Three months passed speedily in this way and she knew that the pills the doctor had given her had not worked. She told herself not to panic. Women had been caught in worse situations before. Francis would only laugh and say: 'I thought you were being clever, getting the cap behind my back.' She had been through the worst. Even his beatings and slappings did not move her any more. She did not know where she got her courage from, but she was beginning to hit him back, even biting him when need be. If that was the language he wanted, well, she would use it. Was she not the greatest biter in her school? Francis threatened to break all her teeth for her, and grew his nails as long as those of a tiger, so whenever Adah opened her mouth to bite, Francis would dig his tiger nails into her flesh, almost choking her. Then the thought struck her that she could be killed and the world would think it was an accident. Just a husband and wife fighting. She still hit back occasionally when she knew she was near the door or out of danger, but she gave in to his demands for the sake of peace. They were like the demands of a wicked child who enjoys torturing a live animal given to him as a pet.

Adah wanted to know the truth from the doctor before she started looking for a room for herself and her children. Mr Noble was fed up with their fights and had asked them to move. To cap it all, the women in the house wrote Adah an open petition begging her to control her husband, because he was chasing them all. The letter was posted unsealed, and sent to the wrong branch of the library. So other library assistants could read it if they liked. Adah was not worried, she was going anyway.

She waited patiently for her turn at the surgery, then went in. The doctor greeted her and asked her how she was and she said, 'The child is sitting there pretty. It did not come out as you made me believe it was going to.' Her voice was low and panicky for the first time.

The look the doctor gave her was terrible. It seemed to chill her blood. His dark Indian skin seemed to have gone a shade darker. He was making an effort to speak but the anger inside him was choking him so that he gobbled feebly just like a kettle on the boil . . . then just like a kettle he spluttered: 'I did not give you the pills to abort the child.'

Adah recoiled like a frightened snake, but again, like a snake, she was gathering all her inner energy ready to attack this frightened little man. What did he mean? Adah asked with a voice that had a tinge of brutal harshness in it. She felt like digging her teeth into those eyes that were popping out like a dead fish's.

'All right, so I am having the baby. But I'll tell you this, the pills you gave me were abortive and you know it and I know it, because I carry the child and know what happened the first few weeks you gave them to me. If my child is imperfect in any way, you are responsible. You know that.'

She walked out of the surgery, not to her own home, but to a park near Gospel Oak village and then sat down, thinking. She had suspected something like this would happen, but to have it confirmed this way made her feel a traitor. She cried for herself, she cried for her children, and she cried for the unborn child. Suppose the child was born imperfect, just like those unfortunate thalidomide babies, what was she going to do then? Her thoughts went to her brother, Boy, who had sent her all his savings, asking her to leave Francis and his children and come back to Nigeria where her work at the Consulate would be waiting for her. Boy, poor Boy, he was very much annoyed over the cap issue which Francis had written to his parents about. This child would give them another song to sing. They would ask why, if she was on birth-control, which she went and got herself, did she then become pregnant? They would say the child was not her husband's, that it'd probably be a white child. You know, like the people who fitted the cap. And then everybody would laugh. Her own people would cover their faces in shame. She found herself being grateful that her parents were dead. This would have killed them. She had raised everybody's hopes when she was at the Methodist Girls' High School, she had raised their hopes higher when she got strings of 'A' levels by taking correspondence courses, and the hopes were being realized when she was in a good job at the American Consulate. If only she had stopped then. She could have passed the rest of her examinations by correspondence. After all, was Ibadan University not a branch of the great *London* University she was so mad about?

But would her children have been in this kind of nursery school where they were then? She got confused. Had it all been worth it?

Then a hand touched her shoulder. The hand was a black man's. Adah jumped. Sitting there, thinking and shedding silent tears, she had not heard the man cross the park. He was an African, a Nigerian. And when he spoke, Adah knew he was Ibo.

'You've had a fight with your husband?'

Adah did not answer. Then the man went on: 'My name is Okpara, and I know you are Ibo because of the marks on your face. I don't want to hear anything. Let's go and beg his forgiveness. He would let you in.' Typical Ibo psychology; men never do wrong, only the women; they have to beg for forgiveness, because they are bought, paid for and must remain like that, silent obedient slaves.

Adah showed him the way to her house. Had not the magic pass word 'Ibo' been uttered? The man talked all the way about this and that. He had a wife, too, with a baby boy, and he had read Law. They had been here some time and were getting ready to go home in about four months. His wife was a secretary and he worked in the Civil Service here. He had now finished his studies. But, he told Adah, they still quarrelled, though he would never beat his wife. He had outgrown that, but they still quarrelled. These quarrels did not mean the end of marriage. He reminded Adah of an old Ibo saying.

'Don't you remember, or have you forgotten, the saying of our people, that a husband and his wife always build their home for many things but particularly for quarrels? A home is where you quarrel in.' Adah nodded, she did remember.

She should have asked Mr Okpara whether the old people lived in one room, whether the men gave babies to their wives in such quick succession. Had not her Ma told her that during her time they used to nurse and breast-feed a child for at least three years? At least those men, the men of the time Mr Okpara was talking about, had other amusements. They had their tribal dances, they had their age-group meetings from which they arrived too drunk with palm-wine to have the energy to ask for their wives. Superstition played a big role in the lives of those people; if you slept with your wife when she was nursing a child, the child would die, so husbands abstained from their nursing wives for a period of three years. Many men were polygamous for this reason. They would build a separate hut for the nursing wife, pension her off for that long period and take in a childless one. These people could afford to build a house in which to quarrel.

But not in London, where her Francis sat all week in the same room by the same kitchen table turning the pages of this book and that book, getting up only to eat or go down to the Nobles to watch their television. Francis could never have a mind as healthy as those men. Again it struck her that their plan had failed, and that it had all been her fault. She should not have agreed to work all the time. She should have encouraged Francis to work, just like this man's wife, whom she had not seen, had encouraged her husband to work. Francis would have met other men, like this one, and he would have copied them. It was not too late, she consoled herself. That was what she was going to try to do. It might even still save the marriage. After all had not Mr Okpara studied privately in the evenings and still gained a certificate instead of going to watch the television from six o'clock to close-down?

To Mr Okpara she said nothing because she still maintained to herself that failure to make her marriage work was her own affair. She did not mind listening to the story of a successful one, and maybe getting some tips on how to make hers work, but she was not letting this stranger know. Why did she allow Mr Okpara to come home with her? Adah herself did not know the answer. She did not tell the man anything, even though her mind was crying for someone to listen to her, to understand her. Yet she felt that by talking to this stranger, although he was kind and an Ibo like herself, she would be betraying her husband, her family, her children. You don't tell people your troubles when you are still in the midst of them, otherwise it makes them bigger, more insoluble. You tell people when it's all over, then others can learn from your mistakes, and then you can afford to laugh over it. Because by then they have stopped hurting, you have passed them all, have graduated from them.

They got into their room. The scene that met their eyes was comical, and that was an understatement. Vicky was sitting on the settee, waving his wet nappy in the air like a flag. Titi was perched on the bed, looking thoughtfully at Vicky and their father. Bubu was lying flat on his back in the cot, listening to the songs Francis was singing to his children from the Jehovah's Witnesses handbook, looking as untidy as ever. His unshaved face became more noticeable now that Mr Okpara was in the room.

The latter was darker than Francis; he was not tall, about five foot eight, the same height as Francis, but he was immaculate. His white shirt was dazzling, and the fact that he was very black pronounced the whiteness still further. He was wearing a black three-piece suit, and his black shoes shone. His black briefcase added to his dignity somehow and the black rolled umbrella he was carrying completed the image – a black clerk in Britain coming home from the city.

As for Francis, to Adah he did not look like the image of anything. He was just himself, just Francis Obi, and Adah saw then that if she was going to model him on the image of this Mr Okpara, she was going to have a big fight ahead of her. Francis was Francis, not ashamed of being Francis, and was not going to change, even if Adah brought two hundred successful Ibo students to show him. He was proud to be what he was and Adah had better start getting used to him that way or move out.

Francis swore to Mr Okpara that he did not touch Adah. 'She simply went out. I did not know where, but I knew she would come back because she can't bear to leave her children for long. I did not beat her. Did she say that?'

Okpara was not daunted. They were not happy, Adah was not happy and this country was a dangerous place to be unhappy in, because you have nobody to pour out your troubles to, so that was why most lonely African students usually had emotional breakdowns because they had no one to share their troubles with. Did Francis want *his* wife to have such a breakdown? Okpara asked. Would that not be a drain on his purse?

This startled Francis and Adah. She did not know that people still lived like that, the husband paying for the doctor's bills. Even in Nigeria, whenever it was necessary for a private doctor to be called, she had always paid. She could not remember Francis ever paying for anything like that. Okpara was out of touch with the problem at hand, and Francis, now confused with anger, shame and disappointment, resented this intrusion into his family life. Adah hurried to make coffee.

She did not know that Francis had come to such a situation that he had told himself subconsciously that he would never pass his examinations. He had as it were told himself that his ever becoming a Cost and Works accountant in this world was a dream. She did not know that for this reason he would do everything to make Adah a failure like himself. He could not help it, it was human nature. He was not a bitter man.

He lashed his tongue at Okpara, told him to go back home and mind his own business. It was then that Adah realized that Okpara was English only on the surface. An English person would have felt insulted and would leave. But not Okpara. He was Ibo, an this was an Ibo family in trouble, and he was not going to leave until he had made them promise to pay a visit, so that they would see how the Okparas lived. He asked Adah if she had relations in London. Could they not intervene for her?

Adah thought this over. She had no close relatives in London, and the few distant ones would simply laugh. They would say: 'We thought she was the educated lady who knew all the answers. Did we not warn her against marrying that man? Did she not make her own bed? Well, let her sleep in it!' So Adah shook her head and said she had nobody.

After coffee, Okpara talked and advised Francis to be a man. Staying at home, and singing to his children from the hymn book of the Jehovah's Witnesses would not feed and clothe his family, to say nothing of his old parents at home. So he must get a job and study in the evenings. After all, the subjects were not completely new to him any more. Otherwise he would lose his manhood, and these children that he was singing to would soon realize that it was their mother that bought them clothes and food.

Francis stared at him as he said this, because it was a great humiliation to an African not to be respected by his own children. Okpara noticed that he had touched a soft spot for he then banged at the kitchen table, just to emphasize his point. He went on and said did Francis not know that the children born in this country get clever right from their mother's stomach? They know and they can remember what goes on around them. So if Francis wanted to hold the respect of his two sons, he'd better know what he was doing. Okpara did not mention Titi, she was only a girl, a second-class human being; it did not matter whether she respected her father or not. She was going to grow into an ordinary woman not a complete human like a man.

In the weeks and months that followed Okpara and his pretty little wife did their best but Francis would always be Francis. He had been used to being worked for, by a woman whom he knew belonged to him by right. Adah could not escape because of the children or so Francis thought.

When she told him she was expecting another child, the laughter that greeted this announcement was like a mad monkey's in the zoo. It was so animal-like, so inhuman, so mirthless, and yet so brutal. Adah was sure she was five months gone before she told him. She had first got over the pain in her own mind, but was still anxious about the perfection of the baby. She worried about that sometimes, but one thing she had learnt from Bubu's confinement was that she was not going to that hospital as a poor nigger woman. Her baby was going to arrive in style. She knitted and sewed, and this time her maternity grant was not going to Francis. She was buying a brand-new pram, a new shawl and a new outfit for herself for when she came out of the hospital. She met a West Indian girl who had had a baby girl by a Nigerian; but the man had not married her because, according to him, the child was not his. It was this girl who showed Adah that you could live on what was called the Assistance until your children grew up and you could get a job. Adah had heard of this Assistance before, in Nigeria; she learnt about it in her Social History lessons. She did not know that she could still claim it. If only she had known, she would have left Francis earlier. But she did not know.

She addressed twenty greeting cards to herself, gave three pounds to Irene, the girl, and told her to post three cards a day after the baby was born. Two big bunches of flowers were to be sent to her, one on her arrival, with Francis's name attached to it with sentimental words. The other one was to arrive at the hospital after her safe delivery. But if she did not survive the birth, Irene was to put Adah's children's names on it and make it into a wreath. Irene got sentimental and started to cry; Adah told her not to, because we all have to die some time. She was sure that if she was going to be operated upon like before, she did not have much chance. But the Indian doctor, now sorry for what he had done, had become Adah's strongest ally. The chances of her not being operated upon were fifty-fifty. Adah knew that if there was one single chance of her not being cut up, she was going to take that one chance. Her body had a way of rejecting anything foreign, she had known that too. So instead of handing over her pay packet to Francis to dole out the two pounds for housekeeping to her she would buy everything the doctors and the midwives told her to eat. Francis raised many rows, but Adah had a more important thing to worry about – her unborn child. It was so small she could hardly feel it. Her figure did not get big like it did when she was having the others. But she kept strictly to the diet prescribed.

It was then that she was introduced to the modern way of relaxation birth. Adah attended all the classes. It all seemed so easy that she regretted the unnecessary pain she had experienced with the other children. She did not lie about the date of her confinement and she was determined to have her four weeks' rest before going into hospital.

The money was not enough to go round and she told Francis, 'From now on, fend for yourself. I know the children are mine, because they need to be fed. You must go out and work. If not, I shall only cater for my children.'

Francis told her that she could not do it. Adah said nothing, but carried out her plans. He must go out to work. She cared about his studies and all that, but the children were growing both in size and in number. They came first. They had a right to happiness as well, not just Francis. He told her to write down the statement that she would not feed him any more. Adah wrote it without any hesitation. If the world was going to blame her for not feeding her able-bodied husband, let it go ahead. She did not care any more. She had three children to think about and soon there would be four.

They were sorry at the Chalk Farm Library that she was going. She was sorry too, but there, in that library, she discovered a hidden talent which she did not know she had before – the uninhibited ability to make friends easily. People had a way of trusting her easily because she was always trying to laugh however bad the situation. She learned to avoid gloomy people; they made her unhappy. So, since she could not avoid seeing Francis and his sad face, she shut him off from her mind's eye. She saw him but her mind did not register him any more. She heard him say that he had reported her to a Ministry or Board or something because she had signed that she would not feed him any more. Adah waited for the Law to come for her, but the Law did not.

He came with her to the hospital in the ambulance, though. On the second morning of her stay, her big bunch of flowers arrived. Her table was gay with cards even before Dada arrived. She came that night, small, but painless, and perfect. Adah was sure that the child arrived in the world smiling and laughing. She was so small, less than five pounds in weight, but beautiful, just like a black doll – and a girl. Adah was thankful for this child, so perfect and so beautiful that she nicknamed her 'Sunshine'.

She came home by herself in a taxi, and did it in style. She made everybody believe that she had wanted it so, to surprise her husband. She did not tell them that Francis had refused to come for her. They would start to pity her, and she could do without that. She tipped the nurses generously and they all laughed and thanked her. When she got home, she wrote a very nice letter to them all thanking them and she could hear them in her mind's ear saying what a nice happy African woman she was. She had no troubles in the world. Because of this attitude her problems became insignificant. They were all part of her life.

Hunger drove Francis to work as a clerical officer in the post office. Adah's hopes rose. This might save the marriage after all. But she was disappointed. Francis would pay the rent and still gave her only two pounds for the six of them and nothing more. Adah did not know how much he was earning or when he was paid. She warned him, though, that she was going into the Civil Service herself, and that she was going to do the same thing. She would not pay the rent, because it was a man's job to do that, she would not contribute to the food budget, because was she not his wife? She would only be responsible for her children, their clothes, the nursery fees and anything else the children needed. But Francis would not know how much she earned or on what date, because he had started it. He told her that she could not do that because she was his wife. He could refuse to allow her to go out to work. Then Adah retorted saying:

'This is England, not Nigeria. I don't need your signature to secure a job for me.'

But Adah hoped and prayed that this new sense of awareness and of pride in himself would continue. He bought himself a suit and shirts, he bought a small transistor radio, which Adah and the children were not allowed to touch and which he carried with him wherever he went, to work and even to the toilet. Adah laughed inside herself, and said how like a small boy Francis could be. She paid for her own food and the children's from the little savings she had collected from her superannuation pay. For the roof over their heads, she paid by being a wife to Francis at night, and by washing his endless shirts.

Her baby grew stronger, and she paid off her conscience by breast-feeding her. She was not going to bottle-feed this one. She had read somewhere that breast-fed babies were more intelligent, and grew stronger, than those fed from the bottle. She learned, too, that there was less likelihood of the mother becoming pregnant again if she did that. So she breast-fed her child.

Things seemed to be working out well, but Adah's money was running short, and the children needed new clothes. She worked out a timetable, and found that she could manage to have three hours of quiet each afternoon. Then her old dream came popping up. Why not attempt writing? She had always wanted to write. Why not? She ran to Foyle's and bought herself a copy of *Teach Yourself to Write* and sat down throughout all those months when she was nursing Dada and wrote the manuscript of a book she was going to call *The Bride Price*.

Zoë Fairbairns

extract from

Daddy's Girls

Christine is a child of the sixties. The elder sister of Janet, she struggles to develop independence in a family where her parents are at war. Her own initiation into sex reflects the emotional chaos of her upbringing.

'I'm very clever,' said my mother. 'He doesn't suspect.'

It was Friday evening. We were at Bleswick Junction, waiting for the train. I was giving myself a sight-test. I chose a single railway line and followed it into the gleaming silver tangle of rails outside the station.

'A wife who suspected wouldn't go off like this, would she?'

My railway line got lost among the other dazzling lines. I shaded my eyes against the early evening sunlight and squinted into the glare.

'A suspicious, nagging wife will drive a man away, Christine. The home should be a haven of peace.'

I couldn't find my railway line. I hoped that didn't mean I was going to need glasses. I would look horrible in glasses. I squinted at the lines till my eyes watered. Through the water a train came into view.

The announcer said, 'Oxford train. Change at Oxford for Birmingham.'

My mother said, 'I met Daddy in Oxford once.'

'Did you?'

'*My* Daddy. He and Mummy were home on leave. They got leave every three years, it was quite good. Lots of people didn't get nearly as much as that. He had to do some research at the Bodleian, so they took furnished rooms. Miss Dolby put me on the train at the end of term and Daddy and Mummy met me at Oxford. I ran the whole length of the platform and he picked me up.'

That seemed to be the end of the story. I followed her on

to the train. It was crowded with people going home from work. They looked tired and fed up. They fidgeted with copies of the *Evening Standard* and the *Evening News*, ran fingers round the insides of grimy shirt collars, and looked out of the window with bleakness in their eyes.

I wanted them to know that tomorrow I was going to see my long lost boyfriend. I was wearing a new dress with red roses because my mother had insisted that I look respectable for her friend Billy. I would have preferred to be wearing something a bit more CND-ish but at least I felt fresh and romantic.

'When he comes to his senses,' whispered my mother at the top of her voice, 'he won't hear a word of reproach from me.'

I begged her with my eyes to be quiet but she said, 'It's not his fault. It's not even her fault. She's a very, very sick girl. I pity her.' As the train picked up speed, so did my mother's pity for Pam. 'There's a certain type of girl, Christine. You can spot them at children's parties. Adorable little things. Rosebuds, with maggots inside. They make up to the little boys and they make up to the Daddies and they get extra pieces of cake. They get everything they want. It's a pity they can't be spotted at birth because that's when they should be strangled.'

'Shall I go and see if there's a buffet?'

'There should be institutions for keeping them out of harm's way. What do you want a buffet for, you're not hungry or thirsty. Nothing'll happen while Janet's around, will it? He wouldn't want to upset Janet, would he?'

'No.'

'I want him to have his fill of her. Have her till he's sick of her.'

'Janet?'

'*Pam*. The novelty'll wear off. He'll see her, warts and all.'

I wished she would lower her voice at least. To set an example I lowered mine. 'She hasn't got warts.'

'She probably has, and a great deal else besides,' said my mother with a mean snigger.

The tired-looking people in the carriage were perking up and listening hard. A man hid behind his *Evening News*, and shook.

I turned my face to the window and pretended to go to sleep. I stared at the gold insides of my eyelids. Silence fell over the carriage. I peeped at her through my eyelashes and saw her writing in her *Household Memoranda* book. I was glad she had stopped talking but there was something embarrassing about the way she chewed her pencil, stared into space and frowned with concentration, like a child doing homework.

I shut my eyes again. I tried to picture Adam's face. We were to meet at nine o'clock tomorrow morning at the headquarters of Construction Not Destruction. I hoped I would recognize him. I couldn't quite remember what he looked like.

'I'm not going to reproach him.' My mother's foot brushed my ankle. The train was slowing down. 'When he comes to his senses he won't hear one word of reproach from me.' We were arriving at Oxford and she was saying what she had been saying shortly before I fell asleep. I looked nervously at the other passengers and wondered if she had been doing Continuous Performances.

'Why should I reproach him? I don't know anything.' We got our things together. Beyond the window the towers and domes of Oxford glowed in the sunset. 'I don't know anything and I never have known anything. That's what's so clever about me.' We got off the train. 'The dreaming spires,' she said. 'I hope Janet will get into Oxford. I don't want her to end up like me.'

'Getting married, you mean? Who'd want her?'

We sat on a bench to wait for our connection. She said,

'Of course I didn't mean not to get married. I'd marry Daddy again ten times over.' Her voice was warm with love. I felt like puking.

'What did you mean then?'

'Nothing really.'

'What did you mean? Why don't you want Janet to end up like you?'

'I don't want either of you to. I want you to fulfil your potential, as I never did.'

'Why didn't you? Why don't you now? Why don't you go back to nursing?'

'Because Daddy –'

'Why don't you go to evening classes?'

'It's not as simple as that.'

'Why? Why isn't it?'

'There you go again. Christine Toms QC for the prosecution.' She opened her handbag and took a photograph out of her wallet. 'Billy,' she said, 'will meet with your approval. She got her SRN *and* her Midwifery. You'll be able to have a long talk with her about how hopeless *I* am.'

The picture showed my mother dressed in wartime nurse's uniform with another nurse at her side. The other one was a head taller than my mother and had a gawky arm round her shoulder. She had wispy hair, thick spectacles and a distinct look of Dilly Dreem the Lovable Duffer.

The platform was filling up. The Birmingham train was announced. My mother said, 'I'd better give you your ticket in case we get separated.' People started to push forward. 'Have I given you any pocket money for the weekend?' She stuffed bits of paper into one of my hands and the handle of my suitcase into the other. She said, 'I'm not the beast of burden.' We ran for the train. I seemed to be losing her in the crush but she mouthed, 'It's all right.' She signalled that she would go to the back of the train and I should go to the front. This doubled the chances of finding at least one seat. I found one, squashed between a nun and a city gent.

The train moved off. I felt uneasy without my mother, though there was no reason. This was normal drill. If my mother didn't find a seat, she would come looking for me and we would share mine. If she had found one she would sit in it and meet me at Birmingham.

The air in the compartment was sweet and stuffy. The nun's habit was touching my clothes. Nuns gave me the creeps. Sharp pain bit into my hand and I wondered if I might be getting a stigmata. What would she think of that? I realized what the trouble was. I was clutching my ticket so tightly that the corner of the cardboard was cutting into my palm. I loosened my hand and saw what else I was holding. I had the photograph of Billy, a pound note and piece of *Household Memoranda* paper with my mother's handwriting on it.

Dear Christine,

I have decided to go home and catch them in the act as all this uncertainty is bad for our family life. Tell Billy and Frank that I have had to have a tooth out unexpectedly but we really must get together soon. From Billy and Frank's house phone home and tell Janet or Daddy or even the Slut if she has the temerity to answer our phone that we have arrived safely. They can settle in for the night all nice and cosy and never imagine that I am nearby waiting for my chance. Sorry for this note but I knew that if I told you what I was going to do you would argue and cross-examine me like the barrister you are at heart and could be if only you would apply yourself and go to university as I never did!

Lots of love from Mummy.

* * *

The sun set. The sky went purple. The train pushed on and on through the countryside. Lights came on in snug farmhouses. The train carried me past them. Towns poked their fingers out into the fields. We went past bomb sites, building sites, gasworks and factories. Floodlights shed their pinkish–yellow glare over acres of gleaming, identical cars with no number plates.

At Snow Hill Station a woman approached me. I recognized her from the photograph but I was surprised at how much older than my mother she seemed. She had lost her gawkiness and looked like a grown woman who might also be a nurse. She said, 'You must be Christine Toms,' and a man tried to take my suitcase.

I snatched it back. The woman said, 'Where's your mother? I'd have known you anywhere. You're her image.'

'I'm not.' I pushed past her. 'You've made a mistake.' I headed towards the exit and the dark city.

'Are you sure?' she cried, and I realized she was as silly as my father had said she was. I looked over my shoulder. She was looking over hers. Frank was looking too, and so was their daughter. I assumed it was their daughter. She had a surly expression. I liked that. If I had been dragged out at ten o'clock at night to meet and make friends with a total stranger just because her mother and my mother were nurses together once, I'd have had a surly expression.

I wanted to reassure her. *It's all right. You won't have to share your room. I'm not here.*

They were still looking at me so I hurried out of the station and found a phone box. I phoned Billy's home and was answered by a girl who I guessed was either another daughter or a babysitter. There was no danger that she would know my voice or my mother's, but I shrieked a bit to be on the safe side. I told her that I and my daughter Christine couldn't come after all because Christine wasn't very well. I tried to make it sound as if what Christine had wrong with her was something to do with her periods, so that the girl wouldn't ask for details. She didn't. She just said, 'They've gone to the station to meet you.'

I said,'I'm so sorry for the inconvenience. We *must* get together soon.'

Opposite the station was a row of bus stops in front of a huge dark church with white gravestones. I looked at the timetables on the bus stops, but none of them mentioned the road where Construction Not Destruction was.

I took a taxi. We seemed to travel a long way through the shadowy city but it was hard to tell whether we were actually getting anywhere. We kept being diverted past roadworks and along one-way streets. I didn't blame my father for not wanting to come to Birmingham, it was all being dug up. Cranes and scaffolding towered above cement mixers and heaps of bricks on bomb sites. The square white beginnings of modern buildings peeped out of the rubble like the tips of new teeth.

We turned down a narrow street. The light from the few lamp posts was dim and greenish yellow. We could hardly read the numbers on the houses, which were small and huddled together in terraces. Their front doors faced straight on to the street. My father would have called them 'omes for the workers.

Some of the houses were boarded up. There were gaps in the terraces. The houses on each side of the gaps were propped up by wooden struts shaped like lopsided letter A's.

One of the gaps had frames in it with dangling ropes. They looked as if they would come in handy for public executions. A sign read 'CONSTRUCTION NOT DESTRUCTION ADVENTURE PLAYGROUND'.

I got out of the cab and waited for the driver to turn into Birmingham's answer to PC Tutsworth and say he wasn't going to leave a nice young girl like me in a place like this. But once he'd taken all my money he drove off at high speed, as if what he really wanted to be was Birmingham's answer to Stirling Moss. He left a smell of petrol in the warm night air where it mixed with soot and dog's muck and a faint hint of flowers.

Nailed to a tree in front of the adventure playground was a sign advertising a CND Poetry and Jazz evening, with today's date and the name of a pub, but no address. I thought that must mean the pub was nearby, and locals would know where it was. All I had to do was find some locals. I peered into the darkness around me but saw no one. I heard running footsteps and a shout of drunken laughter but they were some way off.

I chose a house with a light on. I knocked. A snarling dog hurled itself against the other side of the front door, shaking it till I thought it would give way. I ran.

I heard more drunken voices, and went towards them. I wandered a bit and found the pub. Everyone seemed to be leaving. I ducked into the Saloon Bar where the barmaids were collecting glasses and telling people to drink up. Their accents reminded me of Beryl Reid in *Educating Archie*. I made for the Ladies.

It was half-way up a flight of stairs. From the top of the stairs came the sound of jazz, tantalizing waves of music. I walked towards the waves and they engulfed me, making me tingle.

Smoke curled round a half open door. I peered in. The room was hot, and dark except for a spotlight on three jazz players with embroidered waistcoats and gleaming instruments. Cigarette tips glowed around them.

When the players got to the end of their music, a man wearing a bowler hat over long beatnik hair stood up to read his poem. He spent a lot of time shuffling pieces of paper, but when he got to the poem he seemed to be making it up as he went along. He sounded quite angry and kept saying 'fuck'.

He finished his poem and everybody clapped wildly, which he liked. He was a show-off. He reminded me of Janet. He looked as if he wanted to read us another poem but one of the barmen came up from downstairs and put the lights on. 'Thanks very much, ladies and gents.'

People stretched their limbs and rubbed their eyes as if they were coming out of hibernation. Adam was only a few feet away from me. I recognized him at once, even though his hair was longer than I remembered it and seemed to have gone grey.

He was wearing a frayed jersey and corduroy trousers with paint stains on them. His glasses looked different. The frames were thinner. He was talking to a group of people. Some of them were girls. One of the girls passed a packet of cigarettes. Everyone took one, including Adam. Someone brought out a lighter. They passed it round. Somebody said something that made them laugh. I didn't hear the joke, I just heard the laughter. I felt left out. The sound of the laughter told me that if Adam didn't recognize me I would walk out into the night and never be seen again. If he wasn't pleased to see me I would die. I wouldn't commit suicide, I wouldn't need to, I would simply disappear and die of natural causes.

It must have been a good joke because the laughter went on and on. He rolled his head around. His eyes met mine, went away and came back. He rushed over and hugged me. I hugged him. I didn't care who saw, I was so happy and relieved. He felt small after Miguel, but hard and strong, perhaps from all his building work. Suddenly I was shy. I tried to make the hug go on and on so that I wouldn't have to say anything, or look at him.

His hair smelt of sawdust and paint which explained the greyness and made me sneeze. He said, 'Bless you,' for the sneeze and then looked puzzled. 'I thought you weren't coming till tomorrow.'

'I'll go back then. If you don't want me.'

'Of course I want – but what about you mother and Bertie?'

'*Billy*. Can I have a cigarette?'

'Don't you buy your own yet?'

I took his cigarette and smoked it. He called, 'Jane, have you got a fag?' The girl tossed him one and he lit it from mine.

He said, 'Where's your mother?'

'If I'd known you wanted her, I'd have sent her instead.' I looked as sexy as I could and it worked. He smiled and shrugged and kissed me.

The room was emptying. The barman said, 'Thanks very much, ladies and gents,' put one hand on my back and another on Adam's, and pushed us towards the door.

Adam took my suitcase and we went down the stairs. We had a kiss on each stair. The barman rammed us in the ribs with a tray of glasses. 'Thanks very much, ladies and gents.' Outside the pub, other Poetry and Jazz people were kissing under lamp posts. I looked for Jane but I couldn't see her. Adam walked me into a shadowy corner and we kissed as if we had been starving and had found food. Every time he tried to stop I started another kiss because I didn't want him going after Jane.

* * *

The church hall was near the adventure playground. It reminded me of my father's rugby club, except that the people wandering about inside it looked as if they had brains. Student-type girls and men with beards came and went from the kitchen with mugs of coffee. Paper arrows on the wall showed where males and females were supposed to be sleeping, but no one was going to sleep. They sat on rucksacks, rolled their own cigarettes and had fierce arguments about the Labour Party. Two men were discussing something technical about one of their guitars. They passed the guitar backwards and forwards and strummed a few notes to make their points.

A fussy priest in jeans looked at me, looked at his clip board and looked at me again. 'Hullo! Who's this?'

Adam said, 'It's Chris, she's just arrived. Chris, this is Keith.'

'Pleased to meet you.'

'Chris what? Is she staying?'

'Toms,' I said. 'And yes.'

'The girls sleep up that end.' Keith bustled off.

Adam looked at my dress and my suitcase. 'You have brought a sleeping bag?'

'No.'

'Didn't I say to bring one?'

'I haven't got one.'

He looked at me. 'Has something happened?'

'Billy's children have got scarlet fever.'

'Scarlet –?'

'The whole family's in quarantine. No one's allowed in or out. It's awful.'

He sighed. 'We'd better get you some bedding.' He took me up a flight of stairs to a store-room full of broken pews and boxes of prayer books. On a shelf was a pile of grey blankets and grey pillows. He let go of my hand and scooped up an armful of the bedding. He looked as if he meant to take it downstairs but he stopped, changed his mind and dropped it on the floor.

He held out his arms to me and said, 'Please tell me why you're here.'

'If you don't want me, I'll go away again.'

'I do want you.'

We leaned against a broken pew, kissing. He tasted of paint and smelled of sweat but I didn't mind. I didn't mind my back getting uncomfortable either, but I pretended to. The more uncomfortable I seemed to be, the more he comforted me, and I needed a bit of comforting.

He admired my dress. I let him undo the zip.

Music and talk drifted up from downstairs. He took off my bra. He smiled as if someone had given him a present. He kissed the tip of my left nipple, then my right. They tingled and went hard. They were so hard they hurt. He soothed them. He ran his hands between my breasts and up and down the sides. They felt as if they wanted me to cry, because in all that time with Miguel they had never been properly appreciated and now they were being appreciated again.

He took off his glasses and his jersey. He pressed his hard, skinny chest against my soft, full one. *You'd never think we were the same species.* We were the same species now.

The door opened. A man and a girl stood there looking disappointed. They said, 'Oh, sorry.'

'Don't mention it,' said Adam into my neck.

The girl said, 'You might have put the sign on the door.'

There was a square skylight in the roof. Against its faint glow I could see the blank outline of his head. I couldn't see his features. He could have been anybody.

Anybody at all could have been unhooking my suspenders and rolling my stockings down. He didn't even smell right. Any paint-covered workman could have his hand inside my knickers.

I couldn't believe I was going to do this but I didn't think I was going to stop.

My eyes got used to the darkness. His face was white and devilish. Pews surrounded us like the bars of a cage but we weren't in a cage. We were free. We could do whatever we wanted. I knew what he wanted to do. I knew I was supposed to stop him. He wouldn't stop of his own free will, it was up to me.

He fiddled with the buckle of his belt. It sounded dangerous.

'Don't.'

'You mean I've got to keep my trousers on? What a rotter you are.' He left the buckle alone.

I don't know who's there, I thought.

'It's only me,' he said

I must be safe with him if he can read my mind.

The talking and strumming from downstairs faded into silence. In the silence several hearts thumped. One was Adam's. The others were mine. My main heart had sent little hearts to different parts of my body to thump there. One was in my head. Another was in my stomach. A third thumped in the wetness between my legs.

It retreated from Adam's fingers and went on thumping in safety, deep inside, out of reach.

He said, 'Do you believe I can undo my belt and take my trousers down without using my hands?'

'No.'

'You're right, I can't.' He put his hands on the insides of my thighs. 'So if you can feel my hands, you know I've still got my trousers on.' He opened my thighs and put his face there.

I thought he was going to kiss me, which would have been bad enough. Bad enough for him. I didn't mind it. In fact I quite liked it. I thought he must be hating it, but he sort of settled down, as if he were about to have a good long drink from a river. A swamp was more like it. How could he? I was getting warmer and warmer down there, and up here my breaths were coming fast with little moans at the end of them. I didn't mean to let out those moaning sounds, but there they were. I was embarrassed by the moans and embarrassed by the disgusting thing Adam was doing. He didn't seem to have realised how disgusting it was but he soon would. And when he did he would move away.

I didn't think I could bear that so I moved away first. I got hold of the sides of his head and pushed.

He looked anxious. 'Aren't I doing it right?'

'What?'

His eyes and teeth glowed up towards me. 'Why did you stop me?'

'Well.'

'Are you sufficiently aroused?'

He seemed to want an answer.

I tried out some in my head.

What if I said *yes* and I was wrong?

What if I said *no* and he got angry?

I didn't want to say *no*. I wanted his tongue back. I put my fingers where his tongue had been. They weren't as good as his tongue, but they weren't bad.

He threw his trousers and his underpants over a pew and lay on top of me. I tasted the dust in his hair and felt his penis. My fingers got out of its way, like pedestrians in front of a lorry. I still couldn't believe I was doing this.

He prodded me and made me flinch. That prod spoiled everything. I didn't want to do it after all.

I moved away. He came after me and gave me a long, deep kiss before trying again. He was trembling and gasping. I moved away again. He stopped me. 'I think you're supposed to come towards me. Sort of like this.' He moved his hips about.

'Why?'

'It says in *Modern Woman and* – '

'Why should I hurt myself?'

'If you want to – '

'I don't'.

'Oh.' He looked as if he couldn't believe it. He looked as if he were going to rape me. 'You mean not now? Or never?'

'How should I know?'

He turned away furiously and lit a cigarette. He didn't offer me one. The cigarette calmed him down and he said quietly, 'Either you do this with me now or you'll do it some other time with someone else or you'll be a virgin for the rest of your life. Do you accept my reasoning so far?'

Pompous git, I thought. I nearly said, *Save it for your clever girlfriends at Oxford*, but I didn't want him to save it for them.

He said, 'Is there anyone else you'd prefer?'

'No.'

'And do you want to be a virgin for –'

'No.'

'Well then.' He propped himself up on his elbows again and reared above me. I thought, *This is it*, but he stopped and said, 'There is another possibility. I think you can go to a doctor and have it done under local anaesthetic. Fancy that?'

'Not much.'

He leaned forward and my body gave way.

It hurt a bit but it wasn't nearly as bad as I'd been led to expect by the authoress of *The Second Sex*. Adam seemed to be having a much worse time than I was having. He heaved about, groaned and flopped on top of me as if he had just died.

The French authoress must have been unlucky with her defloration. Whoever had done it, it certainly wasn't Adam. He lit two cigarettes and gave me one. 'Best cigarette in the world,' he said.

I took a few puffs and agreed with him. I watched my smoke-stream mingle with his until there was only one. I could remember a time when I hadn't liked smoking very much and I wondered if sex was like that and you had to get used to it.

As if he had read my mind again, he said, 'Sorry.'

'It's all right, it was nothing.'

He sighed.

'It was lovely,' I lied. 'Especially before.'

'I should have kept going. I hope I'm not doomed to be a premature ejaculator for ever.'

'What's a premature –?'

'Some men can go on for hours.'

I was glad he wasn't one of them but I didn't say anything.

* * *

He fell asleep. I lay with my eyes wide open. I had pins and needles, I felt sore and sticky between my legs, and I was wondering what had happened to my family.

I imagined my mother talking to herself on the train and getting out at Bleswick. She scurried home and hid in the garden. I wondered if she knew that the lilac bush provided the best hiding place. It had a good view of the house and gave off a nice smell.

She waited for darkness. The moon came out. She probably got a bit chilly. She watched to see which lights came on in which windows.

Janet's bedroom light came on first. Janet's going-to-bed routine took about half an hour. She folded her clothes, checked to see that I hadn't been interfering with any of her collections (as if I would), wrote a novel or two and said a thank you prayer for her day's achievements. She got into bed and turned out the light.

Which light would have gone on next? Or lights? If two lights went on – one in the double bedroom and the one in the spare – everything could still be perfectly innocent. But I had a feeling that only the double bedroom light had gone on. The window of the spare room stayed dark.

That would have settled it. I imagined my mother breathing faster and faster. In the window of her own bedroom, the light went out. She gasped with bitterness. They were nice and cosy. She was outside, alone with her jealous rage.

It would have been a rage to scorch the lilac leaves. It would have been a worse rage than any I had ever seen, and I had seen a few. It would be wilder than her Christmas rages, more furious than her slimming rages, or her rages when the boiler wouldn't light, or she couldn't find her handbag, madder than the frenzies in which she begged me to pretend not to know what I knew about my father.

There could be no more pretence after this. But what was *this*? What would she have done? Would she have climbed up the ladder to the bedroom window and caught them in the act?

The act. Adam lay with his head against my beautiful

breasts. It was *our* act. I thought how lucky I was to have him, now that my home was about to become a broken home. If my mother had murdered my father and Pam, or burned the house down or something like that, Janet would probably be put into an orphanage, but I would stay here with Adam.

I woke by myself, itching from the blankets. I could smell bacon frying. I stood up. Wetness trickled like tears between my legs. I ran my hands through my tangled hair and over my face to feel whether it had changed. The skin felt dry but strangely soft. I walked round the store-room, picking my scattered clothes off the pews.

I wanted a full-length mirror to look in, and a bath. I wanted Adam. I put my dress on over my naked body. I pretended it was a négligée. I took my sponge bag out of my case and opened the door of the store-room. At the bottom of the stairs people milled about, rubbing their eyes and clearing up. They wore dungarees and paint-stained overalls which looked as if they had slept in them. I felt rather glamorous. Under my dress I was naked and I knew things. I would know those things for ever, whatever happened.

I followed the smell of bacon into the main hall. The sleeping bags had been cleared away and piled on the stage. There was a trolley with a tea urn and cups. Folding tables and chairs had been set out.

Each table had a catering pack of cornflakes, a pile of bowls and a big metal jug of milk. Through the hatch, I could see Adam in the kitchen with Jane. They both had badges on with the word ORGANIZER, and chefs' hats with CND symbols cut out of them. She wore a pretty apron of purple gingham over tight trousers and a big grey home-knitted jersey. She was frying bacon. He was spreading margarine on slices of Wonderloaf.

I watched them for a long time but they didn't see me. I went to the Ladies. Girls wearing jeans and men's shirts were washing their faces and cleaning their teeth. They stared at me in my dress through eyes that hadn't had enough sleep.

I hadn't had enough sleep either but I had a reason. I had done it. Whatever happened for the rest of my life, I had done *it*. I looked into the eyes of the girl students and guessed which ones had done it and which ones hadn't done anything.

There was no bath so I held my face flannel under a tap, squeezed it out and took it into a cubicle to wipe between my legs. I wondered whether any of the girls had guessed what I was doing and why. I wondered if they disapproved. I didn't care if they did. I wanted them to.

Still barefoot and dressed like a woman of the streets, I went to the kitchen. I said loudly, 'Can I help?'

Adam jumped as if he had been doing something wrong. This made me even more suspicious that he had been. 'Good morning, Chris!'

'Morning.' I picked up a knife.

Jane said, 'You're a weekend volunteer, aren't you? You've got your own rotas.' She was pretending to be friendly but she was looking at the knife and she seemed nervous.

'It's all right.' I spread some margarine. 'I don't mind helping.'

'You don't have to, honestly,' said Adam. 'Have some breakfast. And er –' he smiled – 'get dressed.' He said it as if he didn't want me to think he was ordering me about but he wanted me to do what he said.

Without a word I went back to the store-room and put on jeans and a jersey. If he wanted me to look like everybody else, then I would look like everybody else. Last night he hadn't thought I was like everybody else. As I came back down the stairs I swung my hips in a sexy, automatic sort of way that I seemed to have learnt.

As I queued for breakfast, I felt empty and sad. Why

should I queue up for him? I wanted him to be mine, as I was his. I looked at all the men. I wondered if they realized. I wondered if they were jealous of Adam. I tried to decide which ones I liked. There was one with black hair and a black beard and black curls peeping between his shirt buttons. I wondered what it would be like with somebody like him who was hairy and coarse.

I reached the front of the queue. You had to help yourself to slices of bread and hold them apart while Adam put bacon between them. He did mine very sexily. He gave me an extra rasher and a big smile. I thought he was going to say something but he turned to the next person in the queue.

I got myself some tea and sat with it and my bacon sandwich at one of the tables. The other people at the table were quite nice; they asked where I had come from and when I said Bleswick they pretended to have heard of it. But I couldn't take my eyes off Adam and Jane in the kitchen beyond the hatch.

My sadness had a sickly, familiar feeling. I seemed to know that this always happened after a girl lost her virginity, and it served her right.

I seemed to have done it dozens of times. I seemed to know what to expect. He had lost respect for me and I had lost him.

The priest from last night, who was wearing one of the ORGANIZER badges, banged the side of one of the metal jugs with a spoon. He said, 'I'm not going to preach a sermon,' and the long-termers cheered. He said, 'Thank you. Remember that the whole point of Construction Not Destruction is to provide an answer to the challenge that is so often put to those of us who are against the bomb. What are you *for*? What is your alternative? This weekend, *you* are the alternative.

'Don't ram politics down people's throats. Some of them aren't interested in politics, and that's their privilege. Some of them oppose us, and that's their privilege too. Some of them think ban-the-bombers are sex-crazed drug addicts.' The long-termers cheered again, and Adam winked at me from the kitchen. Keith wasn't laughing. 'This is a serious matter. They've read it in the *Daily Express*, so it must be true. Once again, it's their privilege to suspect what they want, but it is not yours to confirm their suspicions. Remember, you are the ambassadors of the peace movement, and behave accordingly. If our personal behaviour turns people against us, we're wasting our time as far as building our movement is concerned.'

Adam was looking very, very solemn. I was sure I was going to giggle. I kept snorting and blowing my nose. Keith said, 'I'm not saying don't enjoy yourselves. I'm not a killjoy, God knows. But –'

'Make sure no one finds out about it, eh, Keith?' someone suggested.

'Make sure *I* don't find out.' He looked as if the joke had gone far enough.

* * *

I was down on the rota to do Slum Renovation with four strangers. I said to Adam, 'Why can't I be with you?'

'You will be.' He kissed me, but he was in a rush. 'Tonight.' He wasn't my lover any more, he was an Organizer, a long-term volunteer, a big shot.

'Why not today?'

'I'm staying here,' he said. 'Cleaning and catering.'

'I could do that.'

'Housework? You?'

I pointed at the rota. 'I don't know these people.'

He was completely unsympathetic. 'Get to know them. You're a big girl now.'

'You sound like my mother.'

'Which reminds me,' he said.

'What?' I edged away.

'Where is she?'

'Stop going on about that.'

'You still haven't told me why you changed your plans.'

'Look, do you want me to go on this rota or not?'

The others in my group were a fierce-faced Italian girl called Marcella who had a red hammer-and-sickle badge with Russian lettering pinned to her blue pullover, an engaged couple from Sussex University called Tim and Rachel, and Lawrence who was in charge.

Lawrence turned out to be the hairy one from the breakfast queue. He gave the orders while the rest of us loaded stepladders, dust sheets, rolls of wallpaper and tins of paint into a van. We climbed in after them.

Lawrence drove and talked to us over his shoulder. 'We're going to see the Trentons. They're a problem family.'

Marcella said, 'It is the capitalist system that is the problem.'

'Yes, love. Have any of you done any painting or decorating before?'

'Of course.' Marcella sounded as if she thought Lawrence ought to know that she was an expert.

Rachel said, 'We've done a bit, haven't we, Tim? Only I wasn't very good.'

'What about you, Chris? Have you had any experience?'

I didn't answer. I was thinking about my own problem family, and how pleased my mother would be if a team of volunteers were to turn up and decorate 79 Manor Road, Bleswick. If she hadn't burned it down, that was.

Lawrence said, 'I don't think Chris is going to tell us whether she's had any experience or not. I think she prefers to keep quiet about it.' He chuckled into his beard and his eyes glittered at me in the driving mirror. He stopped the van, came round the back and opened the doors. He offered his hand to Marcella, who ignored it and jumped down by herself. I tried to do the same but he got hold of me round my waist and held on for much longer than he had to. Rachel was helped down by Tim.

We were parked in front of a terrace of sooty little houses in a windy street. Lawrence knocked at one of the doors, *bang-tiddy-bang-bang, bang-bang*, and a fat woman with bad teeth and lots of children let us in.

We carried our equipment into the house. The air smelt of nappies, fish and BO. The furniture was odd and old and broken, and frayed bits of carpet were sticky underfoot.

Lawrence showed us the work that had been done so far. Construction Not Destruction had put in a bathroom and an inside toilet, and had re-plastered one of the bedrooms. The bedroom now needed painting and wallpapering. Lawrence put Tim and Marcella in charge of this because they had experience. Rachel didn't look at all pleased about Tim being on his own in the bedroom with Marcella, even if the beds were covered with dust sheets. Lawrence said, 'Rachel and Chris can make a start on the kitchen,' and Rachel looked at me with dislike in her eyes.

'What do we do?' I asked him.

'Strip,' he said meaningfully. 'Rub down and make good.' The kitchen looked as if it would take all day to clear up, never mind decorate. Mrs Trenton said to Lawrence, 'I'm sorry, love, I'm all behind this morning.'

'We're here to help, Mrs T,' he said. 'You get your feet up.' He put his hand under her elbow and gallantly took her out of the room.

The sink and the draining board were covered with empty tins. Rachel carried them out to the bin in the yard. I started clearing dirty plates off the table.

'There's not much point in doing that,' said Rachel, with her hands full of tins. 'There's nowhere to put anything.'

'What shall I do then?'

She gave me the usual look of women who got exasperated when I didn't know what housework to do, but who weren't prepared to tell me. 'Can't you *see*?'

Stuck to the greasy wallpaper were picture postcards, family snaps and portraits of the Queen and President Kennedy cut out of magazines. I started to take them down, peeling back the sellotape. I thought that was one job I couldn't mess up.

I was wrong. A piece of sellotape brought a long strip of the soggy wallpaper away with it. I went on pulling and part of the wall came too, with stones and dust and chunks of plaster. Rachel said, 'You should have put dust sheets down before you started that. Why don't you help me with the washing-up?'

I would have loved to, but I didn't dare let go of the paper. If I didn't keep it pressed against the wall, the avalanche started again. I almost wished my father would walk in. He knew about walls.

'Help,' I said.

'Oh, honestly,' said Rachel. '*Lawrence!*'

He grinned at me. He said, 'You *haven't* done it before, have you?' He stood close behind me and took the wall-paper out of my hand. He didn't exactly stop the avalanche so much as leave it to subside. At least I wasn't responsible for it any more. I felt his breath on my neck.

Mrs Trenton looked in to see how we were getting on. The dust made her cough, and she stared in alarm at the hole in her wall. The wallpaper hung off it like skin round a wound. I thought she was probably thinking that it was all very well for us to spend a weekend smashing up her house when we had homes of our own to go to at the end of it.

The trouble was, I didn't know whether I had.

I said, 'Please, Mrs Trenton, can I use your phone?'

'What phone?' she replied, and Lawrence looked as if I should have known and shouldn't have asked. He said, 'Is it something urgent?'

'No.'

Mrs Trenton said, 'There's a call box at the shop.'

Lawrence said, 'I've got a better idea. My lodgings are just round the corner. There's a phone there.'

'It's all right. It doesn't matter.'

'Come on, love.' He put his hand on my shoulder. 'I'll take you.'

Rachel called after us, 'That's right, leave me to do everything.'

His room was at the back and the top of a tall house. It had a steep fire escape with missing steps. We had to keep stopping for breath.

'Home sweet home,' he said. He nodded at the phone. 'Help yourself.' I thought he might leave me to make my phone call in peace but there was nowhere for him to go. It didn't matter. There was nothing to listen to. The phone rang and rang in Bleswick but there was no reply. I got the operator to check the line. He said it was all right.

I waited and waited and gave up. I wished I hadn't tried. I wanted to go back to the Trentons and knock walls down. I wished I had the kind of face that didn't show things. I wished I could be casual, but I couldn't. I was in a panic, and Lawrence saw. He came over to where I was sitting. He took my hands in his hard, dirty ones and raised me to my feet. His arms went round me in a lovely strong restful hug. I supposed I shouldn't really be letting him hug me, but no one else seemed to be sympathetic. Adam was too busy with his precious Jane.

Lawrence sat me down on the bed. He kissed me fiercely, biting my lips. His breath was stale and his beard tasted of alcohol but I let him run it all over my face until I couldn't see anything except black hairy darkness.

I couldn't see what was happening so nothing could be. When he started to unzip my jeans, he didn't do it seductively or gently or mischievously as Adam would have done it, he did it casually as if they were his own jeans. Perhaps they were his. I didn't feel as if I had any right to tell him what he could or couldn't do with them.

His breath came in fast, sour, hissing gasps. He left my zip for a moment and fumbled with his fly buttons. This gave me a chance to start pulling my zip back up but he stopped me. 'You know you want it, love.' It sounded like a favour he was about to do me. I would be ungrateful to refuse. He opened the front of his trousers and let his penis out. It was the first one I had ever seen in daylight. I was astonished at how painful it looked, even for him, never mind what it would do to me while I was still sore.

I tried to move away. He said, 'You can't get out of it now.' It had stopped being a favour. It was a punishment, though I didn't know what for.

Outside, the fire escape was clanging as if an athlete or some other very energetic person were racing up it. A shadow appeared against the glass top of the outside door. I would have recognized the shape of the shadow even if I hadn't heard the vigorous footsteps. Lawrence said, 'Fuck,' and let go of me. I did up my clothes and opened the door to my mother.

Nadine Gordimer

Blinder

Rose lives in the backyard. She has lived there from the time when she washed the napkins of the children in the house, who are now university students. Her husband had disappeared before she took the job. Her lover, Ephraim, who works for Cerberus Security Guards, has lived with her in the yard for as long as anyone in the house can remember. He used to be night watchman at a parking garage, and the children, leaving for school in the morning after Rose had cooked breakfast for them, would meet 'Rose's husband' in his khaki drill uniform, wheeling his bicycle through the gateway as he came off shift. His earlobes were loops that must once have been filled by ornamental plugs, his smile was sweetened by splayed front teeth about which, being what he was, who he was, he was quite unselfconscious.

That is what they remember, the day they hear that he is dead. The news comes by word-of-mouth, as all news seems to in the backyards of the suburb; who is in jail, caught without a pass, and must be bailed out, who has been told to leave a job and backyard at the end of the month, who has heard of the birth of a child, fathered on annual leave, away in the country. There is a howling and keening in the laundry and the lady of the house thinks Rose is off on a blinder again. In her forties Rose began to have what the family and their friends call a drinking problem. Nothing, in the end, has been done about it. The lady of the house thought it might be menopausal, and had Rose examined by her own doctor. He found she had high blood pressure and treated her for that, telling her employer the drinking absolutely must be stopped, it exacerbated hypertension. The lady of the house made enquiries, heard of a Methodist Church that ran a non-racial Alcoholics Anonymous as part of its community programme, and delivered Rose by car to the weekly meetings in a church hall. Rose calls the AA euphemistically 'my club' and is no longer sloshed and juggling dishes by the family's dinner-hour every night, but she still goes off every two months or so on a week's blinder. There is nothing to be done about it; the lady of the house – the family, the grown children for whom Rose is the innocence of childhood – can't throw her out on the street. She has nowhere to go. If dismissed, what kind of reference can be given her? One can't perjure oneself on the most important of the three requirements of prospective employers: honesty, industry, sobriety.

Over the years, Ephraim has been drawn into discussions about Rose's drinking. Of course, if anyone is able to help her, it should be he, her lover. Though to talk of those two as lovers . . . The men always must have a woman, the women always seem to find a man; if it's not one, then another will do. The lady of the house is the authority who has gone out to the yard from time to time to speak to Ephraim. The man of the house has no time or tact for domestic matters.

Ephraim, what are we going to do about Rose?

I know, madam.

Can't you get her to stop? Can't you see to it that she doesn't keep any of the stuff in the room?

(It is a small room; with two large people living there, Rose and Ephraim, there can't be much space left to hide brandy and beer bottles.)

But she goes round the corner.

(Of course. Shebeens in every lane.)

So what can we do, Ephraim? Can't you talk to her?

What I can do? I talk. Myself, I'm not drinking. The madam ever see me I'm drunk?

I know, Ephraim.

And now Ephraim is dead, they say, and Rose is weeping and gasping in the laundry. The lady of the house does not know whether Rose was in the laundry when one of Ephraim's brothers (as Rose says, meaning his fellow workers) from Cerberus Security Guards came with the news, or whether the laundry, that dank place of greasy slivers of soap, wire coat-hangers and cobwebs, was her place to run to, as everyone has a place in which the package of misery is to be unpacked alone, after it is delivered. Rose sits on an upturned bucket and the water from her eyes and nose makes papier mâché heads, in her fist, out of the Floral Bouquet paper handkerchiefs she helps herself to (after such a long service, one can't call it stealing) in the lady of the house's bathroom. Ephraim has been dead a week, although the news comes only now. He went home last week on leave to his village near Umzimkulu. The bus in which he was travelling overturned and he was among those killed. His bicycle, a chain and padlock on the back wheel, is there where he stored it safely against his return, propped beside the washing machine with its murky submarine eye.

It is a delicate matter to know how to deal with Rose. The ordinarily humane thing to do – tell her not to come back into the house to prepare dinner, take off a few days, recover from the shock – is not the humane thing to do, for her. Under that bed of hers on its brick stilts there quickly will be a crate of bottles supplied by willing 'friends'; it is quite natural that someone with her history will turn to drink. So the lady of the house makes a pot of tea and gently calls Rose to their only common ground, the kitchen, and sits with her a while, drinking tea with her on this rare occasion, just as she will go to visit a friend she hasn't seen for years, if he is dying, or will put in a duty appearance at a wedding in some branch of kin from which she has distanced herself in social status, tastes and interests.

Flesh and tears seem to fuse naturally on Rose's face; it is a sight that causes the face itself to be seen afresh, dissolved of so long a familiarity, here in the kitchen, drunk and sober, cooking a leg of lamb as only she can, or grovelling awfully, little plaited horns of dull hair sticking out under the respectability of her maid's cap fallen askew as she so far forgets herself, in embarrassing alcoholic remorse, to try to kiss the hand of the lady of the house. That face – Rose's face – has changed, the lady of the house notices, just as she daily examines the ageing of her own. The fat smooth brown cheeks have resting upon them beneath the eyes two hollowed stains, the colour of a banana skin gone bad. The drinking has stored its poison there, its fatigue and useless repentance. The body is what the sea recently has been discovered to be: an entity into which no abuse can be thrown away, only cast up again.

Rose doesn't ask, what's for dinner? – not tonight. She is scrubbing potatoes, she has taken the T-bone steaks out of the refrigerator, as if this provides a ritual in place of mourning. It is best to leave her to it, the calm of her daily task. The grown children, when they arrive at different intervals later in the afternoon or evening, go one by one back to childhood to put their arms around Rose, this once, again, in the kitchen, and there are tears again from her. They talk about Ephraim, coming home to the backyard early in the morning, just as they were leaving for school, and she actually laughs, a spluttery sob, saying: I used to fry for him some bread and eggs in the fat left from your bacon! – A collusion between the children and the servant over something the lady of the house didn't know, or pretended never to have known. The grown children also recall for Rose how one or other of them, riding a motorcycle or driving a car, passed him only the other day, where he singled himself out, waving and calling a greeting from the uniformed corps in the Cerberus

Security Guards transport vehicle. The daughter of the house recently happened to enter the headquarters of a mining corporation, where he was on duty in the glassy foyer with his shabby wolf of a guard dog slumped beside him. She had said, poor thing, put out a hand to stroke it, and Ephraim had expertly jerked the dog away to a safe distance, laughing, while it came to life in a snarl. He's very good with those dogs, Rose says, that dog won't let anyone come near him, *any*one . . .

But it is over. Ephraim has been buried already; it's all over. She has heard about his death only after he has been buried because she is not the one to be informed officially. He has – had, always had – a wife and children there where he came from, where he was going back to, when he was killed. Oh yes. Rose knows about that. The lady of the house, the family, know about that; it was the usual thing, a young man comes to work in a city, he spends his whole life there away from his home because he has to earn money to send home, and so – the family in the house privately reasoned – his home really is the backyard where his town woman lives? As a socio-political concept the life is a paradigm (the grown child who is studying social science knows) of the break-up of families as a result of the migratory labour system. And that system (the one studying political science knows) ensures that blacks function as units of labour instead of living as men, with the right to bring their families to live in town with them.

But Ephraim deluded himself, apparently, that this backyard where he was so much at home was not his home, and Rose, apparently, accepted his delusion. This was not the first time he had gone home to his wife and children of course. Sometimes the family in the house hadn't noticed his absence at all, until he came back. Rose would be cooking up a strange mess, in the kitchen: Ephraim had brought a chunk of some slaughtered beast for her; she nibbled his gift of sugar-cane, spitting out the fibre. Poor old Rose. No wonder she took to drink (yes, the lady of the house had thought of that, privately) made a convenience of by a man who lived on her and sent his earnings to a wife and children. Now the man dies and Rose is nothing. Nobody. The wife buries him, the wife mourns him. Her children get the bicycle; one of his brothers from Cerberus Security Guards comes to take it from the laundry and bandage it in brown paper and string, foraged from the kitchen, for transport by rail to Umzimkulu.

When the bus flung Ephraim out and he rolled down and died in the brilliant sugar-cane field, he was going home because there was trouble over the land. What land? His father's land, his brothers' land, his land. Rose gives a garbled version anyone from that house, where at least two newspapers a day are read, can interpret: the long-service employee of Cerberus Security Guards was to be spokesman for his family in a dispute over ancestral land granted them by their local chief. Boundary lines have been drawn by government surveyors, on one side there has been a new flag run up, new uniforms put on, speeches made – the portion of the local chief's territory that falls on that side is no longer part of South Africa. The portion that remains on the other side now belongs to the South African government and will be sold to white farmers – Ephraim's father's land, his brothers' land, his land. They are to get some compensation – money, that disappears in school fees and food, not land, that lasts for ever.

The lady of the house never does get to hear what happened, now that Ephraim is dead. Rose doesn't say; isn't asked; probably is never told. She appears to get over Ephraim's death very quickly, as these people do, after the first burst of emotion – perhaps it would be better to assume she has to take it philosophically. People whose lives are not easy, poor people, to whom things happen but who don't have the resources to make things happen, don't have the means, either, to extricate themselves from what has happened. Of the remedies of a change of scene, a different job, another man, only the possibility of another man is open to her, and she's no beauty any longer, Rose, even by tolerant black standards. That other remedy – drink – one couldn't say she turns to that, either. Since Ephraim has disappeared from the backyard she drinks neither more nor less. The lady of the house, refurbishing it, thinks of offering an old club armchair to Rose. She asks if there is place in her room, and Rose says, Oh yes! Plenty place.

There is the space that was occupied by Ephraim, his thick spread of legs in khaki drill, his back in braces, his Primus stove and big chromium-fronted radio. Rose spends the whole afternoon cleaning the upholstery with carbon tetrachloride, before getting one of the grown children to help her move the chair across the yard. The lady of the house smiles; there was never any attempt to clean the chair while this was part of the duty of cleaning the house.

On Saturdays, occasionally, all members of the family are home for lunch, as they never are on other days. There is white wine this Saturday, as a treat. Rose has baked a fish dish with a covering of mashed potato corrugated by strokes of a fork and browned crisp along the ridges – it is delicious, the kind of food promoted to luxury class by the everyday norm of cafeterias and fast-food counters. In the middle of the meal, Rose appears in the dining-room. The clump of feet that has preceded her gives away that there is someone behind her, out of sight in the passage. The dark hollows under Rose's eyes are wrinkled up with excitement, she shows off: Look who I've got to see you! Look who is here!

The lady of the house is taking good, indulgent, suspicious stock of her, she knows her so well she can tell at once whether or not she's been at the bottle. No – the lady of the house signals with her eyes to the others – Rose is not drunk. Everyone stops eating. Rose is cajoling, high, in her own language, and gesturing back into the passage, her heavy lifted arm showing a shaking jowl of flesh through the tear in her overall – Rose can never be persuaded to mend anything, like the drinking, there is nothing to be done . . .

She loses patience – making a quick, conniving face for the eyes of the family – and goes back into the passage to fetch whoever it is. Heads at table return to plates, hands go out for bread or salt. Wine goes to a mouth. Rose shushes and pushes into the room a little group captured and corralled, bringing with them – a draught from another place and time suddenly blowing through the door – odours that have never been in the house before. Hair ruffles along the small dog's back; one of the grown children quickly and secretly puts a hand on its collar. Smell of wood-smoke, of blankets and clothes stored on mud floors between mud walls that live with the seasons, shedding dust and exuding damp that makes things hatch and sprout; smell of condensed milk, of ashes, of rags saved, of wadded newspapers salvaged, of burning paraffin, of thatch, fowl droppings, leaching red soap, of warm skin and fur, cold earth: the family round the table pause over their meal, its flavour and savour are blown away, the utensils they've been eating with remain in their hands, the presence of a strangeness is out of all proportion to the sight of the black country woman and her children, one close beside her, one on her back. The woman never takes her eyes off Rose, who has set her down there. The baby under the blanket closed over her breast with a giant safety-pin cannot be seen except for a green wool bonnet. Only the small child looks round and round the room; the faces, the table, dishes, glasses, flowers, wine bottle; and seems not to breathe. The dog rumbles and its collar is jerked.

Rose is leaning towards the woman, smiling, hands on the sides of her stomach, and encourages her in their language. She displays her to the assembly caught at table. You know who this is, madam? You don't know? She's from Umzimkulu. It's Ephraim's wife. (She swoops up the small child, stiff in her hands.) Ephraim's children. Youngest and second youngest. Look – the baby; it's a little girl. – And she giggles, for the woman who won't respond, can't respond to what is being said about her.

The lady of the house has got up from her chair. She's

waiting for Rose to stop jabbering so that she can greet the woman. She goes over to her and puts out her hand, but the woman draws her own palms together and claps them faintly, swaying politely on her feet, which are wearing a pair of men's shoes below thick beaded anklets. So the lady of the house puts a hand on the woman's back, on the blanket that holds the lump of baby, and says to Rose, Tell her I'm very glad to meet her.

As if they were children again, the young people at the table recite the ragged mumble of a greeting, smiling, the males half-rising. The man of the house draws his eyebrows together and nods absently.

She's here about the pension, Rose says, they say she can get a pension from Cerberus Security Guards.

She laughs at the daring, or simpleton trust? – she doesn't know. But the heads around the table know about such things. The children have grown up so clever.

The lady of the house has always been spokesman and diplomat: Did she get anything?

Not yet, they didn't give . . . But they'll write a letter, maybe next month, Rose says, and – this time the performance is surely for the benefit of the country woman instead of the family – leans across to the fruit bowl on a side table and twists off a bunch of grapes which she then pokes at the belly of the small child, who is too immobilized by force of impressions to grasp it. Rose encourages him, coyly, in their language, setting him down on his feet.

Rose, says the lady of the house, give them something to eat, mmh? There's cold meat . . . or if you want to take eggs . . .

Rose says, thank you, mam – procedurally, as if the kitchen were not hers to dispense from, anyway.

The woman has been got in, now there is the manoeuvre of getting her out; she stands as if she would stand for ever, with her baby on her back and her child holding a bunch of grapes that he is afraid to look at, while nobody knows whether to go on eating or wait till Rose takes her away.

The lady of the house is used to making things easy for others: Tell her – thank her for coming to see us.

Rose says something in their language and, after a pause, the woman suddenly begins to speak, turned to Rose but obviously addressing the faces at table through her, through the medium, the mediator of that beer-bloated body, that face ennobled with the bottle's mimesis of the lines and shadings of worldly wisdom. Rose follows with agreeing movements of lips and head, reverberating hum of punctuation. She says: She thanks you. She says goodbye.

Hardly has Rose removed her little troupe when she is back again. Perhaps she remembers the family is eating lunch, has come to ask if they'll want coffee? But no. With exaggerated self-effacement, not looking at anyone else, she asks whether she can talk to the madam a moment?

Now?

Yes, please, now.

The lady of the house follows her into the passage.

Can you borrow me ten rands, please madam.

(This will be an advance on her monthly wages.)

Right away?

Please, mam.

So, interrupting her family meal, the lady of the house goes upstairs and fetches two five rand notes from her purse. She sees Rose, as she comes back down the stairs, waiting in the passage like one of the strangers whose knock at the front door Rose herself will answer but whom she does not let into the living-rooms and keeps standing while she goes to call the lady of the house.

Two fives all right? The lady of the house holds out the notes.

Thank you, thanks very much; Rose pushes the money into her overall pocket, that is ripped away at one corner.

For the bus, Rose says, by way of apology for the urgency. Because she's going back there, now, to that place, Umzimkulu.

Georgina Hammick

People for Lunch

'I must get up,' Mrs Nightingale said, but did not move. During the night she had worked her way down the bed so that her feet were now resting on the brass rail at its end. Two years ago today it had been Edward's feet striking this same brass rail with peculiar force that had woken her. 'I don't feel well,' he'd said, and she'd replied – sleepily? sharply? – she needed to know but could not remember – 'Then you'd better not go to work today.' When he'd gone on, haltingly, to murmur: 'No. I can't,' she'd sat up, wide awake and afraid. For Edward was a workaholic. Nothing prevented him going to the office. She'd leant over him and seen that his face and neck were beaded with sweat. She'd touched his forehead and found it as cold and green as marble. 'I've got a pain,' he said, 'in my chest.' Each word was a single, concentrated effort. 'I can't breathe.' Stumbling to the telephone which lived on Edward's side of the bed, she'd started to panic. How could she explain to the doctor, probably still in bed and asleep, how serious it was with Edward lying beside her listening? It was then that she'd begun to shake, and her teeth to rattle in her jaw like pebbles in a bag. She'd knocked the telephone directory on to the floor and misdialled the number half a dozen times. (It was not true that anxious, panicky people proved themselves level-headed, under fire.) 'Be calm, Fanny. Go at it slowly,' Edward had said, lying still, his eyes unfocussed on the ceiling.

*

A shuddering sigh on Mrs Nightingale's left made her turn her head. Lying close on the adjoining pillow was the face of Bone. The dog's small body was concealed by the duvet, as was Mrs Nightingale's own. Mrs Nightingale stared at Bone's black nose, at the white whiskers that sprouted from her muzzle and chin, at her short sandy eyelashes. Bone's eyes were shut, but the left ear was open, its flap splayed on the pillow to reveal an intricacy of shiny and waxy pink coils. Mrs Nightingale leant across and blew gently in this ear. Bone opened one eye and shut it again. Mrs Nightingale put her arms round Bone and laid her head against the dog's neck. It smelt faintly of chicken soup. Bone jerked her head away and stretched her legs so that her claws lodged themselves in Mrs Nightingale's stomach. Mrs Nightingale kissed Bone on the muzzle just above the black, shiny lip. Bone opened her jaws wide in a foetid yawn and stretched again and went back to sleep. Mrs Nightingale got out of bed and left Bone, still covered to her neck by the duvet, sleeping peacefully.

Bone was not allowed in beds, only on them, and she reminded the dog of this. 'I don't like dogs,' she added untruthfully. The house was very quiet. Mrs Nightingale walked out bare-footed on to the uncarpeted landing and stood for a moment listening to the inharmonious ticking of the clocks downstairs. There was no sound from her children's bedrooms and their doors were uninvitingly shut. 'I hate being a widow,' she said aloud.

The bathroom door was blocked by a wrinkled dustbin sack full to overflowing with clothes intended for a jumble sale. She dragged it out of the way. From its torn side hung the yellowing arm of a Viyella cricket shirt. From its top protruded a brown Harris tweed skirt. Liza's name was still stitched to the tiny waistband. Had she ever really been that size? Mrs Nightingale had meant, before the move, to unpick the nametape from Liza's old uniform and take it back to the school for resale, but there had never been the time. This black sack was one of many about the house. Before moving she'd labelled them as to contents, but on examination recently they all contained the same things: out-grown clothes, single football boots, curtains originally made for Georgian sash windows that would not fit the small casements here, curtain hooks, picture hooks, bent wire coat hangers.

Lying motionless in the bath Mrs Nightingale saw Edward on the stretcher being carried into the ambulance. He had joked with the ambulance men. She would never forgive him for that. It had been his joking, and the doctor saying on arrival, just before he'd sent her out of the room: 'If you move, Edward, you're a dead man. If you lie still and do exactly what I say, you'll be all right,' that had given her hope. She could see Edward now, calling out from the stretcher to the twins, shivering in their night things on the front door step: 'Be good, monkeys. I'll be back soon.' And she could see herself, wrapped in his dressing gown, bending down to kiss his cold cheek before the ambulance doors closed. She'd wanted to go with him, she'd needed to go with him, but had had to wait for her mother to come and look after the twins.

The bath water was by now tepid and Mrs Nightingale's finger ends were white and shrunk. As she lay there, unable to move, the church bells began a faint tolling through the shut window and at once the image of the ambulance with its frenetic blue light turning out of the drive was replaced by a picture of dead tulips and lilac in the vase beneath the lectern. She'd seen these on Friday when she'd gone to the church to check the Flower Rota List and found her name down for this Sunday. She forced herself out of the bath and pounded down the passage to Liza's room. She shook the mound of bedclothes.

'Liza – did you remember to do the church flowers yesterday?'

Liza was gliding through a dark lake on the back of a

sea-serpent. She opened blank blue eyes for a second and then shut them again.

'Did you do the church flowers?'

The eyes opened again, flickered and then closed. Waking was a trial for Liza.

'Liza –'

'No. I didn't. Sorry.'

'You're the absolute end.' Mrs Nightingale was furious. 'You asked what you could do to help and I said –'

'Sorry, Mum.'

'You're not asked to do much. And you're eighteen, not six.'

'Don't flap,' – Liza's voice sounded as though it had been dredged from the bottom of a deep lake – 'the congregation's geriatric. No one will notice if the flowers are dead.' She yawned. 'You're sopping wet,' she said incuriously to her mother.

'I need your help,' Mrs Nightingale cried. 'Get up at once, now, before you fall asleep again.' She stood for a moment awaiting results, but as there were none, left the room banging the door behind her.

Mrs Nightingale visited the twins' room next. They were fast asleep on their backs. Lily, on the camp bed they took turns for, was snoring.

'Wake up, both of you,' Mrs Nightingale said. She trampled over their discarded clothes. 'Wake up now.' They sat up slowly, looking hurt and puzzled. 'It's late,' Mrs Nightingale said, 'Nine o'clock. They'll be here by half past twelve and there's a lot to do. You must get up. Now.'

'Who'll be here?' Poppy asked.

'Nine o'clock isn't late, it's early,' Lily said. 'It's Sunday.'

'Now,' Mrs Nightingale said and left the room.

When Mrs Nightingale opened Dave's door he was propped on one elbow, reading. His hair, which had been recently cut by a fellow student using blunt nail scissors, stuck out in stiff tufts. Here and there patches of scalp were visible. They'd had a row about the hair when he arrived. Usually Mrs Nightingale cut Dave's hair, and when she did he looked very nice. This present cut, which he'd admitted he wasn't that keen on himself, was an example of the perversity her son was given to and that Mrs Nightingale found exasperating and incomprehensible. He glanced up at her as she came in.

'Hallo, Mamma. How are you, darlin'?'

The question took Mrs Nightingale off-guard. Suddenly, she wanted to tell him. She wanted to say: 'Daddy died two years ago today.' She wanted to collapse on Dave's bed and howl, perhaps all day, perhaps for ever. Instead she stayed in the middle of the room and stared at the row of hats that hung from hooks above Dave's bed and which, together with the accents – foreign, regional – he adopted, formed part of her son's disguise kit.

'If you're awake, why aren't you up?' Mrs Nightingale heard herself say.

'Stay cool,' Dave said. 'I'm just tucking into Elizabeth Bishop.' He waved a paperback in the air that his mother recognised as her own and removed from its shelf without permission.

'How do you rate her? Compared to Lowell. . .?'

'Get up, please,' Mrs Nightingale said.

'Okay, Marlene. Tuck in.'

Marlene, the second syllable of which was pronounced to rhyme with Jean, was not Mrs Nightingale's name, which was Frances. Marlene, which sometimes became Marlena, second syllable to rhyme with Gina, was the name Dave had bestowed on his mother some years ago when she'd started regularly cutting his hair. 'I'm due for a visit to Marlene's salon,' he'd say, ringing her from Leeds. 'Is the head stylist available?'

Mrs Nightingale moved backwards to Dave's door and fell over the bicycle wheel she'd noted on her way in and taken care to avoid.

'Shit. And your room's in shit, Dave.'

'Cool it.'

'Look, it is in shit and it smells. Do you have to sleep with the window shut? Why are you wearing that tee-shirt in bed?'

'I haven't any pyjamas, that's why,' Dave said reasonably.

'I know if I leave now you'll just go on reading –' Mrs Nightingale was getting desperate '– so get out now, while I'm here.'

'I will as soon as you go. I've got nothing on below this tee-shirt, and the sight of my amazing, user-friendly equipment might unsettle you for the day. Tuck in, Marlene.' He yawned, showing a white tongue and all his fillings, and stretched his huge arms above his head.

Mrs Nightingale returned to her bedroom and dressed herself in scruffy, everyday clothes. Then she pulled Bone out of the bed and swept the bottom sheet with her hands. Being white, Bone's hairs did not show up well against the sheet but Mrs Nightingale knew they were there, and sure enough they flew around the room and settled on the floorboards like snowflakes in a paperweight snowstorm. Mrs Nightingale straightened the duvet and banged the pillows while Bone sat on her haunches, sorrowfully watching. As soon as the lace cover was on Bone leapt back on the bed and made herself comfortable among the cushions. Mrs Nightingale looked at her watch. This time two years ago she had just arrived at the hospital having driven at ninety most of the way. There'd been nowhere to park so she'd parked in one of the doctors' spaces. 'You can't park there,' an old man planting out geraniums by the hospital steps had told her, having watched her manoeuvre. Three floors up, on Harnham Ward, Sister had looked up from her notes and said: 'The specialist has examined your husband and would like to see you now.' Mrs Nightingale suddenly remembered the specialist's nose, aquiline and messily freckled. She'd stared at it as they sat opposite each other, divided by a desk. 'He's on the edge of a precipice,' the specialist had said. 'It was an almost total infarct – that means the supply of blood and oxygen to the heart has been severely reduced. A large part of the heart muscle is already dead. The next forty-eight hours will be crucial. If he survives, and I can give you no assurances, the dead muscle will be replaced in time by scar tissue, which is very tough and can do the same sort of job –'

I hate doctors, Mrs Nightingale thought as she went downstairs. Hate them. She took one look at the kitchen, then shut the door and went into the drawing-room, a room too poky to deserve the title that, from the habit of a lifetime, she had given it. It smelled of soot and damp and cigarettes, and of something indefinable that might have been the previous owners. Mrs Nightingale got down on her knees in front of the fireplace and swept the wood ash and cigarette stubs she found there into a dome. She stuck a firelighter on top of this, but the log baskets were empty except for two pieces of bark and several families of woodlice, so she got up again and started to punch the sofa cushions into shape. Dave came in while she was doing this. He was still wearing the tee-shirt but to his lower half he'd now added an Indian tablecloth which he'd wrapped twice round himself and tucked in at the waist.

'You left a filthy mess in the kitchen last night,' Mrs Nightingale said, remembering the slag heap of coffee grounds decorated by a rusty Brillo pad on the kitchen table. 'I thought you were going to get dressed.'

'Liza's in the bathroom.' Dave scratched his armpit, then sat down heavily on the sofa cushions and rested his head on his knees.

'Dave, I've just done that sofa. We've got people for lunch –'

'Yup. Sure thing. Sorry. What can I do?' He stayed where he was and Mrs Nightingale stared, mesmerized, at his large yellow feet. The toenails were black and torn. Black wire sprouted from his big toes. The same wire twined his calves, visible beneath the tablecloth. It stopped at the ankles, but continued, Mrs Nightingale knew, beyond his knees to his thighs, where it no longer twined, but curled. It was impossible that this huge male person had ever been inside her body. 'Well, the log baskets are empty, as you see,' Mrs Nightingale said, 'so when you're dressed –'

'Sure, sure.'

'I did ask you, you know,' Mrs Nightingale bravely continued, 'when you arrived, if you'd be responsible for getting the wood in, and you said –'

'Yeah. Yeah. Sure. Yup. Tuck in.' He sat for a moment longer and then got up, hitching the tablecloth which had slipped a little. He looked round the room. 'I like your little house, Marlene.'

'It isn't *my* house.' Mrs Nightingale was hurt by Dave's choice of possessive adjective. 'It's *our* house. It's home.'

'Yup.'

'No chance, I suppose,' she said as he padded to the door, 'of your wearing your contact lenses at lunch?' Dave stopped dead in his tracks and turned sharply. 'What's wrong with my specs?' He whipped them off and examined them myopically, close to his nose. They were bright scarlet with butterfly sides, the sort typists wore in the fifties. One arm was attached to the frame by a grubby selotape bandage.

'Nothing's wrong with them. It's just that you look nicer without them. You're quite nice looking, so it seems a shame –'

'Oh Christ,' Dave said and then hit his head on the beam above the door. 'Fuck. I hit my head everywhere I go in this fucking house. Cottage. Hen coop. Hovel.'

By the time Mrs Nightingale had finished scrubbing the potatoes they were all down in the kitchen with her. The kitchen was too small for five people comfortably to be in at one time. She had once, when they were all tripping over each other, made this observation and had received a long lecture from Dave on the living conditions of the average farm-labourer and his family in the latter part of the nineteenth century. Her son was nothing if not inconsistent, Mrs Nightingale thought, remembering the hen coop remark.

'Who's finished the Shreddies?' Poppy was on her knees on the brick floor, peering in a cupboard.

'Dave had them last night – don't you remember?' Liza said, sawing at a grapefruit with the bread knife. A pool of cloudy juice and pips spread over the table, soaking an unpaid telephone bill. Mrs Nightingale snatched it up.

'Here, have this' – Liza plonked the grapefruit halves into bowls and handed one of them to Poppy. 'This is better for you. You're too fat for cereal.'

'Speak for yourself, you great spotty oaf. At least I haven't got suppurating zits all over my face –'

'You will soon,' Dave interrupted cheerfully. 'You're into a pubescent exploding-hormone situation. Tuck in.'

'If you had, they might detract from your nose which, by the way' – Liza glanced at it casually – 'is one big blackhead.'

There was a skirmish. Mrs Nightingale caught the milk bottle as it leapt from the table.

'Cool it, girls.' Dave had seen his mother's face. 'Marlene's trying to get organized. Aren't you, Marlene?' He was propped against the Rayburn, dressed now in one of his father's city shirts and scarlet trousers, the bottoms of which were tucked into old school games stockings, one brilliantly striped, the other grey, and shovelling Weetabix into his mouth from a bowl held within an inch of his face. Each time the spoon went in it banged horribly against his teeth. 'Is the Rayburn *meant* to be off?' he asked, mock-innocently, between mouthfuls.

Mrs Nightingale was about to burst into tears.

'What? Out of my way please.' She pushed the red legs to one side, and knelt on the dog bed in front of the stove. Inside an erratic flame flickered. She turned the thermostat as high as it would go.

'Why's the heat gone down?'

'How the fuck should I know? The wind, probably –'

'Don't swear, Mummy,' Poppy said, grabbing a banana from the fruit bowl and stripping it.

'Put that banana back! It's for lunch.'

'We've got rhubarb crumble for lunch. I made it yesterday, remember.' Poppy took a bite out of the banana, folded the skin over the end and replaced it in the fruit bowl on top of a shrivelled orange.

'Look,' Mrs Nightingale said, 'we'll never be ready at this rate. Couldn't you all just –'

'Keep calm, Mamma. Sit down a moment and drink this.' Liza handed her mother a mug of coffee. 'There's nothing to do. Really. They won't be here till one at the earliest. All we've got to do is get the joint in –'

'Are we eating animals? Yuk. Unreal. Animals are people –'

'Shut up, Lily. – Do the spuds and the veg and lay the table and light the fire and pick some flowers – five minutes at the most.'

'The whole house is in chaos,' Mrs Nightingale said, 'it's composed of nothing but tea chests and plastic bags.'

'They're not coming to see the house. They know we've only just moved. They're coming to see *you*.'

'Actually, they're coming to inspect our reduced circumstances,' Dave said in a prissy voice. He picked up a piece of toast and stretched for the marmalade. Mrs Nightingale pushed it out of his reach. 'No, you've had enough.'

'Daddy couldn't bear them,' Lily said, staring into space.

'Couldn't bear who?' Poppy paused at the door.

'The Hendersons, stupid.'

'The Hendersons? Are *they* coming to lunch? Unreal.'

'Where do you think you're going to, Poppy? You haven't cleared up your breakfast things –'

'I'm going to the lav, if you must know. I'm coming back.'

'While you're up there, Fatso, take some of the gunge off your face!' Dave shouted at her.

'Have you got the logs in?' Mrs Nightingale asked Dave, knowing that he hadn't.

'I'm just about to. We shouldn't *need* a fire in May,' he said, resentfully as though his mother were to blame for the weather. 'Right, Marlena.' He rubbed his hands. 'Here we go-o,' he added in the manner of an air hostess about to deposit a snack on the knees of a passenger. He sat down on Poppy's chair and pulled a pair of canvas boots from under the table. A lace snapped as he put them on.

'Are you going to shave before they arrive?' Mrs Nightingale asked, eyeing him.

'Dunno. Oi moigh' – Dave rubbed his chin so that it rasped – 'an' yere agine oi moigh 'na'. Don't you like me looking manly and virile?' Mrs Nightingale said No, she didn't much. No.

'Mrs Henderson will, though. She's got a yen for me. She'll really tuck in.'

'Oh ha ha,' Liza snorted from the sink.

'Mr Henderson has too. He's always putting his arm round my shoulder. Squeezing me. Kissing –'

'I don't suppose he's that desperate to get herpes. He hasn't seen you since you were about ten –'

'Do something for me, Lil, would you,' Mrs Nightingale said, as Dave minced from the room flexing his biceps. Lily sighed. Did she know what today was? Mrs Nightingale thought perhaps she did. It was impossible to get near Lily at the moment. She resented everything her mother said and did, prefacing her argument with 'Daddy always said' or 'Daddy would have agreed with me that . . .' She'd been in a sulk since the move because the cottage was thatched, i.e. spooky, witchy, bug-infested – and because her father had never been in it. 'Wake up, there,' – Mrs Nightingale waved her hand slowly up and down in front of Lily's face. Lily managed not to blink.

'Go and get Bone off my bed and put her out. She hasn't had a pee yet.' Lily went on sitting there, expressionless. Then all of a sudden she leapt up, scraping back her chair, and ran out of the room.

'Bone, Bone, my darling one, I'm coming.' They could hear her clattering up the stairs, calling 'Bone, beloved angel, Bone –'

'She's mad,' Liza said, stacking plates in the rack. 'All my family's mad. And Dave is completely off the wall.' Mrs Nightingale kissed Liza's spotty face, pink and damp with steam. 'I love you, Lize,' she said.

As Mrs Nightingale rootled in the kitchen drawer looking for enough knives to lay the dining-room table with, Dave's face appeared at the window above the sink. He flattened his nose against the pane and drummed on it with his fingers. 'Open up! Open up!' he shouted. Liza leaned across the taps and biffed the window. It opened in a rush. Dave's face disappeared for a second, and then reappeared half in the window. 'Ladies,' he said with a South London inflexion and in confidential tones, holding up what looked like a piece of string and dangling it from between his fingers and thumb, 'do your hubbies' jock-straps pass the window test? If not –' he leered and let go of the jock-strap which fell across the sill and draped itself over the hot tap, and then held up a packet of something: 'Try new Weedol! Fast-acting, rainproof and guaranteed to eradicate all biological stains for an entire season. Just one sa*chette*' – he paused to consult the packet – 'treats 160 yards, or – if you ladies prefer a more up-to-date terminology – 135 square metres, of normally soiled jock-straps.' He backed away from the window, creased with laughter, and tripped over a flower pot.

'Pathetic,' Liza said, tugging at the window catch, 'quite pathetic.'

'Logs!' Mrs Nightingale shouted at him, just before the window jerked to, scattering them with raindrops, 'Logs, logs, logs!'

Mrs Nightingale did her best with the dining-room which, not being a room they had so far needed to use, had become a dumping ground. There were ten full tea chests stacked in one corner, her husband's golf clubs in a khaki bag, a clothes horse, innumerable lampshades and a depressed-looking cockatoo under a glass dome. Beneath the window precariously stacked books awaited the bookshelves Dave had promised to put up in the summer holidays. Everything in the room, including a dining-table much too large for it, was deep in dust. Mrs Nightingale looked at her watch. This time two years ago she'd sat beside Edward, who'd lain on his back without pillows, his chest and arms wired to a machine. Attached to the machine was a cardiograph that measured and recorded his heartbeat. The signal had gone all over the place, sometimes shooting to the top of the screen, and the bleeps, at each beat, had been similarly erratic – six, say, in succession followed by a silence which, each time it occurred, she'd felt would never be broken. 'The heroin was delicious,' Ed had murmured in a moment of consciousness, 'it took all the pain away, but they won't let me have any more in case I get hooked.' Why couldn't you have died at once, Mrs Nightingale thought, remembering her agony watching the nurse adjusting the drip, which had kept getting stuck, and checking the leads on Ed's chest which, because he rolled around a lot, were in constant danger of coming loose. This had happened once, when there'd been no nurse in the room. She'd been on the edge of her chair, her eyes alternately on Ed, and on the screen, when suddenly the bleeps had stopped and the signal had flattened into a straight, horizontal line.

A red light had come on at the side of the machine and with it a whine like the unobtainable tone when you dial. He's dead, she'd thought. Sister had rushed in at once and checked Ed's pulse and then the leads and after a minute or two the crazy signal was back and the bleeps. 'Try not to worry, dear,' Sister had said. 'Worrying doesn't help.'

Mrs Nightingale forced herself out of her chair and went in search of a duster.

'The joint's in the oven,' Liza said. She had an apron on which bore the message I Hate Cooking, and was standing at the stove stirring a saucepan. 'I'm making onion sauce.' She looked up. 'Are you okay, Ma?' By way of an answer Mrs Nightingale enquired if anyone had seen the silver anywhere. Poppy knew. She and Lily were scraping carrots and glaring at each other across the kitchen table. She got up and helped her mother drag the despatch box from under the sink in the washroom. Back in the dining-room she stood and watched her mother dust the table.

'Mum – can I have a friend to stay – Julia, I mean, in the holidays?'

'Maybe. If we're straighter by then.' Mrs Nightingale didn't like Julia. On the child's last visit Mrs Nightingale had caught her in her clothes cupboard, examining the labels and checking to see how many pairs of Gucci shoes Mrs Nightingale owned, which was none. Mrs Nightingale didn't own a Gucci watch, either, and evidently wasn't worth speaking to: Julia hadn't addressed one word to her in five days. She'd managed a few indirect hits, though, as when at breakfast one morning, having accepted without comment the plate of scrambled eggs Mrs Nightingale had handed her, she'd leaned on one elbow to enquire of Poppy: 'Presumably your mother will be racing at Goodwood next week?' Mrs Nightingale was damned if she'd have Julia to stay again.

'I get bored without a friend,' Poppy moaned on. Mrs Nightingale wasn't having any of that. 'You can't be bored,' she said, 'and you've got Lily.' She unwrapped a yellowing candlestick from a piece of yellowing newspaper. 'Here, take this.'

'We don't get on,' Poppy said. 'We've got nothing in common.' That was rubbish, Mrs Nightingale told her.

'It isn't rubbish. She's so moody. She never speaks – just sits and stares.'

Since the truth of this could not be denied, Mrs Nightingale changed tack. 'As a matter of fact you don't deserve to have a friend to stay.'

Poppy put down the spoon she'd been tentatively rubbing with a duster and stared at her mother with her mouth open.

'Your half-term report is the worst yet,' Mrs Nightingale continued, 'and we ought to discuss it. Not now. I don't mean now. Later. This evening, perhaps, when they've gone.'

'Miss Ansell doesn't like me. It's not my fault.'

'It isn't just Miss Ansell,' Mrs Nightingale said, more in sorrow than in anger. 'No one, no one – apart from Miss Whatsername – you know, games mistress – had a good word to say about you. You won't get a single "O" Level at this rate. Lily, on the other hand –'

'*Don't* compare me with her. She's quite different to me.'

'Different *from* me. Yes. She knows how to work, for one thing. And she reads. You never open a book.'

'I do.'

'The Beano annual. And you're *thirteen*.'

Poppy grinned sheepishly at that. 'Oh, Muzkin,' she said, and sidled up to her mother and put her arms round her waist.

'Muzkin nothing,' Mrs Nightingale said, disentangling herself. For it really was worrying. Poppy never did open a book. If ever she happened by some mischance to pick one up, she'd drop it again as soon as she'd realized her mistake. As a result of this her ignorance went wide and deep. Mrs Nightingale spent sleepless nights discussing the problem with Bone.

Liza's head appeared round the dining-room door.

'Bone's eaten the Brie, I'm afraid,' Liza said, 'so there's only mousetrap for lunch.'

'Where is she? I'll kill her!' Mrs Nightingale cried preparing to do so.

'I've already beaten her,' Liza said. 'It's my business, she's my dog.'

Not when it comes to spending millions of pounds a year on Chum and Butch and Winalot and vet's bills, Mrs Nightingale thought. Not when it comes to clearing up mountains of dog sick and dog shit. Then she's my dog. She followed Liza back to the kitchen. 'Where's Dave?' she asked crossly. 'Where's the wood?'

'He's gone to get some milk and the papers,' Liza said, knowing what her mother's reaction would be.

'*What?*'

'I asked him to go because we're out of milk and you'll want the papers so that the Hendersons can read them after lunch.'

'Has he taken my car?' Mrs Nightingale was beside herself.

'Of course he's taken your car. How else would he go?'

Mrs Nightingale hated Dave taking her car. She hated him taking it because being stuck up a track with rusty bicycles the only means of escape made her feel a prisoner. She hated him taking it because he hadn't asked permission and because she didn't trust him not to drive like a racing driver – i.e. a maniac. It was her car. She hated Dave too because he ought to have remembered what the day was. There was something wrong with him that he hadn't. Something very wrong indeed.

'He has no business to take my car,' she said, 'he'll be gone for hours.'

Liza was taking glasses out of a cupboard. 'Don't be stupid,' she said briskly. 'He'll be back in a minute. He's only gone for the papers, for God's sake. He was *trying* to be helpful.' She held a glass up to the light. 'These glasses are filthy. I'd better wash them.'

'Get up, Lily,' Mrs Nightingale was now in a state of rage and panic. Lily was lying in the dog bed on top of Bone, kissing Bone's ears. 'Get up! Have you made your bed and tidied your room?'

'You can't make a camp bed.' Lily got up reluctantly, her navy angora jersey now covered with dog hairs.

'Answer that, would you, on your way,' Mrs Nightingale snapped as the telephone rang from the drawing-room. Lily returned almost at once.

'It's Granny. She wants to talk to *you*.'

'Fuck,' Mrs Nightingale said. 'Didn't you tell her we've got people for lunch?' Lily shrugged. 'Well, go back and tell her I'm frantic –'

'I'll say,' murmured Liza, putting glasses on a tray. 'These glasses are gross – did you get them from the garage?'

'– and that I'll ring her after tea. Go *on*. Hurry.'

'Granny sounded a bit hurt,' Lily said when she came back, 'She said to tell you she was thinking about you today.'

'What for?' Liza said.

What for, Mrs Nightingale repeated to herself, what for –? 'What can Dave be doing?' she said, 'He's been gone for hours.' She opened the oven door. The joint seemed to be sizzling satisfactorily.

'Stop flapping,' Liza said.

'Did you put garlic on the joint? And rosemary? I couldn't see any.'

'Of course. Stop flapping.'

'Poppy, you're *soaked*! Couldn't you have worn a mac?' Poppy squelched into the kitchen and dumped a collection of sodden wild flowers on the table.

'*I* was going to do the flowers,' Liza said.

'God, the gratitude you get in this place,' Poppy fingered the limp cluster. 'What are these?'

'Ladies' smocks. *Must* you do that in here?' Liza said as Poppy found an assortment of jugs and lined them up on the table. 'I'm trying to get lunch. You can't put wallflowers in with that lot,' she added in disgust.

'Why can't I?' Poppy wanted to know.

'Because they're orange, stupid.'

'Piss off. I like them. I like the *smell*.'

Mrs Nightingale left her daughters to it and took the tray of glasses into the dining-room. Perhaps Dave *had* had an accident. Perhaps, at this very moment, firemen were fighting to cut his lifeless body from the wreckage. That was all she needed. It was typical of him to put her in this position of anxiety today of all days. 'If he's alive I'll kill him,' she thought aloud, knowing that when – please God – he did walk in she'd feel nothing but relief. As she went back into the kitchen he came in by the other door, accompanied by a smell of deep frying. The Sunday papers and two cartons of long-life milk were crushed against his chest. He uncrossed his arms and unloaded their contents into the watery mess of broken stems and leaves on the kitchen table.

'Hey – mind my flowers,' Poppy said. She sniffed. 'I can smell chips.'

'Whoops. Sorry.' Dave straightened up and caught sight of his mother. 'Hi there, Marlene.' He licked his fingers, slowly and deliberately. 'Finger fuckin' good,' he said when he'd finished. There was a silence, succeeded by a snort of laughter from Liza, succeeded by another silence.

'Dave, could I have a word with you, please –' Mrs Nightingale spoke through clenched teeth. She jerked her thumb towards the door. 'Outside.'

'Righto, Marlena.' He snatched up the *Observer* and followed his mother into the hall.

'Watch out, Dave,' Poppy sang out after him. 'You're in deep trouble, Boyo.'

'What are you so screwed-up about?' Dave asked when Mrs Nightingale, determined that they shouldn't be overheard, had shut the drawing-room door. Dave plonked himself into the nearest arm chair.

'Get up out of that chair! Put that newspaper down!' Dave got up, very slowly. 'Take that smirk off your face!' Mrs Nightingale shouted. He towered above her, shifting from one foot to the other, while his eyes examined the ceiling with interest. 'I've had you,' Mrs Nightingale went on, her voice shaking. 'I wish you weren't here. You're twenty years old. You're the only so-called man in this house. I should be able to look to you for help and support. You had no business to take my car without asking –'

'Liza said we were out of milk –'

'It's not her car. It's *mine*. And *I*'d asked you to get the wood in. That's *all* I asked you to do. All all *all*!'

'Oh come *on* –'

'I won't come on.' Mrs Nightingale's voice rose. 'You were gone for hours while everyone else was working. Did you really eat chips, by the way?'

'I was hungry, I'm a big boy,' Dave said, perhaps hoping to appeal to that need (he supposed all women had) to mother and protect huge grown men as though they were babies.

'You didn't have breakfast till ten. And it'll be lunchtime any minute. You can't have been hungry.' Dave said nothing. He was bored with this interview and showed it by jiggling his knee. 'That finger business wasn't funny,' Mrs Nightingale said. 'It was disgusting. How could you, in front of Lily and Poppy?'

'Lily wasn't in the kitchen, actually,' Dave said. He started to pace about with his head down, a sure sign that he was losing his temper.

'Don't be pedantic with me, Dave.' Dave stopped pacing

and swung round and pointed his finger at his mother in a threatening fashion.

'Fuck *you*,' he said. 'You're a complete hypocrite. No one in this house uses filthier language than you. It's "shit this" and "bugger that" all fucking day. We took the words in with your milk –' There was a pause, during which Mrs Nightingale considered reminding him that the twins, at least, had been bottle-fed, but Dave was quite capable of turning this fact to his advantage, so she said nothing. 'Well, I'm sick of your dramas and panics,' he continued, warming to his theme of self-justification. 'I can't stand the atmosphere in this place. I can't *work* here. I'm going back to Leeds. My tutor didn't want me to take time off to help you, and I've missed two important lectures already.' He made for the door.

'Typical,' Mrs Nightingale said, taking care not to say 'fucking well typical' as she would normally have done. 'You can't take any sort of criticism, ever. You just shout abuse and then walk out – it's too easy. What's more, you haven't been any help to me at all. You haven't lifted a finger –'

'Mum' – Liza's head appeared round the door as Dave reached it. He took two steps backwards – 'shouldn't you be putting your face on? It's after twelve.'

'Go away,' Mrs Nightingale said, 'I'm talking to Dave.'

'Sounds like it. Poor Dave.' Liza's head withdrew. The door banged shut.

Mrs Nightingale and her son stood in silence, both waiting for something. Dave stared at the floor and at the front page of the *Observer* which lay at his feet. He pushed at it with the toe of one green canvas boot.

'Sorry I was rude,' he said at last without looking up.

Mrs Nightingale gave a sigh. Dave was good at apologies – much better than she was – and sometimes indulged in them for days after a particularly bloody row, castigating himself and telling anyone who'd listen what a shit he'd been. The trouble was, the apologies changed nothing, as Mrs Nightingale had learned. They never prevented his being rude and aggressive (and unfair, she thought, *unfair*) next time round. She didn't want his apologies. She wanted him to stop the behaviour that made them necessary. She watched him now get down on his knees and take off his specs and rub them on a dirty red-and-white spotted handkerchief and put them back on his nose. He picked up the *Observer* with his left hand and then struck at it with the fist of his right.

'I'm going to kill Mrs Thatcher,' he said, 'listen to this –' Oh dear, thought Mrs Nightingale.

Dave and newspapers did not mix. Cruise missiles, violence in inner cities, child abuse, drug abuse, vivisection, famine, rape, murder, abortion, multiple births, divorce rate, pollution, terrorism, persecution of Blacks and homosexuals, sex discrimination, unemployment, pornography, police brutality, rate capping – the stuff that newspapers were made of – were a daily cross he bore alone. 'You can't take the whole burden of the world on your shoulders,' she'd tell him when he rang from a Leeds call box desperate over the destruction of South American rain forests, or the plight of the latest hijack victims. 'The world has always been a terrible place,' she'd say, 'we just know more about it now because of the media. Horror used to be more *local*.' Then – since it seemed important to end on a positive note – she'd go on to remind him of ways in which the world had changed for the better, instancing the huge advances made in medicine this century (T.B. and polio virtually wiped out, infant mortality and death in childbirth negligible, etc.) and reminding him that there were salmon in the Thames these days, and that people could fall into the river and swallow whole bucketfuls of its waters and not die. 'Try and get a sense of proportion,' she'd say, something she'd never managed herself. She knew that when she lectured Dave it was herself she was trying to comfort. The world was a far nastier place than it had been when she was a child, even though there'd been a world war going on for some of that time. Far nastier.

Thinking about all this she was spared hearing Mrs Thatcher's latest pronouncement, although it was impossible to miss the passion in Dave's recital of the same. She came to when he stopped in mid-sentence, and put the paper down.

'It's the twenty-third today,' he said, 'Did you realise?'

'I know,' Mrs Nightingale said.

'Oh, Mum, I'm sorry. Why didn't you say?'

Dave, on his knees, began to rock backwards and forwards, his arms folded across his stomach. 'Poor old Dad, poor old Dad,' he said. Then he burst into tears. Mrs Nightingale got down on her knees beside her son. She put her arm round his shoulders which reeked of wet wool and chipped potatoes. She sensed that he did not want her arms round him but did not know how to extricate himself. After several minutes he blew his nose on the red-spotted handkerchief and licked at the tears which were running down his chin.

'I must get the wood in and light the fire.' He disengaged himself and got up. 'Then I'll shave. Sorry, Mum.' He gave her a pale smile. At the door he turned, and said in a sharper tone: 'But I still don't understand why you didn't *say*. And why didn't we go to church this morning – or did you, before we were up?'

'No,' Mrs Nightingale said.

'And why are the fucking Hendersons coming to lunch? You don't like them and Pa couldn't stand them. None of it makes sense.' He shook his head, spraying the room with water like a wet dog.

'Look, Dave,' Mrs Nightingale began. She explained that she hadn't asked the Hendersons, they'd asked themselves. She couldn't put them off for ever. Also she'd thought that having people to lunch might make the day easier in some way. And as for church – well, he didn't like Rite A any more than she did. It always put them into a rage, so there was no point, was there, in going.

'True,' Dave said.

It *was* true, she told him. But what she thought they might do, once they'd got rid of the Hendersons, was drive up to the churchyard and take Poppy's flowers perhaps, and put them on Daddy's grave.

Dave's eyes started to fill again. '. . . and then go to Evensong in the Cathedral, if there's time. It'll be a proper service with proper singing and anthems and sung responses.'

'Yup. Cool.'

'All right, sweetheart?' Dave nodded and fiddled with his watchstrap, a thin piece of canvas, once red-and-white striped. 'I suppose you realize,' Mrs Nightingale lied, 'that when I asked you to give me a hand this week, it was just an excuse for wanting you here today. I needed you.' But perhaps it was not a lie, she thought. Perhaps, subconsciously, she had needed him.

'I'm getting the wood now,' Dave said. He peered out of a dismal mullioned window, against which a yew branch flapped in the gale. 'I think the rain's stopping.'

The kitchen when Mrs Nightingale entered it was clean and tidy, everything washed up and put away. Liza was taking off her apron.

'All done,' she said.

She was a wonder, Mrs Nightingale told her, a real star.

'Mum, you must get changed, they'll be here –'

Mrs Nightingale stopped in the doorway. 'Liz – do you know what today is?'

'It's the day Daddy died,' Liza said. 'Go on, Mum, I'll come and talk to you when I've done the ice.'

The back door banged as Mrs Nightingale climbed the

stairs. She could hear Dave's grunts as he humped the log baskets into the hall. It was a relief to be on her own for five minutes. She needed to be alone with Edward who – she stood on the dark landing and peered at her watch – this time two years ago had been about to leave her. Suddenly, without warning and without saying goodbye. Not even a look. Not even a pressure of the hand. She'd hated him for this, until it had dawned on her that it was inevitable. He'd been hopeless at partings. The number of times she'd driven him to Heathrow and been rewarded not with hugs and the 'I'll miss you, darlings' and 'take care of your precious selves' other people seemed to get, but with a preoccupied peck and then his back view disappearing through the barrier. 'Turn round and wave, you bugger,' she used to will him, but he never did.

'You two ready?' she called, in hopeless competition with Madness, through the twins' bedroom door. Then she opened her own. The room looked as though burglars had visited it. The drawers of both clothes chests had been wrenched out; garments spilled from them on to the floor. A brassière, its strap looped round a wooden drawer knob, trailed greyly to the rug where two leather belts lay like coiled springs. Mrs Nightingale turned her gaze to the dressing-table. Here unnumbered treasures drooped from every drawer and orifice. The surface of the table was littered with screws of cotton wool and with unstoppered scent bottles, from which all London, Paris and New York disagreeably breathed. A cylinder of moisturizing lotion lay on its side oozing cucumber extract into the contents of her jewel case which sat, open and empty, on the stool. Three cotton wool buds, their ends clotted with ear wax, had been placed in the china tray which normally housed Mrs Nightingale's lipsticks. Only two lipsticks remained in the tray; the rest, which had been torn apart and abandoned with their tongues protruding, were jumbled up with beads and cotton wool. Mrs Nightingale recognized her daughter Poppy's hand in all this. She opened her mouth wide in anger and despair, but no sound came. Instead, the telephone screamed from the table by her bed. When after the eighth ring no one had answered downstairs, Mrs Nightingale picked up the receiver.

'Mrs Nightingale? Mr Selby-Willis here.'

'Oh hallo, Jerry,' Mrs Nightingale said. (Fuck fuck fuck fuck fuck.) 'How are you?'

'How are *you*?' Jerry Selby-Willis asked, in his best bedroom drawl.

'Well if you must know, I'm frantic. I've got people arriving for lunch any minute.'

'One normally does on a Sunday. Grania's just gone off to the station to meet our lot. I can't imagine *you* being frantic about anything –'

'It just goes to show how little –'

'When are you going to have luncheon with me?' Jerry Selby-Willis interrupted her. 'Or dinner?'

'Jerry, I've only *just* moved house –' Mrs Nightingale began. She had accepted none of his invitations. 'Then you're in need of a nice, relaxing dinner. Tuesday. Have you got your diary there?'

'No. Look, I'm afraid I must go. I haven't got my face on –'

'I'll ring you tomorrow, from the office.'

She must remember to leave the telephone off the hook tomorrow, Mrs Nightingale thought, as she wrenched garments from hangers, tried them on, examined the result in the looking glass, and tore them off again. Or else get the children to answer the telephone and say she was out.

'I've got nothing to wear!' she wailed, as Liza came into the room.

'That looks fine,' Liza said. 'Where's your hairbrush?'

While Liza brushed her mother's hair, Mrs Nightingale perched on the dressing-table stool and searched for her blue beads.

'I can't find my blue beads,' she said, turning out another drawer.

'Poppy's wearing them,' Liza said. 'She said you said she could. Time you dyed your hair, I think, or else made with the *Grecian 2000*,' she said kindly, putting the brush down.

'I think I heard a car,' Mrs Nightingale said, 'do you think you could round everyone up and go down and tell the Hendersons I'm coming. Give them a drink.'

Alone, Mrs Nightingale looked at her watch. It was ten past one. Edward was dead. He'd been dead a full quarter of an hour. At five to one, no doubt when she'd been fending off Jerry Selby-Willis, the signal on the cardiograph had flattened into a straight line for real this time, and the bleeps had ceased. She had not kept vigil; she had not been with him, holding his hand. She sat on the stool, twisting her wedding ring round and round her finger, for comfort. When at last she lifted her head she caught her reflection in the glass and was dismayed to see how pinched and wary and closed her face had become. 'Things have got to get better,' she said aloud. 'I must make them better.' There was a little moisturizer left in the bottle. She squeezed some into her palm and rubbed it into her forehead and cheeks, into the slack skin under her chin, into her crêpey neck. 'I am alive,' she said, 'I am not old. I am a young woman. I could live for another forty years yet.' She fumbled for the blusher, and worked it into her cheeks. 'I am a *person*,' she said threateningly into the glass. 'I am me, Frances.'

There was a thundering on the stairs, followed by Dave, out of breath at the door.

'Hi, folks, it's Lamborghini time,' he hissed. 'The Hendersons are in an arriving situation.' He had not shaved, after all, but on the other hand he was not wearing his red secretary spectacles either. You could not have everything, Mrs Nightingale supposed.

'Hurry up, Marlene,' he said. 'You can't leave us alone with them.' He vanished, and then immediately reappeared. 'You should know that Mrs H. is wearing a salmon two-piece, with turquoise accessories. Tuck in.'

Mrs Nightingale grabbed a lipstick from the table and stretched her mouth into the grimace that, with her, always preceded its application. At the first pressure the lipstick, which had been broken by Poppy earlier and stuck back by her into its case, toppled and fell, grazing Mrs Nightingale's chin as it did so with a long gash of *Wicked Rose*.

Patricia Highsmith

Something You Have to Live With

'Don't forget to lock all the doors,' Stan said. 'Someone might think because the car's gone, nobody's home.'

'All the doors? You mean two. You haven't asked me anything – aesthetic, such as how the place looks now.'

Stan laughed. 'I suppose the pictures are all hung and the books are in the shelves.'

'Well, not quite, but your shirts and sweaters – and the kitchen. It looks – I'm happy, Stan. So is Cassie. She's walking all around the place purring. See you tomorrow morning then. Around eleven, you said?'

'Around eleven. I'll bring stuff for lunch, don't worry.'

'Love to your mom. I'm glad she's better.'

'Thanks, darling.' Stan hung up.

Cassie, their ginger-and-white cat aged four, sat looking at Ginnie as if she had never seen a telephone before. Purring again. Dazed by all the space, Ginnie thought. Cassie began kneading the rug in an ecstasy of contentment, and Ginnie laughed.

Ginnie and Stan Brixton had bought a house in Connecticut after six years of New York apartments. Their furniture had been here for a week while they wound things up in New York, and yesterday had been the final move of smaller things like silverware, some dishes, a few pictures, suitcases, kitchen items and the cat. Stan had taken their son Freddie this morning to spend the night in New Hope, Pennsylvania, where Stan's mother lived. His mother had had a second heart attack and was recuperating at home. 'Every time I see her, I think it may be the last. You don't mind if I go, do you, Ginnie? It'll keep Freddie out of the way while you're fiddling around.' Ginnie hadn't minded.

Fiddling around was Stan's term for organizing and even cleaning. Ginnie thought she had done a good job since Stan and Freddie had taken off this morning. The lovely French blue-and-white vase which reminded Ginnie of Monet's paintings stood on the living room bookcase now, even bearing red roses from the garden. Ginnie had made headway in the kitchen, installing things the way she wanted them, the way they would remain. Cassie had her litter pan ('What a euphemism, litter ought to mean a bed,' Stan said) in the downstairs john corner. They now had an upstairs bathroom also. The house was on a hill with no other houses around it for nearly a mile, not that they owned all the land around, but the land around was farmland. When she and Stan had seen the place in June, sheep and goats had been grazing not far away. They had both fallen in love with the house.

Stanley Brixton was a novelist and fiction critic, and Ginnie wrote articles and was now half through her second novel. Her first had been published but had had only modest success. You couldn't expect a smash hit with a first novel, Stan said, unless the publicity was extraordinary. Water under the bridge. Ginnie was more interested in her novel-in-progress. They had a mortgage on the house, and with her and Stan's freelance work they thought they could be independent of New York, at least independent of nine-to-five jobs. Stan had already published three books, adventure stories with a political slant. He was thirty-two and for three years had been overseas correspondent for a newspaper syndicate.

Ginnie picked up a piece of heavy twine from the living room rug, and realized that her back hurt a little from the day's exertions. She had thought of switching on the TV, but the news was just over, she saw from her watch, and it might be better to go straight to bed and get up earlyish in the morning.

'Cassie?'

Cassie replied with a courteous, sustained, 'M-wah-h?'

'Hungry?' Cassie knew the word. 'No, you've had enough. Do you know you're getting middle-aged spread? Come on. Going up to bed with me?' Ginnie went to the front door, which was already locked by its automatic lock, but she put the chain on also. Yawning, she turned out the downstairs lights and climbed the stairs. Cassie followed her.

Ginnie had a quick bath, second of the day, pulled on a nightgown, brushed her teeth and got into bed. She at once realized she was too tired to pick up one of the English weeklies, political and Stan's favourites, which she had dropped by the bed to look at. She put out the lamp. *Home*. She and Stan had spent one night here last weekend during the big move. This was the first night she had been alone in the house, which still had no name. *Something like White Elephant maybe*, Stan had said. *You think of something*. Ginnie tried to think, an activity which made her instantly sleepier.

She was awakened by a crunching sound, like that of car tyres on gravel. She raised up a little in bed. Had she heard it? Their driveway hadn't any gravel to speak of, just unpaved earth. But –

Wasn't that a *click*? From somewhere. Front, back? Or had it been a twig falling on the roof?

She had locked the doors, hadn't she?

Ginnie suddenly realized that she had not locked the back door. For another minute, as Ginnie listened, everything was silent. What a bore to go downstairs again! But she thought she had better do it, so she could honestly tell Stan that she had. Ginnie found the lamp switch and got out of bed.

By now she was thinking that any noise she had

heard had been imaginary, something out of a dream. But Cassie followed her in a brisk, anxious way, Ginnie noticed.

The glow from the staircase light enabled Ginnie to find her way to the kitchen, where she switched on the strong ceiling light. She went at once to the back door and turned the Yale bolt. Then she listened. All was silent. The big kitchen looked exactly the same with its half modern, half old-fashioned furnishings – electric stove, big white wooden cupboard with drawers below, shelves above, double sink, a huge new fridge.

Ginnie went back upstairs, Cassie still following. Cassie was short for Cassandra, a name Stan had given her when she had been a kitten, because she had looked gloomy, unshakeably pessimistic. Ginnie was drifting off to sleep again, when she heard a bump downstairs, as if someone had staggered slightly. She switched on the bedside lamp again, and a thrust of fear went through her when she saw Cassie rigidly crouched on the bed with her eyes fixed on the open bedroom door.

Now there was another bump from downstairs, and the unmistakable rustle of a drawer being slid out, and it could be only the dining-room drawer where the silver was.

She had locked someone in with her!

Her first thought was to reach for the telephone and get the police, but the telephone was downstairs in the living-room.

Go down and face it and threaten him with something – or them, she told herself. Maybe it was an adolescent kid, just a local kid who'd be glad to get off unreported, if she scared him a little. Ginnie jumped out of bed, put on Stan's bathrobe, a sturdy blue flannel thing, and tied the belt firmly. She descended the stairs. By now she heard more noises.

'Who's *there*?' she shouted boldly.

'Hum-hum. Just me, lady,' said a rather deep voice.

The living-room lights, the dining-room lights were full on.

In the dining-room Ginnie was confronted by a stocking-hooded figure in what she thought of as motorcycle gear: black trousers, black boots, black plastic jacket. The stocking had slits cut in it for the eyes. And the figure carried a dirty canvas bag like a railway mailbag, and plainly into this the silverware had already gone, because the dining-room drawer gaped, empty. He must have been hiding in a corner of the dining-room, Ginnie thought, when she had come down to lock the back door. The hooded figure shoved the drawer to carelessly, and it didn't quite close.

'Keep your mouth shut, and you won't get hurt. All right?' The voice sounded like that of a man of at least twenty-five.

Ginnie didn't see any gun or knife. 'Just what do you think you're doing?'

'What does it look like I'm doing?' And the man got on with his business. The two candlesticks from the dining-room table went into the bag. So did the silver table lighter.

Was there anyone else with him? Ginnie glanced towards the kitchen, but didn't see anyone, and no sound came from there. 'I'm going to call the police,' she said, and started for the living-room telephone.

'Phone's cut, lady. You better keep quiet, because no one can hear you around here, even if you scream.'

Was that true? Unfortunately it was true. Ginnie for a few seconds concentrated on memorizing the man's appearance: about five feet eight, medium build, maybe a bit slender, broad hands – but since the hands were in blue rubber gloves, were they broad? – rather big feet. Blond or brunette she couldn't tell, because of the stocking mask. Robbers like this usually bound and gagged people. Ginnie wanted to avoid that, if she could.

'If you're looking for money, there's not much in the

house just now,' Ginnie said, 'except what's in my handbag upstairs, about thirty dollars. Go ahead and take it.'

'I'll get around to it,' he said laughing, prowling the living-room now. He took the letter-opener from the coffee table, then Freddie's photograph from the piano, because the photograph was in a silver frame.

Ginnie thought of banging him on the head with – with what? She saw nothing heavy enough, portable, except one of the dining-room chairs. And if she failed to knock him out with the first swat? Was the telephone really cut? She moved towards the telephone in the corner.

'Don't go near the door. Stay in sight!'

'Ma-wow-wow-*wow*!' This from Cassie, a high-pitched wail that to Ginnie meant Cassie was on the brink of throwing up, but now the situation was different. Cassie looked ready to attack the man.

'Go back, Cassie, take it easy,' Ginnie said.

'I don't like cats,' the hooded man said over his shoulder.

There was not much else he could take from the living-room, Ginnie thought. The pictures on the walls were too big. And what burglar was interested in pictures, at least pictures like these which were a few oils done by their painter friends, two or three watercolours – Was this really happening? Was a stranger picking up her mother's old sewing basket, looking inside, banging it down again? Taking the French vase, tossing the water and roses towards the fireplace? The vase went into the sack.

'What's upstairs?' The ugly head turned towards her. 'Let's go upstairs.'

'There's *nothing* upstairs!' Ginnie shrieked. She darted towards the telephone, knowing it would be cut, but wanting to see it with her own eyes – cut – though her hand was outstretched to use it. She saw the abruptly stopped wire on the floor, cut some four feet from the telephone.

The hood chuckled. 'Told you.'

A red flashlight stuck out of the back pocket of his trousers. He was going into the hall now, ready to take the stairs. The staircase light was on, but he pulled the flashlight from his pocket.

'Nothing *up* there, I tell you!' Ginnie found herself following him like a ninnie, holding up the hem of Stan's dressing-gown so she wouldn't trip on the stairs.

'Cosy little nook!' said the hood, entering the bedroom. 'And what have we here? Anything of interest?'

The silver-backed brush and comb on the dresser were of interest, also the hand mirror, and these went into the bag, which was now dragging the floor.

'Aha! I like that thing!' He had spotted the heavy wooden box with brass corners which Stan used for cufflinks and handkerchiefs and a few white ties, but its size was apparently daunting the man in the hood, because he swayed in front of it and said, 'Be back for that.' He looked around for lighter objects, and in went Ginnie's black leather jewellery box, her Dunhill lighter from the bedside table. 'Ought to be glad I'm not raping you. Haven't the time.' The tone was jocular.

My God, Ginnie thought, you'd think Stan and I were rich! She had never considered herself and Stan rich, or thought that they had anything worth invading a house for. No doubt in New York they'd been lucky for six years – no robberies at all – because even a typewriter was valuable to a drug addict. No, they weren't rich, but he was taking all they had, all the *nice* things they'd tried over the years to accumulate. Ginnie watched him open her handbag, lift the dollar bills from her billfold. That was the least of it.

'If you think for one minute you're going to get away with this,' Ginnie said. 'In a small community like *this*?

You haven't a prayer. If you don't leave those things here tonight, I'll report you so quick –'

'Oh, shut up, lady. Where's the other rooms here?'

Cassie snarled. She had followed them both up the stairs.

A black boot struck out sideways and caught the cat sharply in the ribs.

'Don't touch that cat!' Ginnie cried out.

Cassie sprang growling on to the man's boot top, at his knee.

Ginnie was astounded – and proud of Cassie – for a second.

'Pain in the ass!' said the hood, and with a gloved hand caught the cat by the loose skin on her back and flung her against a wall with a backhand swing. The cat dropped, panting, and the man stomped on her side and kicked her on the head.

'You *bastard!*' Ginnie screamed.

'So much for your stinking – yowlers!' said the beige hood, and kicked the cat once again. His voice had been husky with rage, and now he stalked with his flashlight into the hall, in quest of other rooms.

Dazed, stiff, Ginnie followed him.

The guest-room had only a chest of drawers in it, empty, but the man slid out a couple of drawers anyway to have a look. Freddie's room had nothing but a bed and table. The hood wasted no time there.

From the hall, Ginnie looked into the bedroom at her cat. The cat twitched and was still. One foot had twitched. Ginnie stood rigid as a column of stone. She had just seen Cassie die, she realized.

'Back in a flash,' said the hooded man, briskly descending the stairs with his sack which was now so heavy he had to carry it on one shoulder.

Ginnie moved at last, in jerks, like someone awakening from an anaesthetic. Her body and mind seemed not to be connected. Her hand reached for the stair rail and missed it. She was no longer afraid at all, though she did not consciously realize this. She simply kept following the hooded figure, her enemy, and would have kept on, even if he had pointed a gun at her. By the time she reached the kitchen, he was out of sight. The kitchen door was open, and a cool breeze blew in. Ginnie continued across the kitchen, looked left into the driveway, and saw a flashlight's beam swing as the man heaved the bag into a car. She heard the hum of two male voices. So he had a pal waiting for him!

And here he came back.

With sudden swiftness, Ginnie picked up a kitchen stool which had a square formica top and chromium legs. As soon as the hooded figure stepped on to the threshold of the kitchen, Ginnie swung the stool and hit him full on the forehead with the edge of the stool's seat.

Momentum carried the man forward, but he stooped, staggering, and Ginnie cracked him again on the top of the head with all her strength. She held two legs of the stool in her hands. He fell with a great thump and clatter on to the linoleum floor. Another whack for good measure on the back of the stockinged head. She felt pleased and relieved to see blood coming through the beige material.

'Frankie? – You okay? – *Frankie*!'

The voice came from the car outside.

Poised now, not at all afraid, Ginnie stood braced for the next arrival. She held a leg of the stool in her right hand, and her left supported the seat. She awaited, barely two feet from the open door, the sound of boots in the driveway, another figure in the doorway.

Instead, she heard a car motor start, saw a glow of its lights through the door. The car was backing down the drive.

Finally Ginnie set the stool down. The house was silent again. The man on the floor was not moving. Was he dead?

I don't care. I simply don't give a damn, Ginnie said inside herself.

But she did care. What if he woke up? What if he needed a doctor, a hospital right away? And there was no telephone. The nearest house was nearly a mile away, the village a good mile. Ginnie would have to walk it with a flashlight. Of course if she encountered a car, a car might stop and ask what was the matter, and then she could tell someone to fetch a doctor or an ambulance. These thoughts went through Ginnie's head in seconds, and then she returned to the facts. The fact was, he *might* be dead. Killed by her.

So was Cassie dead. Ginnie turned towards the living-room. Cassie's death was more real, more important than the body at her feet which only might be dead. Ginnie drew a glass of water for herself at the kitchen sink.

Everything was silent outside. Now Ginnie was calm enough to realize that the robber's chum had thought it best to make a getaway. He probably wasn't coming back, not even with reinforcements. After all, he had the loot in his car – silverware, her jewellery box, all the nice things.

Ginnie stared at the long black figure on her kitchen floor. He hadn't moved at all. The right hand lay under him, the left arm was outstretched, upward. The stockinged head was turned slightly towards her, one slit showing. She couldn't see what was going on behind that crazy slit.

'Are you *awake*?' Ginnie said, rather loudly.

She waited.

She knew she would have to face it. Best to feel the pulse in the wrist, she thought, and at once forced herself to do this. She pulled the rubber glove down a bit, and gripped a blondish-haired wrist which seemed to her of astonishing breadth, much wider than Stan's wrist, anyway. She couldn't feel any pulse. She altered the place where she had put her thumb, and tried again. There was no pulse.

So she had murdered someone. The fact did not sink in.

Two thoughts danced in her mind: she would have to remove Cassie, put a towel or something around her, and she was not going to be able to sleep or even remain in this house with a corpse lying on the kitchen floor.

Ginnie got a dishtowel, a folded clean one from a stack on a shelf, took a second one, went to the hall and climbed the stairs. Cassie was now bleeding. Rather, she had bled. The blood on the carpet looked dark. One of Cassie's eyes projected from the socket. Ginnie gathered her as gently as if she were still alive and only injured, gathered up some intestines which had been pushed out, and enfolded her in a towel, opened the second towel and put that around her too. Then she carried Cassie down to the living-room, hesitated, then laid the cat's body to one side of the fireplace on the floor. By accident, a red rose lay beside Cassie.

Tackle the blood now, she told herself. She got a plastic bowl from the kitchen, drew some cold water and took a sponge. Upstairs, she went to work on hands and knees, changing the water in the bathroom. The task was soothing, as she had known it would be.

Next job: clothes on and find the nearest telephone. Ginnie kept moving, barely aware of what she was doing, and suddenly she was standing in the kitchen in blue jeans, sneakers, sweater and jacket with her billfold in a pocket. Empty billfold, she remembered. She had her house keys in her left hand. For no good reason, she decided to leave the kitchen light on. The front door was still locked, she realized. She found she had the flashlight in a jacket pocket too, and supposed she had taken it from the front hall table when she came down the stairs.

She went out, locked the kitchen door from the outside with a key, and made her way to the road.

No moon at all. She walked with the aid of the flashlight along the left side of the road towards the village, shone the torch once on her watch and saw that it was twenty past one. By starlight, by a bit of flashlight, she saw one house far to the left in a field, quite dark and so far away, Ginnie thought she might do better to keep on.

She kept on. Dark road. Trudging. Did *everybody* go to bed early around here?

In the distance she saw two or three white streetlights, the lights of the village. Surely there'd be a car before the village.

There wasn't a car. Ginnie was still trudging as she entered the village proper, whose boundary was marked by a neat white sign on either side of the road saying EAST KINDALE.

My God, Ginnie thought. *Is this true? Is this what I'm doing, what I'm going to say?*

Not a light showed in any of the neat, mostly white houses. There was not even a light at the Connecticut Yankee Inn, the only functioning hostelry and bar in town, Stan had remarked once. Nevertheless, Ginnie marched up the steps and knocked on the door. Then with her flashlight, she saw a brass knocker on the white door, and availed herself of that.

Rap-rap-rap!

Minutes passed. *Be patient*, Ginnie told herself. *You're over-wrought*.

But she felt compelled to rap again.

'Who's there?' a man's voice called.

'A neighbour! There's been an accident!'

Ginnie fairly collapsed against the figure who opened the door. It was a man in a plaid woollen bathrobe and pyjamas. She might have collapsed also against a woman or a child.

Then she was sitting on a straight chair in a sort of living-room. She had blurted out the story.

'We'll – we'll get the police right away, ma'am. Or an

ambulance, as you say. But from what you say –' The man talking was in his sixties, and sleepy.

His wife, more efficient looking, had joined him to listen. She wore a dressing-gown and pink slippers. 'Police, Jake. Man sounds dead from what the lady says. Even if he isn't, the police'll know what to do.'

'Hello, Ethel! That you?' the man said into the telephone. 'Listen, we need the police right away. You know the old Hardwick place? . . . Tell 'em to go there . . . No, *not* on fire. Can't explain now. But somebody'll be there to open the door in – in about five minutes.'

The woman pushed a glass of something into Ginnie's hand. Ginnie realized that her teeth were chattering. She was cold, though it wasn't cold outside. It was early September, she remembered.

'They're going to want to speak with you.' The man who had been in the plaid robe was now in trousers and a belted sports jacket. 'You'll have to tell them the time it happened and all that.'

Ginnie realized. She thanked the woman and went with the man to his car. It was an ordinary four-door, and Ginnie noticed a discarded Cracker Jack box on the floor of the passenger's seat as she got in.

A police car was in the drive. Someone was knocking on the back door, and Ginnie saw that she'd left the kitchen light on.

'Hya, Jake! What's up?' called a second policeman, getting out of the black car in the driveway.

'Lady had a house robbery,' the man with Ginnie explained. 'She thinks – Well, you've got the keys, haven't you, Mrs Brixton?'

'Oh yes, yes.' Ginnie fumbled for them. She was gasping again, and reminded herself that it was a time to keep calm, to answer questions accurately. She opened the kitchen door.

A policeman stooped beside the prone figure. 'Dead,' he said.

'The – Mrs Brixton said she hit him with the kitchen stool. That one, ma'am?' The man called Jake pointed to the yellow formica stool.

'Yes. He was coming *back*, you see. You see –' Ginnie choked and gave up, for the moment.

Jake cleared his throat and said, 'Mrs Brixton and her husband just moved in. Husband isn't here tonight. She'd left the kitchen door unlocked and two – well, one fellow came in, this one. He went out with a bag of stuff he'd taken, put it in a waiting car, then came back to get more, and that's when Mrs Brixton hit him.'

'Um-*hum*,' said the policeman, still stooped on his heels. 'Can't touch the body till the detective gets here. Can I use your phone, Mrs Brixton?'

'They cut the phone,' Jake said. 'That's why she had to walk to my place.'

The other policeman went out to telephone from his car. The policeman who remained put on water for coffee (or had he said tea?), and chatted with Jake about tourists, about someone they both knew who had just got married – as if they had known each other for years. Ginnie was sitting on one of the dining-room chairs. The policeman asked where the instant coffee was, if she had any, and Ginnie got up to show him the coffee jar which she had put on a cabinet shelf beside the stove.

'Terrible introduction to a new house,' the policeman remarked, holding his steaming cup. 'But we all sure hope –' Suddenly his words seemed to dry up. His eyes flickered and looked away from Ginnie's face.

A couple of men in plainclothes arrived. Photographs were taken of the dead man. Ginnie went over the house with one of the men, who made notes of the items Ginnie said were stolen. No, she hadn't seen the colour of the car, much less the licence plate. The body on the floor was wrapped and carried out on a stretcher. Ginnie had only a glimpse of that, from which the detective even tried to shield her. Ginnie was in the dining-room then, reckoning up the missing silver.

'I didn't mean to kill him!' Ginnie cried out suddenly, interrupting the detective. 'Not *kill* him, honestly!'

Stan arrived very early, about 8 a.m., with Freddie, and went to the Inn to fetch Ginnie. Ginnie had spent the night there, and someone had telephoned Stan at the number Ginnie had given.

'She's had a shock,' Jake said to Stan.

Stan looked bewildered. But at least he had heard what happened, and Ginnie didn't have to go over it.

'All the nice things we had,' Ginnie said. 'And the cat –'

'The police might get our stuff back, Ginnie. If not, we'll buy more. We're all safe, at least.' Stan set his firm jaw, but he smiled. He glanced at Freddie who stood in the doorway, looking a little pale from lack of sleep. 'Come on. We're going home.'

He took Ginnie's hand. His hand felt warm, and she realized her own hands were cold again.

They tried to keep the identity of the dead man from her, Ginnie knew, but on the second day she happened to see it printed – on a folded newspaper which lay on the counter in the grocery store. There was a photograph of him too, a blondish fellow with curly hair and a rather defiant expression. *Frank Collins, 24, of Hartford . . .*

Stan felt that they ought to go on living in the house, gradually buy the 'nice things' again that Ginnie kept talking about. Stan said she ought to get back to work on her novel.

'I don't want any nice things any more. Not again.' That was true, but that was only part of it. The worst was that she had killed someone, stopped a life. She couldn't fully realize it, therefore couldn't believe it somehow, or understand it.

'At least we could get another cat.'

'Not yet,' she said.

People said to her (like Mrs Durham, Gladys, who lived a mile or so out of East Kindale on the opposite side from the Brixtons), 'You mustn't reproach yourself. You did it in defence of your house. Don't you think a lot of us wish we had the courage, if someone comes barging in intending to rob you . . .'

'I wouldn't hesitate – to do what you did!' That was from perky Georgia Hamilton, a young married woman with black curly hair, active in local politics, who lived in East Kindale proper. She came especially to call on Ginnie and to make acquaintance with her and Stan. 'These hoodlums from miles away – Hartford! – they come to rob us, just because they think we still have some family silver and a few *nice* things . . .'

There was the phrase again, the *nice* things.

Stan came home one day with a pair of silver candlesticks for the dining-room table. 'Less than a hundred dollars, and we can afford them,' Stan said.

To Ginnie they looked like bait for another robbery. They were pretty, yes. Georgian. Modern copy, but still beautiful. She could not take any aesthetic pleasure from them.

'Did you take a swat at your book this afternoon?' Stan asked cheerfully. He had been out of the house nearly three hours that afternoon. He had made sure the doors were locked, for Ginnie's sake, before he left. He had also bought a metal wheelbarrow for use in the garden, and it was still strapped to the roof of the car.

'No,' Ginnie said. 'But I suppose I'm making progress. I have to get back to a state of concentration, you know.'

'Of course I know,' Stan said. 'I'm a writer too.'

The police had never recovered the silverware, or Ginnie's leather box which had held her engagement ring (it had become too small and she hadn't got around to having it enlarged), and her grandmother's gold necklace and so forth. Stan told Ginnie they had checked all the known pals of the man who had invaded the house, but hadn't come up with anything. The police thought the dead man might have struck up acquaintance with his chum very recently, possibly the same night as the robbery.

'Darling,' Stan said, 'do you think we should *move* from this house? I'm willing – if it'd make you feel – less –'

Ginnie shook her head. It wasn't the house. She didn't any longer (after two months) even think of the corpse on the floor when she went into the kitchen. It was something inside her. 'No,' Ginnie said.

'Well – I think you ought to talk to a psychiatrist. Just one visit even,' Stan added, interrupting a protest from Ginnie. 'It isn't enough for neighbours to say you did the natural thing. Maybe you need a professional to tell you.' Stan chuckled. He was in tennis shoes and old clothes, and had had a good day at the typewriter.

Ginnie agreed, to please Stan.

The psychiatrist was in Hartford, a man recommended to Stan by a local medical doctor. Stan drove Ginnie there, and waited for her in the car. It was to be an hour's session, but Ginnie reappeared after about forty minutes.

'He gave me some pills to take,' Ginnie said.

'Is *that* all? – But what did he say?'

'Oh.' Ginnie shrugged. 'The same as they all say, that – nobody blames me, the police didn't make a fuss, so what –' She shrugged again, glanced at Stan and saw the terrible disappointment in his face as he looked from her into the distance through the windshield.

Ginnie knew he was thinking again about 'guilt' and abandoning it, abandoning the word again. She had said no, she didn't feel guilty, that wasn't the trouble, that would have been too simple. She felt disturbed, she had said many times, and she couldn't do anything about it.

'You really ought to write a book about it, a novel,' Stan said – this for at least the fourth time.

'And how can I, if I can't come to terms with it myself, if I can't even analyse it first?' This Ginnie said for at least the third time and possibly the fourth. It was as if she had an unsolvable mystery within her. 'You can't write a book just stammering around on paper.'

Stan then started the car.

The pills were mild sedatives combined with some kind of mild picker-uppers. They didn't make a change in Ginnie.

Two more months passed. Ginnie resisted buying any 'nice things', so they had nothing but the nice candlesticks. They ate with stainless steel. Freddie pulled out of his period of tension and suppressed excitement (he knew quite well what had happened in the kitchen), and in Ginnie's eyes became quite normal again, whatever normal was. Ginnie got back to work on the book she had started before moving to the house. She didn't ever dream about the murder, or manslaughter, in fact she often thought it might be better if she did dream about it.

But among people – and it was a surprisingly friendly region, they had all the social life they could wish – she felt compelled to say sometimes, when there was a lull in the conversation, 'Did you know, by the way, I once killed a man?'

Everyone would look at her, except of course those who had heard her say this before, maybe three times before.

Stan would grow tense and blank-minded, having failed once more to spring in in time before Ginnie got launched. He was jittery at social gatherings, trying like a fencer to dart in with something, anything to say, before Ginnie made her big thrust. *It's just something they, he and Ginnie, had to live with*, Stan told himself.

And it probably would go on and on, even maybe when Freddie was twelve and even twenty. It had, in fact, half-ruined their marriage. But it was emphatically not worth divorcing for. He still loved Ginnie. She was still

Ginnie after all. She was just somehow different. Even Ginnie had said that about herself.

'It's something I just have to live with,' Stan murmured to himself.

'What?' It was Georgia Hamilton on his left, asking him what he had said. 'Oh, I know, I know.' She smiled understandingly. 'But maybe it does her good.'

Ginnie was in the middle of her story. At least she always made it short, and even managed to laugh in a couple of places.

Ruth Prawer Jhabvala

How I Became
a Holy Mother

On my twenty-third birthday when I was fed up with London and all the rest of it – boyfriends, marriages (two), jobs (modelling), best friends that are suddenly your best enemies – I had this letter from my girl friend Sophie who was finding peace in an ashram in South India:

> . . . oh Katie you wouldn't know me I'm such a changed person. I get up at 5 – *a.m.*!!! I am an absolute vegetarian let alone no meat no eggs either and am making fabulous progress with my meditation. I have a special mantra of my own that Swamiji gave me at a special ceremony and I say it over and over in my mind. The sky here is blue all day long and I sit by the sea and watch the waves and have good thoughts . . .

But by the time I got there Sophie had left – under a cloud, it seemed, though when I asked what she had done, they wouldn't tell me but only pursed their lips and looked sorrowful. I didn't stay long in that place. I didn't like the bitchy atmosphere, and that Swamiji was a big fraud, anyone could see that. I couldn't understand how a girl as sharp as Sophie had ever let herself be fooled by such a type. But I suppose if you want to be fooled you are. I found that out in some of the other ashrams I went to. There were some quite intelligent people in all of them but the way they just shut their eyes to certain things, it was incredible. It is not my role in life to criticize others so

I kept quiet and went on to the next place. I went to quite a few of them. These ashrams are a cheap way to live in India and there is always company and it isn't bad for a few days provided you don't get involved in their power politics. I was amazed to come across quite a few people I had known over the years and would never have expected to meet here. It is a shock when you see someone you had last met on the beach at St Tropez now all dressed up in a saffron robe and meditating in some very dusty ashram in Madhya Pradesh. But really I could see their point because they were all as tired as I was of everything we had been doing and this certainly was different.

I enjoyed myself going from one ashram to the other and travelling all over India. Trains and buses are very crowded – I went third class, I had to be careful with my savings – but Indians can tell when you want to be left alone. They are very sensitive that way. I looked out of the window and thought my thoughts. After a time I became quite calm and rested. I hadn't brought too much stuff with me, but bit by bit I discarded most of that too till I had only a few things left that I could easily carry myself. I didn't even mind when my watch was pinched off me one night in a railway rest-room (so-called). I felt myself to be a changed person. Once, at the beginning of my travels, there was a man sitting next to me on a bus who said he was an astrologer. He was a very sensitive and philosophical person – and I must say I was impressed by how many such one meets in India, quite ordinary people travelling third class. After we had been talking for a time and he had told me the future of India for the next forty years, suddenly out of the blue he said to me, 'Madam, you have a very sad soul.' It was true. I thought about it for days afterwards and cried a bit to myself. I did feel sad inside myself and heavy like with a stone. But as time went on and I kept going round India – the sky always blue like Sophie had said, and lots of rivers and fields as well as desert – just quietly travelling and looking, I stopped feeling like that. Now I was as a matter of fact quite light inside as if that stone had gone.

Then I stopped travelling and stayed in this one place instead. I liked it better than any of the other ashrams for several reasons. One of them was that the scenery was very picturesque. This cannot be said of all ashrams as many of them seem to be in sort of dust bowls, or in the dirtier parts of very dirty holy cities or even cities that aren't holy at all but just dirty. But this ashram was built on the slope of a mountain, and behind it there were all the other mountains stretching right up to the snow-capped peaks of the Himalayas; and on the other side it ran down to the river which I will not say can have been very clean (with all those pilgrims dipping in it) but certainly looked clean from up above and not only clean but as clear and green as the sky was clear and blue. Also along the bank of the river there were many little pink temples with pink cones and they certainly made a pretty scene. Inside the ashram also the atmosphere was good which again cannot be said of all of them, far from it. But the reason the atmosphere was good here was because of the head of this ashram who was called Master. They are always called something like that – if not Swamiji then Maharaj-ji or Babaji or Maharishiji or Guruji; but this one was just called plain Master, in English.

He was full of pep and go. Early in the morning he would say, 'Well what shall we do today!' and then plan some treat like all of us going for a swim in the river with a picnic lunch to follow. He didn't want anyone to have a dull moment or to fall into a depression which I suppose many there were apt to do, left to their own devices. In some ways he reminded me of those big business types that sometimes (in other days!) took me out to dinner. They too had that kind of superhuman energy and seemed to be stronger than other people. I forgot to say that Master was a big burly man, and as he didn't wear all that many clothes – usually only a loincloth –

you could see just how big and burly he was. His head was large too and it was completely shaven so that it looked even larger. He wasn't ugly, not at all. Or perhaps if he was one forgot about it very soon because of all that dynamism.

As I said, the ashram was built on the slope of a mountain. I don't think it was planned at all but had just grown: there was one little room next to the other and the Meditation Hall and the dining hall and Master's quarters – whatever was needed was added and it all ran higgledy-piggledy down the mountain. I had one of the little rooms to myself and made myself very snug in there. The only furniture provided by the ashram was one string bed, but I bought a handloom rug from the Lepers Rehabilitation Centre and I also put up some pictures, like a Tibetan Mandala which was very colourful. Everyone liked my room and wanted to come and spend time there, but I was a bit cagey about that as I needed my privacy. I always had lots to do, like writing letters or washing my hair and I was also learning to play the flute. So I was quite happy and independent and didn't really need company though there was plenty of it, if and when needed.

There were Master's Indian disciples who were all learning to be swamis. They wanted to renounce the world and had shaved their heads and wore an orange sort of toga thing. When they were ready, Master was going to make them into full swamis. Most of these junior swamis were very young – just boys, some of them – but even those that weren't all that young were certainly so at heart. Sometimes they reminded me of a lot of school kids, they were so full of tricks and fun. But I think basically they were very serious – they couldn't not be, considering how they were renouncing and were supposed to be studying all sorts of very difficult things. The one I liked the best was called Vishwa. I liked him not only because he was the best looking, which he undoubtedly was, but I felt he had a lot going for him. Others said so too – in fact, they all said that Vishwa was the most advanced and was next in line for full initiation. I always let him come and talk to me in my room whenever he wanted to, and we had some interesting conversations.

Then there were Master's foreign disciples. They weren't so different from the other Europeans and Americans I had met in other ashrams except that the atmosphere here was so much better and that made them better too. They didn't have to fight with each other over Master's favours – I'm afraid that was very much the scene in some of the other ashrams which were like harems, the way they were all vying for the favour of their guru. But Master never encouraged that sort of relationship, and although of course many of them did have very strong attachments to him, he managed to keep them all healthy. And that's really saying something because, like in all the other ashrams, many of them were not healthy people; through no fault of their own quite often, they had just had a bad time and were trying to get over it.

Once Master said to me, 'What about you, Katie?' This was when I was alone with him in his room. He had called me in for some dictation – we were all given little jobs to do for him from time to time, to keep us busy and happy I suppose. Just let me say a few words about his room and get it over with. It was *awful*. It had linoleum on the floor of the nastiest pattern, and green strip lighting, and the walls were painted green too and had been decorated with calendars and pictures of what were supposed to be gods and saints but might as well have been Bombay film stars, they were so fat and gaudy. Master and all the junior swamis were terribly proud of this room. Whenever he acquired anything new – like some plastic flowers in a hideous vase – he would call everyone to admire and was so pleased and complacent that really it was not possible to say anything except, 'Yes very nice.'

When he said, 'What about you, Katie?' I knew at once

what he meant. That was another thing about him – he would suddenly come out with something as if there had already been a long talk between you on this subject. So when he asked me that, it was like the end of a conversation, and all I had to do was think for a moment and then I said, 'I'm okay.' Because that was what he had asked: was I okay? Did I want anything, any help or anything? And I didn't. I really was okay now. I hadn't always been but I got so travelling around on my own and then being in this nice place here with him.

This was before the Countess came. Once she was there, everything was rather different. For weeks before her arrival people started talking about her: she was an important figure there, and no wonder since she was very rich and did a lot for the ashram and for Master when he went abroad on his lecture tours. I wondered what she was like. When I asked Vishwa about her, he said, 'She is a great spiritual lady.'

We were both sitting outside my room. There was a little open space round which several other rooms were grouped. One of these – the biggest, at the corner – was being got ready for the Countess. It was the one that was always kept for her. People were vigorously sweeping in there and scrubbing the floor with soap and water.

'She is rich and from very aristocratic family,' Vishwa said, 'but when she met Master she was ready to give up everything.' He pointed to the room which was being scrubbed: 'This is where she stays. And see – not even a bed – she sleeps on the floor like a holy person. Oh Katie, when someone like me gives up the world, what is there? It is not such a great thing. But when *she* does it –' His face glowed. He had very bright eyes and a lovely complexion. He always looked very pure, owing no doubt to the very pure life he led.

Of course I got more and more curious about her, but when she came I was disappointed. I had expected her to be very special, but the only special thing about her was that I should meet her *here*. Otherwise she was a type I had often come across at posh parties and in the salons where I used to model. And the way she walked towards me and said, 'Welcome!' – she might as well have been walking across a carpet in a salon. She had a full-blown, middle-aged figure (she must have been in her fifties) but very thin legs on which she took long strides with her toes turned out. She gave me a deep searching look – and that too I was used to from someone like her because very worldly people always do that: to find out who you are and how usable. But in her case now I suppose it was to search down into my soul and see what that was like.

I don't know what her conclusion was, but I must have passed because she was always kind to me and even asked for my company quite often. Perhaps this was partly because we lived across from each other and she suffered from insomnia and needed someone to talk to at night. I'm a sound sleeper myself and wasn't always very keen when she came to wake me. But she would nag me till I got up. 'Come on, Katie, be a sport,' she would say. She used many English expressions like that: she spoke English very fluently though with a funny accent. I heard her speak to the French and Italian and German people in the ashram very fluently in their languages too. I don't know what nationality she herself was – a sort of mixture I think – but of course people like her have been everywhere, not to mention their assorted governesses when young.

She always made me come into her room. She said mine was too *luxurious*, she didn't feel right in it as she had given up all that. Hers certainly wasn't luxurious. Like Vishwa had said, there wasn't a stick of furniture in it and she slept on the floor on a mat. As the electricity supply in the ashram was very fitful, we usually sat by candlelight. It was queer sitting like that with her on the floor with a stub of candle between us. I didn't have to do much talking as she did it all. She used her arms a lot, in sweeping gestures, and I can still see them weaving around there by candlelight as if she was doing a dance with them; and her eyes which were big and baby-blue were stretched wide open in wonder at everything she was telling me. Her life was like a fairy-tale, she said. She gave me all the details though I can't recall them as I kept dropping off to sleep (naturally at two in the morning). From time to time she'd stop and say sharply, 'Are you asleep, Katie?' and then she would poke me till I said no I wasn't. She told me how she first met Master at a lecture he had come to give in Paris. At the end of the lecture she went up to him – she said she had to elbow her way through a crowd of women all trying to get near him – and simply bowed down at his feet. No words spoken. There had been no need. It had been predestined.

She was also very fond of Vishwa. It seemed all three of them – i.e. her, Master, and Vishwa – had been closely related to each other in several previous incarnations. I think they had been either her sons or her husbands or fathers, I can't remember which exactly but it was very close so it was no wonder she felt about them the way she did. She had big plans for Vishwa. He was to go abroad and be a spiritual leader. She and Master often talked about it, and it was fascinating listening to them, but there was one thing I couldn't understand and that was why did it have to be Vishwa and not Master who was to be a spiritual leader in the West? I'd have thought Master himself had terrific qualifications for it.

Once I asked them. We were sitting in Master's room and the two of them were talking about Vishwa's future. When I asked, 'What about Master?' she gave a dramatic laugh and pointed at him like she was accusing him: 'Ask him! Why don't you ask him!'

He gave a guilty smile and shifted around a bit on his throne. I say throne – it really was that: he received everyone in this room so a sort of dais had been fixed up at one end and a deer-skin spread on it for him to sit on; loving disciples had painted an arched back to the dais and decorated it with stars and symbols stuck on in silver paper (hideous!).

When she saw him smile like that, she really got exasperated. 'If you knew, Katie,' she said, 'how I have argued with him, how I have fought, how I have begged and pleaded on my *knees*. But he is as stubborn as – as –'

'A mule,' he kindly helped her out.

'Forgive me,' she said (because you can't call your guru names, that just isn't done!); though next moment she had worked herself up again. 'Do you know,' she asked me, 'how many people were waiting for him at the airport last time he went to New York? Do you know how many came to his lectures? That they had to be turned away from the *door* till we took a bigger hall! And not to speak of those who came to enrol for the special three-week Meditation-via-Contemplation course.'

'She is right,' he said. 'They are very kind to me.'

'Kind! They want him – need him – are crazy with love and devotion –'

'It's all true,' he said. 'But the trouble is, you see, I'm a very, very lazy person.' And as he said this, he gave a big yawn and stretched himself to prove how lazy he was: but he didn't look it – on the contrary, when he stretched like that, pushing out his big chest, he looked like he was humming with energy.

That evening he asked me to go for a stroll with him. We walked by the river which was very busy with people dipping in it for religious reasons. The temples were also busy – whenever we passed one, they seemed to be bursting in there with hymns, and cymbals, and little bells.

Master said, 'It is true that everyone is very kind to me in the West. Oh they make a big fuss when I come. They have even made a song for me – it goes – wait, let me see –'

He stopped still and several people took the opportunity to come up to ask for his blessing. There were many other holy men walking about but somehow Master stood out. Some of the holy men also came up to be blessed by him.

'Yes it goes: "*He's here! Our Masterji is here Jai jai Master! Jai jai He!*" They stand waiting for me at the airport, and when I come out of the customs they burst into song. They carry big banners and also have drums and flutes. What a noise they make! Some of them begin to dance there and then on the spot, they are so happy. And everyone stares and looks at me, all the respectable people at the airport, and they wonder, "Now who is this ruffian?"'

He had to stop again because a shopkeeper came running out of his stall to crouch at Master's feet. He was the grocer – everyone knew he used false weights – as well as the local moneylender and the biggest rogue in town, but when Master blessed him I could see tears come in his eyes, he felt so good.

'A car has been bought for my use,' Master said when we walked on again. 'Also a lease has been taken on a beautiful residence in New Hampshire. Now they wish to buy an aeroplane to enable me to fly from coast to coast.' He sighed. 'She is right to be angry with me. But what am I to do? I stand in the middle of Times Square or Piccadilly, London, and I look up and there are all the beautiful beautiful buildings stretching so high up into heaven: yes I look at them but it is not them I see at all, Katie! Not them at all!'

He looked up and I with him, and I understood that what he saw in Times Square and Piccadilly was what we saw now – all those mountains growing higher and higher above the river, and some of them so high that you couldn't make out whether it was them with snow on top or the sky with clouds in it.

Before the Countess's arrival, everything had been very easy-going. We usually did our meditation, but if we happened to miss out, it never mattered too much. Also there was a lot of sitting around gossiping or trips to the bazaar for eats. But the Countess put us on a stricter régime. Now we all had a timetable to follow, and there were gongs and bells going off all day to remind us. This started at 5 a.m. when it was meditation time, followed by purificatory bathing time, and study time, and discussion time, and hymn time, and so on till lights-out time. Throughout the day disciples could be seen making their way up or down the mountainside as they passed from one group activity to the other. If there was any delay in the schedule, the Countess got impatient and clapped her hands and chivied people along. The way she herself clambered up and down the mountain was just simply amazing for someone her age. Sometimes she went right to the top of the ashram where there was a pink plaster pillar inscribed with Golden Rules for Golden Living (a sort of Indian Ten Commandments): from here she could look all round, survey her domain as it were. When she wanted to summon everyone, she climbed up there with a pair of cymbals and how she beat them together! Boom! Bang! She must have had military blood in her veins, probably German.

She had drawn up a very strict timetable for Vishwa to cover every aspect of his education. He had to learn all sorts of things; not only English and a bit of French and German, but also how to use a knife and fork and even how to address people by their proper titles in case ambassadors and big church people and such were drawn into the movement as was fully expected. Because I'd been a model, I was put in charge of his deportment. I was supposed to teach him how to walk and sit nicely. He had to come to my room for lessons in the afternoons, and it was quite fun though I really didn't know what to teach him. As far as I was concerned, he was more graceful than anyone I'd ever seen. I loved the way he sat on the floor with his legs tucked under him; he could sit like that without moving for hours and hours. Or he might lie full-length on the floor with his head supported on one hand and his ascetic's robe falling in folds around him so that he looked like a piece of sculpture you might see in a museum. I forgot to say that the Countess had decided he wasn't to shave his hair any more like the other junior swamis but was to grow it and have long curls. It wasn't long yet but it was certainly curly and framed his face very prettily.

After the first few days we gave up having lessons and just talked and spent our time together. He sat on the rug and I on the bed. He told me the story of his life and I told him mine. But his was much better than mine. His father had been the station master at some very small junction, and the family lived in a little railway house near enough the tracks to run and put the signals up or down as required. Vishwa had plenty of brothers and sisters to play with, and friends at the little school he went to at the other end of town; but quite often he felt like not being with anyone. He would set off to school with his copies and pencils like everyone else, but half way he would change his mind and take another turning that led out of town into some open fields. Here he would lie down under a tree and look at patches of sky through the leaves of the tree, and the leaves moving ever so gently if there was a breeze or some birds shook their wings in there. He would stay all day and in the evening go home and not tell anyone. His mother was a religious person who regularly visited the temple and sometimes he went with her but he never felt anything special. Then Master came to town and gave a lecture in a tent that was put up for him on the Parade Ground. Vishwa went with his mother to hear him, again not expecting anything special, but the moment he saw Master something very peculiar happened: he couldn't quite describe it, but he said it was like when there is a wedding on a dark night and the fireworks start and there are those that shoot up into the sky and then burst into a huge white fountain of light scattering sparks all over so that you are blinded and dazzled with it. It was like that, Vishwa said. Then he just went away with Master. His family were sad at first to lose him, but they were proud too like all families are when one of them renounces the world to become a holy man.

Those were good afternoons we had, and we usually took the precaution of locking the door so no one could interrupt us. If we heard the Countess coming – one good thing about her, you could always *hear* her a mile off, she never moved an inch without shouting instructions to someone – the moment we heard her we'd jump up and unlock the door and fling it wide open: so when she looked in, she could see us having our lesson – Vishwa walking up and down with a book on his head, or sitting like on a dais to give a lecture and me showing him what to do with his hands.

When I told him the story of *my* life, we both cried. Especially when I told him about my first marriage when I was only sixteen and Danny just twenty. He was a bass player in a group and he was really good and would have got somewhere if he hadn't freaked out. It was terrible seeing him do that, and the way he treated me after those first six months we had together which were out of this world. I never had anything like that with anyone ever again, though I got involved with many people afterwards. Everything just got worse and worse till I reached an all-time low with my second marriage which was to a company director (so-called, though don't ask me what sort of company) and a very smooth operator indeed besides being a sadist. Vishwa couldn't stand it when I came to that part of my story. He begged me not to go on, he put his hands over his ears. We weren't in my room that time but on top of the ashram by the Pillar of the Golden Rules. The view from here was fantastic, and it was so high up that you felt you might as well be in heaven, especially at this hour of the evening when the sky was turning all sorts of colours though mostly gold from the sun setting in it. Everything I was telling Vishwa seemed very far away. I can't say it was as if it had never happened, but it seemed like it had happened in someone else's life. There were tears on Vishwa's lashes, and I couldn't help myself, I had to kiss them away. After which we kissed properly. His mouth was as soft as a flower and his breath as sweet; of course he had never tasted meat nor eaten anything except the purest food such as a lamb might eat.

The door of my room was not the only one that was locked during those hot afternoons. Quite a few of the foreign disciples locked theirs for purposes I never cared to enquire into. At first I used to pretend to myself they were sleeping, and afterwards I didn't care what they were doing. I mean, even if they weren't sleeping, I felt there was something just as good and innocent about what they actually *were* doing. And after a while – when we had told each other the story of our respective lives and had run out of conversation – Vishwa and I began to do it too. This was about the time when preparations were going on for his final Renunciation and Initiation ceremony. It's considered the most important day in the life of a junior swami, when he ceases to be junior and becomes a senior or proper swami. It's a very solemn ceremony. A funeral pyre is lit and his junior robe and his caste thread are burned on it. All this is symbolic – it means he's dead to the world but resurrected to the spiritual life. In Vishwa's case, his resurrection was a bit different from the usual. He wasn't fitted out in the standard senior swami outfit – which is a piece of orange cloth and a begging bowl – but instead the Countess dressed him up in the clothes he was to wear in the West. She had herself designed a white silk robe for him, together with accessories like beads, sandals, the deer-skin he was to sit on, and an embroidered shawl.

Getting all this ready meant many trips to the bazaar, and often she made Vishwa and me go with her. She swept through the bazaar the same way she did through the ashram, and the shopkeepers leaned eagerly out of their stalls to offer their salaams which she returned or not as they happened to be standing in her books. She was pretty strict with all of them – but most of all with the tailor whose job it was to stitch Vishwa's new silk robes. We spent hours in his little shop while Vishwa had to stand there and be fitted. The tailor crouched at his feet, stitching and restitching the hem to the Countess's instructions. She and I would stand back and look at Vishwa with our heads to one side while the tailor waited anxiously for her verdict. Ten to one she would say, 'No! Again!'

But once she said not to the tailor but to me, 'Vishwa stands very well now. He has a good pose.'

'Not bad,' I said, continuing to look critically at Vishwa and in such a way that he had a job not to laugh.

What she said next however killed all desire for laughter: 'I think we could end the deportment lessons now,' and then she shouted at the tailor: 'What is this! What are you doing! What sort of monkey-work do you call that!'

I managed to persuade her that I hadn't finished with Vishwa yet and there were still a few tricks of the trade I had to teach him. But I knew it was a short reprieve and that soon our lessons would have to end. Also plans were now afoot for Vishwa's departure. He was to go with the Countess when she returned to Europe in a few weeks' time; and she was already very busy corresponding with her contacts in various places, and all sorts of lectures and meetings were being arranged. But that wasn't the only thing worrying me: what was even worse was the change I felt taking place in Vishwa himself, especially after his Renunciation and Initiation ceremony. I think he was getting quite impressed with himself. The Countess made a point of treating him as if he were a guru already, and she bowed to him the same way she did to Master. And of course whatever she did everyone else followed suit, specially the foreign disciples. I might just say that they're always keen on things like that – I mean, bowing down and touching feet – I don't know what kick they get out of it but they do, the Countess along with the rest. Most of them do it very clumsily – not like Indians who are *born* to it – so sometimes you feel like laughing when you look at them. But they're always very solemn about it and afterwards, when they stumble up again, there's a sort of holy glow on their faces. Vishwa looked down at them with a benign expression and he also got into the habit of blessing them the way Master did.

Now I stayed alone in the afternoons, feeling very miserable, specially when I thought of what was going on in some of the other rooms and how happy people were in there. After a few days of this I couldn't stand being on my own and started wandering around looking for company. But the only person up and doing at that time of day was the Countess who I didn't particularly want to be with. So I went and sat in Master's room where the door was always open in case any of us needed him any time. Like everybody else, he was often asleep that time of afternoon but it didn't matter. Just being in his presence was good. I sat on one of the green plastic benches that were ranged round his room and looked at him sleeping which he did sitting upright on his throne. Quite suddenly he would open his eyes and look straight at me and say, 'Ah Katie,' as if he'd known all along that I was sitting there.

One day there was an awful commotion outside. Master woke up as the Countess came in with two foreign disciples, a boy and a girl, who stood hanging their heads while she told us what she had caught them doing. They were two very young disciples; I think the boy didn't even have to shave yet. One couldn't imagine them doing anything really evil, and Master didn't seem to think so.

He just told them to go away and have their afternoon rest. But because the Countess was very upset he tried to comfort her which he did by telling about his early life in the world when he was a married man. It had been an arranged marriage of course, and his wife had been very young, just out of school. Being married for them had been like a game, specially the cooking and housekeeping part which she had enjoyed very much. Every Sunday she had dressed up in a spangled sari and high-heeled shoes and he had escorted her on the bus to the cinema where they stood in a queue for the one-rupee seats. He had loved her more than he had ever loved anyone or anything in all his life and had not thought it possible to love so much. But it only lasted two years at the end of which time she died of a miscarriage. He left his home then and wandered about for many years, doing all sorts of different jobs. He worked as a motor mechanic, and a salesman for medical supplies, and had even been in films for a while on the distribution side. But not finding rest anywhere, he finally decided to give up the world. He explained to us that it had been the only logical thing to do. Having learned during his two years of marriage how happy it was possible for a human being to be, he was never again satisfied to settle for anything less; but also seeing how it couldn't last on a worldly plane, he had decided to look for it elsewhere and help other people to do so with him.

I liked what he said, but I don't think the Countess took much of it in. She was more in her own thoughts. She was silent and gloomy which was *very* unusual for her. When she woke me that night for her midnight confessions, she seemed quite a different person: and now she didn't talk about her fairy-tale life or her wonderful plans for the future but on the contrary about all the terrible things she had suffered in the past. She went right back to the time she was in her teens and had eloped with and married an old man, a friend of her father's, and from there on it was all just one long terrible story of bad marriages and unhappy love affairs and other sufferings that I wished I didn't have to listen to. But I couldn't leave her in the state she was in. She was crying and sobbing and lying face down on the ground. It was eerie in that bare cell of hers with the one piece of candle flickering in the wind which was very strong, and the rain beating down like fists on the tin roof.

The monsoon had started, and when you looked up now, there weren't any mountains left, only clouds hanging down very heavily; and when you looked down, the river was also heavy and full. Every day there were stories of pilgrims drowning in it, and one night it washed over one bank and swept away a little colony of huts that the lepers had built for themselves. Now they no longer sat sunning themselves on the bridge but were carted away to the infectious diseases hospital. The rains came gushing down the mountain right into the ashram so that we were all wading ankle-deep in mud and water. Many rooms were flooded and their occupants had to move into other people's rooms resulting in personality clashes. Everyone bore grudges and took sides so that it became rather like the other ashrams I had visited and not liked.

The person who changed the most was the Countess. Although she was still dashing up and down the mountain, it was no longer to get the place in running order. Now she tucked up her skirts to wade from room to room to peer through chinks and see what people were up to. She didn't trust anyone but appointed herself as a one-man spying organization. She even suspected Master and me! At least me – she asked me what I went to his room for in the afternoon and sniffed at my reply in a way I didn't care for. After that one awful outburst she had, she didn't call me at night any more but she was certainly after me during the day.

She guarded Vishwa like a dragon. She wouldn't even let me pass his room, and if she saw me going anywhere in that direction, she'd come running to tell me to take the other way round. I wasn't invited any more to accompany them to the bazaar but only she and Vishwa set off, with her holding a big black umbrella over them both. If they happened to pass me on the way, she would tilt the umbrella so he wouldn't be able to see me. Not that this was necessary as he never seemed to see me anyway. His eyes were always lowered and the expression on his face very serious. He had stopped joking around with the junior swamis, which I suppose was only fitting now he was a senior swami as well as about to become a spiritual leader. The Countess had fixed up a throne for him at the end of Master's room so he wouldn't have to sit on the floor and the benches along with the rest of us. When we all got together in there, Master would be at one end on his throne and Vishwa at the other on his. At Master's end there was always lots going on – everyone laughing and Master making jokes and having his fun – but Vishwa just sat very straight in the lotus pose and never looked at anyone or spoke, and only when the Countess pushed people to go and touch his feet, he'd raise a hand to bless them.

With the rains came flies and mosquitoes, and people began to fall sick with all sorts of mysterious fevers. The Countess – who was terrified of germs and had had herself pumped full of every kind of injection before coming to India – was now in a great hurry to be off with Vishwa. But before they could leave, he too came down with one of those fevers. She took him at once into her own room and kept him isolated in there with everything shut tight. She wouldn't let any of us near him. But I peeped in through the chinks, not caring whether she saw me or not. I even pleaded with her to let me come in, and once she let me but only to look at him from the door while she stood guard by his pillow. His eyes were shut and he was breathing heavily and moaning in an awful way. The Countess said I could go now, but instead I rushed up to Vishwa's bed. She tried to get between us but I pushed her out of the way and got down by the bed and held him where he lay moaning with his eyes shut. The Countess shrieked and pulled at me to get me away. I was shrieking too. We must have sounded and looked like a couple of madwomen. Vishwa opened his eyes and when he saw me there and moreover found that he was in my arms, *he* began to shriek too, as if he was frightened of me and that perhaps I was the very person he was having those terrible fever dreams about that made him groan.

It may have been this accidental shock treatment but that night Vishwa's fever came down and he began to get better. Master announced that there was going to be a Yagna or prayer-meet to give thanks for Vishwa's recovery. It was to be a really big show. Hordes of helpers came up from the town, all eager to take part in this event so as to benefit from the spiritual virtue it was expected to generate. The Meditation Hall was repainted salmon pink and the huge holy *OM* sign at one end of it was lit up all round with coloured bulbs that flashed on and off. Everyone worked with a will, and apparently good was already beginning to be generated because the rains stopped, the mud lanes in the ashram dried up, and the river flowed back into its banks. The disciples stopped quarrelling which may have been partly due to the fact that everyone could move back into their own rooms.

The Countess and Vishwa kept going down into the town to finish off with the tailors and embroiderers. They also went to the printer who was making large posters to be sent abroad to advertise Vishwa's arrival. The Countess often asked me to go with them: she was really a good-natured person and did not want me to feel left out. Especially now that she was sure there wasn't a dangerous situation working up between me and Vishwa. There she was right. I wasn't in the least interested in him and felt that the less I saw of him the better. I couldn't forget the way he had shrieked that night in the Countess's room as if I was something impure and dreadful. But on the contrary to me it seemed that it had been *he* who was impure and dreadful with his fever dreams. I didn't even like to think what went on in them.

The Great Yagna began and it really was great. The Meditation Hall was packed and was terribly hot not only with all the people there but also because of the sacrificial flames that sizzled as more and more clarified butter was poured on them amid incantations. Everyone was smiling and singing and sweating. Master was terrific – he was right by the fire stark naked except for the tiniest bit of loincloth. His chest glistened with oil and seemed to reflect the flames leaping about. Sometimes he jumped up on his throne and waved his arms to make everyone join in louder; and when they did, he got so happy he did a little jig standing up there. Vishwa was on the other side of the Hall also on a throne. He was half reclining in his spotless white robe; he did not seem to feel the heat at all but lay there as if made out of cool marble. He reminded me of the god Shiva resting on top of his snowy mountain. The Countess sat near him, and I saw how she tried to talk to him once or twice but he took no notice of her. After a while she got up and went out which was not surprising for it really was not her scene, all that noise and singing and the neon lights and decorations.

It went on all night. No one seemed to get tired – they just got more and more worked up and the singing got louder and the fire hotter. Other people too began to do little jigs like Master's. I left the Hall and walked around by myself. It was a fantastic night, the sky sprinkled all over with stars and a moon like a melon. When I passed the Countess's door, she called me in. She was lying on her mat on the floor and said she had a migraine. No wonder, with all that noise. I liked it myself but I knew that, though she was very much attracted to Eastern religions, her taste in music was more for the Western classical type (she loved string quartets and had had a long *affaire* with a cellist). She confessed to me that she was very anxious to leave now and get Vishwa started on his career. I think she would have liked to confess more things, but I had to get on. I made my way uphill past all the different buildings till I had reached the top of the ashram and the Pillar of the Golden Rules. Here I stood and looked down.

I saw the doors of the Meditation Hall open and Master and Vishwa come out. They were lit up by the lights from the Hall. Master was big and black and naked except for his triangle of orange cloth, and Vishwa was shining in white. I saw Master raise his arm and point it up, up to the top of the ashram. The two of them reminded me of a painting I've seen of I think it was an angel pointing out a path to a pilgrim. And like a pilgrim Vishwa began to climb up the path that Master had shown him. I stood by the Pillar of the Golden Rules and waited for him. When he got to me, we didn't have to speak one word. He was like a charged dynamo; I'd never known him like that. It was more like it might have been with Master instead of Vishwa. The drums and hymns down in the Meditation Hall also reached their crescendo just then. Of course Vishwa was too taken up with what he was doing to notice anything going on round him, so it was only me that saw the Countess come uphill. She was walking quite slowly and I suppose I could have warned Vishwa in time but it seemed a pity to interrupt him, so I just let her come on up and find us.

Master finally settled everything to everyone's satisfaction. He said Vishwa and I were to be a couple, and whereas Vishwa was to be the Guru, I was to embody the Mother principle (which is also very important). Once she caught on to the idea, the Countess rather liked it. She designed an outfit for me too – a sort of flowing white silk robe, really quite becoming. You might have seen posters of Vishwa and me together, both of us in these white robes, his hair black and curly, mine blonde and straight. I suppose we do make a good couple – anyway, people seem to like us and to get something out of us. We do our best. It's not very hard; mostly we just have to sit there and radiate. The results are quite satisfactory – I mean the effect we seem to have on people who need it. The person who really has to work hard is the Countess because she has to look after all the business and organizational end. We have a strenuous tour programme. Sometimes it's like being on a one-night stand and doing your turn and then packing up in a hurry to get to the next one. Some of the places we stay in aren't too good – motels where you have to pay in advance in case you flit – and when she is very tired, the Countess wrings her hands and says, 'My God, what am I doing here?' It must be strange for her who's been used to all the grand hotels everywhere, but of course really she likes it. It's her life's fulfilment. But for Vishwa and me it's just a job we do, and all the time we want to be somewhere else and are thinking of that other place. I often remember what Master told me, what happened to him when he looked up in Times Square and Piccadilly, and it's beginning to happen to me too. I seem to *see* those mountains and the river and temples; and then I long to be there.

Rosamond Lehmann

extract from

Invitation to the Waltz

Olivia, just past her seventeenth birthday, is longing for the evening when she can accompany her older sister, Kate, to a grown-up party for the first time. This is 1920 and the major event in the social life of the village where the girls live is the annual dance given by Lady Spencer at Meldon Towers. It proves to be an education for Olivia.

The elderly gentleman with the thick white wavy hair approached her. She had noticed him before, dancing with the youngest girls in the room one after the other; the girls drooping a little, pressed to his paunch.

'Would you be so very very kind as to spare a dance for an old fogy?'

'Oh yes, of course I will.'

'What? You will? Oh, how kind!'

He clasped her to him and set off with slow, rather laboured but elegant strides.

He repeated, 'How kind to spare a dance for old Methuselah.'

'Oh, but you're not old.'

She gave him an encouraging smile. His skin was puckered and wrinkled, tortoise-like, under the chin, his cheeks puffy and veined with purple, his eyes a bit glazed and bloodshot. Otherwise he didn't look bad. His hair was beautiful.

'What? Oh, come now – you're trying to flatter me – aren't you . . . Not that I feel my age. Not a bit of it. Far from it.'

'It's what you feel that matters, isn't it?'

'Ah, very true, very true. What a clever little lady. You've hit the nail on the head this time. It's what you feel that matters. I feel as young as ever, and that's a fact. If the heart stays young, why, then *you* stay young, whatever the calendar has to say about it – eh?'

'Yes, of course.'

Gathering impetus from this reflection, he crushed her to him and swung heavily, vigorously round on a corner . . . 'Shall I tell you a secret? Eh?'

'Yes, do.'

She beamed at him, all attention.

'I only took up dancing again two years ago. Before that – ah, well – circumstances were different. I'd have said my dancing days were done . . . over and done . . .' He blew a gusty sigh down her neck.

'Oh, really?' After a few more steps, she added, 'And now you've started again?'

'I have,' he said gravely. 'The ladies are very kind to me – especially the young ladies. They don't seem to mind dancing with me. They don't object.'

'I should think not,' she said warmly.

He must have had a Great Sorrow, and put it behind him. His voice was brave and ringing.

'I must confess I had my qualms at first. I thought the old machinery might creak a bit. Ha! Ha! Ha!' He swung again, quite wildly, to show how well the old machinery was working. 'As a matter of fact I took a few lessons on the quiet, just to get the hang of this jazz, you know. I was very lucky in my teacher. Doreen Delaval her name was. A thoroughly cheery soul – you know, a real jolly girl, as keen as mustard – pretty girl, too – a lady, of course. Belonged to an old county family. Fell on bad times, had to sell their place up. This little girl Doreen, she'd always had a turn for dancing, so she pulled up her socks and took to it for a living. Plucky thing to do.'

'Does she manage to – to make a living all right?'

'What? M'yes, yes. She's all right. She's doing well.'

He was beginning to breathe a trifle heavily. She ventured, 'Just say when you'd like to stop.'

'Stop? Do you want to stop?'

'Oh no, rather not. I just thought perhaps you might like to.'

'Not a bit of it. I can dance all night and feel the better for it. And that's a fact.'

'Can you really?'

She looked up at him admiringly, for he was still a bit put out, suspicious.

'Yes, and I don't lie abed next morning. I don't coddle myself – never have. That's what's kept me fit. But of course if you want a rest . . .'

'Oh *no*. I'd much rather go on.'

'Afraid I don't know many of these new-fangled steps. I don't get much practice.'

'Oh, I don't mind. I'm not a bit well up in them either.'

But this wasn't the right answer. A silence ensued, and she amended, 'As a matter of fact, you dance beautifully. You're so frightfully easy to dance with.'

'What? Do you think so? Ah, I'm afraid you're a flatterer. What? Aren't you?'

'Not at all.'

Curious: he had a sort of family likeness to Major Skinner; but – owing perhaps to the loftier moral tone – he was somehow more cloying, more slippery; and far more uneasy and exacting.

'Ah, well, I dare say some folk would call me an old fool.'

'Why should they?'

'What? Undignified, you know. Making myself ridiculous.'

'How absurd. I'm sure nobody could think so.'

'What? D'you think it's absurd? Well, so do I. But folk are apt to get in a groove as they grow older, you know. They lose their resilience, their elasticity. Their horizons contract.'

'I expect they forget they were young themselves once.'

'Ah, that's it.' He was delighted. 'They forget. They get narrow-minded.'

'Narrow-minded people are such a bore. I don't think

it matters what they say. They're not worth bothering about. Where I live I shock some of the old frumps dreadfully because I go for walks without my hat on.'

'Oh, so you're unconventional too, are you? Then you and I'll get on like a house afire. I thought we should. We've got a lot in common. I felt it directly I saw you.' He pressed her to him, sighed richly. 'The gods were good to me, little lady. They granted me a spirit that can never grow old. Whatever they denied me, they granted me that. I suppose that's why you young folk don't seem to mind my company.' He paused, but this time she failed him and remained silent, and soon he added with another, thinner sigh, 'All the same, one feels lonely sometimes.'

'I hope you're not lonely,' she said politely.

'What? Lonely? Ah well, I can't complain. Life can be very rich in spite of everything. One can be alone and yet not lonely, can't one? One has one's philosophy.'

She tried to give him a look of bright interest, but it was getting harder. He does need so much bolstering up.

'All the same, there are times when one longs for real companionship – for the touch of a vanished hand . . .' He lowered his voice to add, 'I lost my dear wife three years ago. We were everything to each other.'

What was it in the way he said this that froze the springs of sympathy? Perhaps the way he dropped his voice; or a sort of glibness, as if there were a crack, an unsound place concealed . . . But of course it must have been a terrible grief.

'I'm so sorry. How awful for you.'

'Thank you. I knew you were sympathetic. Your voice told me so. Gentle and low, an excellent thing in woman.' He pressed her again. 'Ah, sympathy's a wonderful gift.'

The band stopped. He released her, clapped enthusiastically, mopped his face. He was perspiring freely.

'Ah, that was splendid – splendid. Now what about an ice? Eh?' He looked at her roguishly. 'That 'ud slip down nicely, wouldn't it? Come on now. Let's see how many we can account for. I'll take you on!'

She followed him, wanly simpering. His schoolboy spirits weren't infectious.

* * *

Tony said, 'Look here, don't you ever ride?'

'No,' said Kate. 'I never do. When I was very small we had a pony. But the truth is – since the war we haven't been able to afford anything much.'

'How sickening for you. You would so love it.'

'I'm sure I would. It's always been one of the things I wanted most – to have a horse of my own.'

He said with his quick engaging diffidence, 'You'd look corking on a horse. You're simply made for it.'

'Am I?'

She smiled, looking over his shoulders with shining unseeing eyes.

'I could teach you in no time.'

'Do you think you could?'

'I know I could.' He continued eagerly, 'And I could mount you too. I've got the very horse for a beginner. An old mare of my father's, as comfortable and quiet as anything. . . . Why not?'

'Well, for one thing I haven't any clothes.'

'Oh, bother clothes. We'll find you a pair of breeches.'

'All right. I'd love to.'

'I'll take you a few times round our big field for a start, and then as soon as you've got confidence we could go up on to the downs.'

'Oh, how glorious!'

They looked at one another, radiant.

* * *

Dance after dance with an old fogy. Three running now, pressed to his paunch. It seemed as if it might go on for ever. Not even Reggie to the rescue. Reggie must be at the buffet with the Martins. Neither he nor they had appeared upon the floor for a considerable time. No hope, no help. Programme a blank right on till Number 19, and that seemed now distant and improbable as a dream.

His name was Mr Verity. He spoke of the little shack he had recently acquired in the vicinity; of the wonder of the sunsets viewed from his study window. He mentioned his best friends, his books, and quoted more than once from the Poet. Gather ye rosebuds, he said. Also, Then come kiss me sweet and twenty. Also, Si joonesse savvy. He asked her if she would take tea one day with a lonely old man; his housekeeper, dear devoted old soul, would make her welcome. He talked a good deal too about people with titles whom he fished and shot with.

Her senses shrank away from him. They seemed to shout their frantic distaste into his heedless, his leathery ear. I don't like you. I don't like touching you. I hate dancing with you. I can't bear you. She gave up smiling; almost gave up answering. Her face set stiffly, in utter dejection. Next dance I'll say I'm booked and go and hide in the cloakroom. But he'll know it's an excuse. It'll hurt his feelings. He'll go away and think, I'm a lonely old man. Oh, help! help! Will no one help?

As she accompanied him for the fourth time towards the ballroom, Marigold appeared suddenly from nowhere, caught at her arm; whisked her aside, drew her far away without a word to him or a backward look.

'I thought you needed rescuing.'

'Oh, I *did*! You angel!'

She clasped Marigold's hand in pure relief and gratitude.

'I thought sudden tactics would be the most effictitious . . . You did look down-hearted.'

'I thought I'd never get away from him.'

'I know what he's like – the old octopus . . .' Her voice was harsh with contempt. 'He fished and fished for an invitation to this. He's our neighbour, worse luck. He's taken that cottage by the south gate. He tells everyone Daddy and he were lads together at Cambridge, and that Daddy begged him to come and settle near him. I call him Johnny Walker. Did he ask you to tea?'

'Yes. He did.'

'I thought as much. He's always trying that on. Mum thinks he's harmless, but of course he's not likely to be up to any of his tricks with her. They talk politics and county together, and he butters her up, and she thinks he's so sensible and so fond of young people and so picturesque and old-world with his white hair. In fact she was quite umbrageous with me when I called him a dirty old man. But of course Mum's hopeless. She thinks virgins are sacred to all men – you know, all the Tennyson flower stuff. Of course he's the most infernal snob too, but she can't see that. Still, I must admit he's quite different with the elderly ones. You wouldn't know him. It's the young ones that rouse him – especially the ones in their teens.'

'How queer . . . Have you been to tea with him?'

'Catch me. He did try it on once, but I said could I bring my governess, so he changed the subject.'

'What d'you suppose he'd do?'

'Oh, fumble about a bit, I expect – you know, feel your muscle and mess about with your hands pretending he's a fortune-teller, and measure how tall you were against him – that sort of feeble pawing. It's a sort of disease old men get, I believe.'

'Yes, I think it must be.'

'They go native. Honestly it's a warning. Did he tell you he'd got a grown-up son and daughter?'

'No, he didn't. He kept on hinting he was all alone in the world.'

'He would. But he's got two children, and they won't live with him. Mum thinks it's this modern selfishness, but I bet the trouble was he was too sprightly for them. Fancy having a lasciverous old father prodding and stroking every girl you brought into the house. Mine's not like that – not yet, anyway. Is yours?'

'Oh no. Not in the least.'

Dad prodding young girls . . . Olivia giggled.

'Though he adores a mild flirt with the pretty ones.'

'I don't think mine even does that,' said Olivia, after reflection.

She saw Johnny Walker standing alone by the ballroom door, pretending not to watch them out of the corner of his eye. He knows we're talking about him. How was it that Marigold, so sheltered, so well brought up, knew so much, in such a shrewd cynical, coarse-grained way, about the facts of life? – had on the tip of her tongue the best sort of snub for a tiresome old man, so that he knew it was no go, so that he feared her? Whereas oneself, one would never know what to say, one never spotted hidden motives, swallowed any story, trusted everybody, would very likely land oneself in a mess one day . . . Even now, seeing him furtively watch Marigold's pert expressive face, feeling him brood sheepishly over the ungracious, the wanton, flouting way they'd left him in the lurch, yet not dare to approach them, feeling the sickly collapse of his self-esteem, even now she was tempted to reassure him somehow, apologise, show him she was sorry. For it was Major Skinner all over again – the painfulness of seeing an old white-haired person humiliated before youth, ashamed of wanting the thing he wanted. He'd never get it. It was too late. He was old and done for. How his heart must ache . . . Oh dear! I wish I could want to comfort you . . . She saw the faintly stricken expression on his face. He stood there representing the pathos, the indignity of being old; of the dancing days being done. Oh, maidens! he cried in vain. He wouldn't dare ask any more of them to dance tonight. Soon he would creep off home. And Marigold had done this to him without an instant's compunction or compassion . . . out of kindness to, pity for, oneself? . . . out of pure malice and scorn for him? A strange impulse, a curious action – one of Marigold's. Why, whence, out of her new estrangement and excitement, had she noticed, and darted?

'There's Rex waiting for me. I must fly. Are you enjoying yourself? Have you had lots of partners?'

'I haven't got very much more booked,' admitted Olivia. 'Only Number nineteen.'

'Oh, you must fill up or he'll pounce again.' She gave a chuckle. 'Who d'you fancy? Oh, there's Timmy Douglas. He's so sweet. He's my favourite man – almost – no, quite. He's sure not to be full up, poor darling. When his wife's dancing with someone else, he mostly just stands and waits. Come on, I'll introduce you.'

She saw, against the wall inside the ballroom, a young man, tall, pale, standing and waiting. He seemed to be smiling; but on a closer view, it seemed not to be a smile after all. It was a queer taut set of the muscles round his mouth.

'He's a marvellous dancer,' said Marigold. 'You'd never dream he's . . .' She lowered her voice abruptly as they came near to him, and her last words were inaudible – stone something or other, it sounded like.

She cried, 'Timmy, hullo!'

He had been looking towards her without recognition, but now his face lit up faintly.

'Marigold?'

His voice had an edge of question. He put his hand out in a wooden way, straight in front of him, and she clasped it in both her own.

'Timmy darling, I meant to come and find you ages ago.

But I've been so whizzed about all the evening. Are you happy?'

Her voice had a softer, more caressing note than one had ever heard before. He answered with not quite convincing enthusiasm, 'Yes, rather.' He waited a moment, then said hesitatingly: 'When can I have a dance, Marigold?'

Then he waited again. His face became suddenly patient and listening. His voice was patient too, quiet, flat, rapid. He didn't look at her.

'Oh, darling! I'm so full up. Isn't it sickening?'

'That's bad luck – for me.'

Patient and cheerful.

'Timmy, I've brought Olivia Curtis to dance with you.' He turned his head slightly and sharply; out came his hand again. His eyes, upon which the full lids constantly opened and fell with a long spasmodic movement, were opaque, navy blue in colour, like those of a new-born baby.

'How d'you do?'

The smile that wasn't a smile tightened the muscles of mouth and cheek.

'Olivia's very nice with her practically black hair turned round each side of her face in a plaited bun, and a red dress.'

Had she really said that? The dream had come on again.

'I must fly, Timmy darling. I'll come back later, for sure and certain.' Brushing past Olivia, her fingers clung for a second on her arm, she whispered fiercely, '*Did you hear*? He's . . .' but again the last word, sharply muted, was lost as she fled on.

He stood without moving, his head a little bent as if he were listening to her going. He said in his pleasant flat voice, 'She's got more vitality than half a dozen ordinary people. She just leaves it in the air around her, wherever she's been.'

It was quite true. It was the secret of Marigold, that one had never been able to define. She agreed, pleased, surprised. It was an unusual thing to say.

'It's a marvellous possession,' he said. 'The only gift I'd trouble a fairy godmother for. If you've got it, you can't be beaten. What's more, you make other people imagine they can't be . . .'

He smiled now, a real smile, but faint. He himself looked as if he lacked vitality. He was pale and thin, rather worn-looking. He had beautifully cut long delicate features and straight light hair growing rather far back above a high frail prominent forehead. He gave an impression of scrupulous cleanness and neatness.

'Would you care to dance?' he said. 'I'm afraid I'm apt to barge into people. The room's pretty full, isn't it?'

'Rather full.'

She looked at him, puzzled. Once again he had turned an obvious statement into a question. She looked at him, and in a sudden stab flash of realization, saw him as one isolated, remote, a figure alone in a far place. He was . . .

'However if you don't mind steering a bit. I generally manage more or less.'

He stood and waited, crooking his right arm ready to receive her. She saw that he was blind. She led him out on to the floor and they started to dance.

I'll guide you, I'll look after you. Depend on me . . . Blinded in the war? There wasn't a scar – nothing to proclaim it – only the opaque swimming irises between the heavily twitching lids; and the set of his face. His hand, holding hers, vibrated as if it had a separate, infinitely sensitive life – long fingers, exquisite nails. He'll guess what I'm like from my voice, from touching me. What will he guess? They say blind people always know, you can't deceive them.

They collided badly with another couple, who looked at him in cold surprise.

'Sorry,' he said pleasantly, 'my fault.'

He waited while they moved on. She saw the girl's face alter suddenly, not in pity, but in a look of avid curiosity. She whispered something to her partner, they both turned to stare at him. How dare they stare like that! . . .

'I'm sorry,' she said. 'I never saw them. You dance so beautifully, I just forgot to steer.'

He looked a little bit pleased.

'We used to dance a lot at the place I was – St Dunstan's, you know. I don't do much in that line now. Molly's awfully keen on it. I wish she got more.'

'Is that your wife?'

'Yes, she's dancing, I think – I believe she's dancing with Rollo Spencer.'

'Oh yes, I see her.'

She saw Rollo quite close to them, dancing with a shortish person in rather a dowdy royal-blue dress – quite commonplace, quite insignificant. She had a good deal of straight brown hair, inclined to wispiness at the sides, blue eyes, some moles on her face, a weather-beaten skin without powder or make-up. There was nothing one could say about her, think about her. Olivia searched in vain for traces of spiritual intensity, renunciation, suffering, such as might fitly mark the face of one devoting, sacrificing all to a blind husband. She looked sensible, capable, her eyes clear and hard. Rollo must be dancing with her out of niceness. She glanced at her husband and his partner, but only for a minute, without apparent interest. I suppose you get used – I suppose you soon get used. . . . It all depends how you let yourself think about it. Even now, already, it was getting quite easy to behave towards him as his simplicity, his utter non-assumption of the role of martyr, his rather negative, low-pitched but unforced cheerfulness demanded – to treat him as one like other men. It was as if he were tacitly demonstrating: You see, it isn't a tragedy at all. You needn't be sorry for me. . . .

Yet the first image persisted in the background of her mind: a figure in its essence far apart.

'The Spencers are most frightfully nice, aren't they?' he said. 'They've been most awfully decent to us.'

'Do you live near?'

'Oh yes, I'm one of their tenants. We've got that little house beyond the church – about a mile away. Do you know it? Cherry Tree Cottage it's called – and it's actually got a cherry tree too.' His voice was more lively now. He liked talking about his house. 'Lady Spencer's helped us no end – Sir John too . . . We're chicken-farmers. Thanks to them, we've worked up quite a big connection – that's the right term, isn't it? We supply all the eggs and poultry for the house too.'

'Do you like doing it?'

'Oh yes, I like it all right. There's more in chickens than you'd think.' He smiled. 'I used to think they were the most ghastly feeble animals. If anybody'd told me I'd be keeping them for a living, I'd have – well, I don't know what. As a matter of fact, I wanted to be an architect – that's what I was keen on. But if you really take up a thing you can't help getting interested – don't you think?'

'Oh yes, I quite agree.'

She searched his face – it was placid; his voice, now he was surer of his ground, equable and very young-sounding. How did one look after chickens when one was blind?

'Molly's awfully keen on it, luckily. In fact it was she who got the whole thing going. She's awfully practical and good at running things. She does most of the dirty work, really. It keeps us busy. It's all jolly scientific these days, a proper chicken farm, I can tell you.'

'Is it? How frightfully interesting.'

'Molly's always lived in the country, but I'm a London bird. I didn't think I'd like it at first, but I've got quite used to it. I must say one does feel better – don't you think? Sort of more peaceful. It's nice for the infant too, to be brought up in the country. She loves animals. She's got a pet duckling that follows her everywhere.'

His smile spread clear over his face.

'Have you got a little girl?'

'Rather.'

'How old is she?'

'Getting on for two. She runs about like anything, and chatters all day. She's pretty forward, I think.'

'What's her name?'

'Elizabeth. Molly wanted Marjorie and I wanted Susan, so we split the difference with Elizabeth. It's a good name, don't you think?'

'Yes. I love the old English names.'

She was moved by his simple pride and pleasure in his possessions – his family, his farm, everything that told him he was a man with a background, a place in the world; a successful grown-up man who had by his own labours established his security. But he looked so young to be a husband and father – not more than twenty-two. Molly didn't look nearly so young. Perhaps she'd been his nurse. Probably he'd never seen her. . . . He'd never see his daughter either. One must try not to let that seem too pathetic. It was the sort of thing that brought a too-easy sob in the throat. It doesn't matter, it doesn't matter really.

'Marigold rides over to see us pretty often,' he said. 'We look forward to that.' (It was queer really that Marigold had never mentioned him. . . . But she was so secretive.) 'She'd buck anybody up, wouldn't she? She's so frightfully amusing, isn't she? Really witty. . . . Otherwise it's a quiet life. Not that I mind. I play the gramophone a lot in the evenings. I like music awfully. But I wish Molly got out more. It's dull for her.'

She plucked up courage to say timidly: 'Do you – can you find your way about – fairly well in your house?'

'Oh Lord, yes. Anywhere. Like a cat, you know. I see in the dark.' He smiled at his joke, adding mildly but emphatically, 'Oh, Molly's not tied like that – not to that extent. I can do pretty well everything for myself.'

She saw him going up and downstairs, dressing, undressing, feeding himself, patiently listening to his gramophone, changing the needle, walking over his farm, scattering grain to the hens, painstakingly independent, giving no trouble.

She murmured, 'I know – I'm sure – you're simply . . . It's so difficult to realize there's anything wrong. I hadn't an idea.'

'Oh well,' he said equably, 'it's all a question of one's point of view, isn't it? One's taught not to – well, not to think of it as a misfortune, you know.'

'When were you – how long ago . . .?'

'June 1918.' His voice was even. 'I went out from school. I only had three months of it. A sniper got me plunk behind the eyes.'

She was silent. War, a cloud on early adolescence, weighing not too darkly, long lifted. . . . A cousin in the flying corps killed, the cook's nephew gone down at Jutland, rumour of the death of neighbours' sons (that included Marigold's elder brother) and, among the village faces, about half a dozen familiar ones that had disappeared and never come back . . . and butter and sugar rations; and the lawn dug up for potatoes (the crop had failed); and knitting scratchy mittens and mufflers; and Dad being a special constable and getting bronchitis from it: that was about all that war had meant. And during that safe, that sheltered unthinking time, he had gone out to fight, and had his eyes destroyed. She saw him reel backwards, his hands on his face, crying; I'm blind . . . or coming to in hospital, not realizing, thinking it was the middle of the night. . . . Imagination stretched shudderingly towards his experience. She had a moment's dizziness, a moment's wild new conscious indignation and revolt, thinking for the first time: This was war – never, never to be forgiven or forgotten, for his sake.

I'd stay with you, I'd look after you. I'd be your eyes and show you everything. Oh – is she nice enough to you? But if it was me, I'd be too sorry, I'd upset him. She's sensible, she's matter-of-fact, she takes it for granted. How dare she. . . . She keeps his life practical and orderly, keeps him cheerful. They've got a child. So he must love her. And it doesn't matter to him that she's not young or pretty. . . . Yes, all his gratitude, all his solicitude were for her.

The band stopped.

'Thank you very much indeed,' he said. 'I'm just getting the hang of the room. It's jolly big, isn't it?'

'Yes, very big, with big mirrors in the panels, and chandeliers. It's very bright – the light, I mean.'

'I can remember photographs of this house in some paper. I remember it quite well. It's a beautiful house. A perfect specimen, but just unconventional enough to have a character of its own.'

He stood in the middle of the room, thinking about it.

She said nervously, 'What would you like to do? Shall we go and sit somewhere?'

'Rather. Anything you like . . .'

'Would you like an ice – or anything?'

'Yes, what about an ice? A drink anyway – I could do with a drink.'

He laid his fingers on the tip of her elbow, and she led him to the dining-room. He walked with a light quick step straight on his course, his touch on her arm almost imperceptible; not at all like one's idea of the shuffle and grope of a blind man. Only his head looked somehow vulnerable and wary. She felt important, self-assured, helping him, not shy or self-conscious in spite of people staring.

'Here's a beautiful armchair,' she said.

'Thanks.'

He lowered himself into it after a second's hesitation.

'Wait here, I'll get you a drink. What would you like?'

'Oh, anything cool, thanks. I'm a teetotaller these days.'

Waiting at the buffet for orangeade, she watched him take out his silver case and a matchbox and light his cigarette, slowly and carefully. Then he smoothed his hair, adjusted his tie, brushed his sleeve, his shoulders. In case I've left any mark, powder, a hair or anything. He's afraid of looking slovenly, neglected, ridiculous, and not knowing it. That's why he's neater, more polished up than anybody else. He didn't smoke his cigarette, but let it burn away between his long fingers. He sat back, his head slightly bent, the muscles taut in his face, waiting.

Now he looks like a blind man.

He was very easy to talk to. She chatted to him without effort or embarrassment until the next dance began, and his wife came strolling towards them. She walked with her square shoulders hunched. The skin of her neck and arms was rather rough and red, and her legs were short, muscular, slightly bandy. She looked like a hockey-playing cross-country-striding person, in striking contrast to his pallor, his elegant narrow-hipped length.

'Hullo!' she said. Her voice was rather rough too, with a twang in it.

He stirred without lifting his face.

'Oh hullo, Molly!' He added politely to Olivia, 'Can I introduce my wife?'

She smiled, meeting Olivia's shy and eager beam. Her smile was limited, but direct and pleasant, and her eyes were nice too, a clear bright blue.

Reggie was approaching. He looked a little congested about the face. He mustn't meet Timmy.

'Goodbye,' she said, and walked away.

She heard him say after a moment: 'Has she gone?'

It was just a question. No suspicion, regret, or relief in it. No interest.

Doris Lessing

The New Man

About three miles on the track to the station a smaller overgrown road branched to the Manager's House. This house had been built by the Rich Mitchells for their manager. Then they decided to sell a third of their farm, with the house ready for its owner. It stood empty a couple of years, with sacks of grain and ox-hides in it. The case had been discussed and adjudicated on the verandas of the district: no, Rich Mitchell was not right to sell that part of his farm, which was badly watered and poorish soil, except for a hundred acres or so. At the very least he should have thrown in a couple of miles of his long vlei with the lands adjacent to it. No wonder Rich Mitchell was rich (they said); and when they met him their voices had a calculated distance: 'Sold your new farm yet, Mich?' No, he hadn't sold it, nor did he, for one year, then another. But the rich can afford to wait. (As they said on the verandas.)

The farm was bought by a Mr Rooyen who had already gone broke farming down Que Que way. The Grants went to visit, Mrs Grant in her new silk, Mr Grant grumbling because it was the busy season. The small girl did not go, she refused, she wanted to stay in the kitchen with old Tom the cookboy, where she was happy, watching him make butter.

That evening, listening with half an ear to the parents' talk, it was evident things weren't too good. Mr Rooyen hadn't a penny of his own; he had bought the farm through the Land Bank, and was working on an eight-hundred pounds loan. What it amounted to was, it was a gamble on the first season. It's all very well,' said Mr Grant, summing up with the reluctant critical note in his voice that meant he knew he would have to help Mr Rooyen, would do so, but found it all too much. And, sure enough, in the dry season the Rooyen cattle were running on Grant land and using the Grant well. But Mr Rooyen had become 'the new man in the Manager's House'.

The first season wasn't too bad, so the small girl gathered from the talk on the verandas, and Mr Rooyen might make out after all. But he was very poor. Mrs Grant, when they had too much cheese or butter, or baked, sent supplies over by the cook. In the second year Mr Grant lent Mr Rooyen two hundred pounds to tide him over. The small girl knew that the new neighbour belonged for ever to that category of people who, when parting from the Grants, would wring their hands and say in a low, half-ashamed voice, 'You've been very good to me and I'll never forget it.'

The first time she saw the new farmer, who never went anywhere, was when the Grants went into the station and gave Mr Rooyen a lift. He could not afford a car yet. He stood on the track waiting for the Grants, and behind him the road to his house was even more overgrown with bushes and grass, like a dry river-bed between the trees. He sat in the back, answering Mr Grant's questions about how things were going. She did not notice him much, or rather refused to notice him, because she definitely did not like him, although he was nothing she had not known all her life. A tallish man, dressed in bush khaki, blue eyes inflamed by the sun, he was burned – not a healthy reddish brown – but a mahogany colour, because he was never out of the sun, never stopped working. This colour in a white man, the small girl already knew, meant a desperate struggling poverty and it usually preceded going broke or getting very ill. But the reason she did not like him, or that he scared her, was the violence of his grievance. The hand which lay on the back of the car seat behind Mr Grant trembled slightly; his voice trembled as he spoke of Rich Mitchell, his neighbour, who had a vlei seven miles long and would neither sell nor rent him any of it. 'It isn't right,' he kept saying. 'He doesn't make use of my end. Perhaps his cattle graze there a couple of weeks in the dry season, but that's all.' All this meant that his cattle would be running with the Grants' again when the grass was low. More: that he was appealing, through Mr Grant, for justice, to the unconstituted council of farmers who settled these matters on their verandas.

That night Mr Grant said, It's all very well! a good many times. Then he rang up Mr Matthews (Glasgow Bob) from the Glenisle Farm; and Mr Paynter (Tobacco Paynter) from Bellevue; and Mr Van Doren (The Dutchman) from Blue Hills. Their farms adjoined Rich Mitchell's.

Soon after, the Grants went into the station again. At the last minute they had remembered to ring up and ask Mr Rooyen if he wanted a lift. He did. It wasn't altogether convenient, particularly for the small girl, because two-thirds of the back seat was packed to the roof with plough parts being sent into town for repair. And beside Mrs Grant on the front seat was a great parcel full of dead chickens ready for sale to the hotel. 'It's no bother,' said Mrs Grant, to Mr Rooyen, 'the child can sit on your knee.'

The trouble was that the small girl was definitely not a child. She was pretty certain she was no longer a small girl, either. For one thing, her breasts had begun to sprout, and while this caused her more embarrassment than pleasure, she handled her body in a proud gingerly way that made it impossible, as she would have done even a season before, to snuggle in on to the grown-up's lap. She got out of the car in a mood of fine proud withdrawal, not looking at Mr Rooyen as he fitted himself into the narrow space on the back seat. Then, with a clumsy fastidiousness, she perched on the very edge of his bare bony knees and supported herself with two hands on the back of the front seat. Mr Rooyen's arms were about her waist, as if she were indeed a child, and they trembled, as she had known they would – as his voice still trembled, talking about Rich Mitchell. But soon he stopped talking. The car sped forward through the heavy, red-dust-laden trees, rocking and bouncing over the dry ruts, and she was jerked back to fit against the body of Mr Rooyen, whose fierceness was that of lonely tenderness, as she knew already, though never before in her life had she met it. She longed for the ride to be over, while she sat squeezed, pressed, suffering, in the embrace of Mr Rooyen, a couple of feet behind the Grants. She ignored, so far as was possible, with politeness; was stiff with resistance; looked at the backs of her parents' heads and marvelled at their blindness. 'If you only knew what your precious Mr Rooyen was doing to your precious daughter. . . .'

When it was time to come home from the station, she shed five years and became petulant and wilful: she would sit on her mother's knee, not on Mr Rooyen's. Because now the car was stacked with groceries, and it was a choice of one knee or the other. 'Why, my dear child,' said the fond Mrs Grant, pleased at this rebirth of the charming child in her daughter. But the girl sat as stiffly on her mother's knee as she had on the man's, for she felt his eyes continually returning to her, over her mother's shoulder, in need, or in fear, or in guilt.

When the car stopped at the turning to the Manager's House, she got off her mother's knee, and would not look at Mr Rooyen. Who then did something really not allowable, not in the code, for he bent, squeezed her in his great near-black hairy arms and kissed her. Her mother laughed, gay and encouraging. Mr Grant said merely, 'Good-bye, Rooyen,' as the tall forlorn fierce man walked off to his house along the grass-river road.

The girl got into the back seat, silent. Her mother

had let her down, had let her new breasts down by that gay social laugh. As for her father, she looked at his profile, absorbed in the business of starting the car and setting it in motion, but the profile said nothing. She said, resentful, 'Who does he think he *is*, kissing me.' And Mrs Grant said briskly, 'My dear child, why ever not?' At which Mr Grant gave his wife a quick, grave look, but remained silent. And this comforted the girl, supported her.

She thought about Mr Rooyen. Or rather, she felt him – felt the trembling of his arms, felt as if he were calling to her. One hot morning, saying she was going for a walk, she set off to his house. When she got there she was overheated and tired and needed a drink. Of course there was no one there. The house was two small rooms, side by side under corrugated iron, with a lean-to kitchen behind. In front was a narrow brick veranda with pillars. Plants stood in painted paraffin tins, and they were dry and limp. She went into the first room. It had two old leather armchairs, a sideboard with a mirror that reflected trees and blue sky and long grass from the low window, and an eating table. The second room had an iron bed and a chest-of-drawers. She looked, long and thoughtful, at the narrow bed, and her heart was full of pity because of the lonely trembling of Mr Rooyen's arms. She went into the tiny kitchen. It had an iron Carron Dover stove, where the fire was out. A wooden table had some cold meat on it with a piece of gauze over it. The meat smelled sourish. Flies buzzed. Up the legs of the table small black ants trickled. There was no servant visible. After getting herself a glass of tepid-tasting water from the filter, she walked very slowly through the house again, taking in everything, then went home.

At supper she said, casual, 'I went to see Mr Rooyen today.'

Her father looked quickly at her mother, who dropped her eyes and crumbled bread. That meant they had discussed the incident of the kiss. 'How is he?' asked Mrs Grant, casual and bright. 'He wasn't there.' Her father said nothing.

Next day she lapsed back into her private listening world. In the afternoon she read, but the book seemed childish. She wept enjoyably, alone. At supper she looked at her parents from a long way off, and knew it was a different place where she had never been before. They were smaller, definitely. She saw them clear: the rather handsome phlegmatic man at one end of the table, brown in his khaki (but not mahogany, he could afford not to spend every second of his waking hours in the sun). And at the other end a brisk, airy, efficient woman in a tailored striped dress. The girl thought: I came out of them; and shrank away in dislike from knowing how she had. She looked at these two strange people and felt Mr Rooyen's arms call to her across three miles of veld. Before she went to bed she stood for a long time gazing at the small light from his house.

Next morning she went to his house again. She wore a new dress, which her mother had made. It was a childish dress that ignored her breasts, which is why she chose it. Not that she expected to see Mr Rooyen. She wanted to see the small, brick, ant and fly-ridden house, walk through it, and come home again.

When she got there, there was not a sign of anyone. She fetched water in a half-paraffin tin from the kitchen and soaked the half-dead plants. Then she sat on the edge of the brick veranda with her feet in the hot dust. Quite soon Mr Rooyen came walking up through the trees from the lands. He saw her, but she could not make out what he thought. She said, girlish, 'I've watered your plants for you.'

'The boy's supposed to water them,' he said, sounding angry. He strode on to the veranda, into the room behind and out at the back in three great paces shouting, 'Boy! Boy!'

A shouting went on, because the cook had gone to sleep under a tree. The girl watched the man run himself a glass of water from the filter, gulp it down, run another, gulp that. He came back to the veranda. Standing like a great black hot tower over her, he demanded, 'Does your father know you're here?'

She shook her head, primly. But she felt he was unfair. He would not have liked her father to know how his arms had trembled and pressed her in the car.

He returned to the room, and sat, knees sprawling apart, his arms limp, in one of the big ugly leather chairs. He looked at her steadily, his mouth tight. He had a thin mouth. The lips were burned and black from the sun, and the cracks in them showed white and unhealthy.

'Come here,' he said, softly. It was tentative and she chose not to hear it, remained sitting with her back to him. Over her shoulder she asked, one neighbour to another, 'Have you fixed up your vlei with Mr Mitchell yet?' He sat looking at her, his head lowered. His eyes were really ugly, she thought, red with sun-glare. He was an ugly man, she thought. For now she was wishing – not that she had not come – but that he had not come. Then she could have walked, secretly and delightfully, through the house, and gone, secretly. And tomorrow she could have come and watered his plants again. She imagined saying to him, meeting him by chance somewhere, 'Guess who was watering your plants all that time?'

'You're a pretty little girl,' he said. He was grinning. The grin had no relationship to the lonely hunger of his touch on her in the car. Nor was it a grin addressed to a pretty little girl – far from it. She looked at the grin, repudiating it for her future, and was glad that she wore this full, childish dress.

'Come and sit on my knee,' he tried again, in the way people had been saying through her childhood: come and sit on my knee. She obligingly went, like a small girl, and balanced herself on a knee that felt all bone under her.

His hands came out and gripped her thin arms. His face changed from the ugly grin to the look of lonely hunger. She was sitting upright, using her feet as braces on the floor to prevent herself being pulled into the trembling man's body. Unable to pull her, he leaned his face against her neck, so that she felt his eyelashes and eyebrows hairy on her skin, and he muttered, 'Maureen, Maureen, Maureen, my love.'

She stood up, smoothing down her silly dress. He opened his eyes, sat still, hands on his knees. His mouth was half-open, he breathed irregularly, and his eyes stared, not at her, but at the brick floor where tiny black ants trickled.

She sat herself on the chair opposite, tucking her dress well in around her legs. In the silence the roof cracked suddenly overhead from the heat. There was the sound of a car on the main road half a mile off. The car came nearer. Neither the girl nor the man moved. Their eyes met from time to time, frowning, serious, then moved away to the ants, to the window, anywhere. He still breathed fast. She was full of revulsion against his body, yet she remembered the heat of his face, the touch of his lashes on her neck, and his loneliness spoke to her through her dislike of him, so that she longed to assuage him. The car stopped outside the house. She saw, without surprise, that it was her father. She remained where she was as Mr Grant stepped out of the car, and came in, his eyes narrowed because of the glare and the heat under the iron roof. He nodded at his daughter, and said, 'How do you do, Rooyen?' There being only two chairs, the men were standing; but the girl knew what she had to do, so she went out on to the veranda, and sat on the hot rough brick, spreading her blue skirts wide so that air could come under them and cool her thighs.

Now the two men were sitting in the chairs.

'Like some tea, Mr Grant?'

'I could do with a cup.'

Mr Rooyen shouted, 'Tea, boy!' and a shout came back from the kitchen. The girl could hear the iron stove being banged and blown into heat. It was nearly midday and she wondered what Mr Rooyen would have for lunch. That rancid beef?

She thought: if I were Maureen I wouldn't leave him alone, I'd look after him. I suppose she's some silly woman in an office in town. . . . But since he loved Maureen, she became her, and heard his voice saying: Maureen, Maureen, my love. Simultaneously she held her thin brown arms into the sun and felt how they were dark dry brown, she felt the flesh melting off hard lank bones.

'I spoke to Tobacco Paynter last night on the telephone, and he said he thinks Rich Mitchell might very well be in a different frame of mind by now, he's had a couple of good seasons.'

'If a couple of good seasons could make any difference to Mr Mitchell,' came Mr Rooyen's hot, resentful voice. 'But thank you, Mr Grant. Thank you.'

'He's close,' said her father. 'Near. Canny. Careful. Those North Country people are, you know.' He laughed. Mr Rooyen laughed too, after a pause – he was a Dutchman, and had to work out the phrase 'North Country'.

'If I were you,' said Mr Grant, 'I'd get the whole of the lands on either side of the vlei under mealies the first season. Rich has never had it under cultivation, and the soil'd go sixteen bags to the acre for the first couple of seasons.'

'Yes, I've been thinking that's what I should do.'

She heard the sounds of tea being brought in.

Mr Rooyen said to her through the door, 'Like a cup?' but she shook her head. She was thinking that if she were Maureen she'd fix up the house for him. Her father's next remark was therefore no surprise to her.

'Thought of getting married, Rooyen?'

He said bitterly, 'Take a look at this house, Mr Grant.'

'Well, you could build on a couple of rooms for about thirty, I reckon. I'll lend you my building boy. And a wife'd get it all spick-and-span in no time.'

Soon the two men came out, and Mr Rooyen stood on the veranda as she and her father got into the car and drove off. She waved to him, politely, with a polite smile.

She waited for her father to say something, but although he gave her several doubtful looks, he did not. She said, 'Mr Rooyen's in love with a girl called Maureen.'

'Did he say so?'

'Yes, he did.'

'Well,' he said, talking to her, as was his habit, one grown person to another, 'I'd say it was time he got married.'

'Yes.'

'Everything all right?' he inquired, having worked out exactly the right words to use.

'Yes, thank you.'

'Good.'

That season Rich Mitchell leased a couple of miles of his big vlei to Mr Rooyen, with a promise of sale later. Tobacco Paynter's wife got a governess from England, called Miss Betty Blunt, and almost at once Mr Rooyen and she were engaged. Mrs Paynter complained that she could never keep a governess longer than a couple of months, they always got married, but she couldn't have been too angry about it, because she laid on a big wedding for them, and all the district was there. The girl was asked if she would be a bridesmaid, but she very politely refused. On the track to the station there was a new signpost pointing along a well-used road which said: 'The Big Vlei Farm C. Rooyen.'

Olivia Manning

extract from

The Spoilt City

The first book of Olivia Manning's Balkan trilogy, The Great Fortune, *introduces her two main characters, Guy and Harriet Pringle. Recently married and not yet entirely at ease with each other they are drawn closer by the dangers of their situation. It is 1940 and the 'phoney war' is coming to an end. Guy is a gregarious, impulsive man, a lecturer in English at the University of Bucharest. Harriet often feels excluded from his world and resents the demands of his many friends. Her own fears about the impending crisis are heightened by a sense of isolation.*

In the second volume of the trilogy, The Spoilt City, *from which this extract is taken, events are closing in on the pair and those they have befriended, especially Guy's half-Jewish student, Sophie, the exuberantly parasitic Prince Yakimov and young Sasha Drucker, the saddest of the three, whose father and family fortune are now both lost to him.*

Yakimov had played Pandarus in Guy's production of *Troilus and Cressida*. The play over, his triumph forgotten, he was suffering from a sense of anti climax and of grievance. Guy, who had cosseted him through it all, had now abandoned him. And what, he asked himself, had come of the hours spent at rehearsals? Nothing, nothing at all.

Walking in the Calea Victoriei, in the increasing heat of midday, his sad camel face arun with sweat, he wore a panama hat, a suit of corded silk, a pink silk shirt and a tie that was once the colour of Parma violets. His clothes were very dirty. The hat was brim-broken and yellow with age. His jacket was tattered, brown beneath the armpits, and so shrunken that it held him as in a brace.

During the winter he had felt the ridges of frozen snow through the holes in his shoes: now he felt, just as painfully, the flagstones' white candescence. Steadily edged out to the kerb by the vigour of those about him, he caught the hot draught of cars passing at his elbow. He was agitated by the clangour of trams, by the flash of windscreens, blaring of horns and shrieking of brakes – all at a time when he would ordinarily have been safe in the refuge of sleep.

He had been wakened that morning by the relentless ringing of the telephone. Though from the lie of the light he could guess it was no more than ten o'clock, apparently even Harriet was out. Damp and inert beneath a single sheet, he lay without energy to stir and waited for the ringing to stop. It did not stop. At last, tortured to full consciousness, he dragged himself up and found the call was for him. The caller was his old friend Dobbie Dobson of the Legation.

'Lovely to hear your voice,' Yakimov said. He settled down in anticipation of a pleasurable talk about their days together in *Troilus*, but Dobson, like everyone else, had put the play behind him.

'Look here, Yaki,' he said, 'about those transit visas . . .'

'What transit visas, dear boy?'

'You know what I'm talking about.' Dobson spoke with the edge of a good-natured man harassed beyond endurance. 'Every British subject was ordered to keep in his passport valid transit visas against the possibility of sudden evacuation. The consul's been checking up and he finds you haven't obtained any.'

'Surely, dear boy, that wasn't a serious order? There's no cause for alarm.'

'An order is an order,' said Dobson. 'I've made excuses for you, but the fact is if you don't get those visas today you'll be sent to Egypt under open arrest.'

'*Dear boy*! But I haven't a bean.'

'Charge them to me. I'll deduct the cost when your next remittance arrives.'

Before he left the flat that morning, it had occurred to Yakimov to see if he could find anything useful in it. Guy was careless with money. Yakimov had more than once picked up and kept notes which his host had pulled out with his handkerchief. He had never before actually searched for money, but now, in his condition of grievance, he felt that Guy owed him anything he could find. In the Pringles' bedroom he went through spare trousers and handbags, but came upon nothing. In the sitting-room he pulled out the drawers of sideboard and writing-desk and spent some time looking through the stubs of Guy's old cheque-books which recorded payments made into London banks on behalf of local Jews. In view of the fact Drucker was awaiting trial on a technical charge of black-market dealing, he considered the possibility of blackmail. But the possibility was not great. Use of the black market was so general that, even now, the Jews would laugh at him.

In the small central drawer of the writing-desk he came on a sealed envelope marked 'Top Secret'. This immediately excited him. He was not the only one inclined to suspect that Guy's occupation in Bucharest was not as innocent as it seemed. Affable, sympathetic, easy to know, Guy would, in Yakimov's opinion, make an ideal agent.

The flap of the envelope, imperfectly sealed, opened as he touched it. Inside was a diagram of a section through – what? A pipe or a well. Having heard so much talk of sabotage in the English Bar, he guessed that it was an oil well. A blockage in the pipe was marked 'detonator'. Here was a simple exposition of how and where the amateur saboteur should place his gelignite.

This was a find! He resealed and replaced the empty envelope, but the plan he put into his pocket. He did not know what eventual use he might make of it, but he would have some fun showing it around the English Bar as proof of the dangerous duties being exacted from him by King and country. He felt a few moments of exhilaration. Then as he trudged off to visit the consulates the plan was forgotten, the exhilaration was no more.

The consulates, taking advantage of the times, were charging high prices. Yakimov, disgusted by the thought of money wasted on such things, obtained visas for Hungary, Bulgaria and Turkey. That left only Yugoslavia, the country that nine months before had thrown him out and impounded his car for debt. He entered the consulate with aversion, handed over his passport and was – he'd expected nothing better – kept waiting half an hour.

When the clerk returned the passport, he made a movement as though drawing a shutter between them. '*Zabranjeno*,' he said.

Yakimov had been refused a visa.

It had always been at the back of his mind that when he could borrow enough to remit the debt, he would reclaim his Hispano-Suiza. Now, he saw, they would prevent him doing so.

As he wandered down the Calea Victoriei, indignation grew in him like a nervous disturbance of the stomach. He began to brood on his car – the last gift of his dear old friend Dollie; the last souvenir – apart from his disintegrating wardrobe – of their wonderful life together. Suddenly, its loss became grief. He decided to see Dobson. But first he must console himself with a drink.

During rehearsals, to keep a hold on him, Guy had bought Yakimov drinks at the Doi Trandifuri, but Guy was a simple soul. He drank beer and *ţuica* and saw no reason why Yakimov should not do the same. Yakimov had longed for the more dashing company of the English Bar. As soon as the play was over, he returned to the bar in expectation of honour and applause. What he found there bewildered him. It was not only that his entry was ignored, but it was ignored by strangers. The place was more crowded than he had ever known it. Even the air had changed, smelling not of cigarettes, but cigars.

As he pushed his way in, he had heard German spoken on all sides. Bless my soul, German in the English Bar! He stretched his neck, trying to see Galpin or Screwby, and it came to him that he was the only Englishman in the room.

Attempting to reach the counter, he found himself elbowed back with deliberate hostility. As he breathed at a large man 'Steady, dear boy!' the other, all chest and shoulders, threw him angrily aside with '*Verfluchter Lümmell*'.

Yakimov was unnerved. He lifted a hand, trying to attract the attention of Albu, who, because of his uncompromising remoteness of manner, was reputed to be the model of an English barman. Albu had no eyes for him.

Realizing he was alone in enemy-occupied territory, Yakimov was about to take himself off when he noticed Prince Hadjimoscos at the farther end of the bar.

The Rumanian, who looked with his waxen face, his thin, fine black hair and black eyes, like a little mongoloid doll, was standing tiptoe in his soft kid shoes and lisping in German to a companion. Relieved and delighted to see a familiar face, Yakimov ran forward and seized him by the arm. 'Dear boy,' he called out, 'who *are* all these people?'

Hadjimoscos slowly turned his head, looking surprised at Yakimov's intrusion. He coldly asked; 'Is it not evident to you, *mon prince*, that I am occupied?' He turned away, only to find his German companion had taken the opportunity to desert him. He gave Yakimov an angry glance.

To placate him, Yakimov attempted humour, saying with a nervous giggle; 'So many Germans in the bar! They'll soon be demanding a plebiscite.'

'They have as much right here as you. More, in fact, for they have not betrayed us. Personally, I find them charming.'

'Oh, so do I, dear boy,' Yakimov assured him. 'Had a lot of friends in Berlin in '32,' then changing to a more interesting topic; 'Did you happen to see the play?'

'The play? You mean that charity production at the National Theatre? I'm told you looked quite ludicrous.'

'Forced into it, dear boy,' Yakimov apologized, knowing himself despised for infringing the prescripts of the idle. 'War on, you know. Had to do m'bit.'

Hadjimoscos turned down his lips. Without further comment, he moved away to find more profitable companionship. He attached himself to a German group and was invited to take a drink. Watching enviously, Yakimov wondered if, son of a Russian father and an Irish mother, he could hint that his sympathies were with the Reich. He put the thought from his mind. The British Legation had lost its power here, but not, alas, over him.

*

The English Bar was itself again. The English journalists had re-established themselves and the Germans, bored with the skirmish, were drifting back to the Minerva. The few that remained were losing their audacity.

Hadjimoscos was again willing to accept Yakimov's company, but cautiously. He would not join him in an English group – that would have been too defined an attachment in a changing world – but if Yakimov had money he would stand with him in a no man's land and help him to spend it.

Yakimov, though not resentful by nature, did occasionally feel a little sore at this behaviour. Practised scrounger though he was, he was not as practised as Hadjimoscos. When he had money, he spent it. Hadjimoscos, whether he had it or not, never spent it. With his softly insidious and clinging manner, his presence affected men like the presence of a woman. They expected nothing from him. By standing long enough, first on one foot then on the other, he remained so patiently, so insistently *there*, that those to whom he attached himself bought him drinks in order to be free to ignore him.

Yakimov, entering the bar that morning, saw Hadjimoscos with his friend Horvatz and Cici Palu, all holding empty glasses and watching out for someone to refill them.

He bought his own drink before approaching them. Seeing them eye the whisky in his hand, he began, in self-defence, to complain of the high cost of the visas he had been forced to buy. Hadjimoscos, smiling maliciously, slid forward a step and put a hand on Yakimov's arm. '*Cher prince*,' he said, 'what does it matter what you spend your money on, so long as you spend it on yourself?'

Palu gave a snigger. Horvatz remained blank. Yakimov knew, had always known, they did not want his company. They did not even want each other. They stood in a group, bored by their own aimlessness, because no one else wanted them. To Yakimov there came the thought that he was one of them – he who had once been the centre of entertainment in a vivacious set. He attempted to be entertaining now: 'Did you hear? When the French minister, poor old boy, was recalled to Vichy France, Princess Teodorescu said to him; "*Dire adieu, c'est mourir un peu.*"'

'Is it likely that the Princess of all people would be so lacking in tact?' Hadjimoscos turned his back, attempting to exclude Yakimov from the conversation as he said, 'Things are coming to a pretty pass! What do I learn at the *cordonnier* this morning? Three weeks to wait and five thousand to pay for a pair of hand-made shoes!'

'At the *tailleur*,' said Palu, 'it is the same. The price of English stuff is a scandal. And now they declare meatless days. What, I ask, is a fellow to eat?' He looked at Yakimov, for all the world as though it were the British and not the Germans who were plundering the country.

Yakimov attempted to join in. 'A little fish,' he meekly suggested, 'a little game, in season. Myself, I never say no to a slice of turkey.'

Hadjimoscos cut him short with contempt: 'Those are *entrées* only. How, without meat, can a man retain his virility?'

Discomfited, casting about in his mind for some way of gaining the attention he loved, Yakimov remembered the plan he had found that morning. He took it out. Sighing, he studied it. The conversation faltered. Aware of their interest, he lowered the paper so it was visible to all. 'What will they want me to do next?' he asked the world.

Hadjimoscos averted his glance. 'I advise you, *mon prince*,' he said, 'if you have anything to hide, now is the time to hide it.'

Knowing he could do nothing to please that morning, Yakimov put the plan away and let his attention wander. He became aware that a nearby stranger had been attempting to intercept it. The stranger smiled. His shabby, tousled appearance did not give much cause for hope, but Yakimov, always amiable, went forward and held out his hand. 'Dear boy,' he said, 'where have we met before?'

The young man took his pipe out from under his big, fluffy moustache and spluttering like a syphon in which the soda level was too low, he managed to say at last, 'The name's Lush. Toby Lush. I met you once with Guy Pringle.'

'So you did,' agreed Yakimov, who had no memory of it.

'Let me get you a drink. What is it?'

'Why, whisky, dear boy. Can't stomach the native rot-gut.'

Neighing wildly at Yakimov's humour, Lush went to the bar. Yakimov, having decided his new acquaintance was 'a bit of an ass', was surprised when he was led purposefully over to one of the tables by the wall. He did not receive his glass until he had sat down and he realized something would be demanded in return for it.

After a few moments of nervous pipe-sucking, Lush said, 'I'm here for keeps this time.'

'Are you indeed? That's splendid news.'

With his elbows close to his side, his knees clenched, Lush sat as though compressed inside his baggy sports-jacket and flannels. He sucked and gasped, gasped and spluttered, then said, 'When the Russkies took over Bessarabia, I told myself: 'Toby, old soul, now's the time to shift your bones.' There's always the danger of staying too long in a place.'

'Where do you come from?'

'Cluj. Transylvania. I never felt safe there. I'm not sure I'm safe here.'

It occurred to Yakimov that he had heard the name Toby Lush before. Didn't the fellow turn up for a few days in the spring, having bolted from Cluj because of some rumour of a Russian advance? Yakimov, always sympathetic towards fear, said reassuringly, 'Oh, you're all right here. Nice little backwater. The Germans are getting all they want. They won't bother us.'

'I hope you're right.' Lush's pale, bulging eyes surveyed the bar. 'Quite a few of them about though. I don't feel they like us being here.'

'It's the old story,' said Yakimov, 'infiltrate, then complain about the natives. Still, it was worse last week. I said to Albu, "Dry Martini", and he gave me three martinis.'

Squeezing his knees together, Lush swayed about, gulping with laughter. 'You're a joker,' he said. 'Have another?'

When he returned with the second whisky, Lush had sobered up, intending to speak what was on his mind. 'You're a friend of Guy Pringle, aren't you?'

Yakimov agreed. 'Very old and dear friend. You know I played Pandarus in his show?'

'Your fame reached Cluj. And you lodge with the Pringles?'

'We share a flat. Nice little place. You must come and have a meal with us.'

Lush nodded, but he wanted more than that. 'I'm looking for a job,' he said. 'Pringle runs the English Department, doesn't he? I'm going to see him, of course, but I thought perhaps you'd put in a word for me. Just say, "I met Toby Lush today. Nice bloke," something like that.' Toby gazed earnestly at Yakimov, who assured him at once; 'If I say the word, you'll get the job tomorrow.'

'If there's a job to be got.'

'These things can always be arranged.' Yakimov emptied his glass and put it down. Lush rose, but said with unexpected firmness, 'One more, then I have to drive round to the Legation. Must make my number.'

'You have a car? Wonder if you'd give me a lift?'

'With pleasure.'

Lush's car was an old mud-coloured Humber, high-standing and hooded like a palanquin.

'Nice little bus,' said Yakimov. Placing himself in an upright seat from which the wadding protruded, he thought of the beauties of his own Hispano-Suiza.

The Legation, a brick-built villa in a side-street, was hedged around with cars. On the dry and patchy front lawn a crowd of men – large, practical-looking men in suits of khaki drill – were standing about, each with an identical air of despondent waiting. They watched the arrival of the Humber as though it might bring them something. As he passed among them, Yakimov noted with surprise that they were speaking English. He could identify none of them.

Lush was admitted to the chancellery. Yakimov, as had happened before, was intercepted by a secretary.

'Oh, Prince Yakimov, can I help you?' she said, extruding an elderly charm. 'Mr Dobson is so busy. All the young gentlemen are busy these days, poor young things. At their age life in the service should be all parties and balls, but with this horrid war on they have to work like everyone else. I suppose it's to do with your *permit de séjour*?'

'It's a personal matter. *Ra*-ther important. I'm afraid I must see Mr Dobson.'

She clicked her tongue, but he was admitted to Dobson's presence.

Dobson, whom he had not seen since the night of the play, raised his head from his work in weary inquiry. 'Hello, how are you?'

'Rather the worse for war,' said Yakimov. Dobson gave a token smile, but his plump face, usually bland, was jaded, his eyes rimmed with pink; his whole attitude discouraging. 'We've had an exhausting week with the crisis. And now, on top of everything, the engineers have been dismissed from the oil-fields.'

'Those fellows outside?'

'Yes. They've been given eight hours to get out of the country. A special train is to take them to Constanza. Poor devils, they're hanging around in hope we can do something!'

'So sorry, dear boy.'

At the genuine sympathy in Yakimov's tone, Dobson let his pen drop and rubbed his hands over his head. 'H.E.'s been ringing around for the last two hours, but it's no good. The Rumanians are doing this to please the Germans. Some of these engineers have been here twenty years. They've all got homes, cars, dogs, cats, horses . . . I don't know what. It'll make a lot of extra work for us.'

'Dear me, yes.' Yakimov slid down to a chair and waited until he could introduce his own troubles. When Dobson paused, he ventured, 'Don't like to worry you at a time like this, but . . .'

'Money, I suppose?'

'Not altogether. You remember m'Hispano-Suiza. The Jugs are trying to prig it.' He told his story. 'Dear boy,' he pleaded, 'you can't let them do it. The Hispano's worth a packet. Why, the chassis alone cost two thousand five hundred quid. Body by Fernandez – heaven knows what Dollie paid for it. Magnificent piece of work. All I've got in the world. Get me a visa, dear boy. Lend me a few thou. I'll get the car and flog it. We'll have a bean-feast, a royal night at Cina's – champers and the lot. What d'you say?'

Dobson, listening with sombre patience, said, 'I suppose you know the Rumanians are requisitioning cars.'

'Surely not British cars?'

'No.' Dobson had to admit that the tradition of British privilege prevailed in spite of all. 'Mostly Jewish cars. The Jews are always unfortunate, but they *do* own the biggest cars. What I mean is, this isn't a good time to sell. People are unwilling to buy an expensive car that might be requisitioned.'

'But I don't really want to sell, dear boy. I love the

old bus. . . . She'd be useful if there were an evacuation.'

Dobson drew down his cheek and plucked at his round pink mouth. 'I'll tell you what! One of us is going to Belgrade in a week or so – probably Foxy Leverett. You've got the receipt and car key and so on? Then I'll get him to collect it and drive it back. I suppose it's in order?'

'She was in first-class order when I left her.'

'Well, we'll see what we can do,' Dobson rose, dismissing him.

Outside the Legation, the oil-men were still standing about, but the Humber had gone. As Yakimov set out to walk back through the sultry noonday, he told himself, 'No more tramping on m'poor old feet. And,' he added on reflection, 'she's worth money. I'd make a packet if I sold her.'

* * *

A week after the visit to the park café, Harriet, drawn out to the balcony by a sound of rough singing, saw a double row of marching men rounding the church immediately below her. They crossed the main square.

Processions were not uncommon in Bucharest. They were organized for all sorts of public occasions, descending in scale from grand affairs in which even the cabinet ministers were obliged to take part, to straggles of schoolchildren in the uniform of the Prince's youth movement.

The procession she saw now was different from any of the others. There was no grandeur about it, but there was a harsh air of purpose. Its leaders wore green shirts. The song was unknown to her, but she caught one word of it which was repeated again and again on a rising note: '*Capitanul, Capitanul. . . .*'

The Captain. Who the captain was she did not know.

She watched the column take a sharp turn into the Calea Victoriei, then, two by two, the marchers disappeared from sight. When they were all gone, she remained on the balcony with a sense of nothing to do but stand there.

The flat behind her was silent. Despina had gone to market. Yakimov was in bed. (She sometimes wished she could seal herself off, as he did, in sleep.) Sasha – for he was still with them despite her decree of 'one night only' – was somewhere up on the roof. (Like Yakimov, he had nowhere else to go.) Guy, of course, was busy at the University.

The 'of course' expressed a growing resignation. She had looked forward to the end of the play and the end of the term, imagining she would have his companionship and support against their growing insecurity. Instead, she saw no more of him than before. The summer school, planned as a part-time occupation, had attracted so many Jews awaiting visas to the States, he had had to organize extra classes. Now he taught and lectured even during the siesta time.

On the day the oil engineers were expelled from Ploesti, the Pringles, like other British subjects, received their first notice to quit the country. Guy was just leaving the flat when a buff slip was handed him by a *prefectura* messenger. He passed it over to Harriet. 'Take it to Dobson,' he said. 'He'll deal with it.'

He spoke casually, but Harriet was disturbed by this order to pack and go. She said, 'But supposing we have to leave in eight hours?'

'We won't have to.'

His unconcern had made the matter seem worse to her, yet he had been proved right. Dobson had had their order rescinded, and that of the other British subjects in Bucharest, but the oil engineers had had to go.

At different times during the day, Harriet had seen

their wives and children sitting about in cafés and restaurants. The children, becoming peevish and troublesome, had been frowned on by the Rumanians, who did not take children to cafés. The women, uprooted, looked stunned yet trustful, imagining perhaps that, in the end, it would all prove a mistake and they would return to their homes. Instead, they had had to take the train to Constanza and the boat to Istanbul.

Despite the Rumanian excuse that the expulsion had been carried out on German orders, the German Minister was reported to have said, 'Now we know how Carol would treat us if we were the losers.'

Well, the engineers, however unwillingly they may have gone, had gone to safety. Harriet could almost wish Guy and she had been forced to go with them.

While she stood on the balcony with these reflections in mind, the city shook. For an instant, it seemed to her that the balcony shelved down. She saw, or thought she saw, the cobbles before the church. In terror she put out her hand to hold on to something, but it was as though the world had become detached in space. Everything moved with her and there was nothing on which to hold. An instant – then the tremor passed.

She hurried into the room and took up her bag and gloves. She could not bear to be up here on the ninth floor. She had to feel the earth beneath her feet. When she reached the pavement, that burnt like the Sahara sand, her impulse was to touch it.

Gradually, as she crossed the square and saw the buildings intact and motionless, the familiar crowds showing no unusual alarm, she lost her sense of the tremor's supernatural strangeness. Perhaps here, in this inland town with its empty sky ablaze and the sense of the land-mass of Europe lying to the west, earthquakes were common enough. But when, in the Calea Victoriei, she came on Bella Niculescu, she cried out, forgetting the check on their relationship, 'Bella, did you feel the earthquake?'

'Didn't I just?' Bella responded as she used to respond. 'It scared me stiff. Everyone's talking about it. Someone's just said it wasn't an earthquake at all, but an explosion at Ploesti. It's started a rumour that British agents are blowing up the oil-wells. Let's hope not. Things are tricky enough for us without that.'

The first excitement of their meeting over, Bella looked disconcerted and glanced about her to see who might have witnessed it. Harriet felt she had done wrong in accosting her friend. Neither knowing what to say, they were about to make excuses and separate when they were distracted by a lusty sound of singing from the distance. Harriet recognized the refrain of '*Capitanul*'. The men in green shirts were returning.

'Who are they?' Harriet asked.

'The Iron Guard, of course. Our local fascists.'

'But I though they'd been wiped out.'

'*That's* what we were told.'

As the leaders advanced, lifting their boots and swinging their arms, Harriet saw they were the same young men she had observed in the spring, exiles returned from training in the German concentration camps. Then, shabby and ostracized, they had hung unoccupied about the street corners. Now they were marching on the crown of the road, forcing the traffic into the kerb, filling the air with their anthem, giving an impression of aggressive confidence.

Like everyone else, the two women, silenced by the uproar of '*Capitanul*', stood and watched the column pass. It was longer than it had been that morning. The leaders, well dressed and drilled, gained an awed attention, but this did not last. The middle ranks, without uniforms, were finding it difficult to keep in step, while the rear was brought up by a collection of out-of-works, no doubt converted to Guardism that very morning. Some were in rags. Shuffling, stumbling, they gave nervous side-glances and grins at the bystanders and their only contribution to the song was an occasional shout of '*Capitanul*'. This was too much for the Rumanian sense of humour. People began to comment and snigger, then to laugh outright.

'Did you ever see the like!' said Bella.

Harriet asked, 'Who is this "*capitanul*"?'

'Why, the Guardist leader – Codreanu: the one who was 'shot trying to escape', on Carol's orders, needless to say. A lot of his chums were shot with him. Some got away to Germany, but the whole movement was broken up. Who would have thought they'd have the nerve to reappear like this? Carol must be losing his grip.'

From the remarks about them, it was clear that other onlookers were thinking the same. The procession passed, the traffic crawled after, and people went on their way. From the distance the refrain of '*Capitanul*' came in spasms, then died out.

Bella was saying, 'They tried to make a hero of that Codreanu. It would take some doing. I saw him once. He looked disgusting with his dirty, greasy hair hanging round his ears. *And* he needed a shave. Oh, by the way,' she suddenly added, 'you were talking about that Drucker boy. Funny you should mention him. A day or two after, I got a letter from Nikko and he'd been hearing about him too. Apparently they only took him off to do his military service. (I bet old Drucker had been buying his exemption. Trust *them*!) Anyway, the boy's deserted and the military are on the look-out. They've had orders to find him at all costs. I suppose it's this business of the fortune being in his name. They'll make him sign the money over.'

'Supposing he refuses?'

'He wouldn't dare. Nikko says he could be shot as a deserter.'

'Rumania's not at war.'

'No, but it's a time of national emergency. The country's conscripted. Anyway, they're determined to get him. And I bet, when they do, he'll disappear for good. Oh, well!' Bella dismissed Sasha with a gesture. 'I'm thinking of going to Sinai. I'm sick of stewing in this heat waiting for something to happen. My opinion is, nothing will happen. You should get Guy to take you to the mountains.'

'We can't get away. He's started a summer school.'

'Will he get any students at this time of the year?'

'He has quite a number.'

'Jews, I bet?'

'Yes, they are mostly Jews.'

Bella pulled down her mouth and raised her brows. 'I wouldn't encourage that, my dear. If we're going to have the Iron Guard on the rampage again, there's no knowing what will happen. They beat up the Jewish students last time. But they're not only anti-Semitic, they're anti-British.' She gave a grim, significant nod, then, when she was satisfied that she had made an impression, her face cleared. 'Must be off,' she cheerfully said. 'I've an appointment with the hairdresser.' She lifted a hand, working her fingers in farewell, and disappeared in the direction of the square.

Harriet could not move. With the crowd pushing about her, she stood chilled and confused by perils. There was the peril of Sasha under the same roof as Yakimov, a potential informer – she did not know what the punishment might be for harbouring a deserter, but she pictured Guy in one of the notorious prisons Klein had described; and there was the more immediate threat from the marching Guardists.

Her instinct was to hurry at once to Guy and urge him to close down the summer school, but she knew she must not do that. Guy would not welcome her interference. He had put her out of his production on the grounds that no man could 'do a proper job with his wife around'. She wandered on as a preliminary to action, not knowing what action to take.

When she reached the British Propaganda Bureau, she came to a stop, thinking of Inchcape, who could, if he wished, put an end to the summer school. Why should she not appeal to him?

She stood for some minutes looking at the photographs of battleships and a model of the Dunkirk beaches, all of which had been in the window a month and were likely to remain, there being nothing with which to replace them.

She paused, not from fear of Inchcape but of Guy. Once before by speaking to Inchcape she had put a stop to one of Guy's activities and by doing so had brought about their first disagreement. Was she willing to bring about another?

Surely, she told herself, the important point was that her interference in the past had extricated Guy from a dangerous situation. It might do so again.

She entered the Bureau. Inchcape's secretary, knitting behind her typewriter, put up a show of uncertainty. Domnul Director might be too busy to see anyone.

'I won't keep him a moment,' Harriet said, running upstairs before the woman could ring through. She found Inchcape stretched on a sofa with the volumes of *A la Recherche du Temps Perdu* open around him. He was wearing a shirt and trousers. Seeing her, he roused himself reluctantly and put on the jacket that hung on the back of a chair.

'Hello, Mrs P.,' he said with a smile that did not hide his irritation at being disturbed.

Harriet had not been in the office since the day they had come here to view Calinescu's funeral. Then the rooms had been dilapidated and the workmen had been fitting shelves. Now everything was painted white, the shelves were filled with books and the floor close-carpeted in a delicate shade of grey-blue. On the Biedermeier desk, among other open books, lay some Reuter's sheets.

'What brings you here?' Inchcape asked.

'The Iron Guard.'

He eyed her with his irritated humour. 'You mean that collection of neurotics and nonentities who trailed past the window just now? Don't tell me they frightened you?'

Harriet said, 'The Nazis began as a collection of neurotics and nonentities.'

'So they did!' said Inchcape, smiling as though she must be joking. 'But in Rumania fascism is just a sort of game.'

'It wasn't a game in 1937 when Jewish students were thrown out of the University windows. I'm worried about Guy. He's alone there except for the three old ladies who assist him.'

'There's Dubedat.'

'What good would Dubedat be if the Guardist broke in?'

'Except when Clarence puts in an appearance, which isn't often, I'm alone here. I don't let it worry me.'

She was about to say, 'No one notices the Propaganda Bureau,' but stopped in time and said, 'The summer school is a provocation. All the students are Jews.'

Although Inchcape retained his appearance of urbane unconcern, the lines round his mouth had tightened. He shot out his cuffs and studied his garnet cuff-links. 'I imagine Guy can look after himself,' he said.

His neat, Napoleonic face had taken on a remote expression intended to conceal annoyance. Harriet was silenced. She had come here convinced that the idea of the summer school had originated with Guy – now she saw her mistake. Inchcape was a powerful member of the organization in which Guy hoped to make a career. Though she did not dislike him – they had come to terms early on – she still felt him an unknown quantity. Now she had challenged his vanity. There was no knowing what he might not say about Guy in the reports which he sent home.

When in the past, she had been critical of Inchcape, saying, 'He's so oddly mean: he economizes on food and drink, yet spends a fortune on china or furniture in order to impress his guests,' Guy had explained that Inchcape's possessions were a shield that hid the emotional emptiness of his life. Whatever they were, they were a form of self-aggrandizement. She realized the summer school was, too.

Knowing he could not be persuaded to close it, she decided to placate him. 'I supposed it *is* important,' she said.

He glanced up, pleased, and at once his tone changed. 'It certainly is. It's a sign that we're not defeated here. Our morale is high. And we'll do better yet. I have great plans for the future . . .'

'You think we have a future?'

'Of course we have a future. No one's going to interfere with us. Rumanian policy has always been to keep a foot in both camps. As for the Germans, what do they care so long as they're getting what they want? I'm confident that we'll keep going here. Indeed, I'm so confident that I'm arranging for an old friend, Professor Lord Pinkrose, to be flown out. He's agreed to give the Cantecuzene Lecture.'

Meeting Harriet's astonished gaze, Inchcape gave a grin of satisfaction. 'This is a time to show the flag,' he said. 'The lecture usually deals with some aspect of English literature. It will remind the Rumanians that we have one of the finest literatures in the world. And it is a great social occasion. The last time, we had eight princesses in the front row.' He started to lead her towards the door. 'Of course, it calls for a lot of organization. I've got to find a hall and I'll have to book Pinkrose into an hotel. I'm not sure yet whether he'll come alone.'

'He may bring his wife?'

'Good heavens, he has no wife.' Inchcape spoke as though marriage were some ridiculous custom of primitive tribes. 'But he's not so young as he was. He may want to bring a companion.'

Inchcape opened the door and said in parting, 'My dear child, we must maintain our equilibrium. Not so easy,

I know, in this weather, when one's body seems to be melting inside one's clothes. Well, goodbye.'

He shut the door on her, and she descended to the street with a sense of nothing achieved.

Shortly before the Guardists passed the University, Sophie Oresanu had come to see Guy in his office. The office had once been Inchcape's study, and the desk at which Guy sat still held Inchcape's papers. The shelves around were full of his books.

Sophie Oresanu, perched opposite Guy on the arm of a leather chair, had joined the summer school with enthusiasm. She now said, 'I cannot work in such heat,' leaning back with an insouciance that displayed her chief beauty, her figure. She pouted her heavily darkened mouth, then sighed and pushed a forefinger into one of her full, pasty cheeks. 'At this time the city is terrible,' she said.

Guy, viewing Sophie's languishings with indifference, remembered a conversation he had overheard between two male students: '*La* Oresanu is not nice, she is *le* "cock-tease"'. '*Ah, j'adore le "cocktease."*'

He smiled as she wriggled about on the chair-arm, flirting her rump at him. Poor girl! An orphan without a dowry, possessed of a freedom that devalued her in Rumanian eyes, she had to get herself a husband somehow. Remembering her grief when he had returned to Bucharest with a wife, he said the more indulgently, 'The other students seem to be bearing up.'

She shrugged off the other students. 'My skin is delicate. I cannot tolerate much sun.'

'Still, you're safer in the city this summer.'

'No. They say now the Russians are satisfied there will be no more troubles. Besides' – she made a disconsolate little gesture – 'I am not happy at the summer school. All the students are Jews. They are not nice to me.'

'Oh, come!' Guy laughed at her. 'You used to complain

that because you are half-Jewish, it was the Rumanians who were "not nice" to you.'

'It is true,' she agreed. 'No one is nice to me. I don't belong anywhere. I don't like Rumanian men. They live off women and despise them. They are so conceited. And the women here are such fools! They want to be despised. If the young man gives them *un coup de pied*, they do like this.' She wriggled and threw up her eyes in a parody of sensual ecstasy. 'Me, I wish to be respected. I am advanced, so I prefer Englishmen.'

Guy nodded, sympathizing with this preference. He had avoided marrying her himself, but he would have been delighted could he have married her off to a friend with a British passport. He had attempted to interest Clarence in her unfortunate situation, but Clarence had dismissed her, saying, 'She's an affected bore,' while of Clarence she said, 'How terrible to be a man so unattractive to women!'

'Besides,' she went on, 'it is expensive, Bucharest. Every quarter my allowance goes, pouf! Other summers, for an economy, I let my flat and go to a little mountain hotel. Already I would have taken myself there, but my allowance is spent.'

She paused, looking at him with a pathetic tilt of the head, expecting his usual query: 'How much do you need?'

Instead, he said, 'You'll get your allowance next month. Wait until then.'

'My doctor says my health will suffer. Would you have me die?'

He smiled his embarrassment. Harriet had forced him to recognize Sophie's wiles and now he wondered how he had ever been taken in by them. Before his marriage, he had lent Sophie what he could not afford, seeing these loans, which were never repaid, as the price of friendship. With a wife as well as parents dependent on him, he had been forced to refuse her. His refusal had kept her at bay for the last few months and he was acutely discomforted at the prospect of having to refuse her again.

Leaning forward with one of the persuasive gestures she had effectively used in *Troilus*, she said, 'I worked hard for the play. It was nice to have such a success, but I am not strong. It exhausted me. I have lost a kilo from my weight. Perhaps you like girls that are thin, but here they say it is not pretty.'

So that was it! She wanted a return for services rendered. He looked down at his desk, having no idea, in the face of this, how to reject her claim. He could only think of Harriet, not certain whether the thought came as a protection or a threat. Anyway, he could use her as an excuse. Sophie knew she could get nothing out of Harriet.

He was beginning to recognize that Harriet was, in some ways, stronger than himself. And yet perhaps not stronger. He had a complete faith in his own morality and he would not let her override it. But she could be obdurate where he could not, and though he stood up to her, knowing if he did not he would be lost, he was influenced by her clarity of vision; unwillingly. It was probably significant that he was physically short-sighted. He could not recognize people until almost upon them. Their faces were like so many buns. Good-natured buns, he would have said, but Harriet did not agree. She saw them in detail and did not like them any the better for it.

He was troubled by her criticism of their acquaintances. He preferred to like people, knowing this fact was the basis of his influence over them. The sense of his will to like them gave them confidence: so they liked in return. He could see that Harriet's influence, given sway, could undermine his own successful formula for living and he felt bound to resist it. Yet there were occasions when he let her be obdurate for him.

While these thoughts were in his mind Sophie's chatter had come to a stop. Looking up, he found her watching him, puzzled and hurt that he let her talk on without the expected interruption.

As she concluded in a small, dispirited voice, 'And I need only perhaps fifty thousand, not any more,' she dropped all her little artifices and he saw the naïveté behind the whole performance. He had often, in the past, thought Sophie unfairly treated by circumstances. She had been forced, much too young, to face life alone with nothing but the weapons her sex provided. He thought, 'The truth is, she's not much more than a scared kid,' thankful nevertheless that he did not have fifty thousand to lend her.

He said as lightly as he could, 'Harriet looks after the family finances now. She's better at it than I am. If anyone asks me for a loan I have to refer them to her.'

Sophie's expression changed abruptly. She sat upright, affronted that he should bring Harriet in between them. She rose, about to take herself off in indignation when a sound of marching and singing distracted her. They heard the repeated refrain '*Capitanul*'.

'But that is a forbidden song,' she said.

They reached the open window in time to see the leading green shirts pass the University. Sophie caught her breath. Guy, having talked with David's informants, was less surprised than she by this resurgence of the Iron Guard. He expected an appalled outcry from her, but she said nothing until the last stragglers had passed, then merely, 'So! We shall have troubles again!'

He said, 'You must have been at the University during the pogroms of 1938?'

She nodded. 'It was terrible, of course, but I was all right. I have a good Rumanian name.'

Remembering her annoyance with him, she turned suddenly and went without another word. She apparently had not been much disturbed by the spectacle of the marching Guardists, but Guy, when he returned to his desk, sat for some time abstracted. He had seen a threat made manifest and knew exactly what he faced.

When they had discussed the organization of the summer school, Guy had said to Inchcape, 'There's only one thing against it. It will give rise to a concentration of Jewish students. With the new anti-Semitic policy, they might be in a dangerous position.'

Inchcape had scoffed at this. 'Rumanian policy has always been anti-Semitic and all that happens is the Jews get richer and richer.'

Guy felt he could not argue further without an appearance of personal fear. Inchcape, who had retained control of the English department, wanted a summer school. His organization must do something to justify its presence here. More than that, there was his need to rival the Legation. Speaking of the British Minister, he would say, 'The old charmer's not afraid to stay, so why should I be?' If anyone pointed out that the Minister, unlike Inchcape and his men, had diplomatic protection, Inchcape would say, 'While the Legation's here, we'll be protected too.'

Guy knew that Inchcape liked him and, because of that, he liked Inchcape. He also admired him. With no great belief in his own courage, he esteemed audacious people like Inchcape and Harriet. Yet he tended to pity them. Inchcape he saw as a lonely bachelor who had nothing in life but the authority which his position gave. If a summer school made Inchcape happy, then Guy would back it to the end.

Harriet, he felt, must be protected from the distrust that had grown out of an unloved childhood. He would say to himself, 'Oh, stand between her and her fighting soul,' touched by the small, thin body that contained her spirit. And he saw her unfortunate because life, which he took easily, was to her so unnecessarily difficult.

He picked up a photograph which was propped against the inkstand on his desk. It had been taken in the Calea Victoriei: one of those small prints that had to be provided when one applied for a *permit de séjour*. In it Harriet's face – remarkable chiefly for its oval shape and the width of the eyes – was fixed in an expression of contemplative sadness. She looked ten years older than her age. Here was something so different from her usual vivacity that he said when he first saw it, 'Are you really so unhappy?' She had denied being unhappy at all.

Yet, he thought, the photograph betrayed some inner discontent. He believed it to be the discontent of the confused and the undedicated. He replaced the photograph with a sense of regret. He could help her if she would let him; but would she let him?

He remembered that when he had set about her political education, she had rebuffed him with, 'I cannot endure organized thought,' and, having taken up that position, refused to be moved from it.

Before she married, she had worked in an art gallery and been the friend of artists, mostly poor and unrecognized. He had pointed out to her that were they working in the Soviet Union they would be honoured and rewarded. She said, 'Only if they conformed.' He had argued that in every country everyone had to conform in some way or other. She said, 'But artists must remain a privileged community if they're to produce anything important. They can't just echo what they're told. They have to think for themselves. That's why totalitarian countries can't afford them.'

He had to admit that she, too, thought for herself. She would not be influenced. Feminine and intolerant though she might be in particular, she could take a wide general view of things. Coming from the narrowest, most prejudiced class, she had nevertheless declassed herself. The more the pity, then, that she had rejected the faith which gave his own life purpose. He saw her muddled and lost in anarchy and a childish mysticism.

What did she want? The question was for him the more difficult because he was content. He wanted nothing for himself. Possession he found an embarrassment, a disloyalty to his family that had to survive on so little. While he was taking his degree, he had worked as a part-time teacher. His mother had also worked. Between them they had paid the rent and kept the family together.

He had envied no one except the men without responsibilities who had been free to go and fight in Spain. These men of the International Brigade had been his heroes. He would still recite their poetry to himself, with emotion:

From small beginnings mighty ends:
From calling rebel generals friends,
From being taught at public schools
To think the common people fools,
Spain bleeds, and Britain wildly gambles
To bribe the butcher in the shambles.

The marching Guardists that morning had brought to his mind the Blackshirts and their 'Monster Rally' in his home town. That was when his friend Simon had been beaten up and he had recognized the fact that one day he, too, would have to pay for his political faith.

Simon had arrived late and sat by himself. When the rest of them, sitting in a body, attempted to break up the meeting they were frog-marched into the street. Simon, left alone, had with a fanatical, almost hysterical courage, carried on the interruptions unsupported. The thugs had had him to themselves. They had dragged him out through a back door to a garage behind the hall. There he was eventually found unconscious.

At that time the stories of fascist savagery were only half believed. It was a new thing in the civilized world. The sight of Simon's injured and blackened face had appalled Guy. He told himself he knew now what lay ahead – and from that time had never doubted that his turn would come.

While he sat now at his desk, confronting his own

physical fear, his door opened. It opened with ominous slowness. He stared at it. A tousled head appeared.

With playful solemnity, Toby Lush said, 'Hello, old soul! I'm back again, you see!'

Harriet, walking home with all her fears intact, allayed them with the determination to act somehow. If she could not surmount one danger, she must tackle another. There was the situation at home – at least she need not tolerate that.

She must make it clear to Guy that they could not keep both Yakimov and Sasha. He had brought them into the flat. Now it was for him to decide which of the two should remain, and to dismiss the other.

When, however, she entered the sitting-room and found Yakimov there, awaiting his luncheon, she decided for herself. Sasha was the one who needed their help and protection. As for Yakimov, only sheer indolence kept him from fending for himself. And she was sick of the sight of him.

Her mind was made up. He must go. She would tell him so straightaway.

Yakimov, sprawled in the armchair, was drinking from a bottle of *ţuica* which Despina had brought in that morning. He moved uneasily at the sight of her and, putting a hand to the bottle, excused himself. 'Took the liberty of opening it, dear girl. Came in dropping on m'poor old feet. The heat's killing me. Why not have a snifter yourself?'

She refused, but sat down near him. Used to being ignored by her, he became flustered and his hand was unsteady as he refilled his glass.

Her idea had been to order him, there and then, to pack and go, but she did not know how to begin.

His legs were crossed and one of his narrow shoes dangled towards her. His foot shook. Through a gap between sole and upper, she could see the tips of his toes and the rags of his violet silk socks. His dilapidation reproached her. He lay back, pretending nonchalance, but his large, flat-looking, green eyes flickered apprehensively, looking at her and away from her, so she could not speak.

He tried to make conversation, asking, 'What's on the menu today?'

She said, 'It is a meatless day. Despina bought some sort of river fish.'

He sighed. 'This morning,' he said, 'I was thinking about *blinis*. We used to get them at Korniloff's. They'd give you a heap of pancakes. You'd spread the bottom one with caviare, the next with sour cream, the next with caviare, and so on. Then you'd cut right through the lot. Ouch!' He made a noise in his throat as at a memory so delicious it was scarcely to be endured. 'I don't know why we don't get them here. Plenty of caviare. The fresh grey sort's the best, of course.' He gave her an expectant look. When she made no offer to prepare the dish, he glanced away as though excusing her inhospitality with, 'I admit there's nothing to compare with the Russian Beluga. Or Osetrova, for that matter.' He sighed again and, on a note of yearning, asked, 'Do you remember ortolans? Delicious, weren't they?'

'I don't know. Anyway, I don't believe in killing small birds.'

He looked puzzled. 'But you eat chickens! All birds are birds. What does the size matter? Surely the important thing is the taste?'

Finding this reasoning unanswerable, she glanced at the clock, causing him to say, 'The dear boy's late. Where *does* he get to these days?' His tone told Harriet that, having been dropped from Guy's scheme of things, he was feeling neglected.

She said, 'He's started a summer school at the University. I expect you miss the fun of rehearsals?'

'They were fun, of course, but the dear boy did keep us at it. And, in the end, what came of it all?'

'What could come of it? I mean, so far from home and

with a war on, you could not hope to make a career of acting?'

'A career! Never thought of such a thing.'

His surprise was such, she realized he had probably looked for no greater reward than a lifetime of free food and drink. The fact was, he had never grown up. She had thought once that Yakimov was a nebula which, under Guy's influence, had started to evolve. But Guy, having set him in motion, had abandoned him to nothingness, and now, like a child displaced by a newcomer, he scarcely knew what had happened to him.

He said, 'Was happy to help the dear boy.'

'You'd never acted before, had you?'

'Never, dear girl, never.'

'What did you do before the war? Had you a job of any sort?'

He looked slightly affronted by the question and protested, 'I had m'remittance, you know.'

She supposed he lived off a show of wealth: which was as good a confidence trick as any.

Conscious of her disapproval, he tried to improve things. 'I did do a little work now and then. I mean, when I was a bit short of the ready.'

'What sort of work?'

He shifted about under this inquiry. His foot began to shake again. 'Sold cars for a bit,' he said. 'Only the best cars, of course: Rolls-Royces, Bentleys. . . . M'own old girl's an Hispano-Suiza. Finest cars in the world. Must get her back. Give you a run in her.'

'What else did you do?'

'Sold pictures, bric-à-brac . . .'

'Really?' Harriet was interested. 'Do you know about pictures?'

'Can't say I do, dear girl. Don't claim to be a professional. Helped a chap out now and then. Had a little flat in Clarges Street. Would hang up a picture, put out a bit of bric-à-brac, pick up some well-heeled gudgeon, indicate willingness to sell. "Your poor old Yaki's got to part with family treasure." You know the sort of thing. Not work, really. Just a little side-line.' He spoke as though describing a respected way of life, then, as his shifting eye caught hers, his whole manner suddenly disintegrated. He struggled upright in his seat and, with head hanging, gazing down into his empty glass he mumbled, 'Expecting m'remittance any day now. Don't worry. Going to pay back every penny I owe. . . .'

They were both relieved to hear Guy letting himself into the flat. He entered the room, smiling broadly as though he were bringing Harriet some delightful surprise. 'You remember Toby Lush?' he said.

'It's wonderful to see you again! Wonderful!' Toby said, gazing at Harriet, his eyes bulging with excited admiration, giving the impression that theirs was some eagerly awaited reunion.

She had met him once before and barely remembered him. She did her best to respond but had never been much impressed by him. He was in the middle twenties, heavy-boned and clumsy in movement. His features were pronounced, his skin coarse, yet his face seemed to be made of something too soft and pliable for its purpose.

Sucking at his pipe, he turned to Guy and jerked out convulsively, 'You know what she always makes me think of? Those lines of Tennyson: "She walks in beauty like the night of starless climes and something skies."'

'Byron,' said Guy.

'Oh, crumbs!' Toby clapped a hand over his eyes in exaggerated shame. 'I'm always doing it. It's not that I don't know: I don't remember.' He suddenly noticed Yakimov and crying, 'Hello, hello, hello,' he rushed forward with outstretched hand.

Harriet went into the kitchen to tell Despina there would be a guest for luncheon. When she returned, Toby, with many irrelevant guffaws, was describing the situation in the Transylvanian capital from which he had evacuated himself.

Although Cluj had been under Rumanian rule for twenty years, it was still an Hungarian city. The citizens only waited for the despised regime to end.

'It's not that they're pro-German,' he said, 'they just want the Hunks back. They shut their eyes to the fact that when the Hunks come the Huns'll follow. If you point it out, they make excuses. A woman I know, a Jewess, said, "We don't want it for ourselves, we want it for our children." They think it'll happen any day now.'

Toby was standing by the open French window, the dazzle of out-of-doors limning his ragged outline. 'I can tell you,' he said, 'the only Englishman among that lot, I had to keep my wits about me. And what do you think happened before I left? The Germans installed a Gauleiter – a Count Frederich von Flügel. "Get out while the going's good," I told myself.'

'Freddi von Flügel!' Yakimov broke in in delighted surprise. 'Why, he's an old friend of mine. A dear old friend.' He looked happily about him. 'When I get the Hispano, we might all drive to Cluj and see Freddi. I'm sure he'd do us proud.'

Toby gazed open-mouthed at Yakimov, then his shoulders shook as though giving some farcical imitation of laughter. 'You're a joker,' he said and Yakimov, though surprised, seemed gratified to be thought one.

While they were eating, Harriet asked Toby, 'Will you remain in Bucharest?'

'If I can get some teaching,' he said. 'I'm a freelancer, no organization behind me. Came out on my own, drove the old bus all the way. Bit of an adventure. The fact is, if I don't work, I don't eat. Simple as that.' He gazed at Guy, supplicant and inquiring. 'Hearing you were short-staffed, I turned up on the doorstep.'

The question of his employment had obviously been

raised already, for Guy merely nodded and said, 'I must see what Inchcape says before taking anyone on.'

Harriet looked again at Toby, considering him not so much as a teacher as a possible help in time of trouble. She had noticed his heavy brogues. He was wearing grey flannel trousers bagged at the knees and a sagging tweed jacket, much patched with leather. It was the uniform of most young English civilians and yet on him it looked like a disguise. 'The man's man!' The last time he had arrived in Bucharest, during one of the usual invasion scares, he had fled from Cluj in a panic: but she was less inclined to condemn panic since she had experienced it herself. How would he react to a sudden Guardist attack? All this pipe-sucking masculinity, this casual costume, would surely require him, when the time came, to prove himself 'a good man in a tight corner'. She looked to Guy, who was saying, 'If Inchcape agrees, I might be able to give you twenty hours a week. That should keep you going.'

Toby ducked his head gratefully, then asked, 'What about lectures?'

'I would only need you to teach.'

'I used to lecture at Cluj – Mod. Eng. Lit. I must say, I enjoy giving the odd lecture.' Toby, from behind his hair and moustache, gazed at Guy like an old sheepdog confident he would be put to use. Harriet felt sorry for him. He probably imagined, as others had done before him, that Guy was easily persuadable. The truth was, that in authority Guy could be inflexible. Even if he needed a lecturer, he would not choose one who mistook Byron for Tennyson.

'The other day,' Yakimov suddenly spoke, slowly and sadly, out of his absorption in his food, 'I was thinking, strange as it must seem, I haven't seen a banana for about a year.' He sighed at the thought.

The Pringles had grown too used to him to react to his chance observations, but Toby rocked about, laughing as though Yakimov's speech had been one of hilarious impropriety.

Yakimov modestly explained, 'Used to be very fond of bananas.'

When luncheon was over and Yakimov had retired to his room Harriet looked for Toby's departure, but when he eventually made a move Guy detained him saying, 'Stay to tea. On my way back to the University, I'll take you to the Bureau to meet Inchcape.'

Harriet went into the bedroom. Determined to incite him to act while the power to incite was in her, she called Guy in, shut the door of the sitting-room and said, 'You must speak to Yakimov. You must tell him to go.'

Mystified by the urgency of her manner and unwilling to obey, he said, 'All right, but not now.'

'Yes, *now*.' She stood between him and the door. 'Go in and see him. It's too risky having him here with Sasha around. He must go.'

'Well, if you say so.' Guy's agreement was tentative, a playing for time. He paused, then said, 'It would be better if you spoke to him.'

'You brought him here, you must get rid of him.'

'It's a difficult situation. I was glad to have him here while he was rehearsing. He worked hard and helped to make the show a success. In a way, I owe him something. I can't just tell him to go now the show's over, but it's different for you. You can be firm with him.'

'What you mean is, if there's anything unpleasant to be done, you prefer that I should do it?'

Cornered, he reacted with rare exasperation. 'Look here, darling, I have other things to worry about. Sasha is up on the roof. Yakimov's not likely to see him and probably wouldn't be interested if he did see him. So why worry? Now I must go back and talk to Toby.'

She let him go, knowing nothing more would be gained by talk. And she realized it would always be the same. If action had to be taken, she would have to be the one to take it. That was the price to be paid for a relationship that gave her more freedom than she had bargained for. Freedom, after all, was not a basic concept of marriage. As for Guy, he did not want a private life: he chose to live publicly. She said to herself, 'He's crassly selfish' – an accusation that would have astounded his admirers.

She went over to the window and leant out. Looking down the drop of nine floors to the cobbles below, she thought of the kitten that had fallen from the balcony five months before. The scene dissolved into a marbling of blue and gold as her eyes filled with tears, and she suffered again the outrageous grief with which she had learnt of the kitten's death. It had been her kitten. It had acknowledged her. It did not bite her. She was the only one who had no fear of it. Possessed by memory of the little red-golden flame of a cat that for a few weeks had hurtled itself, a ball of fur and claws, about the flat, she wept, 'My kitten. My poor kitten,' feeling she had loved it as she could never again love anything or anybody. Guy, after all, did not permit himself to be loved in this way.

She did not return to the room until she heard Despina taking in the tea things. Toby was saying, 'But someone's certain to march in here sooner or later. I suppose the Legation'll give us proper warning?'

Guy did not know and did not seem much to care. He said, 'The important thing is not to panic. We must keep the school going.'

Toby ducked his head in vehement agreement. 'Still,' he said, 'one must keep the old weather eye open.'

Yakimov had appeared for tea in his tattered brocade dressing-gown and when Guy and Toby went off to see Inchcape there he still was, his apprehensions forgotten, comfortably eating his way through the cakes and sandwiches that were left. Well, here was her opportunity to say, 'You have been living on top of us since Easter. I've had enough of you. Please pack your bags and go.' At which Yakimov, with his most pitiful expression, would ask, 'But where can poor Yaki go?' There had been no answer to that question four months before, and there was no answer now. He had exhausted his credit in Bucharest. No one would take him in. If she wanted to get rid of him, she would have to pack his bags herself and lock him out. And if she did that, he would probably sit on the doorstep until Guy brought him back in again.

When he had emptied the plates he stretched and sighed, 'Think I'll take a bath.' He went, and she had still said nothing. Knowing herself no more capable than Guy was of throwing Yakimov out, she had thought of a different move. She would go and see Sasha. The boy probably imagined that they, like the diplomats, were outside Rumanian law. She could explain to him that by sheltering him Guy ran the same risk as anyone else. Then what would Sasha do?

The problem of their responsibility lay between desperation and desperation. The only loophole was the possibility that Sasha could think of a friend who might shelter him, perhaps a Jewish schoolfriend. Or there was his stepmother, who was claiming maintenance from the Drucker fortune. Someone surely would take him in.

She went out to the kitchen. Despina was on the fire-escape, bawling down to other servants who had a free hour or so before it was time to prepare dinner. Feeling anomalous in these regions, Harriet slipped past her and started to ascend the cast iron ladder, but Despina missed nothing. 'That's right,' she called out. 'Visit the poor boy. He's lonely up there.'

Despina had adopted Sasha. Although Despina had been told that he must not come into the flat, Harriet had several times heard them laughing together in the kitchen. Despina scoffed at her fears, saying she could pass the boy off to anyone as her relative. Sasha was settling into a routine of life here and would soon, if undisturbed, become, like Yakimov, an unmovable part of the household.

The roof, high above its neighbours, was in the full light of the lowering sun. The sun was still very warm. Heat not only poured down on to the concrete but rose from it.

A row of wooden huts, like bathing-boxes, stood against the northern parapet, numbered one for each flat. Harriet, as she reached the roof-level, could see Sasha sitting outside his hut, holding a piece of stick which he had been throwing for a dog. The dog, a rough, white mongrel, apparently lived up here.

As soon as he saw her, Sasha got to his feet while the dog remained expectant, swaying a tail like a dirty feather.

She explained her visit by saying, 'How are you managing up here? Is Despina looking after you?'

'Oh, yes.' He was eagerly reassuring, adding thanks for all that was done for him. The fact of his presence being a danger to them seemed not to have occurred to him.

While he talked she looked beyond him through the open door of the hut where he was living. The hut had no window and was ventilated by a hole in the door. On the floor was a straw pallet that Despina must have borrowed for him, a blanket, some books Guy had brought up and a stub of candle.

Before she left England she would have believed it impossible for a human being to survive through the freezing winter, the torrid summer, in a cell like this. She had discovered in Rumania that there were millions to whom such shelter would be luxury. She took a step towards it but, repelled by the interior smell and heat, came to a stop saying, 'It's very small.'

Sasha smiled as though it were his place to apologize. He had been here only a few days but he was already putting on weight. When she had seen him on the night of his reappearance, she had been repelled by his abject squalor. Now, clean, wearing a shirt and trousers Guy had given him, the edge of fear gone from his face, his hair beginning to show like a shadow over his head, he was already the boy she had first met in the Drucker flat.

He was rather an ugly boy with his long nose, close-set eyes and long, drooping body, but there was an appeal about his extreme gentleness of manner, which on their first meeting had made her think of some nervous animal grown meek in captivity. Because of this, he seemed completely familiar to her.

Feeling no restraint with him, she put out her hand and said, 'Let us sit on the wall,' and, jumping up, she settled herself on the low parapet that surrounded the roof. From here she could see almost the whole extent of the city, the roofs gleaming through a heat-mist that was beginning to grow dense and golden with evening. Sasha came and leant against the wall beside her. She asked him what he passed for among the servants who slept in the other huts.

He said, 'Despina says I come from her village.'

He looked nothing like a peasant, but he might be the son of some Jewish tallyman. Anyway, no one, it seemed, took much notice of him. Despina said the kitchen quarters of Bucharest harboured thousands of deserters.

'How long had you been in Bucharest when we met you?' she asked.

'Two nights.' He told her that he had separated from his company in Czernowitz and stowed away in a freight train that brought him to the capital. On the night of his arrival, he had slept under a market stall near the station, but had been turned out soon after midnight by some beggars whose usual sleeping place it was. The next night he had tried to sleep in the park, but there had been one of the usual spy scares on. The police, in their zeal, had tramped about all night, forcing him repeatedly to move his position.

He had not known what had happened to his family. When in Bessarabia, he had written to his aunts but received no reply. When he reached Bucharest, he had looked up at the windows of the family flat and, seeing the curtains changed, realized the Druckers were not there. In the streets he had caught sight of people he knew, but in his fear of re-arrest dared approach no one until he saw Guy.

While he talked, he glanced shyly aside at her, smiling, all the misery gone from his gaze.

She said, 'You know that your family have left Rumania?'

'Guy told me.' If he knew they had taken flight immediately, without a backward glance for him or his father, he did not seem much concerned.

She decided the time had come to mention the possibility of his finding another shelter. She said, 'Your stepmother is still here, of course. Don't you think she could help you? She might be willing to let you live with her.'

He whispered, 'Oh, no,' startled and horrified by the suggestion.

'She wouldn't hurt you, would she? She wouldn't give you away?'

'Please don't tell her anything about me.'

His tone was a complete rejection of his stepmother. So much for her. Then what about the possible friends? She said, 'You must have known a lot of people in Bucharest. Isn't there anyone who would give you a better hiding-place than this?'

He explained that, having been at an English public school, he had no friends of long standing here. She asked, what about his University acquaintances? He simply shook his head. He had known people, but not well. There seemed to be no one on whom he could impose himself now. Jews did not make friends easily. They were suspicious and cautious in this anti-Semitic society, and Sasha had been enclosed by a large family. The Druckers formed their own community, one which depended on Drucker's power for its safety. His arrest had been the signal for flight. If they had hesitated, they might all have suffered.

Watching him, wondering what they were to do with him, Harriet caught Sasha's glance and saw her questions had disturbed him. He had again the fearful, wary look of the hunted, and she knew she was no better than Guy at displacing the homeless. Indeed, she was worse for, unlike Guy, she had been resolved and had failed. When it came to a battle of human needs, her resolution did not count for much.

Glancing away from her, Sasha saw the dog, stick in mouth, patiently awaiting his attention. He put out his hand to it.

The extreme gentleness of his gesture moved her. She suddenly felt his claim on her and knew it was the claim of her lost red kitten, and of all the animals to whom she had given her love in childhood because there had been no one else who wanted it. She wondered why Yakimov had not moved her in this way. Was it because he lacked the quality of innocence?

She said to Sasha, 'There's someone living with us in the flat, a Prince Yakimov. We have to keep him for the moment, he has nowhere else to go, but I don't trust him. You must be careful. Don't let him see you.' She slid down from the wall, saying as she left him, 'This is a wretched hut. It's the best we can do for the moment. If Yakimov leaves – and I hope he will – you can have his room.'

Sasha smiled after her, his fears forgotten, content like a stray animal that, having found a resting-place, has no complaint to make.

Next morning only *Timpul* mentioned the 'trickle of riff-raff in green shirts that provoked laughter in the Calea Victoriei'. By evening this attitude had changed. Every paper reported the march with shocked disapproval, for the King had announced that were it repeated the military would be called out to fire on the marchers.

The Guardists went under cover again, but this, people said, was the result not of the King's threat but an address made to the Guardists by their chief, Horia Sima, who was newly returned from exile in Germany. He advised them to leave off their green shirts and sing '*Capitanul*' only in their hearts. The time for action was not yet come.

Their leading spirits again hung unoccupied about the streets, sombre, shabby, malevolent, awaiting the call. These men, whom it seemed only Harriet had noticed in the spring, suddenly became visible and significant to everyone, giving rise to fresh excitements and apprehensions, and renewed terror among the Jews.

Biographical Notes

Judy Cook, *Editor of this anthology*
was born in Wiltshire in 1983 and educated at King's College, University of London. She lectured in modern literature in the Extra-Mural Department, University of London and in the USA and became Head of the English Department at Richmond College, Surrey. In 1981 she founded *The Fiction Magazine* which she edited until its demise in 1987, when she published a collection of stories, essays and poems by its contributors, *The Best of the Fiction Magazine*. She is now a freelance editor and is working on a paperback series for the British Council; co-edited with Malcolm Bradbury, the first issue of *New Writing* is to be launched in Spring 1992. She writes critical articles, reviews fiction regularly for the *Guardian* and has published short stories and a novel, *New Road*.

Deborah Moggach
was born in 1948, one of four sisters in a family of writers. Her nine novels include *Hot Water Man* (1982), *Porky* (1983), *Driving in the Dark (1989) and Stolen* (1990). Her latest novel, *The Stand-In*, was published in Spring 1991. Her short stories have been broadcast by the BBC and published in various anthologies including *Best British Stories* 1986, 1988 and 1991. A collection of stories, *Smile*, was published in 1988. She also writes TV scripts. She lives in London with her two teenage children.

Atwood, Margaret 1939–
Canadian poet, novelist and short story writer. Born in Ottawa and educated at the University of Toronto and at Radcliffe College. She has been writer in residence at several universities in Canada and the United States. Her first volume of poetry, *Circle Game*, was published in 1966, followed by collections which include *Selected Poems* (1976) and *Interlunar* (1983). Her novels include *The Edible Woman*

(1969), *Surfacing* (1972), *Lady Oracle* (1976), *Life Before Man* (1979) *Bodily Harm* (1981), *The Handmaid's Tale* (1985) and *Cat's Eye* (1989).

Bowen, Elizabeth 1899–1973
Anglo-Irish novelist and short story writer. Born in Dublin, she spent much of her childhood at the family home in County Cork, which she inherited in 1930 and described in *Bowen's Court* (1942). Her first collection of stories, *Encounters*, was published in 1923; her *Collected Stories* in 1980. Novels include *The Hotel* (1927), *The Death of the Heart* (1938), *The Heat of the Day* (1949) and *Eva Trout* (1969).

Brookner, Anita 1928–
Born in London, she trained as an art historian and taught at the Courtauld Institute, where she was reader in the History of Art at the University of London. In 1988 she left the Courtauld to concentrate on writing fiction. Her novels include *Family and Friends* (1985), *Hotel du Lac* (1984), *Look At Me* (1983), *A Start In Life* (1981), *The Latecomers* (1988) and *Lewis Percy* (1989). She is also the author of *Watteau, the Genius of the Future*, *Greuze* and *Jacques-Louis David*.

Carter, Angela 1940–
Novelist, short story writer and journalist. Born in London, she was educated at Bristol University, spent two years living in Japan and from 1976–78 was Fellow in Creative Writing at Sheffield University. Her first novel, *Shadow Dance*, was published in 1965. Other novels include *The Magic Toyshop* (1967), *Heroes and Villains* (1969), *The Infernal Desires of Dr Hoffman* (1972) and *Nights at the Circus* (1984). Her short story collections include *The Bloody Chamber* (1979) and *Black Venus* (1985).

Colette (Sidonie Gabrielle) 1873–1954
French novelist and short story writer who had early success as a music hall artist. Among her best known works are *Chéri* (1920), *La Maison de Claudine* (1922), *Le Kepi* (1943) and *Gigi* (1943). *Gigi* was turned into a successful musical by Alan Jay Lerner and Frederick Loewe.

Desai, Anita 1937–
Novelist and short story writer. Born in India of a Bengali father and German mother and educated in Delhi, she now lives in Bombay. Her work includes *Fire on the Mountain* (1977), a collection of short stories, and the novels *Games of Twilight* (1978), *Clear Light of Day* (1980), *In Custody* (1984) and *Baumgartner's Bombay* (1988).

Drabble, Margaret 1939–
Novelist and biographer. Born in Sheffield, she was educated at the Mount School, York, and at Newnham College, Cambridge. Her novels include *A Summer Birdcage* (1963), *The Garrick Year* (1964), *The Millstone* (1965), *The Ice Age* (1977), *The Radiant Way* (1987) and *A Natural Curiosity* (1989). She has also written studies of Wordsworth and Arnold Bennett and is now working on a biography of Angus Wilson.

Du Maurier, Dame Daphne 1907–90
Novelist and short story writer, born in London and educated in Paris. She later lived in the West Country which provided the background to many of her novels, including *Rebecca* (1938) and *Frenchman's Creek* (1941). Adaptations of her work for film include *Rebecca* and two short stories, both thrillers, *The Birds* and *Don't Look Now*.

Duras, Marguerite 1914–
French novelist born in Indo-China. At eighteen she came to Paris where she studied mathematics, law and political science. Her novels include *La Vie Tranquille* (1944), *Le Marin Gibraltar* (1952), *Hiroshima Mon Amour* (1961), *L'Amante Anglaise* (1967) and *The Lover* (1985).

Emecheta, Buchi 1944–
Nigerian novelist. Born in Lagos, she moved to London in 1962. Her first two novels, *In The Ditch* (1972) and *Second Class Citizen* (1974), were published together as *Adah's Story* in 1983. Her later novels, several set in West Africa, include *The Bride Price* (1976) and *The Rape of Shavi* (1983). She has also written for children and for television.

Fairbairns, Zoë 1948–
Novelist and short story writer. Born in Kent, she studied history at the University of St Andrews. Her novels include *Benefits* (1979), *Here Today*, which won the 1985 Fawcett Book prize, and *Daddy's Girls* (1991). She has also contributed to a range of short story collections including *Tales I Tell My Mother* and *The Seven Deadly Sins*.

Gordimer, Nadine 1923–
South African short story writer and novelist, born in Springs, Transvaal. Her collections of stories include *Face To Face* (1949), *The Soft Voice of the Serpent* (1952), *A Soldier's Embrace* (1980) and *Something Out There* (1984). Among her novels are *A Guest of Honour* (1970), *The Conservationist* (1974), *Burger's Daughter* (1979) and *July's People* (1981).

Hammick, Georgina 1939–
Short story writer. Born in Hampshire, she was educated at boarding schools in England and Kenya and at the Académie Julian in Paris. Her first book, *People for Lunch*, a widely acclaimed collection of short stories, was published in 1987.

Highsmith, Patricia 1921–
American novelist and short story writer, educated at Barnard College and Columbia University, New York. Her crime novel *The Talented Mr Ripley* (1956) was the first in a series of books featuring her anti-hero Ripley, including *Ripley Underground* (1971) and *Ripley's Game* (1974). Other works include *Strangers on a Train* (1950), *Little Tales of Misogyny* (1977), *Edith's Diary* (1977) and *Tales of Natural and Unnatural Catastrophes* (1987).

Jhabvala, Ruth Prawer 1927–
Novelist, short story writer and screenwriter. Born in Germany of Polish parents, she arrived in London a refugee. Resident in India from 1951, she moved to New York in 1975. Her novels include *Esmond in India* (1958), *Heat and Dust* (1975), *In Search of Love and Beauty* (1983). Her collection of stories, *How I Became a Holy Mother*, was published in 1976. As a screenwriter she has been associated with the films of Ismail Merchant and James Ivory. Her screen credits include *Shakespeare Wallah*, *The Bostonians* and *Room with a View*.

Lehmann, Rosamond 1901–90
Born in Buckinghamshire and educated privately and at Girton College, Cambridge. Her first novel, *Dusty Answer*, was a *succès de scandale*. Other novels include *Invitation to the Waltz* (1932) and its sequel *The Weather in the Streets* (1936); *The Ballad and the Source* (1944) and *The Echoing Grove* (1953). *The Swan in the Evening: Fragments of an Inner Life* (1967) is a short autobiographical account of her reactions to her daughter's sudden death and her own subsequent conversion to spiritualism.

Lessing, Doris 1917–
Novelist and short story writer. Born to English parents in Persia, she grew up on a farm in Southern Rhodesia and worked at various jobs until in 1949 she arrived in England, bringing with her the manuscript of her first book. This was the novel *The Grass Is Singing*, which was published in 1950, followed by her first collection of short stories, *This Was the Old Chief's Country* (1951). Novels include the Martha Quest sequence, collectively titled *The Children of Violence* and consisting of *Martha Quest (1959), A Proper Marriage* (1954), *A Ripple From the Storm*, (1958), *Landlocked* (1965) and *The Four-Gated City* (1969). *The Golden Notebook* (1962) is one of her major works, exploring new territories in narrative. Lessing's later work includes *Briefing for a Descent into Hell* (1972) and five novels in her space fiction series, 'Canopus In Argos'. She returned to realistic narrative in two novels published under the pseudonym of Jane Somers, *The Diary of a Good Neighbour* (1983) and *If The Old Could* (1984). The novels *The Good Terrorist* and *The Fifth Child* were published in 1985 and 1988 respectively.

Manning, Olivia 1908–80
Born into a naval family, her early life was spent in Portsmouth. Her first novel, *The Wind Changes*, was published in 1937. During the war she travelled to Bucharest, Greece, Egypt and Jerusalem, and these experiences form the background to *The Balkan Trilogy*: *The Great Fortune* (1960), *The Spoilt City* (1962), *Friends and Heroes* (1965). This was followed by *The Levant Trilogy*: *The Danger Tree* (1977), *The Battle Lost and Won* (1978) and *The Sum of Things* (1980). Her collections of short stories are *Growing Up* (1948) and *A Romantic Hero* (1966).